Coming Apart

"A touching story of one family's struggle during the Great Depression—not only for survival, but for connection and meaning in the midst of a dark time. Heenan has an instinct for tender connection between her characters and a great understanding of human nature." - Olivia Hawker, author of *The Ragged Edge of Night* and *One for the Blackbird, One for the Crow*

"Rich with historical detail, *Coming Apart* is a poignant and personal tale of two courageous sisters surviving the Great Depression—one strong-willed, proud, and determined to keep her family together despite the brutal realities of life in a coal mining town, and the other poised and quietly strong, holding her heartache close while striving to find her place among Philadelphia's privileged upper class. Heenan's sisters captivate and inspire in this story of sacrificial love, resilience, and hope." - Paulette Kennedy, author of *The Witch of Tin Mountain*

"*Coming Apart* is a touching story of sisterhood in all its raw, messy, challenging, triumphant beauty." - Gabriella Saab, author of *The Last Checkmate*

"Filled with beautiful prose and enchanting detail, Heenan's story of two sisters struggling with their private demons in an era filled with hardship, is both poignant and real. A touching story filled with perseverance and hope." - Noelle Salazar, author of *Flight Girls*

Coming Apart

KAREN HEENAN

~CONTENT WARNING~

This story is intended for mature audiences. This story contains situations that some readers may find objectionable, including childbirth, miscarriage, post-partum depression, accidental death/disaster (on and off-page), and mention of sexual assault on a minor (brief, mostly implied or off-page).

E-book ISBN: 978-1-957081-08-3
Paperback ISBN: 978-1-957081-09-0
Audiobook ISBN: 978-1-957081-10-6

Cover design and illustration ©2022 Rebecca F. Kenney.
All rights reserved.

Interior Layout ©2022 Karen Heenan
Typeset in Garamond and Lemon Tuesday

Coming Apart

KAREN HEENAN

Also by Karen Heenan

The Tudor Court Series

Songbird – Book I
A Wider World – Book II
Lady, in Waiting – Book III

Ava and Claire

From This Day Forward (newsletter exclusive novella)
Coming Apart – Book I
Coming Closer – Book II (spring 2023)

For my dad, who loved his dangerous job.
For my mom, who coped with it.

Part One

November 1931 - December 1931

1

Ava

Mama's breathing is shallow as she ascends the ladder to the heaven she believes in so fervently. Pearl and little Thelma pray at her bedside, and I close my eyes and try to pray with them, but my girls have more faith in the Almighty than I do at this moment.

It's hard to believe in a God who would put an old woman through so much pain.

In these last months, the loudest sound in our house has been my mother struggling to breathe. It drowns out all the other noises: doors banging, kids shouting. Kids crying, inevitably. The thud of Daniel's work boots on the stairs. The clatter as the stove is filled with wood. The mine whistle, which tells the time as surely as the bells from St. Stanislaus.

Now her struggle is coming to an end, and we are gathered around the narrow bed in the front room where she chose to sleep, ever since Daniel came home from the war and we began our marriage. She wanted to give us privacy, but she also liked to be at the center of everything. Mama never stopped running the house, even as her eyesight failed and her health followed. Watching her lying there, working so hard at dying, I feel no older than Thelma.

A mere child. *Her* child.

Does this long smothering press down on her, the way it does the rest of us? It's been three days since she last spoke, and then it was only to pray. Her voice left her in the middle of a Hail Mary. It's only right, I suppose, but I would have preferred some guidance instead.

A long, rattling breath. Is this one shorter?

There aren't many people in this world that I like, much less love, but I would die for every person in this room. Kill for them, if need be. Maybe that's why Daniel and I made so many kids, so I'd have more people to care about.

Only one is missing: Dandy, my firstborn. He should be here, but if he was, then his father would be gone. They never work the same shift at the mine; if something happens, that way only one of them will be lost.

A persistent kicking under my breastbone reminds me there's yet another soul in the room, and I put a hand on the hard swelling of this latest child. That's another worry: without Mama, we'll need to pay for a midwife.

The silence, when it comes, is louder than her breathing. We all wait to see if she gasps to life again. It's happened before.

This time she stays quiet. Gone.

Across from me, Daniel looks up, and I see on his unguarded face a grief as deep as my own. Mama had treated him as one of her own even before we were married, and he'd been with her longer than most of her own brood.

"Well, that's it, then." His chair scrapes on the scarred linoleum. "Are you okay?"

Once, when I was ten, Mary-Ora Rettinger had punched me in the stomach so hard it took my breath. That's how I feel now.

"We'll be fine." I manage a tight smile. "You go on up to the store and let Frank know."

He shrugs into his patched gray coat and rests his hands on my shoulders. "Sure you'll be all right?"

I tilt my head back and slide my hands over his, letting his unspoken comfort seep into me. "We'll be fine."

The words are meant to reassure, but I have no idea how I'm going to manage without her. I'm thirty-two years old, with five kids and another on the way, and I'm scared to death, though I will barely admit it to myself. Mama raised me not to give in to hard times, and I'm raising our kids the same way. I just wish there weren't so many opportunities for us to practice.

"Boys, kiss your granny and go outside." I look at my daughter. "Pearl and I have work to do."

Toby and George are crying a little, but the only thing that truly upsets boys that age—six and eight—is an empty belly. They're scuffling and fighting over a ball before they're off the front porch steps.

Pearl glares after them; her close bond with Mama only increased during this last year. "They're so disrespectful."

Echoes of my girlhood, when I complained about Jake and Teddy. I repeat Mama's words. "Let them be kids while they can."

Daniel lingers at the door, watching the boys in the road. "Ava, should I…?"

I know what he's not asking. I've avoided thinking about my sister these last few days, but I can't put it off any longer. "Go ahead."

"I'll fetch the good soap," I say as Pearl hauls me from the chair. "You get a basin of warm water ready for me."

The narrow stairs loom steep, but I force myself to climb them often, afraid I might otherwise end up giving birth on the kitchen table. Also, it's a moment alone, and those are few and far between.

The soap is tucked in my dresser drawer. Lilac scented, wrapped in matching tissue. Claire and her damn fool gifts. Mama never would use it. It was too good, too precious.

Until now. Mama will go to her rest smelling of lilacs.

It is suddenly too much: the baby, Mama, the neighbors who will come to call as soon as word spreads of her death.

Claire.

Folding my arms on the dresser, I rest my head on them, letting the weight of the baby hang until my low back screams with strain. I cry until it hurts to breathe, and then I cry some more, sobs all the more painful because they are silent. Mama taught me how to be a mother. How to be a miner's wife, too. I have her lessons in my bones, and one of them is that with small children to care for, and a husband whose employer demands sixty hours each week, sadness is a luxury I can't afford.

"Do you need help, Mama?"

"I'll be right there." My voice is steady; my competence closes around me like a shell. It makes me hard, but the people who matter know there is softness inside. Even so, I am afraid to let my kids see how gutted I am by this completely expected loss. I wipe my eyes and see the faint smudge of coal dust on my faded yellow sleeve.

Why *had* Mary-Ora punched me? I remember suddenly and smile through my tears. It was Daniel. She'd had a crush on him, but even then it was too late. We were mated for life by the time we were six years old.

Before covering the mirror with the dresser scarf, I check my reflection. My eyes are puffy, but I'm eight months pregnant. *All* of me is puffy. No one will notice.

I drop the soap into my apron pocket and start down, leaning hard on the rail. A stitch nags in my side, and I stop to let it pass.

"Are you okay, Mama?" Thelma peers over the back of her chair.

I take another step. "Just slow as a turtle, baby."

By the time I'm downstairs, Pearl has brought the basin to the bedside. The front of her dress is damp from her battle with the balky pump, but the water is the perfect temperature. She leans over and sniffs the soap. "Yummy."

She's at an age where nice things start to matter. I'll save the leftover soap for our baths before the funeral.

Turning back the quilt and the mended sheet beneath, I am confronted by the reality of my mother's body, in a flannel gown so old it is sheer in spots. I undo the tiny pearl buttons, exposing skin soft and creased as the tissue folded around Claire's soap, and fight the sob rising in my throat.

I can do this. I've prepared bodies for burial before. It's easier to think of her that way, as a collection of frail bones and pale, spotted skin, covered by a faded wedding ring quilt of her own making, than as my mother.

Dip the rag into the water, swipe it over the soap. Her hands must have been so pretty before work hardened them and arthritis thickened her knuckles. Her wedding band is worn thin as wire. Someday mine will look like that.

"Is Granny a ghost now?" Thelma's voice quavers, just a little.

"Don't be silly," Pearl says. "Ghosts aren't real."

I'm not so sure. I can feel Mama, hanging in the corners of the front room. Not her ghost, maybe, but a spirit that isn't quite ready to stop watching over us.

Thelma clambers out of her seat and puts a small hand on Mama's shoulder, still damp from my tending. "Granny will go to heaven."

"Of course, she will." I glance at Pearl. "Will you do a reading at the funeral?" The sheet is pulled up, Mama's decency restored until we get her into her traveling clothes. "She'd like that."

"Really?" Her face lights up. "Won't Daddy want to? Or Uncle Frank?"

"Your daddy would want you to do it." Daniel's pride in Pearl knows no bounds, and he doesn't read well enough to be comfortable with public reading, anyway. "We'll see if your uncle wants to say a word."

Mama's three dresses hang neatly on pegs. I evaluate how much wear is left in each, already knowing which I will choose. It's wasteful, burying Mama in her dark blue church dress, but disrespectful not to. It would never fit me, anyway. Even not pregnant, I outweighed her by twenty pounds. I could cut it down for Pearl, but I can't send my mother off to meet her maker wearing feed-sack calico so my daughter can have a new dress.

Out of nowhere, Pearl smiles. "Good thing Granny wasn't an ancient Egyptian."

"What?"

"We'd have to bury her with everything she owned," she explains. "That's what they did, the Egyptians, buried their dead in pyramids with all their worldly goods."

I don't ask where she learned this; my bookworm child is chock-full of strange facts. "I guess we're lucky, then, because we need her worldly goods. I'll cut her other dresses down for you, and make yours over for Thelma."

"What about her unders?" Pearl rubs the blue cloth between her fingertips.

I sigh. I'm exhausted, and the day is far from over. "Only drawers. Her slip is too good."

Pearl nods, accepting, and helps me maneuver the dress into place. Once we're finished, I lace Mama's beads through her fingers. She might lack proper underwear, but Lillie Kovaleski will be buried with the rosary she brought from Ireland.

Thelma and Pearl bow their heads and this time I pray with them: that we will get through this time of sorrow, that the baby won't come until after we've paid for the funeral, and, selfishly, that my sister has car trouble.

Claire

My nails dig into my palm as Daniel relates the news of my mother's death. "Tell Ava I'm thinking of her—of all of you. We'll be there tomorrow."

I put the phone down, but remain seated in the alcove under the stairs, staring unseeing at the hideous Egyptian revival wallpaper and moving only when I hear precise footsteps coming from the second floor. I wipe my sleeve across my face in the hopes that Irene won't see I've been crying, but she misses nothing.

"Your eyelashes are all over your face." Her voice is crisp, as if the most logical way to comfort an upset daughter-in-law is to point out the flaws in her makeup. "Do tidy yourself. Harry will be home soon."

According to her, my main role in her son's life is decorative, and so there can be no worse crime than to be caught looking less than my best. "That was my sister's husband," I tell her. "My mother is dead."

"What a shame. Are you finished with the telephone? I need to call Mrs. Leadbetter to tell her I'll be late for her bridge party." She lingers until I move out of her way. "I assume you plan to attend the funeral?"

"Of course." I have disliked my mother-in-law almost since the beginning, but never as much as I do at this moment. "Please don't let me keep you from your call."

I take the stairs slowly, not breaking into a run until I reach the hall. The haven of my bedroom beckons, but when I fall through the door, the room is already occupied by Katie, our maid.

She turns, duster in hand. "It was bad news?" Seeing my face, she makes no judgment about the wreckage of my makeup, and instead takes my arm and leads me toward the tufted boudoir chair. "Mr. Kimber sounded upset."

"My mother," I begin to say, and tears overtake me again. I find myself gathered against Katie's bony shoulder.

"Shh, Mrs. Claire, you just cry it out," she murmurs, rubbing my back and humming under her breath as I sob. At least I won't leave marks on her black uniform.

Finally, my sobs taper into hiccups and she eases me into the chair. "What can I get you, ma'am? Would a cup of tea help?"

"It might." I sniff, and she hands me a handkerchief from the box on my vanity. "It couldn't hurt." As she opens the door, I call after her, "Could you have Baxter fetch our bags down from the luggage room? Mr. Warriner and I will be away for a few nights."

After she leaves, I consider calling Harry to ask him to come home early but decide against it. It will take all the time until his return to get myself into a state fit to be seen. I wonder if there's time for Katie to run a bath.

It feels ridiculous—frivolous, even—to be thinking of my husband's reaction to my swollen eyes when my mother is dead, but Harry's satisfaction is a constant worry, and it will keep me from thinking too much about what I will find when I return home.

She can't be dead. As I think into the lilac-scented bubbles, I turn over the bare facts of Daniel's call.

"Lillie's dead. The funeral is Friday morning. Ava thought you should know."

There were other words, but not many. My sister married a man whose first language is silence. She understands what he cannot be bothered to say, but it is not so easy for the rest of the world.

The gist of it is that my mother had been ill for some time; now she is dead, and the funeral is in two days. I choose not to think about the fact that my sister thought I should be told. If I was a good daughter, I would have known already. I would have been there, or even brought her to Philadelphia to be treated by competent doctors.

But I hadn't. I had never even offered, fearing what Irene would say, and that Mama would pity me when she saw I was no more than an unwelcome visitor in my own grand house.

Lord only knows what my family thinks of me. It is likely no better than what I think myself.

Ava

Between wrangling the kids and getting Mama laid out, there's little time to think before Daniel returns. I'm grateful to be kept busy, but I need him with me—he knows how I feel, and we won't have to talk about it.

But he's hardly ever here when I need him. It's not his fault, and I'm not discounting what he does. You couldn't get me down into the Gracie if you held a gun to my head. The mine is Daniel's world, where he's most comfortable, despite the dangers we know all too well.

Life on the topside is little better. In good times, a miner makes decent money for the risks he takes. Right now, though, the times aren't so good and it's my job to make his salary stretch, which is as hard in its own way as clawing rock from the coal face.

We've always been poor, but we've managed, until now. I didn't think the Depression would make much difference, but I was wrong. Though people will always need coal, the only ones making money these days are the mine owners. They've cut hours and wages, but prices at the store are the same, and Mr. Callum is less likely to grant credit. He just shakes his head—"Sorry, Mrs. Kimber, there's not enough on the books"—and I choose what we'll do without until next week.

When he's marked down my purchases, he turns away with a smile that I recognize. People look at you funny if you have too many kids. I just tilt my chin up, the way Mary-Ora said made me look like a snob. You can't go around apologizing for your life. They won't respect you any more for it.

The fact that my husband works a job that pays in scrip means we'll always be poor. Even if they paid cash, we couldn't shop anywhere else, because there are no other stores in town. The company doesn't allow it. There's no other industry, either. Men get extra work doing repairs or helping out local farmers, but if they don't want to work in the mine, they have to leave.

Each July fourth, the company throws a picnic for the miners and their families. The price of admission is pretending to pay attention to old Mr. Scovill as he lectures us on making good choices and living within our means. As if he's ever had to live within his means! Every woman in town could teach him ten different ways to exist on no money. Perhaps then he would understand that our bad choices aren't really choices at all.

I keep quiet because that spouting old man pays my husband's wages, but I always have indigestion after the picnic from swallowing my rage.

By the time Daniel gets back, I'm stretched out on the davenport, trying to catch my breath. Thelma is curled at my feet and Pearl hovers over me like a gnat, a dust cloth in her hand. "I stopped in at the church," he says, pulling off his cap and shaking the damp from his coat. "The priest says Friday at eleven for the funeral, and he's sorry he wasn't here when she passed."

Father Dennis gave her the last rites yesterday when it appeared the end was coming; I am content with that, though I hope he calls in before the neighbors arrive. Like my husband, the priest is someone who will not make me talk about my feelings. "Did you reach everyone?"

"I sent a telegram to Frank and spoke to Claire." Daniel is wary where my sister is concerned. "She'll be here tomorrow. Her and His Lordship."

"They mean well." My tone carries a warning. *Not in front of the kids.*

Daniel's dark hair curls over his forehead, making him look no older than the boy I fell in love with. If I could sit up more easily, I would brush it out of his eyes.

"I'm sure they do. We just never see them." He leans down and gives me a quick kiss of apology. "And neither did Lillie."

Rain drips through the ceiling, sizzling on the hot stove. "Who forgot to empty the bucket?" Pearl shouts.

Feet pound up the stairs and in a moment, a sluice of water passes the window and the bucket clanks back into place. The roof needs to be patched before winter. Mr. Henderson, the agent, is aware of the problem, but when I press him on it, he just mouths excuses and busies himself with his books. I feel like the boy with his finger in the dike, except there are more leaks than I have fingers.

The whistle cuts the air, shrill but on time. It's when it screams between shifts that my heart stops. That means an accident—in the breaker or underground. Dandy won't be home for a while, but I want to catch him before he walks in and sees his grandmother.

Half an hour later, he comes trudging up the road with the others, his oversized lunch pail swinging from one hand. In the fading light, with his black hair and stooped shoulders, it would be easy to mistake him for his father. He comes in the kitchen door, still covered in filth, and Pearl hastens to heat water for him. Grief wars with bravado when he hears our sorry news, but he continues to shuck his clothes until he stands by the tub in his long johns.

"I'm sorry I wasn't here." He kisses me carefully, though the lower half of his face is relatively clean because of the bandana he ties over his mouth and nose. "What do you need me to do?"

My boy can make me smile even on this dark day. "Get cleaned up, first of all. Why are you still so dirty?"

He shrugs. "I didn't want to wait in line at the wash house."

"You could go with your father to pick up the coffin," I suggest.

"If he goes on his own, they'll help." Dandy motions for us to leave. "Let me stay here and be useful."

When he emerges in clean clothes, with his hair slicked back, he goes to the bedside and says a private farewell to Mama, then looks around. The house is untidy, normal chores abandoned during the death watch. "Where should I start?"

I set him to shifting furniture so I can sweep. Pearl washes the floor, using bucket after bucket of water to try to bring the linoleum up to a color other than dark gray. Mama's bed is moved to the center of the room for ease of visiting, and Dandy corrals the boys before they can escape, and orders them to fill the wood box and the coal bin.

When he still wants occupation, I point toward the vinegar jug and let him wash the front windows. One pane is cracked, and he cleans it carefully, then twitches the curtain so it's less noticeable.

Pearl took the boys out earlier and they returned with baskets of berry-laden branches, colorful leaves, and a few bedraggled flowers from someone's garden. Thelma arranges them in canning jars around the head of the bed. They make a pretty sight, the closest we can manage to flowers with winter coming on and no money to spend on such things.

The house is shabby, but it's as clean as anything can be in a coal town. I want to be a woman who has nice things, but that doesn't seem likely. There's no point in wishing—anything new would only be ruined by the black dust that seeps through every crack and crevice. If we're lucky, it will stay tidy until everyone leaves on Friday.

"The Queen of England could come to tea and I wouldn't be embarrassed." I sink down, my low back threatening to spasm.

"How about Aunt Claire?" Pearl's freckled face is skeptical.

Kids hear things, no matter how little we say. "Your Aunt Claire isn't the Queen of England. She was born here, same as the rest of us."

And having been born here, Claire—if she comes—will recognize every stick of furniture in this house. Some of it has been mended, some painted to hide the wear, but all of it is old. She will also see the wet patch on the ceiling. I'll bet her roof doesn't leak. If it does, some poorly-paid man would be scrambling up a ladder before the clouds were gone from the sky.

"But she lives in Philadelphia now." Dandy, finally still, sits on the hassock at my feet. "With Uncle Harry, in a big house."

The stairs creak. "Most houses are bigger than ours," Daniel says, coming down from his pre-work nap. "Their house is a palace compared to this."

"This is *our* palace," Pearl says quickly.

While she checks the dinner warming on the stove, I hold out my hands and let Daniel pull me to my feet. The baby might not be due for weeks, but I'm as slow and ungainly as a woman in her ninth month.

The warming fragrance of soup fills the small kitchen: vegetables from my garden with a beef bone for flavor. A half loaf of bread hides under a cloth, and Pearl cuts slices for everyone. The kettle whistles as she hands around the last of the bowls, and she transfers the hot water into Mama's brown china pot and puts it in front of me.

The sugar bowl is near-empty; one of the kids will have to run up to the store in the morning. I add the last two teaspoons to Daniel's cup before he can object. Working nights, he needs every bit of energy he can get. The smaller kids get milk with a slosh of tea, while Pearl, Dandy, and I drink it black.

I spoon up the last of my soup. "This was good, Pearl."

She smiles with pleasure, then asks, "Where are they going to stay? Aunt Claire and Uncle Harry?"

"At the Mansion House," Daniel tells her. "It's good enough for Mr. Scovill when he comes to town."

"They might stay in Scranton." I lean to one side so she can take my bowl. "It's more of a drive, but they'd likely prefer it."

"I don't remember Auntie Claire." George flips his spoon in the air and catches it.

"You were just little." Toby rubs his spoon on his nose to make it stick. "I remember her, kind of."

"Last time she was here, Thelma wasn't a year old." We didn't know there was anything wrong yet, and Claire cooed over our beautiful baby girl, ignoring the older kids until I reminded her of their existence. "I'm surprised you remember."

Pearl takes the basin of warm water from the oven and hauls Toby up by his collar, handing him a towel. "They still don't have any kids of their own?"

"Not yet."

There were a lot of hasty weddings during the war, but Claire's wasn't one of them—unlike Daniel, Harry wasn't a soldier. She and I didn't talk much by then. I assumed she wanted to tie him down before he thought too hard about marrying a girl from a coal patch.

"Why not?"

"Some people have babies and some don't," I tell her. "Maybe they don't want kids."

2

Claire

"We'll stay at the Searle, of course." Harry turns from the dresser. I don't have to look to know he has placed his change, watch, and cufflinks in precise order on its polished surface.

"There's always the hotel in town." My voice is even; I have learned, for the most part, to control my emotions. People die all the time. Even mothers. Even mine. "We'd be closer to my family."

He buttons his pajama top—crisp blue-and-white striped cotton with blue piping—and stretches. "And the mines." His gold-rimmed spectacles are placed on the bedside table, within easy reach; he can see nothing without them. "I'd prefer not to wake to the sound of the breaker."

"As you wish." I ignore the headache nestled at the base of my skull and watch as he settles the blanket up to his chin. Our beds are separated by a small table with a silver bowl of hothouse roses. I inhale their lush scent and it soothes me, just a bit.

I don't mind staying at the Searle; it was where we met, and I enjoy going back as a guest, remembering my days as the assistant desk clerk, answering phones and greeting men in suits who either ignored me or looked at me like I ought to be included in the price of their room.

Except for one man.

Harry Warriner *saw* me. From the moment he walked through the brass-trimmed double doors, past the lobby boys in their dark-red uniforms, he saw me as something more than a pretty face behind the counter. I checked him in and sent his luggage up with one of the boys. When he lingered at the desk, I worked up the nerve to speak.

"How were the trains?" I asked. "They all seem to be full of soldiers." My cheeks grew hot, hoping he didn't think I watched the trains to look at them. I didn't. Those boys would give me nothing I couldn't get at home.

"I came up from Philadelphia," he said, "so they weren't crowded. I'm sure the journey back will be different."

I looked down at the register, letting the lobby lights gleam off my bent head. "I wish you a pleasant stay, Mr. Warriner."

He stayed a few extra days, talking to me each time we met—and I made sure we met frequently. Growing up around men who brawled as easily as they breathed, his mannered calm was a new experience. On what should have been his last day, he asked me to walk with him when I finished my shift.

In the back room, I pinned on my pale blue straw hat and pinched my cheeks to bring up the color. Working indoors kept me pale, but perhaps Mr. Warriner would be attracted to a little country freshness?

"Going somewhere, are you?" one of the maids asked. Her shift over, she dropped her apron on the bench and knuckled the tightness from her shoulders.

"To make my fortune."

Everyone laughed, but I wasn't joking. I hadn't left home just to work in the city. I was the quick one, the pretty one; I'd known it from a young age, just as I'd known I wasn't going to spend my life in Scovill Run, at the mercy of the mines and the men who worked in them.

At first, the Searle seemed like a palace, though I learned later it wasn't even Scranton's *best* hotel. A year later, having worked my way from waitress (too much bottom pinching) to the telephone desk (better, but I would never meet a man by transferring a call to his room) to the front desk, I still loved walking through the marble-floored lobby every morning, pretending it was my own grand house.

Harry Warriner belonged at the Searle. He was tall, with slicked-back brown hair and a narrow mustache. His suits fit beautifully; his shoes were polished to a high shine; his nails were trimmed, with no half-moons of dirt under them. He looked like someone had taken him out of a bandbox and pushed him through the hotel doors, straight at me.

My mother would have said he was a gift from God.

We walked down the street from the hotel, turning onto Lackawanna Avenue, busy with motor cars and wagons full of goods, and eventually ending at the river. My hand rested on his arm, lightly but with a feeling of possession. He talked steadily, and I heard most of it—his business in Scranton might be delayed, would I have dinner with him one night if he stayed on? Could I recommend a restaurant other than the one at the hotel, and the others he'd visited with his business associates? He understood it wasn't Philadelphia, there wouldn't be much selection…

Listening, I understood that he was nervous. Had I somehow unsettled him? He was at least thirty-five to my seventeen, but that was fine—I didn't want a callow boy, and those extra years gave him time to establish himself in his business, whatever it was.

"What do you do in Philadelphia?" I hoped he hadn't already told me, and dimpled to take away the sting of my inattention. "I mean, you've said some things, but…"

He flushed. "I have several different businesses," he said, "but I'm in Scranton to purchase a textile mill."

Textiles sounded profitable. Like coal, they were something everyone needed, but it seemed cleaner, safer. "What's it like, working in a mill?"

"You are charming, Miss Kovaleski." His laughter was charming, even if it was at my expense. "I've only ever worked in the offices, during summers and when I finished college. When my father died four years later, I inherited all his concerns, including the mills. When the war started in Europe, I signed a contract with the government to supply cloth for military uniforms."

I smiled again and wound my arm a little more firmly through his. "I've never been to Philadelphia."

We reached the end of the river path and turned back. "Parts of it are quite like Scranton." He gestured toward the city center. "Factories are the same everywhere. Philadelphia is situated between two rivers, so there has always been a lot of industry. I live in the downtown area, quite close to everything."

"In a house or an apartment?" I'd seen pictures of city apartment buildings. They looked glamorous, like what I imagined a grand hotel would be like.

"A house," he said. "It's larger than I need, but it's my family home."

My family's house had always been smaller than we needed, with children everywhere, Mama stepping over them to do her endless chores; Tata coming home filthy and exhausted, claiming a corner of the sleeping room upstairs, bellowing for quiet.

"All that space must be lovely." I'd said the words aloud. This time I didn't need to pinch my cheeks; the blush climbed to my hairline.

Harry Warriner stopped and took my hands. "It's all right," he said. "There's no need to be embarrassed."

His hands were soft; he'd obviously never done manual labor. "I'm not from here," I confessed. "I grew up in Scovill Run."

A blink showed his surprise. "How did you come to Scranton?"

In for a penny. He would either run away or accept me for who and what I was. "When I finished school, I applied for jobs here until I found a place that would take me." I met his eyes. "I don't want my mother's life."

After a moment, he nodded. "We're more alike than you realize. Despite appearances, I don't want to live my father's life. I detest manufacturing. I'd like to go into politics when the war ends."

His words broke the spell of my misstep. "That sounds wonderful. I've never met anyone who wanted to run for office." The light was beginning to fade, and as much as I wanted to talk to him, I had to be back at the boarding house in time for supper. Mr. Warriner hadn't offered to feed me, and I couldn't waste money. "Would you walk me back to my room?"

"If I can see you again," he said with a smile. "It will take a few more days to finalize the purchase of the mill."

We walked in silence all the way to the boarding house. Its shabby appearance made me shy again, but he didn't seem to notice. He knew the worst already and wanted to see me again, so maybe Mrs. Novak's peeling paintwork wasn't important.

"I have the day off on Saturday." Usually, I caught a ride home to spend the day with my family, but I could send a note to explain my absence. They would understand—especially when I told them about Harry Warriner.

Pearl

November 18, 1931

Granny died this afternoon. This is the first chance I've had to write, or to even think about her. Is it wrong that I'm relieved? She's been sick for so long.

Daddy left right away, to let everyone know, and Mama sent the boys out to play. Why is it boys get to be boys until they're men, but girls have to be women long before our bodies catch up?

After they were gone, we washed and dressed Granny. That was hard, because she told me once that no one had seen her naked since she was little. Granny had as many babies as Mama, and while I'm not sure how that works, I know your drawers have to come off. I wanted to ask Mama, but it didn't feel respectful.

Claire

When Harry's steady breathing tells me he is asleep, I slip from my bed to cry in the bath. I did cry a little when I told him, but it was nothing like the hysterics I had when Daniel gave me the news that she was dead.

I'm sad, but it's guilt as much as sadness that keeps me wakeful. It's been four years since I've been home. Four years of knowing she was failing, yet still taking care of Ava's ever-growing family. Why did I keep postponing my visit?

A better question: why had I never tried to bring her to live with us?

Would Lillie Kovaleski have left her home, left Ava and her family, to live in a house with servants? To share the title of Mother with Irene Warriner, who didn't share?

I don't think she would have come, not even for me, but it was a nice dream, especially now that it could never happen. I try to imagine Mama taking the air in Rittenhouse Square with the other ladies her age, but the picture won't come clear, probably because it is unrealistic. She would have found the narrow streets to the south of us instead and talked to the women of her own class—if she left the house at all.

The funeral is Friday. Before that, Daniel said, the family will be at home, which means Mama will be laid out in the front room, in the same place where we'd waked my brother Teddy and my father, later that same year.

I can't do this on my own, which is part of the reason I've never visited without Harry. He gives me strength. He can't conceive of a situation he can't master, and I ride his coattails when I can't manage, which is often.

Staying at the Searle is probably best. It will take no more than five hours to get to Scranton if the roads are clear. We can check in and drive the seven miles further to my mother's house.

Daniel had called collect and would only stay on the phone for a minute, but he managed to mention they had another baby on the way. "Ava probably told you."

She hasn't told me, because we don't write.

My sister's fecundity rankles. Compared to her, I'm a failure. Twelve years of marriage, five miscarriages, and endless stretches of prayer and nothingness in between. This last time, I lost the baby at four months, far enough along that I truly felt pregnant.

Dr. Lyle conducted an exam, poking around in areas examined so frequently that I no longer embarrassed. I put on my clothes, resuming my serene mask, and Harry and I sat down in the doctor's office. "There's nothing wrong to the eye," he said, "but something's amiss. There hasn't been an injury you haven't mentioned? Perhaps a fall, something like that, when you were young?"

I winced, but Harry spoke, his voice cutting, "She's treated as if she's made of glass. Are you saying you can do nothing?"

The doctor shook his head. "I can refer you to a specialist in New York. Beyond that, I'm afraid not."

Harry wants to try again. I'm not sure I can face it. I don't fear the pain of childbirth, but that other pain, the tugging sensation between my hip bones that tells me another child has come loose from my unwelcoming womb.

But if he wants to try again, I will.

Harry is rich and successful; a former member of the city council; a friend of the mayor. He can have anything, but all he wants is children, and I haven't been able to give him one.

I drift off to sleep thinking of my sister's children. Maybe they will be so numerous, so loud, so overwhelming, that he'll change his mind and be content with just me?

3

Ava

Long ago, on the night of my father's vigil, Mama told me, "The dead speak. We just don't always listen." I don't know if Tata said anything to her; I heard nothing, as I hear nothing now.

I sent the kids to bed as early as I could, wanting—needing—to be alone. I miss her with a fierceness that claws at me. Deep inside there is a panicky fear that I won't be able to cope. Whether making a meal out of almost nothing, fixing mustard plasters to nurse Daniel through his winter cough, or delivering my babies, she's always been there. She raised me strong, but she was always there to bolster my strength with hers.

Daniel told me, early on, that he liked living with Mama because it meant I wouldn't be alone if something happened to him. I didn't want to think about that. I'd already been through it with my father and brother. It was too much to ask that I give a husband to the Gracie.

If things had been different, maybe we would have gotten a place of our own. If the war hadn't happened. If I hadn't had Dandy so soon. If any of my other siblings had stayed home. By the time Daniel came back, it was just me and Mama, and I refused to leave her.

Now I have no blood family left, except my sister, Margit, lost years ago to the church, and Frank, who I don't like all that much and who lives ten miles away with his wife and kids. Until Mama took a turn for the worse, we only saw them on holidays.

And Claire, of course. Always Claire.

Growing up, we were as inseparable as we were different. I couldn't imagine leaving Scovill Run, and she couldn't imagine staying. I thought I understood, but her abrupt departure shattered something between us. She wrote every week, one letter addressed to everyone, and visited most Saturdays, but we never found much to say to each other after she left. When she got engaged in the summer of 1918, I was happy for her in the way I would have been happy for a neighbor.

The army didn't release Daniel until the war was well over. Losing my sisters so close together, Margit to holy orders and Claire to Harry, tightened the bond between me and Mama even further. She helped raise my son, and together we figured out ways to get by without a man in the house. So long as we paid the rent, the company let us stay on, and like many women whose men were dead or away at the war, we rented rooms, cleaned houses for the mine managers' wives, and sewed for anyone who could pay us.

They were hard times, but we survived, my son thrived, and when Daniel came home at last, we were waiting for him.

But Claire...does our bond even exist anymore? She deserted the family. That's hard to forgive. When Mama's vision failed, she made Pearl say it was her arthritis that made it difficult to write. That was too much for me, and I added a line informing Claire that our mother had gone blind.

I received a concerned letter in return, but blindness did not merit a visit, and so no one bothered to tell her when the situation got worse. The black lung isn't just for miners; living with that dust for decades, women get it as well. Mama choked and wheezed for years before this last bout of pneumonia.

It's been nineteen years since the mine took my father. My brother, too—though he wasn't underground when he died, the Gracie was still at fault. It's hard to think about Teddy, even now. It's because of him I got so angry when Dandy left school for the mine. Men know what they're about, but boys die still unknowing. Teddy was killed without ever having kissed a girl.

The laws are different now, and sometimes even observed. Dandy didn't start on the breaker until this year. My father started at six, spending years in that hulking beast until he was old enough to go underground. After that, it seemed he only came up for whiskey, baths, and the occasional fierce argument with Mama, all of which probably led to their six children.

Dreams of the mine have haunted me all my life—a close blackness that resembles my memory of being shut in Mama's trunk when I was three. Tons of earth sagging above, waiting to fall. Ridiculous to be terrified by the thing that gives this town life, but there it is. I still wake sweating and wiping invisible soil from my face, sure that the ceiling is coming down. As my breathing slows, I see a sliver of light from the window or hear Daniel snore and realize my mind is playing tricks again.

I hate this town, but I can't bring myself to leave. Is it because Mama never considered going, even after everything she lost? Is it because I will never tear my husband away from the dark place that has taken so much from both of us?

Daniel lost a brother in the same cave-in that took Tata. His father was already dead, his life coughed away before he was forty. It isn't something we talk about, but we grew up with the same memories of empty chairs and mothers forcing back tears. It leaves its mark, something like that.

I circle back to Claire. When did I separate the woman she is now from the girl who was my sister? We'd shared everything—a bed being the least of it. Her hatred of the Gracie was visceral but different than mine. She hated the black dust that coated everything, and that her clothes were never clean. She hated—as I do—that we are owned in all but name by the Scovill Mining Company.

I understood when she took the job in Scranton. At least, I tried to. She always wanted more than our town had to offer. And none of us were surprised when she married Harry Warriner. He was exactly what she was running to when she left us. The wedding—a civil ceremony, since the groom wasn't Catholic—was held at the courthouse. I was her matron of honor, and two alarmingly fashionable girls who were Harry's cousins stood as bridesmaids. Mama and I had new dresses and hats, paid for by the groom, and there was a fancy luncheon afterward at the hotel where Claire worked with expensive, out-of-season flowers.

Despite her objections about Harry's age and religion, Mama defended Claire's choice. "I always knew she was destined for more. She'll end up fine, you watch."

What we had was fine enough. Claire didn't need a rich man who moved her two hundred miles away to prove she was better than us. But that's what she did on her wedding day, getting into a long black car with her new husband while we took the train home.

After the first few years, her visits trickled down to once every summer, then once every other. Now, with Mama gone, I doubt we'll see her again after the funeral. Even her letters will taper off, then stop altogether.

I try not to mind, but I do. This last year, when she was failing, Mama needed Claire. Needed her even more when she was dying. Those square blue envelopes kept arriving, filled with news of parties and visits and the dresses she wore, but never a mention of a visit, or more than a passing question about Mama's health.

My sister, the girl we called Dolly because of her porcelain prettiness, was gone.

It occurs to me, as the sun rises, that I haven't anything to wear. My maternity dresses look as old and tired as I feel. It's silly, like worrying over the lack of flowers, but it hurts all the same. The sewing machine stares reproachfully from across the room: I could make a dress in time for the funeral, but there is no cloth, and no means to buy any. Nor, truth be told, is there time—I can hardly greet the neighbors hunched over the sewing machine.

If I wasn't so far along, I could make do with the dress I wore for Claire's wedding. It's still my second-best, altered time and again as styles changed and waistlines moved up and down. With a sweater, I could leave it open down the back and hope for the best, but it hasn't fit in months.

A light knock, and I push myself from my chair as the door opens. "Morning, Trudy."

Gertrud Metzger, fortyish and capable, shares the other side of our split house with her brother, son, four grandchildren, and an ever-shifting array of bachelor boarders. I feel a kinship with her beyond neighborliness. Her husband died in the same cave-in that killed my father. She grew close to Mama after that and adopted me as a sort of younger sister.

"I'm so sorry about Lillie." Despite coming here as a young woman, she has never lost her accent. "I wouldn't come so early, but I thought you might have need."

She shakes the rain from her shawl and sidles past, crossing herself and saying a silent prayer at Mama's side before turning back to me. From a canvas bag, she pulls a charcoal-gray skirt and a dark flowered blouse. "They are not proper mourning, but the skirt fit Dora when she had her baby. The blouse is mine."

"Thank you." Tears prick my eyes. "I was just wondering what I could wear. Isn't it silly, thinking about clothes at a time like this?"

"You want to show your respect." She turns again and touches Mama's cheek. "She looks at peace."

I hope she is.

"You are worried, my friend."

There is no point in lying to Trudy; I can say things to her I can't share with Daniel or the kids. "It's all on me now."

Her face softens. "Do you think Lillie would have left if she did not believe you could manage?"

"No." There are noises upstairs: the kids are awake, and soon the house will ring with life. Just not hers. I tilt my head toward the coffin. "Last night was only the second night I've ever been apart from her."

The first was my wedding night, spent with Daniel in unaccustomed luxury at the Mansion House. Mama paid for the hotel room from her emergency fund, insisting we have at least one night alone.

Trudy clasps my shoulder. "She will always be with you."

Squabbling breaks out as George and Toby start their day. Pearl's voice rises over theirs, and the quarrel subsides.

"She manages them as well as Mama."

Trudy nods. "She must do even more now."

I want more for my girl than to be a nursemaid to her siblings. Pearl needs an education, but the company school stops at eighth grade. Claire caught a ride every day to the next town over to attend high school, but I don't want Pearl wandering around by herself; the world is a dangerous place for a girl on her own.

The steps creak and groan as the kids tumble downstairs, Toby and George shoving each other, Thelma holding the rail, and Pearl following close behind.

"Good morning, Mrs. Metzger." She reaches out to straighten Toby's collar and cuffs the back of his head when he tries to squirm away. "Mama, do you want me to get them fed? Daddy will be home soon."

"If you could. Where's Dandy? He needs to get ready."

"He went out," Pearl calls from the kitchen. "You were asleep in the chair."

I send Toby next door with Trudy for a half-cup of sugar and join them in the kitchen. The tea is hot and I breathe deeply over the cup. "What's he doing out so early?"

Pearl shrugs. "You know what he's like."

I do. Hard-headed like me, as talkative as his father.

We're done eating when Daniel comes in, Dandy on his heels. Both are wet through. I give Dandy a dark look as he splashes water on his face. Standing at my side, he wolfs a bowl of oatmeal and drinks two cups of tea.

"Where were you?" I keep my voice under the general din.

"Don't worry, Ma." He puts his mug down, reaching for the lunch pail his sister has packed. "I'm off. Will Aunt Claire be here when I get home?"

"I imagine so." The weather doesn't look promising. "If not, you'll see her at the funeral."

Claire

It was raining when we left Philadelphia. Now the sky is the color of slate and the rain has turned to snow. My mood matches the weather, but I force a smile when we stop for lunch. Harry would rather be at the office than driving the Lackawanna Trail; the least I can do is not be gloomy.

"I'm sorry." I slide into the booth and take off my hat, smoothing my hair. The dampness has gotten into it, and I fear for my waves.

"For what?"

"All this." I wiggle my fingers at the glass. "Rain, snow. It'll be dark by the time we get there."

Harry takes my hand across the table. "You can't control the weather, Claire."

Nor can I control my thoughts, or the foolish words that tumble from my mouth. "It feels appropriate," I say. "Sad weather."

Studying the menu, he doesn't respond immediately. "Well, it's a sad day," he says, putting the stiff card on the table. "You only have one mother."

But I still have a mother-in-law. If my luck holds, Harry's mother will live another thirty years. I wonder if he realizes how quickly I would trade Irene for a single day with my mother. We are both fatherless, but his father died of heart failure. I feel the difference in our backgrounds most acutely when I compare the losses our families have suffered—how certain tragedies are avoidable if one has money.

24

"It should only be another hour to Scranton." The waitress takes our order before he continues, "The road is quite good, even with the rain, and it should be smooth sailing until we get close to Scovill Run. God only knows what the roads are like there."

"Not good, unless things have changed." There are few cars other than those belonging to the managers; most of the transport around the mine is done by rail.

"Do things change there?" I don't adjust my expression in time, and his smile fades. "I'm sorry. It's hard to remember you grew up there."

"For me, too." If I count the time in Scranton before my marriage, I've been gone thirteen years. It seems like a century. I ignored the unspoken plea in Mama's letters because facing my past is uncomfortable. After the funeral, there will be no reason to return at all, except to see Ava and her family—and I'm not sure my sister even wants to see me. I miss her like an amputated limb, even as the idea of seeing her fills me with terror.

Two bowls of steaming chicken soup are placed in front of us. "I wish I'd done this sooner." I put my napkin on my lap. "It's been too long."

"Water under the bridge." The heat from the soup makes his lenses steam up. "I don't mean it unkindly, darling. It's just something one learns in business—not to regret what can't be changed, and simply move on from there. It's not a bad way to live one's life."

"Perhaps."

After we finish our sandwiches and a second cup of coffee, Harry retrieves our coats and we run through the snow to the car. Safely inside, I peer into the mirror and frown at the sad state of my cloche. It will have to be steamed into shape when we get home. Thankfully there's another in my luggage. Perhaps it's superficial, but I can't bear the thought of being seen looking like something the cat dragged in.

Ava

When the noon whistle subsides and before the bells of St. Stanislaus have stopped ringing, the first neighbors arrive. Most are women since the day shift doesn't end until four. They offer polite sympathies and head for the kitchen, where Pearl accepts their stuffed cabbage and pierogi and sauerkraut and arranges it on the table. A few bring flowers from their gardens, and they are added to the arrangements at the head of the coffin.

A handful of men, elderly, unemployed, or night shift like Daniel, pay their respects and retreat outside, sheltering under the porch roof to smoke and pass slender bottles fetched from the depths of their coat pockets. Grieving is women's business.

It feels as though half the town passes through the front room. It's heartwarming and panic-inducing at the same time, and I stand between Daniel and Father Dennis, breathing in the comfort that exudes from the priest's very pores. He is a great thick slab of a man with a pink Irish face, curly white hair, and hands like Easter hams. Even in his old age, he radiates energy and strength.

I can see why Mama said he was the handsomest man in town when she arrived. "My man was dead and the next best belonged to God," she said. "At least that meant I could see him often."

By mid-afternoon, my head is swimming and I leave Pearl and Daniel to deal with our visitors. My breasts hurt. My back hurts. I want to lie down. And I have to pee. Again.

I pass through the kitchen, grab my shawl off its hook, and duck out to the outhouse. It's not as cold as I expect, but the snow stings my exposed skin and I make quick work of my business there.

This pregnancy feels so long. They always do, by this point, but this one seems particularly endless. You'd think my body would be used to it by now, but each time it's a new version of the old discomfort.

I try to remember what I looked like before my first baby, and I can't, not without referring to my wedding photograph. I was never as slender as Claire—I got Mama's Irish peasant stock, rather than Tata's more delicate Polish build. My body has served me well, but I don't remember what it's like to have a waist or a bust whose sole purpose isn't to nurse a baby.

Coming back into the kitchen, I stand close to the stove, trying to work up the energy to return to the front room.

"Are you cold, Mama?" Thelma is in the corner; she hides from strangers and I leave her be—no one wants attention just because there's something wrong with them.

"No, baby." I sit beside her. "I'm just sad and all these people make me tired."

Trudy appears in the doorway, her gloved hands wrapped around a cast-iron pot. "Rabbit stew." She winks. "For you, not all of them."

"Thank you." I swing the heavy pot onto the back of the stove, lifting the lid to inhale the rich aroma. "I'm sorry I wasn't out there."

"You have greeted me once today already," she says with a wry face. "Until you greet that baby, you do not have the…patience for all this." She takes off her glove and strokes Thelma's hair. "Hello, my pretty."

I check the window. The light is fading, and snow clings to the corners of the panes. Harry's fancy car isn't equipped to handle these roads in the dark, so they'd better get here soon.

"You have not heard from Claire?" Trudy guesses.

"Not yet." She'll walk in, shed a few decorative tears, and become the center of everyone's sympathy and attention. Which I shouldn't mind, since I want to be left alone. But I will.

The noise level spikes as the men and boys all start talking at once. Nothing but an unfamiliar car would cause that much ruckus. I lean on Trudy and take Thelma's hand. Tired or not, pregnant or not, lame or not, we will greet our guests properly.

We reach the coffin as the front door opens. Daniel takes my hand, and the kids close ranks around me.

4

Claire

The closer we get, the tighter my chest becomes. I regret not coming back to see Mama, but I remember vividly why I didn't want to. My past lives here, and much of it isn't friendly.

We turn off the highway and take the road around the mountain, past the breaker and the blackened mess of culm beyond the mine entrance. The rumble of the breaker reaches us through the closed windows, and I wonder if Daniel is underground.

The town looks the same. Past the mine is the company store, the town hall, the school, two shabby churches, and an open field where men play ball in warm weather. Then comes a short street of nicer houses belonging to the mine supervisors, the men who run the breaker, the rental agent, and the storekeeper. After that, the road turns from gravel to mud, and the miners' dwellings appear, street after street of nearly-identical double houses, most with sagging porches out front and an outhouse and the tattered remains of a garden in the back.

Harry drives carefully around a pothole big enough to drown a cat but misses another, and the car bounces and groans. The Packard is his baby, less than a year old, a long, sleek sedan with gray velvet upholstery and white-walled spare tires mounted on its swooping front bumpers. Baxter usually drives, but Irene required his presence in Philadelphia, which means I won't have to imagine him regaling the other servants with descriptions of my home and family.

The windshield wipers barely make a dent in the fast-falling snow, and Harry swears quietly as the car shudders again. "Even the snow is gray."

I want to defend my home, but the swirling flakes *are* gray, and the fresh snow at the side of the road is already filmed with black dust. I had forgotten just how ugly it was here.

Following the road to its end, we stop at the next to last house. It is indistinguishable from the others but for the tattered black crepe wreath on the door. Figures move before the lit front window, and my stomach drops. The neighbors are visiting.

"I didn't want to make an entrance," I murmur to Harry.

"No way to avoid it." He offers his arm. "Chin up, darling."

I dodge the worst of the puddles, holding tight to his sleeve. On the porch, a cluster of men back away, muttering greetings. The door is ajar, and Harry pushes it open, standing aside so I can enter.

At first, I see nothing but the cheap pine box in the middle of the room. Then the heat hits me. Not from the stove; it's the warmth of too many bodies packed into a small space. Beneath the competing smells of coal smoke, wet wool, and lamp oil, I catch a hint of something floral—lilac? It seems impossible in this place.

I take a steadying breath and look up. Ava is on the other side of the coffin, flanked by Daniel and the children. She looks like a sentimental magazine illustration of a rural Madonna. A brown button-up sweater does not conceal the bulge of advanced pregnancy. Her blue eyes are pale, like chips of ice. She doesn't smile.

I'd never thought we resembled each other, but now it's like looking at myself in an old mirror. Everything about Ava is a little larger, a little softer, blurred by pregnancy and the three years between us.

"Claire!" She approaches, and the children follow like a school of fish. "I was worried you had trouble on the roads."

Everything is a little softer, except her tongue. We are late, and they have been waiting. "Only the last few miles," I say. Hugging her is awkward, the hard bulk of her belly a physical manifestation of the distance between us. "It's really coming down."

"Go on through to the kitchen." She squeezes my hands. "You're freezing."

"It's not too bad in the car." Harry comes forward and kisses Ava's cheek, reaching around her to shake Daniel's hand. "The heater is top-notch."

At the mention of the car, the few males who aren't already at the windows drift in that direction. Ava's little boys are flat up against the glass, and the eldest boy, holding fast to her side, is twitching with curiosity.

"I need to see Mama first." When I approach the coffin, everyone steps back. She's smaller than I remember. Her gray hair is loose on her shoulders, and someone has put a few finger waves at her temples. She wears her dark blue dress with a tatted collar, and her rosary is laced through her fingers.

There are homely flowers and branches at the head of the coffin, which make me glad we ordered a blanket of carnations and lilies to be delivered to the church tomorrow. Mama loved flowers, so I wanted her to have plenty of them.

I touch her hand and am overwhelmed; she is cold and still, my mother who was never either of those things. Ava lays a hand on my back. "Come along, Claire."

"The family should be alone now," a German-accented voice says behind us. "We will come together again in the morning."

Slowly, the room empties, until a final closing of the door leaves me alone with my sister.

"You need a cup of tea." Ava's voice is firm. She pushes me gently into a chair. A young girl pours two cups of tea from Mama's old pot and slides them across the table.

"Pearl, you remember your Aunt Claire, don't you?"

The girl nods. She looks to be about eleven or twelve, ruddy-cheeked, with a dusting of freckles across her nose. Her light brown hair is shingled to her jawline, an unfortunate style for her face. "Last time you came, you brought me a fairytale book."

"So I did." I can't remember if it was Grimm or Anderson. "Of course, you're too old for it now."

"I read it to the littles before bed, after I read Granny's Bible." She turns to Ava. "Are we still going to read the Bible every night?"

"Of course." Ava balances her cup on her belly. "Granny knew that book cover-to-cover, just from hearing it every day. She'd want the same for you all."

The girl scoots out to the front room, and I hear her asking the men if they want tea. She quickly returns. "Mama, Uncle asked me to bring glasses for him and Daddy."

Ava's eyebrows raise. "Did he now?" She looks at me. "And what does Harry want that can't be drunk from teacups?"

"He might have brought a little something for the wake." Prohibition is pretty much ignored in our circle. Harry often meets friends over whiskey at the Union League, and we begin every evening with a civilized cocktail in the living room. But Mama never permitted spirits in the house, because of Tata. I should have remembered.

"Then we'll save it for the wake," Ava says. "Daniel has to go to work soon. The last thing he needs is for them to smell whiskey on his breath." She sends Pearl in with tea and calls after her, "Tell the boys to go upstairs if they aren't going to stop yammering about the car."

"They can't hurt it," I say, knowing she doesn't want my advice. "Let them look."

"They'll have a better chance tomorrow," she says. "But if Harry doesn't mind...I just want them to wear themselves out so we can have some peace."

Pearl conveys the message, and the front door slams before she finishes speaking. The oldest boy leans into the kitchen. He holds the whiskey bottle like it's a bomb. "Uncle asked if you would keep hold of this."

He's probably seen bootleg liquor, but never a whole bottle of the stuff. Harry is giving Ava's son an education, whether she likes it or not.

"On the shelf over the stove," Ava says. "And come say hello to your aunt."

Dandy approaches. He's at the age where boyhood and manhood haven't decided who's in charge. "Last time I saw you, you drew me a picture, do you remember?"

He nods. "I drew a lot then."

"You were good at it." I like his face, a boyish version of Daniel. He hasn't gotten that pinched look around the eyes yet. "Do you still draw?"

"No." His expression darkens, but I don't take the hint.

"Why not?"

He holds out his hands. At first glance, they look like any boy's hands, slightly grubby and too large for his bony wrists, but the resemblance ends there. His fingertips are split and crusted with scabs. Several nails are missing, and fresh blood seeps from cracked knuckles. I realize with horror that he's missing a finger on his left hand.

"My God! What happened?" The sight of his injuries makes me light-headed. "Ava, has he seen the doctor?"

"He's on the breaker, Claire," she says impatiently. "You remember what Teddy's hands were like when he started."

"They'll heal soon enough." Dandy sounds almost eager. "And then I'll be able to work underground like Dad."

31

Ava

I make light of Dandy's missing finger. Even if Claire thinks me heartless, I don't want my son to understand how wrong it is for a child to work until his body is broken, not if there's nothing that can change the situation.

Dandy was the most perfect baby I'd ever seen, with silky black hair and wide eyes that took in the world without seeing how sorry it was. Sometimes when I look at him, I remember how he smelled when he nursed, his head tucked under my chin. I love all my kids, but Dandy is special, there's no getting around it. When Mama delivered him, the pain was like nothing I'd ever imagined, but when she put that squalling, red-purple baby in my arms, it was worth every bit of it.

He was crawling before Daniel returned from the war, so he feels mine in a way the others do not. When they were born, Daniel could be their father right away. I had Dandy to myself for a whole year.

When the time came for him to go to work, I humbled myself and begged Daniel to let me keep him another year. It was Dandy who changed my mind—his friends were on the breaker already, and he didn't want to look like a sissy.

"I'll be a red tip, Mama," he said, "but then my hands will harden up and it won't matter no more."

He's tough, my boy. Those first weeks when he came home with his fingers split and bloodied by the sharp slate, it sickened me. Knowing how I felt, Mama still insisted I take care of him, soaking his hands and smearing them with grease, bandaging them until he wrecked them again the following day.

I wouldn't let Daniel touch me for weeks. It wasn't his fault—he'd been through the same thing, I knew that well enough, having kissed his mutilated fingers when I was no more than eight—but this was my son.

When they brought him home last spring, a seeping bandage wrapped around his left hand, my heart near fell out of my chest. It was Mama, unwrapping it, who said, "Why that's only your pinkie finger. You'll hardly be missing that at all."

And Dandy blinked his swollen eyes and agreed, though I could see the tear tracks through the dirt on his face.

His brothers idolize him, and I thank God every day that they're puny and look no older than the babies they are. They're safe for a few more years.

There is a yawn behind me, and we turn. Thelma is curled in her chair like a kitten. "Thel, baby, wake up. Your aunt's here."

"Hello, auntie." Her eyes are large in her pointed face.

"Darling." My sister opens her arms. "Come give me a hug."

I watch Claire as Thelma hops off the chair and walks unevenly to her. People are unnerved by my daughter—such a beautiful child, with her pale hair and blue eyes, and then that awful limp. We had the doctor in when we realized, but he said whatever was wrong with her had happened too far back for him to fix.

A girl as pretty as Thelma won't have an easy life in a place like this, but as a cripple, she'll be invisible to the kind of men who might otherwise prey on her. Pearl is fierce in her defense of her sister, shouting at the boys when they exclude her for being too slow, and sneaking her extra food from her plate.

Claire scoops Thelma up and cuddles her in a way that looks almost desperate. With her love of babies, I'm surprised she and Harry don't have any after all this time. Daniel just has to smile for me to end up in the family way, so she must be doing something to prevent it. Since she's no longer Catholic, she won't go to hell, at least not for that.

"She likes you."

"I like her." Claire kisses her head. "What would you like me to send you when I go home, Thelma? Do you want a doll? A storybook?"

She gets down and leans against my hip, looking at me for permission. "I don't have a doll."

"Then I'll send you a doll, one with yellow hair and blue eyes just like yours," Claire says. "You look for it by Christmas, all right?"

She nods. "I'm hungry, Mama."

They're probably all hungry. "Pearl—"

"I'll warm up Mrs. Metzger's stew," she says. "Daddy will be late if he doesn't eat soon."

Claire

We retreat to the front room while Pearl starts dinner and the drop in temperature is shocking. It's been a long time since I've done without central heating, and I tuck my hands under my legs when I sit, missing the marvelous cast-iron radiators that keep our house toasty.

"Light the stove, would you?" Ava says to Daniel.

"Don't bother on our account," Harry says. "I thought we'd drop Dan at work on our way to the hotel. Is that all right with you, Claire?"

I glance over at Mama. A few candles flicker among the flowers, and though she's just in the middle of the front room, it feels almost like a church. Harry probably sees the house as dirty, but I think it's miraculous, with everything she's had on her plate, that Ava found the time to clean at all. "We haven't had much chance to talk."

Ava raises an eyebrow. "I'm going to sit up with her again tonight," she says. "Once the kids go to bed. You're welcome to stay."

"I'd like that," I say, without thinking. Do I want to sit up with my mother's body—with my sister?

Harry drops a hand on my shoulder. "If you'd like to stay, I'll bring your change of clothes in the morning."

I turn from Ava to him. "Would you mind?"

"I'll manage." There is a smile in his voice. "I saw Jim Brooks when we checked in. I'll catch up with him. You spend some time with your family."

After dinner, when the men have gone and the younger children are in bed, Ava and I settle into the front room again. She turns up the lamp and moves the mending basket close to her chair, looking surprised when I lean forward and pull something from the pile.

"You don't need to." She threads a needle to replace a button on a striped flannel shirt. "I can manage, or Pearl."

"She's doing homework." I pluck a needle from the tomato cushion. "I'd like to feel useful."

It doesn't take long to regret the shirt I've chosen; the seam is badly frayed, impossible to mend with anything approaching neatness. I wouldn't bother to fix anything in this condition, but clothing is precious here.

"Did I miss Frank today?"

"He'll be here tomorrow." Ava snips the thread and puts the shirt to one side. "He's come every Sunday for months."

Even Frank, who moved away when I was still in school, is a more frequent visitor. With a sigh, I reach for another, simpler task, hoping to regain the comfort I once had in my sister's company, but she sews in silence, her mind elsewhere.

Ava's movements are quick, impatient. Just like her. She's always been this way, but it seems like her natural tendencies have grown sharper with age. Daniel and the kids defer to her, which is just as well because she would run right over them anyway.

My sister has always made me feel small. That's more my problem than hers. I let her manage me, and then I delivered myself into Harry's hands, and he passed me on to his mother. I've never been anything but controlled by my elders. I'm sick of it, but I don't know how to change.

When the basket is empty, Ava folds the finished pieces on the ottoman, lowers the lamp, and sinks back with a pained sigh. "This one could come any day now, but I reckon he's due near Christmas."

"Do you think it's a boy? How can you tell?"

"See how I'm carrying here, all straight out to the front?" She turns in her chair, showing me her profile. "That's how I carried with Dandy and the boys. With Pearl and Thelma, I got fat all over."

"Can I..." My hands twist in my lap. "Can I touch him?"

She shrugs. "He's quiet, because I've been sitting, so you might not feel much. If I was trying to sleep, he'd be turning somersaults."

I place my palm on her belly—it's almost hard, not what I expect. I shake my head. "He's not moving for me."

"Like I said, he's probably asleep. I hope he naps this much when he's on the outside." Pushing herself up using the arms of the chair, she says, "Tea. I'm chilled through." She turns when she realizes I'm not with her. "Claire?"

Mama's sewing machine stands near the window, its high wooden cover latched over the black-and-gold Singer beneath. I run my fingertips over the carved design; it's the most ornate piece of furniture in the house. "Remember when she tried to teach me to use this?"

"You were afraid you were going to sew your fingers."

"I still am," I tell her. "Harry bought me a machine after I told him how much you and Mama loved to sew, and how good you were at it. I've used it once or twice, but it scares me to death." I stroke the wood again and turn away. "Did you know they make electrical machines now? No more treadle."

"Is it fast?" Ava's sternness melts into something very like Toby and George's expressions when they saw the Packard. "What else can it do?"

"It's so fast! The first time I pressed the pedal, it took off like a car." I remember my reaction. "I screamed, and Harry laughed and laughed."

"I'd love to try one of those."

"They're much less expensive now. Mine was only thirty-nine dollars."

Ava laughs so hard she has to clutch her belly. "That's more than Daniel makes in a month—and we don't have electric."

The lamp is arranged so the light falls on Pearl's books. She looks up at our entrance. "Do you want tea, Mama?"

"I want you in bed, my girl." Ava offers her cheek. "You've put in a long day."

Pearl kisses us and vanishes, and I point Ava toward the rocker. "Let me deal with the tea, you sit and warm yourself."

"I won't say no." She settles in, rocking slowly. "I'm exhausted, but I never sleep well by this point."

"You'll be more comfortable after." I stand close to the stove, discreetly holding my hands toward its warmth. Using the coal stove is a luxury, but the boys can always scavenge wood to heat the kitchen.

"Maybe," Ava says, "but I won't sleep then, either. He'll need feeding every few hours, and when he's not eating, he'll be yelling his head off." She rubs her belly with affection. "It's what they do."

"I wish I'd come home sooner."

"So do I." Her voice is matter-of-fact. "But Mama understood."

"Do you?"

Ava is quiet. "Not entirely," she says at last, "but I don't need to. This isn't your home, not anymore." She takes the cup from me. "But she was your mother."

"And you're my sister." Tears brim and I blink them back. Keeping myself always in check is exhausting. "I spend so much time pretending to belong, but no one is fooled. I'm an outsider there, and now I'm one here."

"How are you an outsider?" Her skeptical tone makes me feel an inch tall. "Harry adores you, anyone can see that. And you look like something out of a magazine."

The dress I'm wearing undoubtedly cost more than the entire Kimber family wardrobe. "All it takes to look like this is money, but money doesn't matter when people don't accept you."

"His mother?" Ava guesses. "Is that old bat still around?"

I feel guilty for laughing, but Irene Warriner is over a hundred miles away and can't possibly know we're making fun of her. "I think she'd almost forgive me for taking her son if I gave her a grandchild, but…"

"You haven't yet."

"I've lost five babies." The taste of loss is bitter on my tongue. "They say to put it out of my mind, like they weren't real. I let them think I do, but I can't." I wipe my eyes resolutely, not wanting her pity. "Harry treats them like business deals that fell through, but they're children to me."

Ava takes in my words. Then, instead of sympathy or platitudes, like a normal person, she says, "Do you think it's because of what happened?"

Damn her. "I don't want to talk about that."

She nods. "I understand. But do you think—"

"If it is, what good does it do to think about it now?" My secret has been with me for fifteen years. "I can't carry a child to term. I feel like I've sold Harry a bill of goods because all he wanted was children."

She gets up and clumsily puts her arm around me. "Does he know?"

I jerk away. "No."

Why can't she leave it alone? Ava is the only one who knows what happened—aside from the man who hurt me—and we vowed, long ago, never to speak of it.

"Did you ever tell Daniel?"

"No." Her expression darkens. "I don't like keeping things from him."

I laugh. "It's not like he'd tell anyone. He doesn't talk."

"Mostly he listens," she agrees, her mouth curling. "But we talk about what's important."

Despite the stove, I'm cold again. I rub my hands together, to warm them and to hide their sudden shaking. "The past isn't important."

"Sometimes it is." Ava's hands link under her belly, making me wonder how it feels, to be so big and off-balance. "We shouldn't have kept it from Mama."

A moment of fear before I remember she's dead. "She would have gone to the mine office and demanded his head on a platter, and they would have laughed in her face. And they would have probably sent him to evict us." I remember his sneering face, the tobacco on his breath. His dirty fingernails when he'd grabbed my wrists. "Everyone would have known. I couldn't have endured that."

"Bastard," Ava says quietly.

"Bastard," I agree. I want to be at home, where even slightly uncomfortable conversations are eased with sherry. For this, I need gin, or Harry's whiskey, but all Ava has to offer is tea and not enough sugar.

5

Pearl

Aunt Claire looks like she walked out of a magazine. Thelma will look just like that someday, except that she won't, not really.

Mama's being nicer than I expected. Being sisters is something you don't get over, I guess. She's bristly as a cat, though. I don't know if it's losing Granny or Aunt Claire staying away so long. It's definitely because Uncle Harry brought whiskey into the house.

If drink is illegal, how come it's so easy to get? I smelled it on the porch earlier, too. What the men here drink comes from stills up on the mountain, but what Uncle Harry brought is from a store, with a label that says Scotland. I asked him about it when Mama wasn't around because it's the kind of question she'd say was rude. He says it's not illegal to drink it, only to make it or sell it or ship it.

Since that didn't answer my question, I guess that bottle just fell out of the sky and into his fancy car.

Now I sound like Mama.

Ava

Daniel comes in after five, moving slowly, and we leave him alone to wash. The night shift can't use the wash house, and he is black from head to foot, his eyes and teeth flashing white like a minstrel show I once saw. He emerges soon after with a mug of tea and settles in to doze in the armchair while we return to the kitchen.

"Doesn't he mind the cold?" Claire asks.

"He's used to it." I think of where he's been, and then the walk home in the snowy darkness; the unheated front room is an improvement.

Seeing Claire again is jarring. It isn't that she's so different, more that she's become fixed: too thin, too blonde, too brittle. Her expressions change quickly, as if she is uncertain of the right one for the situation. She appears happy with Harry, and he certainly dotes on her, but something is wrong. It might be the lack of children or the secret we've kept all these years. I don't know. But she'd been such a sunny little girl. I hate seeing that light dimmed, even by her own hand.

When I return from yet another trip to the outhouse, I find a sister who has run out of tears and moved on to practicalities. "What about her headstone?"

"We'll get one." Claire hands me a cup and I let it warm my fingers. "Eventually."

She puffs out a breath. "You don't have to do it all yourself, you know. Let me and Frank chip in. She was our mother, too."

"Frank is already paying half the burial cost." I don't mind taking money from my brother—not as much, anyway.

"Then let us pay for the stone. Please."

Pearl comes soundlessly into the kitchen and ties on an apron. "Mama, they're awake up there. Should I get started?"

I stand, one hand going automatically to my low back. It doesn't like lying down, but it doesn't appreciate sitting up all night either. "I should have already."

"The stove is nice and hot still from Daddy's wash water, you stay put."

I squeeze her shoulders as I maneuver past, addressing my next words to Claire. "Fine. And thank you."

She doesn't gloat, I'll give her that. "I'll have Harry order it before we leave." She hesitates. "How many names?"

"All four, if you're paying," I say wryly. "On our dime, she'd get 'Mother.'"

"Four names?" Pearl turns from the pot of oatmeal.

"Lillie Donohue Flannery Kovaleski," Claire recites. "Her maiden name, her first husband, and your Grandpa."

"Granny was married twice?" Dandy comes in with an armload of stove wood, dropping it into the box with a clatter. "I've filled the coal already and sent Dad upstairs to bed." He leans over Pearl's shoulder until she swats him with a spoon.

"Your granny was married in Ireland," I say. "He came over first, and she followed the next year with the baby."

Claire takes up the tale. "She traveled from Dublin to New York, then got on a train." She looks from Pearl to Dandy. "When she arrived in Scovill Run, she discovered Gerry Flannery was dead. Measles."

"What did she do?" they ask in unison.

"Can you imagine?" Claire is tearful again, picturing sorrows fifty years in the past. "Twenty years old, no family, no friends, no husband."

"What choice did she have?" Mama always said, no matter what happened, you got on with life. That lesson seems to have skipped Claire. "She took a job cooking at the hotel, and the men lined up to court her when they realized she was a widow."

"Even with a baby?" Pearl neglects the oatmeal in her fascination with her granny's story.

"Especially with a baby." I realize too late how that will sound to Claire.

"She married your Grandpa within two months," she says smoothly, not looking at me. "She said she didn't want to marry another Irishman, because the first one hadn't been so lucky."

"Was the baby Uncle Frank?" Judging the oatmeal to be ready, Dandy shoulders Pearl aside and starts dishing it out. "Call them," he says. "They've probably tied Thelma up or something."

"Hang on," Pearl says. "Was it Uncle Frank, Mama?"

"No, the baby was Gerry, after his daddy. He was grown and out of the house by the time I was little." I barely remember him. "He was killed in the war."

Pearl ducks out and calls up the stairs to the kids. "You'd better be dressed right, you two!"

The boys shove each other into the kitchen. Their short pants are clean and their shirts are tucked in, though their ties are crooked, and George's knitted vest has a hole in it. Their light brown hair is damp, marked with the tracks of a comb.

"Very nice." I tweak Toby's tie into place. "What have you done with your sister?"

Daniel hands Thelma in the door. "Are you looking for a fairy princess?" He tips his head toward the stairs. "I'll be back down before you're ready to go."

Pearl passes the bowls around. "Mama," she asks, "did Granny love Grandpa?"

"Of course she did," Claire says immediately.

"Not straight away," I answer at the same time. "But she thought he would be a good provider. She said it was easy to fall in love with a good man."

Not long after we've finished eating, Frank arrives with Polina and his kids. He alights from the beat-up truck he shares with his brother-in-law and feigns shock at the sight of Claire. I get between them before he can say anything upsetting. My careless words have been enough; she's too fragile for his rough tongue.

Everyone shoves into the front room, the kids talking loudly until Pearl shepherds them into the kitchen. "Be quiet or I'll put you all outside."

"Dan still on nights?" Frank accepts a cup of tea. "Poor bastard."

"It's a tough schedule." I look toward the stairs; if he doesn't come down soon, I'll have to wake him. "With Dandy on days, they hardly see each other."

Frank ruffles Dandy's hair. "How're you liking it?"

"It's okay." My son looks uncomfortable in his Sunday clothes, his ragged hands jammed in his pockets. "I'll be underground after the new year."

Daniel appears, wearing his wedding suit. It hasn't fit properly in years, but I've never gotten around to altering it. Since Sunday is his only day off, he rarely attends church, and the suit comes out only for funerals. Like the boys, his hair is wet and freshly combed. Unlike the boys, his tie is straight.

Looking at the clock, he says, "Undertaker should be here soon. Why don't you all go into the kitchen? Frank and I can deal with him."

The words are well-meant, but I want to be here when Mama is carried out. I gather the kids and they kiss her one last time. It's best they don't see; the world is real enough already without watching their grandmother's body taken away.

There's a knock, but instead of the undertaker, it's Harry, with a box of hotel pastries and a suitcase and hatbox for Claire. She takes them and sprints for the stairs. I follow more slowly, letting the men deal with the undertaker after all while Polina watches the kids.

When I make it upstairs, the bed is littered with clothing, but Claire is still, gazing into the uncovered mirror. I put a hand on her shoulder and she jumps. "You were staring into that thing the way you did when you were twelve."

"For a second there, I thought you were Mama, creeping up to scold me for being vain."

I slip behind the screen, hanging my tired cotton dress over the side and stepping into fresh drawers. By this point, everything is uncomfortable. The borrowed skirt barely closes, and I add a safety pin at the waist as an extra precaution. The blouse is better. It isn't pretty, but the abundant tucks at the yoke let the fabric drape over my bulk.

Years fall away as I watch Claire get ready. She steps out of her dress and stands for a moment in her underthings before whipping them off and changing into a fresh set, pale pink satin, the prettiest I've ever seen.

"Lord, Ava, how can you stand this room? I'm practically blue!"

"I don't walk around naked." She always had pretty legs. I watch her wiggle one foot into a sheer black stocking and turn away, strangely embarrassed by my sister's womanhood.

Sliding the pins from my hair, I rub my knuckles against my scalp. I should have remembered to take my hair down last night; keeping it up for too long makes my head ache.

"Let me."

"Don't fuss, Claire." She takes up the brush anyway and I close my eyes. Brushing my hair is one of the few attentions I permit.

"You always had such pretty hair."

I tip my head back. Anyone seeing the two of us side-by-side would know we were related, but they would probably not guess we were so close in age. If anything, I look like Claire's reflection in the old mirror, darker, my outlines uncertain. All Clare's edges are clean—her pointed chin, her smooth jawline, her thin arms and slender legs.

"You got the better color." Is her hair still natural, or is it dyed these days? I cast back, smiling briefly. "Mama called you and Teddy her butter babies because of how blonde you were."

"But your hair is so thick. Mine has always been fine."

"Pregnancy makes it thick." I don't take to compliments, nor see any beauty in the hair that reaches halfway down my back. I'd bob it, but then I'd have to deal with the upkeep, and I don't have the patience for that either.

When Daniel and I married, I wouldn't have said I was pretty, but I was attractive enough, with a defined waist, high breasts, and no stretch marks on my stomach. Now lines trace across my flesh like the silvery tracks of snails, and if there is a lotion or an oil that will reduce them, I've never seen it, and we couldn't afford it anyway. "Remember, I've been pregnant or nursing for the past fourteen years." I stand, ending the moment, and twist my hair back into its knot, stabbing in pins with unnecessary force.

The whole business takes less time than it takes Claire to put on her slip. She's like a dress-up doll, I think, watching as she zips herself into a sleek black dress with godets in the skirt. Her white collar and cuffs glow in the dim room.

"You belong in a magazine." I resist the urge to touch her sleeve to see if the fabric is as nice as it looks.

"Don't be silly." The damp has loosened her waves and she opens the hatbox, removing a dark gray cloche and sliding it over her hair. She applies a fresh Cupid's bow of lipstick and offers the tube. "It would brighten you up some."

It is dark red, the color of blood. "No thanks," I say, retreating. "I'll go as myself."

6

Ava

Scovill Run existed before the mine, but there are few people left who remember when the company didn't rule the town and everyone in it. The breaker is a ramshackle, five-story construction for cleaning and processing the anthracite that emerges from the Gracie no. 2, dug from the ground by men like my husband. It's an ugly thing, and I hate it.

Men and boys walk down these sloping streets each morning and trudge back up at dusk. Children attend school in its shadow, knowing it is their future.

Our house is a mile from the center of town. It is a long mile or short, depending on how you feel. Today, it is a muddy mile, and none of us want to walk, but when Harry suggests taking the car, I shake my head. We won't fit in two vehicles, and it doesn't seem right, straggling into the church in dribs and drabs, so we walk behind the horse-drawn hearse, leaving both car and truck behind.

The church doors are open and Father Dennis paces outside, wearing a mismatched muffler and cap. From a distance, he looks much younger than his mid-seventies. I expect he'll be around to baptize my grandchildren.

He greets me with a kiss and slaps Daniel on the back. His wild gray eyebrows rise when he sees Claire, but he contents himself with, "It's good to have you home, my dear. How long has it been?"

"Too long, I'm sure." She dips her fingers in the holy water and crosses herself. Episcopalian Harry waves his hand over the font and follows her inside.

I see St. Stan's through their eyes: a shabby little church, the stations of the cross painted roughly on the walls, a faded gilt crucifix swaying above the altar. Off to one side are two confessional booths and a shrine to St. Barbara. The swaybacked pews, shiny with polish, are textured with decades of vandalism perpetrated by bored little boys.

If I slide my hand along the last pew, I will find D&A 1908 carved into the seat. That was the year Daniel first asked me to marry him.

Claire

I've almost allowed myself to forget Frank, but back in this place, I remember. His angry, twisted face looming over mine, taunting me for being pretty, for being my father's favorite. Smashing my doll when I told on him.

Why had he disliked me so? Mama said some people just can't abide beauty in an ugly world, and that was Frank. She seemed embarrassed to have such an awful son, but she never could do anything with him. Only Tata could manage Frank, but he chose instead to drink with him.

The day he married Polina and went to live with her family was the happiest day of my childhood.

Watching him now, his face half turned away, I wonder if Frank had seen the same thing in me that *he* had, something that could be easily squashed and dominated. Something he could hurt, for the pleasure of it. Now he eyes me, and the flesh creeps on the back of my neck. Ava gets between us, and the moment passes.

We make our way to the church through streets just as muddy as yesterday. Harry doesn't understand why we can't drive, but I squeeze his hand and he walks silently beside me.

Once we pass Father Dennis and his enthusiastic greeting, the church is dingy and cold, just like I remember. There's a shrine to the miners' saint in an alcove, with candles burning at her feet. It feels strange and spare; the harsh god of my childhood still lives here.

As the eldest, Frank takes the first pew with his family. Ava and Daniel file into the next row with Dandy and sweet little Thelma. Harry and I slide in next to Pearl, whose job is to keep an eye on her younger brothers.

She looks over. "Aunt Claire, can you watch them when I do my reading?"

"Of course." How do you keep an eye on Toby and George, who, even in this sacred place, are poking each other and giggling like small demons. I smile at them, and they break into waves of hilarity.

Harry leans over. "You two." His voice carries enough authority that they stop laughing. "Do you want to clean my car after the funeral? Nickel apiece."

Their eyes widen and they nod.

"Then you'll both sit here quiet as mice." He looks over his glasses. "I'll be watching."

I wouldn't have thought to bribe them, with money or access to the car. After a dozen years, I still have much to learn about my husband.

The coffin stands before the altar, with the simple flowers from Ava's house grouped in front of the brass candlesticks. The blanket of carnations and lilies I ordered covers the entire top of the coffin. Is it too showy? Do they make the other flowers look shabby, or do theirs make ours look ridiculous?

They smell divine, and I focus on their scent as the service begins. Despite attending St. Mark's Episcopal Church for the last dozen years, my body remembers the Catholic service and makes the appropriate responses to Father Dennis's opening prayer.

In front of us, there is a sound—a cough or a laugh—and when I look, Ava has her face buried in her hands, her shoulders shaking. My eyes fill, to see her weeping in public.

When the priest finishes, Pearl rises and walks slowly to the lectern. She's at the worst part of an awkward age. Her socks droop around her ankles, making her plaid skirt look even shorter.

She finds the paper marker in the big Bible. "A reading from the letter of St. Paul to the Romans." Her voice trembles and she takes a breath visible from where we sit. Her intonation, when she speaks, is Mama's, but without the brogue; they must have spent a lot of time together.

"I consider that the sufferings of this present time are as nothing compared with the glory to be revealed for us."

Her voice grows stronger, though her knuckles are white where she grips the lectern.

> *"We know that all creation is groaning in labor pains even until now;*
>   *and not only that, but we ourselves,*
>   *who have the first fruits of the Spirit,*
>   *we also groan within ourselves*
>   *as we wait for adoption, the redemption of our bodies.*
> *The word of the Lord."*

Father Dennis returns to lead us in a psalm, and my mind wanders until he says something that cannot be ignored.

> *"Your wife will be like a fruitful vine within your home,*
> *Your children like young olive plants around your table."*

His words could have been crafted to point out my failure. I am the blighted, barren branch of that fruitful vine, my mother.

I wrench my mind from these dark thoughts and focus on Ava's children. They are undersized, but sturdy enough, except for Thelma. I want to carry her off to a place that will be kinder to her. And Pearl, with that unfortunate shingled haircut. Given her role as second mother to the little ones, perhaps it's for the best; she will have no time for romance.

Dandy is dark and rangy, with the hunched shoulders of a boy who's grown too quickly. The younger boys—sandy and freckled like Ava—are all elbows and knees, and that, along with their inability to keep out of trouble, explains why they're in short pants a week before Thanksgiving.

Abruptly, there is silence and I join in on the "Amen," before anyone can catch me woolgathering.

I am thankful that Father Dennis and Ava between them decided against a full mass with communion. Sitting through the homily is more than enough for me, and for my nephews. Only the threat of losing access to the car is keeping Toby and George in their seats.

This visit hasn't been what I feared, and I regret—again—not coming home sooner. Mama was hardly neglected, not in that crowded house, but it wasn't kind to abandon her, and she raised her children to be kind.

So many children. There had been a stillborn son and at least one miscarriage. Of Mama's seven living children, only three of us are left. Possibly four, but no one has heard from Jake in almost twenty years. He'd been my defender, but he wasn't strong enough to face the mines again after the cave-in.

"I have to go," he said, shoving clothes into a sack. "Now that it's opening up again, I can't refuse. Mama won't let me."

"If you leave, I won't have anyone."

"You won't have me if I die down there." His freckled face was bleak.

The next morning, when his absence was discovered, I bit my lip and feigned ignorance, though I ached for Mama. She thought the worst had already happened, but his disappearance broke something in her. She still smiled, but Jake took her laughter.

Ava

I keep my hands over my face until I am confident I can control myself. Beside me, Daniel is still shaking, and I kick his ankle to make him stop. Bad enough people will see me and think I'm crying; to be caught laughing at my mother's funeral would be unforgivable.

"Did they deliver the wrong flowers?" he whispered. "There's a racehorse somewhere looking at a wreath that says 'Mother.'"

Frank approaches the lectern and I focus on his halting sentences to bring myself back to the proper frame of mind. He reads no better than Daniel, but he doesn't have the self-awareness to realize it.

One of the things I hate most about the mine is that it keeps men ignorant, taking them so young they're unable to read well enough to be informed or entertained when they aren't at work. I think it's deliberate: an educated workforce wouldn't tolerate such treatment, but those who don't know better welcome work at any price.

Father Dennis calls for us to pray and I bow my head, praying for my mother's soul and for some other employer to come to Scovill Run so that my remaining boys—and this baby—will not have to join their father underground.

After the burial, there's a short wake at the town hall, organized with Father Dennis's blessing. Women stand behind a long table with filled cups and pre-cut slices of cake at the ready.

"Thank you for doing this." I watch to make sure Toby and George don't take more than their share.

"You're in no condition to host half the town right now," Alma Cooper says, nodding at my midsection. "Not with this one to worry about."

Alma had been a school friend, though I can't recall the last time we spoke beyond casual greetings at church or the store. She and Bettina Vankirk and Ulla Randall did this for my mother, and I am grateful.

I find a seat along the wall and let people come to me. The baby is a lead weight and I crave silence and a place to nap. Claire and the kids take turns sitting with me, and I have a few moments with Father Dennis, who takes my hands and prays with me. It helps, a bit.

There is only so much sympathy I can take; I need someone who will be normal with me. I look for Trudy and find her standing among her family, her hands curled around a teacup. I wave her over.

"Are you okay?"

"I am fine." She does not look fine at all. This is more than losing Mama.

"What's wrong?"

She sits, heaving a great sigh. Close up, her eyes are red. "My son leaves tomorrow to find work. He takes the two youngest kinder with him, to live with Dora's people."

"I'm so sorry." Karl Metzger has been out of work for months, and the family is getting by on the salary brought in by Trudy's brother, Hermann. Lots of men are going off to look for work these days, but splitting up the children seems particularly harsh. "Can't you change his mind?"

Trudy brushes a wisp of hair from her eyes. "It is what he wants," she says. "You know he has not been himself since..."

Her voice trails off. Dora died six months ago, giving birth to the baby who will now be handed off to her other grandmother in western Pennsylvania, where her father won't have to look at her.

"You should have told me."

"I did not want you to worry," she says. "You have enough on your plate."

My plate is full because I have people to worry about. Trudy's plate is clearing because her worries are being taken away, but at what cost? I would do anything to keep my family together—but so would she, and it hasn't worked.

I take a sip of tea. "These bad times can't last forever."

"Let us hope not." She tries to smile. "I will spend this evening with my family. Let me know if you need me. We will both be lonely, now."

We stay for another hour, and I watch Claire deal with those who gawk at her clothes and her hat and her husband. When it looks to be too much, I catch Daniel's eye. He nods and makes his way to Father Dennis, who raises his booming voice over the general noise.

"I want to thank you all for coming today to honor our dear sister and her family, here from both near and far. When Lillie came to Scovill Run, she was a girl. A mother. A widow. Fifty years later, there's not a family in this town that hasn't been touched by her in one way or another." Wiping his eyes with a large white handkerchief, he adds, "That would be including myself. I'll now offer one last prayer for the departed." He bows his head, and we all do likewise.

As we struggle into coats and hats, Father Dennis joins us. "Go with God," he says, kissing my cheek. "Your mother is with you."

Tears sting; I've felt her close this whole day. "Thank you, Father," I say, and hug him as best as I can.

Warmed by tea and community, we make our slow way home. I wish I had thought to visit the toilet at the hall before we left. This baby has a future as a vaudeville star, the way he's tap dancing on my bladder.

The boys walk between Harry and Claire, their brimming energy in check for once. Perhaps they're more upset than I realized. I pay them no further mind until we reach the house and they skid to a halt, glancing expectantly at their uncle.

Hands in his coat pockets, Harry looks them up and down. "Still want to clean the car?"

"Yes!"

"What's this?" Daniel puts a hand on each boy's shoulder.

"Bribery," Harry confesses with a shrug. "I said they could clean the car if they behaved in church. It will have to be washed when we get home anyway."

The car's gleaming chrome is dulled with mud and coal dust, which, of course, will be transferred to my children, but…in the name of peace, I let it go. "You can do it, but change your clothes first."

"I don't want you paying them," Daniel says. "They'll do it for free."

The boys' faces fall. "But he promised," Toby says. "Mama says it's important to keep your promises."

"You only hear me when it suits you." I cast a glance at my husband. "Let them do it."

Once their church clothes have been swapped for everyday shirts and short pants, the boys raid the rag bin and attack the car with enthusiasm. They are soon joined by other boys, some with buckets, others with more rags. "They'll clean me out, the little robber barons," Harry says, smiling easily. "How do you manage them?"

I put my feet up, something I've wanted to do all this long day. "With a whip and a chair, sometimes."

"When we have to leave them home, Mama says 'don't break anything, don't set anything on fire.'" Pearl is on the davenport beside me, waiting to be of use. "I used to tie them to the porch when they were little, but they always got loose."

"They're good with knots." Daniel inspects their work out the window. "They're mad for cars, especially Toby."

"I don't imagine they see them too often," my sister says over Thelma's head.

We regained something during last night, Claire and I, something I've desperately missed. After the mending and the tea, we sat in the dark with Mama, waiting for Daniel. "You're still my favorite person." There was a wobble in Claire's voice, but it was her words that struck me, taking me straight back to our girlhood, when she would roll toward me in the dark and say that.

She sounded as earnest as she had then, and when I answered, "No, you're *my* favorite," she made a sound like a sob and we agreed wordlessly to retreat to the kitchen for more tea.

Will we be able to maintain that closeness once we're separated again? I want to—without Mama, I need Claire more than ever. After she told me about her lost babies, I shared my fear of having a stranger deliver this one; I am more nervous than I care to admit, even to Daniel.

He passes behind me and puts his hands on my shoulders, rubbing the knots at the base of my neck. "We'd probably have to sell at least three kids to afford a car, right, honey?"

I tilt my head and smile up at him. "At least three. Maybe four."

We polish off the rest of Harry's pastries and some jam-filled horns left over from yesterday. No one mentions the whiskey, and I'm glad. It's the last thing Frank needs; if he starts in on Claire, Daniel and Harry together will pitch him into the road, while I cheer them on.

At three, Harry goes out to check on the boys, jingling the change in his pocket. He returns with George and Toby, swatting them affectionately as he pushes them toward me. "They've robbed me blind."

"He gave us each a quarter!" George says in wonder.

"Which you'll give to your ma," Daniel tells him. "We'll save them for a Christmas treat."

They are pacified by the mention of Christmas and the coins, warm and sticky, are given into my hand.

Claire

"We'd better get on the road." Harry needs to go to work in the morning. "It's not a long drive, but…"

Frank waves a hand through the putrid cigar smoke that encircles him. "Get on your way, dolly. You can forget we exist now."

"Shut it, Frank." Daniel puts himself between us, and I want to kiss him.

Instead, I stumble into Ava's unwieldy embrace. "I've missed you," I tell her. "So much."

"Me too." She hugs me tight. "Write to me? I'll need news from outside."

"I will." I no longer belong here, but I'm not the stranger I thought I was. "Will you be all right? You can always come to us—all of you."

"We'll manage," she says, ignoring my invitation. "One way or another."

"Mama always said we don't know what we're capable of until we're forced to do it." I try to sound hopeful. "I pray everything goes well."

Ava closes her eyes. "She also said family stays together, over and over like it was a goddamn prayer, and you see how well that's worked out."

"We will stay together this time," I vow, taking my coat from her cold hands. "We will."

Harry touches my arm. "Are you ready?" I look from him to Ava. I'm not ready to leave my sister, but she's had as much as she can take for one day. "Yes," I say. "Let's go."

When Scovill Run recedes into the distance, I am filled with a strange blend of emotions: relief at my escape, regret at the sight of Ava and the children waving from the front porch. I returned to say goodbye to my mother, but I'm leaving with my sister restored to me.

"How are you feeling?" He's in a much better mood now that the weather has cleared.

"Better," I say. "Grief is divided if enough people bear it with you."

"Then you should hardly feel a thing." He turns onto the road following the mountain. "That was quite a crowd at the church."

"Mama knew everyone." I thought of all the things I hadn't said to her because of distance, or time, or the fear that my letters might be read aloud. What had I been afraid of? I'd lost so much time.

"Your sister's a strong woman," he says, in lieu of nothing. Except Harry's remarks are never in lieu of nothing, and there is something he wants to say.

"She always has been."

"Daniel's a hard one to warm up to, though." He has one hand on the wheel while the other holds my gloved fingers. "Nice enough fellow, but…"

I love when he holds my hand. Watching Daniel and Ava's casual affection makes me notice my husband's formality. "Ava's the only one who can make him laugh."

"When did he go into the mine?"

I think back. "I had only just started school, so nine or ten? It tore Ava up. She met him every day when his shift ended, to make sure he was still in one piece."

Whatever Harry wanted to say, it appears to have been said. He lapses into silence, focusing his attention on the road.

The car is warm. I remove my hat. My hair is lank from the dampness and the coal dust in the air. First thing tomorrow, I'll call the beauty parlor and schedule a shampoo and set. The least I can do is to provide Harry with an attractive exterior when he comes home. My insides could be feathers—or spiders, for all he knows—but I am fresh and blonde and beautifully dressed, thanks to his money.

"Do you know," I say, "when I was Pearl's age, I thought about joining the church."

He looks briefly at me. "I don't see you as a nun, my dear."

"Neither did I, in the end." Mama tolerated my fervor, but she knew I lacked vocation before I did. "I think I just wanted to get away." I smoothed my gloves, dark gray to match my coat. "Then I realized Father Dennis might have wanted to escape his hometown, and look where he ended up. Joining the church was no guarantee I wouldn't spend my life in someplace equally miserable."

Harry reaches over and claims my hand again. "I'm glad you waited for me to find you."

7

Pearl

November 20, 1931

I read my verse at the funeral and wasn't too nervous. Mama put a bow in my hair, like that changed anything. A plain girl in a bow is still plain.

Aunt Claire left before suppertime. I wonder if we'll see her again? Uncle Frank said something mean and I thought she was going to cry. He makes me feel that way too sometimes. Mama says he's always been a bully. She doesn't think we'll see much of him from now on, without Granny as an excuse. I should be sad, but I'm not. Don't think Mama is either.

Ava

Another wave of grief washes over me as I watch my sister drive away. How did she worm her way back in so quickly? As soon as Frank and Polina leave, Daniel runs upstairs and comes back dressed for work. I look at him, my heart sinking.

"They want me in tonight," he says. "They got word to me at the hall."

"But you were supposed to be off." Dandy was given a day for his grandmother's funeral; surely I can have my husband's comfort for one night.

"I know. But..."

Day men are certain of their employment, but most of the night workers have done something to end up there. It's been years since Daniel was mixed up with the effort to unionize, but the company hasn't forgotten. Backing down and a little public contrition saved his job, but he's been on nights ever since. It's their way of keeping him in his place.

After six years, I still miss having him home. Once the kids are asleep, the evenings stretch long. Without Mama to talk to, I'll be alone with my knitting until I give in and go to sleep.

Pearl would suggest that I read, but I hate to waste the lamp. Anyway, by that time, I'm so exhausted the words swim together on the page. I can knit in near-darkness, rest my eyes, and dream about a life where my husband comes home for supper and sits around and talks in the evening, then goes up to bed with me.

Lord, but I miss sleeping with him. We've mastered the art of silent love—there are always kids in the room or on the other side of the thin walls—and Daniel can bring me to completion with no more than a sigh, while he ends with a short, sharp sound, his face buried in my hair. It isn't just what we do together in bed. His horrible snoring, his hacking cough, his frequent thrashing nightmares are confirmation that the man I love is near. It doesn't matter that I sleep more deeply when he's at work; I sleep better when he's home.

Claire

November 22, 1931

Dear Sister,

We have made it back to Philadelphia, obviously, and I am missing you and the children more than you know. All the comforts of my life do not make up for having people to talk to or care about. I am writing now as proof of my renewed efforts to be a good sister. I am sorry it took Mama's death to bring about our reunion, but she would be happy we are together again. I know I sound silly, and you will probably think I haven't grown up yet, but I was so happy to see you again and know we are still truly sisters. For a long time, I was afraid we weren't.

Telling you my troubles has strangely lightened my mind, and I hope I didn't burden you with them. I am sure I (we) will try again, and if so, I will let you know this time.

In our absence, Irene has been preparing for Thanksgiving. Judging from the state of the house, we could feed half of Scovill

Run with her extravagance. I wish I could put it all on a train and ship it to you.

We are all that is left of this family, you and I, and while I may not be able to bear children, I bear much love for you and yours. Do write and tell me as soon as the baby is born. I long to know if I have a new niece or, as you predict, a nephew.

I know you are proud, but please consider—Harry could at any time find Daniel a job in one of his factories, or elsewhere depending on his inclinations. I would love to have you close so I could spend time with you and your family.

All my love,
Claire

Because it makes me look weak, I do not tell Ava I offered to help Irene with her holiday preparations and was rebuffed. Again. "Leave that to me and Mrs. Fell," she says. "Don't bother yourself about it."

"It's no bother," I protest. "I'm Harry's wife."

Her eyes narrow. "And I am his mother, and his hostess. No one expects you to manage these events."

No matter how I attempt to involve myself, my mother-in-law is in charge of everything. She tells the cook our schedule for the week and they discuss menus in Irene's rooms. When I ask Baxter to pick up something in the car, he checks with her first, to see if there are any errands more important than mine.

I squeeze my eyes shut, forcing back tears. Why can I not just tell her I want to be mistress of my own home?

Because it would do no good, that's why. If I challenge her, she'll go to Harry, and I do not want him to have to choose between us, nor do I wish to know who he would choose.

For a long time, when I was newly married and uncertain of my position, there was safety in being treated like a child; I was not expected to do much, or understand much, and so I did not. But now I am a thirty-year-old woman who is not permitted to manage her household, and it grates.

I hand my letter to Katie and retreat to my sitting room to consider what I have written. Is it mad to suggest that Ava pick up stakes and move her family to Philadelphia to live off my husband's charity? That's how she will see it, whether or not it's the truth. I'm not as scared of Ava as I was, but such an invitation is enough to bring out the worst in her. She's so proud. So stubborn, just like Mama. Both of them willing to let their children suffer rather than ask for help.

It's something I've sworn I will never do, though I will never likely be required to make such decisions. Maybe I would. Ava's not stupid, and neither is Daniel, for all his lack of education. They just can't see past their existence in that awful place, can't see that they could make new lives for themselves, and better futures for their children.

Harry would find a job for Daniel. He'd make one specifically if I asked him to. With his factories and other enterprises, I'm sure there's something my sister's husband could do—if he's capable of dragging coal from the earth at constant risk to his life, a factory job would be nothing for him.

I'd like to move them into our guest rooms and pamper them, especially Thelma. I didn't remember about her legs. Perhaps Ava never mentioned them; it's likely enough. I imagine myself with a little girl like Thelma, in a ruffled dress with white ankle socks and patent-leather shoes, her blonde hair in ribbons.

It would be like having a doll, but better. I close my eyes and picture my niece, my Thelma-doll, and get an idea.

Pearl

November 23, 1931

Aunt Claire either forgot her hat or thought it wasn't worth taking because it got wet. It looked ratty, but Mama just smiled and made me bring our biggest squash in from the back porch. She wrapped it in a towel and steamed the hat back into shape in no time. She says aunt probably has a dozen more like it anyway.

Now I have Mama's old hat, which makes me look very grown up. I wonder should I let my hair grow, so I can put it up? I'd rather pray to Jesus to look like Aunt Claire, but I don't think He grants prayers like that, or every lady would look like Aunt Claire.

Except for Mama. She would stay herself out of sheer hard-headedness.

Ava

Trudy and I combine forces for Thanksgiving. Karl has not returned, and for a few days, my smiling friend is replaced by a sad-eyed woman who looks ten years older. She pulls herself together because Fritz and Hetty, her remaining grandchildren, need her.

In addition to the moral support, a joint dinner means more food for all. One of Daniel's friends managed to shoot a couple of turkeys in the woods north of town, and he brought one home in exchange for helping to fix a roof. The house is perfumed with its rich scent.

Carrying the platter across the back porch to Trudy's kitchen, I think about how this was always Mama's favorite holiday. She was big on gratitude, giving loud thanks for blessings other people might not have recognized as such. I want to be more like her, but I can't help but see that we have a turkey only because Daniel gave up his day off, and a meal meant for family must be shared with others for there to be enough.

I hear Mama's voice, as I often do these days. *Family is whoever you choose to bring under your roof.* Trudy is family, in that sense, as was Dora, her daughter-in-law.

There are thirteen around the table, which is two tables put together and dragged into the front room: Trudy and Hermann, Fritz and Hetty, Daniel and me and our five, and two of Trudy's boarders who were invited at the last minute, soft-spoken men whose contributions are a pie and a packet of tea.

"Bless us, O Lord, and these, Thy gifts which we are about to receive from Thy bounty. Through Christ, Our Lord, amen."

The room falls silent but for "please pass the potatoes" and "may I have more beans?" For once no one worries about holding back for the next day.

One of the men says something to Hermann, and he repeats it to Trudy. She turns to me. "Hans says at such a meal, his family would go around the table and each person says what they are grateful for. Do you think this is good?"

"It sounds like something Mama would have liked."

Her eyes crinkle. "Then we shall do it for Lillie." She explains the idea to everyone and points to the man who suggested it. "Hans, is your idea, so you go first."

Hans blushes and stammers, but manages—with Trudy's translation—to say, "I am thankful to be surrounded by kind people when I am missing my family."

His friend, whose name I didn't catch, echoes him, word for word.

"I'm thankful for turkey!" Toby waves his fork.

"And pie!" George, not to be outdone, points toward the kitchen.

"I'm grateful for my family," Dandy says, ducking his head.

Trudy looks around. "I am thankful for my family that is here, and my family that is not here."

Fritz, his chin quivering, gulps and says, "I am thankful Mama didn't live to see us separated." His grandmother says something sharp in German and the boy shakes his head.

"I'm grateful for Granny," Pearl says, smoothing things over. "I'm grateful we had her as long as we did."

"So am I, honey." I put my hand over hers. "And I'm grateful for everyone at this table today."

"Thelma?" Daniel asks. "What about you?"

She looks up through tousled curls. "I'll be grateful not to be the baby anymore."

There is no night shift on Thanksgiving. Daniel and I huddle together under the quilts, listening to the murmur of the kids' conversation on the other side of the wall. It quiets down soon enough; their bellies are too full for them to stay awake for long.

"You never said what you were thankful for." I roll on my left side, the only position in which I am comfortable.

He curls around me and nuzzles my neck. "Like you have to ask," he says. "I'm thankful for you, and our family. I'm the luckiest man in the goddamn world."

8

Claire

"I'd like to send gifts to the children for Christmas," I say to Harry as we sit by the fire. I've waited until Irene has gone up, so she doesn't pour cold water on my idea. "Their situation struck me as rather dire, and I don't know how much they'll get otherwise. Ava's worried about money once the baby comes."

"They should be worried." Harry lights a cigarette and takes several puffs before continuing. "I don't know how much longer Daniel's going to have a job, the way things are going. Oil heat is the coming thing—I'm considering having our furnace changed over in the spring. It's cleaner than coal, and less expensive, once the burner is installed."

That stops me cold. What happens to Ava's family if the demand for coal disappears? If there aren't two shifts at the mine, Daniel will be out of work. They can't make the rent with Dandy's salary and whatever Ava brings in from sewing.

"Do you think people will stop using coal?" I shift the cut-glass ashtray toward him.

He leans forward, balancing his cigarette on the edge. "Oil is the fuel of the future. Men won't need to risk death underground just so we can keep warm."

"But that's all they know how to do." Scovill Run only exists because of the Gracie mine. "What happens if everyone starts to use this future fuel? What happens to men like Daniel?"

"Good question." Harry's eyes narrow. "If you can wait until Saturday, I'd like to come with you—they're good kids. It might be fun to shop for Christmas presents."

I finish his thought. *Like normal people. Like people with children.*

There are six large department stores in Philadelphia, but Wanamaker's, with its grand chandeliers and marble columns—

decorated for the holidays with enormous wreaths—has always struck me as special. Their pipe organ is the largest in the world, and its tuneful offerings filter through the store. The wide aisles on the ground floor seethe with shoppers, making it difficult to see the counters. On any other day, this would undoubtedly annoy Harry, but he is as excited as a boy to be shopping for Ava's children. "Shall we start in the toy department?"

The elevator hall is as crowded as the rest of the store. We duck into the nearest car and give our destination. "Ninth floor, please."

The car whooshes up and I squeeze Harry's hand. The smartly uniformed operator slides the gate back and we step out into a fancifully-decorated wonderland. Under garlands of lights, a line of children winds across the floor toward a heavily carved throne. Waiting for Santa.

We are the only adults unaccompanied by children. I almost don't mind, it's such a pleasure to watch the little ones, bundled in snowsuits and scarves, their cheeks red with excitement as they squeal and point at the shining black engine pulling a line of open cars filled with toys and gaily-wrapped packages through the snowy Christmas village.

"I never got to see the trains at Christmas." Harry's expression is wistful. "Mother didn't like crowds. Our Christmas was always delivered."

I squeeze his fingers. The occasional glimpse of the boy inside my husband fills me with love. Why couldn't Irene have allowed him such a simple pleasure?

"I wish they could see this." I stop to look at a tableau of ice-skating penguins wearing striped scarves and knitted hats. "They would love it."

"Toby and George would rob the train." Harry's smile is fond; he likes the boys despite their wildness.

When Harry drifts toward the trains, I am drawn to the doll display. It appears endless. There are large dolls, small dolls, dolls with full wardrobes. Dolls that look like women and dolls that look like babies. There are china dolls, and the newer composition ones, which are less breakable but equally pretty. I examine them all, trying to pick the perfect one for Thelma. I consider and discard a sweet-faced walking doll; it seems unkind to draw attention to her lameness with its smooth, mechanical gait.

Closing my eyes, I try to imagine what would have made me happiest at her age, and when I open them again, the doll is right in front of me. She has a porcelain head with abundant golden curls, blue eyes with bristly black lashes, and wears a blue flounced dress and white leather shoes. I amuse myself by selecting a few more outfits, including a fur-trimmed skating costume and a pink satin gown with beads at the neckline.

My purchase fills me with excitement, and I want to keep shopping, to give my nieces and nephews all the things they deserve. While the doll is being wrapped, I choose a small cardboard trunk with brass fittings to hold the extra clothes and shoes.

"My husband and I will be making several more purchases," I say. "Please have everything delivered this evening."

"Of course, Mrs. Warriner," the clerk replies. "That's a lucky little girl, to get all this."

"She's just as pretty as the doll." I hand back the signed receipt, and over the clerk's shoulder, I see the most perfect toy ever made. If I hadn't been so fixated on the dolls, I would have noticed it earlier.

Mounted on a high platform, the rocking horse watches over the toy department with a benign presence. It is exquisite—painted a deep, shining gray, with flashing black eyes and a leather saddle with brass trim. It is also as big as a table.

Ava would kill me if I bought it for the baby.

"The horse," I begin, and the clerk, following my gaze, steps in smoothly.

"Beautiful, isn't it? It's hand-carved, imported from England. The mane and tail are real horsehair."

I don't care about all that. It's a fairy tale horse. A child could wear a suit of armor, a cowboy hat, or—thinking of Thelma, a princess dress—riding on such a beast.

"I don't think I can buy it now. The family doesn't have room in their current situation."

"Such a shame." He returns to my paperwork, disappointed at losing the sale. "It's one of a kind. I'm surprised it's lasted this long."

So am I.

It's ridiculous to think it could fit in their house—and I can't buy it for ours. I've already purchased too many things for a nursery that might never be occupied. Such extravagance would doom my hopes forever.

"Just the doll things," I say. "And whatever my husband has chosen for our nephews."

"Of course. The delivery van will be around by six." There is a line of trucks parked on 13th Street, emblazoned with the scripted Wanamaker's logo, just waiting to be called into action, rather like the elevator operators in their sameness and determination to be of service.

A touch on my arm makes me jump. "Your sister is going to have my head."

That means he did well. "Did you find something for all three?"

"Just the younger ones," he says. "I'm not sure about Dandy."

"I have an idea, but let's look for Pearl's gift first." How many books is too many? She loves to read and there is nothing in the house beyond the Bible and a book of fairy tales. When I was her age, the town library consisted of a shelf of tattered volumes at the store. Even if it has improved beyond measure in the years since I left, it will be nothing like Philadelphia's free library system.

Pearl deserves her own books.

Little Women, certainly. I pull a purple-bound volume off the shelf and admire the colored illustration of the March sisters on the cover. Is she too young for *Jane Eyre*? Perhaps. I didn't read it until I was married, when I tried to consume every book in the library in the hopes of acquiring the polish necessary to be Harry's wife. Nobody ever asked what I read, of course. I was the human equivalent of Thelma's doll; no one expected me to be literate, only pretty.

"Let's add this to the pile." Harry shows me a copy of *Alice's Adventures in Wonderland*.

"Oh, that's nice." What kind of adventures did Pearl dream of?

"She can read it to the boys," he says. "Tweedle-Dee and Tweedle-Dum."

Ava

"Do you need Dandy today?" It's a Saturday in early December, and we're still at breakfast. Dandy's shifts have just been cut, so he's holding up a corner of the table and staring into his mug like any boy his age who'd been roused from his bed for no good reason.

"Pearl and I are baking." The more children I can get out from underfoot, the better. "If you need him, we'll manage."

The four o'clock whistle is fading when the front door opens, but the loaves are cooling by the window and I'm in the rocker with my feet up, a woman of leisure for just a few minutes, so I don't bother to investigate until my husband calls for me to come. I hold out my hands, and Pearl pulls me up, making a sound like a popping cork as I heave myself out of the rocker.

Squeals from Toby, George, and Thelma. Daniel shushes them, laughter in his voice. What has he done?

The front room is dim but for a faint glow on the faces of my clustered family. I come up behind them and see the source: a small Bakelite radio. Daniel feels me behind him and snaps it on. Music floods into the room.

A radio? I can't conceive of it—how many months of groceries did it cost? How much rent? How can he be so extravagant when we don't yet have money for the midwife? "Daniel—"

"I traded for it," he says quickly.

"Traded what?" Despite my misgivings, the music is seeping into my bones. It's wonderful, like rain after a long dry spell.

"Harry's whiskey." He draws me to the side, leaving the kids to inspect the radio. "It was just sitting on the shelf. We don't need that kind of temptation in the house."

I'm impressed by his ingenuity, though there are other things he could have traded for. "Doesn't Callum have his own bootlegger?"

"Apparently Harry's whiskey is better." Daniel is clearly delighted with himself. "He saw the label and his eyes lit up. I let him sample it, and at that point, I think he would have given me the store. I settled for the radio. The house is awful quiet without Lillie."

He's right. We all feel it. Trudy comes over in the evenings sometimes, but it's not the same. I'm filled with a rush of love for my husband. Strangers might think him taciturn, but his care shows in small ways.

Daniel pulls me to him in a quick squeeze, and I'm reminded sharply of the long dry spell between us. "I almost forgot." He rummages in his pocket, handing me a small, paper-wrapped parcel. "Callum gave me these. I think he wants to stay on your good side."

Inside is a box of glinting silver bobbins and a packet of sewing machine needles. Before Mama died, Mrs. Callum had mentioned coming to us for a dress, so this is better news than the radio.

Across the room, Pearl has Dandy locked into a waltz position. "You're older than me!" she scolds. "Someday a girl's going to want to dance with you, you can't dance like a clod."

"I don't want to dance with girls." He tries to twist away.

She hangs on. "You will, and you can thank me then."

Thelma sits by the window, but instead of her usual withdrawn expression, she is staring at the radio with sparkling eyes. Her crooked legs swing back and forth above the floor.

Daniel bows in front of her. "May I have this dance?"

She giggles. "I don't know how, Daddy."

"Your brother doesn't know how, and he's doing okay." Daniel lifts her so she stands on his shoes, and he slowly waltzes her around the room. She tips her head back and laughs, and I feel it like a blow to my heart—I would let him spend our life savings to hear my daughter laugh like that.

Pearl

December 5, 1931

Daddy traded Uncle Harry's bottle for a radio. I can't believe that bitty little bottle got us such a wonderful thing. He set it up in the front room and called us out of the kitchen and it was magic, the dark room and the glowing radio. Even Mama smiled, which is like Christmas come early.

This must be what it feels like to be rich. I wouldn't want it, not all the time. It's more special this way.

Ava

Pearl stops by the cemetery at least twice a week on her way home from school. She's a better person than I am, but I've always suspected that.

It's not that I'm avoiding visiting Mama, though I've no real curiosity to see the headstone Claire has chosen. It's more about not seeing the memorial put up in 1913, with the names of the seventeen men and boys who died in the cave-in, and the stone with the name

Tadeusz Kovaleski, a stone too small to be a proper grave marker, as Teddy was too young to die.

In a place like this, I am constantly reminded of the fragility of life; I do not need to see it set in stone.

I pray every day that no more of my loved ones end up there. If they do, no doubt I will refuse to visit them, as well.

Pearl

December 12, 1931

I visited Granny today again. The stone is in place, and it's beautiful. Pale pink granite, with all her names, just like Aunt Claire promised. I wish Granny had been with us for longer. There wasn't time for me to hear all the stories she must have had. Sometimes I lay in bed thinking about her coming to America with her baby, but in my head, it turns into a happily-ever-after story, which I don't think is how her life was, even though she was never sad. Why can't I just remember things the way they happened?

December 20, 1931

When I went to the store today, Mr. Callum said there was a box for us. I said I'd take it with me and he just laughed. So did I, when I saw it. It's huge! I had to go home for the cart and Toby and George walked on either side so we could get it home.

Aunt Claire said she was going to send Christmas presents, but this is so big I'm afraid Mama will get mad and send it back. Except we can't afford to, so being poor is in our favor this time.

I hope Aunt C sent me a book. Even more, I hope she remembered Thelma's doll.

Ava

Mama always said *we don't need* rather than *we can't afford,* and I've used that phrase myself ever since the kids were old enough to ask for things. They know we don't have any money, but this way they don't feel as deprived. At least I hope they don't because there's not a damn thing we can do about it.

Dandy and Pearl went out after church and came home with evergreen branches and holly. Pearl wove a wreath for the door and used the rest to trim the dresser around the radio. Mama would have said it looks like a pagan altar, and we do worship that Philco like it's a holy thing. With her funeral and Daniel and Dandy's hours reduced, there won't be much in the way of Christmas this year, so the greenery cheers us all up a bit and makes the house look festive.

Today, Claire's gifts arrived from Philadelphia. Not in a box, mind, but a *crate*. The size is worrying—has she completely lost her mind?—but the kids are so excited I let it go. Daniel pries it open and hands out box after box, each one wrapped in pretty paper, their bows slightly squashed. Even I smile when he pulls out a box of chocolates and we decide, decadently, to eat them now instead of waiting for Christmas day.

9

Ava

The cramps wake me before dawn, as clearly as if I've heard a knock on the door. Thelma snores lightly beside me. On my other side is a small, warm body. I determine from the stubbly head that it's George, which means Toby has hogged the covers.

I lay still, listening to my body. The baby is quiet for the first time in months. I put a hand on my belly, waiting for him to turn, or kick. Something. This lack of movement isn't normal.

My breath comes faster. Is the baby all right?

Baby's just resting up for the long journey ahead. Mama's voice.

Still. I arch my back and rub my belly. This brings another twinge, as the baby pokes me with an elbow. That's what I get for waking him. Now I have to pee, but there's no way to get up without disturbing the kids. I settle back, trying to ignore my bladder. Just a few more minutes of peace before the house is awake and Christmas begins.

The sky lightens around the pinned-up blanket at the window, but it has a grayish cast. More snow on the way. Hopefully not too much or the walk to church will be difficult. Daniel and Dandy have promised to go to mass and I'm not letting them off the hook. If Thelma and I can do it, two able-bodied men have no excuse.

Movement in the other room as Dandy makes his way downstairs. Thumping, followed by a clank: he's filled the stove. I'll wait a few minutes before I start breakfast.

"I've got it, Mama." Pearl speaks quietly, just outside the door. "You stay down for a little longer."

I don't object. Another low cramp. Is it labor or the same discomfort I've felt for the last six weeks? After this many babies, I should know, but each pregnancy is different.

"Time to get up." I nudge Thelma and she murmurs and rolls against me. George bolts upright and plunges out of the room. "Toby, get up! It's Christmas!"

I swing my feet out of bed and use the headboard to push myself upright. Biting my lip against another spasm, I call for Dandy. "Carry Thelma down for me? I'll be right there."

When they are gone, I lean on the dresser and look down at my feet. They are only visible when I stand like this. I wait for another cramp. My body remains quiet, and so I wash and dress and go down to join the others.

"Can we open presents now?"

"Let's finish breakfast, Thelma, and wait for your daddy." The kids grumble but don't push me. We do things as a family when we can.

Breakfast is oatmeal and an egg apiece. Fried in butter with salt and pepper, an egg is a gift on such a cold morning. The tea is strong, and there is a small pitcher of milk from Mrs. Wood's goat, in payment for Pearl watching her baby.

I drink my tea, anticipating the day I can have coffee again. I miss coffee even more than I miss seeing my feet, but the smell of it makes me sick when I'm pregnant.

"Can we, Mama!" Toby pushes his plate aside. "Please?"

"Any minute now." I'm about to pour the last of the tea when the kitchen door opens. "There he is," I say, as the children chorus a greeting and begin to clamor for their presents again. "Let the poor man get cleaned up before you jump all over him."

"Morning." He drops his helmet, with its heavy carbide lamp, on the counter and settles his tin lunch pail by the door.

Pearl picks it up again, her arms straining at its unexpected weight. "It's still full!"

Daniel blinks. "I forgot to empty it," he says. "I'm sorry, my girl."

What is on his mind, that he could have forgotten? The clumsy pail holds two gallons of life-saving water, in case he is trapped underground for any length of time.

Pearl tips it into the kettle on the stove. "I'll add it to your bathwater."

"Ava." He holds out a piece of paper, then busies himself with his coat, hiding his face.

It has to be a bonus. Why else would they have a crew working on Christmas Eve? I unfold it with shaking hands and learn that

Daniel is unemployed, effective immediately; his last pay will go on deposit at the store in two days.

"No cash at all?"

"None." Reaching around me, he picks up the nearest mug and drains it. "A day like this, I wish I hadn't traded that whiskey away."

The children are silent. Pearl says, finally, with a quaver in her voice, "Will we be okay?"

He smiles at her. It's a crooked smile, but enough to break the tension. "We'll be okay, Pearlie. Things will just be tight for a while."

Dandy looks skeptical. "They're already tight."

"Well, now they'll be tighter." I stack the bowls on the counter. "It's Christmas. Leave the dishes, let your father get washed up, and then we'll open presents."

We walk slowly to St. Stan's. Daniel carries Thelma and I lean on his other side, Pearl hovering like a third parent. Despite his promise to attend, I would have understood if he decided to stay home, but he readied himself for church with no comment other than to keep the boys in check.

The wind finds its way through the gaping buttons on my winter coat, and I am glad of my shawl. The snow has held off, so all we have to deal with is yesterday's, flattened and dirty, not wet enough to seep into our shoes.

The church doors are open, spilling yellow light into the gray morning. The priests stand on either side of the doors, greeting everyone as they enter. Father Dennis takes Thelma from Daniel. "There you go, Christmas angel," he says, setting her on her feet and smiling as she dips her fingers in the font. "How are you, Daniel?"

"Fine, Father, and yourself?" Like all miners, Daniel is a God-fearing man, but he's not been comfortable in church since he came home from the war.

"Blessed by the Lord." He steps back and looks closely at me. "Do I need to clear the manger?" he asks. "We're here to celebrate the birth of the Baby Jesus, not the latest member of the Kimber family."

I feel another twinge, press my lips together and hope it looks like a smile. "Then let us pray, Father. Let us pray."

The first real contraction comes halfway through mass. It gathers under my breastbone and yanks me forward. I hold tight to the edge of the pew and take a deep breath. I'm not going into labor in church. Not on Christmas Day. I won't allow it.

I close my eyes and compose a thank-you letter to Claire in my head. She'd gone overboard, but the accuracy of her gifts showed the depth of knowledge she'd acquired during her short visit.

Thelma was struck speechless by her doll. Nearly as large as a real baby, it has eyes that open and close, and more clothes than my daughter.

Books for Pearl, of course—three of them, and a pretty lace collar to pin on her best dress. My girl fondled those books like Mama used to pet her Bible, as if just touching the covers gave her comfort.

Toby and George got cowboy and Indian suits, with a bow and arrow and a popgun. I sense Harry's input there and laid down the law immediately that there were to be no old west battles in the house, no matter how cold it was outside.

It was Dandy's gift that threw me. Claire had been distressed that he no longer drew, but I hadn't thought she would send him a camera. Nor had I expected him to flush like he'd seen a pretty girl, and immediately take it out of the box and herd us all together for a family photograph.

I protested, not wanting to be memorialized in such a state, but he insisted. It is difficult for me to resist when he is excited about something. "Fine, but do it quickly," I said. "We're going to be late for church." The kids arranged themselves in front of me and he clicked the shutter before I could change my mind.

The service is almost over when the next contraction hits. This one has intent behind it. My labors have been shorter with each child—what if I can't make it to the end of the carol-singing and Father Dennis's prediction comes to pass?

Trudy is in the row in front of us. I reach out and touch her shoulder. She turns, sees my face, and mouths the word, "Now?"

I nod.

She gets up, stepping around her grandchildren. I do the same. Daniel shifts so I can pass. "I'm going home," I whisper. "Take them next door when this is over."

"Now?"

Why is anyone surprised? I've been lumbering around like a hippopotamus since before Mama died. It has to happen eventually.

"Can I help?" Pearl hands me my shawl and slips her arms into her coat.

"Stay with your father."

"Let her come." Trudy overrules me. "We'll need her."

We leave as the carols begin. Pearl closes the door, but the music follows us into the road, faint in the thin, cold air.

> *What Child is this who, laid to rest*
> *On Mary's lap, is sleeping?*
> *Whom angels greet with anthems sweet*
> *While shepherds watch are keeping?*

It's snowing now, light flakes that stick to our coats like lint. We stop several times, once for a contraction, and twice simply because I can't walk without getting out of breath. "I just want to get in the house before my water breaks."

"*Ja*," Trudy says. "If it breaks out here, it will freeze your feet to the ground."

I smile, glad she can see the bright side again, even if it's the bright side of my misfortunes.

The road feels longer than ever, but I can see the house now. I link my hands under my belly, feeling the frantic activity within. Was it only a few hours ago I worried about his stillness? "Hold on, little one," I gasp. "Not too much further."

"Can I be there?" Pearl asks.

I bite the inside of my cheek to keep from groaning. "You don't need to see this yet."

The front door closes behind us. I've never been happier to see the front room. I pause, leaning on the back of the chair, then reach for the railing. "Pearl, you can tidy up here," I say, hauling myself upstairs. "That'll keep you busy."

Trudy shakes her head. "She should be upstairs. There is nothing like seeing a baby born to keep a girl on a straight path."

Pearl is already on a straight path. As far as I know, she's never even looked at boys—which is more than I can say for myself at eleven. By that age, I'd already been dreaming of my wedding to Daniel. Love happens quick at that age; maybe it won't hurt for her to see that the wages of sin aren't death, but birth.

Claire

Normally, Christmas is my favorite holiday, but this year it is endless. I try to sleep in, but Katie gets me up so I can attend morning service with Harry and Irene. Manners made to the Almighty, we return and eat lunch, then open gifts under the enormous tree. There is a brief moment of peace while Irene makes a few calls, then we drink afternoon tea, open more gifts, and sit down to dinner at six.

I'm tired and nervy, still full from lunch, and with the beginnings of an Irene-inspired headache throbbing at my temples. The house is warm enough that I perspire in my blue velvet. I look forward to undressing so I can open the bathroom window and cool off.

What is happening in Scovill Run? I compare our elaborate celebration with the spare Kimber front room. I wanted to be there when the children opened their presents. I wouldn't even mind leaving the warmth of the stove to walk to church in the snow and listen to Father Dennis, because Christmas is different.

I want a family Christmas. I want *my* family.

There is enough food on the mahogany sideboard to feed a dozen people, but there are only three of us at the table.

Irene's sister, Honora, lives just outside the city, but we rarely see her. She has her own family: a husband and two adult daughters who were my long-ago bridesmaids. From our few interactions, I suspect she shares my opinion of Irene, but a smooth mask hides her thoughts. Irene has the same mask, but it slips when she's at home.

I admire my new bracelet under the edge of the table. White gold, with square-cut diamonds. It's beautiful—Harry's taste in jewelry is exquisite—but I wonder how much it cost. It's been a long time since I've wondered about the cost of anything, just as I forgot what it was like to live without conveniences. Nowadays, light blooms at the flip of a switch, food arrives without my having to cook it, and, best of all, there is heat in the winter and fans to move the hot air in the summer. There is a car, which always starts, and Baxter to drive it.

My life is easy. All I have to do is show up, appropriately dressed, and say the right words to the right people. But I'm bored.

It's worse after two days with Ava and her family. It's not activity I lack, but people. I can read, but there is no one with whom to discuss what I've read. I can visit any number of museums in the city, but that, too, is no fun alone. My husband plans our events and excursions, but while he appreciates art, he isn't going to sit for hours while I stare at French paintings and figure out why they make me feel the way they do.

I have friends—acquaintances, really, wives of Harry's associates—but we meet from convenience, not affection.

My life is divided into before and after: before and after the cave-in; before and after leaving home; before and after my marriage.

There could be another: before and after a child, but I no longer believe that will happen.

10

Ava

Mama delivering my babies was always a comfort. She'd borne so many herself, and knew everything a midwife would know—plus she was my mother. If only she'd lived a few more months! Just long to help bring this child into the world, that would be enough.

But she didn't, and the midwife is off visiting her daughter in Wilkes-Barre, so I need to pull myself together. Trudy is here, but for all I know, she may be no more help than Pearl.

"I want my rosary." I lean my full weight on the bed frame, panting. "It's in my coat pocket."

Pearl sprints back downstairs.

"We have just come from the church," Trudy says. "I think you are in good standing with God."

Taking a deep breath, I hold it for a moment. "It calms me," I tell her on the exhale. "I've always done it."

I drop my clothes on the floor and step away from them. My slip stretches tight, and there are a few popped stitches on the left side seam. It will have to be mended once the baby is born. I pull the nightgown over my head and dispense with my underclothes while Trudy pads the bed with several weeks' worth of newspapers. We can't afford to ruin the mattress, and the waterproof sheet is covering the hole in the roof.

Pearl returns with my beads. "I put water on to boil," she says. "The biggest pot, and the teapot too, in case you're thirsty, Mama."

"Thank you." I have an idea. "What books did your aunt send?"

"*Little Women*." Pearl glows with pleasure. "I only read the first few paragraphs, but it looks wonderful."

Another, longer contraction. I sit down hard and lean forward as much as I am able, expelling a slow breath. "Why don't you read to us? This baby will come when he's ready, not when I am."

While Pearl is gone, Trudy moves swiftly to the foot of the bed and flips my gown above my knees. "Let me take a quick look," she says, "before the girl comes back."

Some things never change; I always forget the pain, and I never forget just how uncomfortable it is to have someone look at me there, a place I've never seen and which Daniel only explores under the covers. Trudy's gaze is dispassionate, almost clinical. She pats my bare thigh as she straightens.

"Coming along," she says. "Let her read, and the time will pass more quickly."

Pearl returns with a thick, purple-bound book with a picture of four girls on the cover. Trudy shoves her toward the stool. "I will go and have a cup of tea," she says. "You call me, I will come."

I sigh with relief. Trudy is a good friend, but I am happy for a few minutes with my daughter. "I'm sorry you have to see this." There is another contraction building, and I search the covers for my beads. "See *me* like this."

"I should see." Pearl closes the book and takes my hand, not flinching as I squeeze her fingers. "You've gone through this for each of us."

"I miss your granny." It sounds weak, wanting my mother.

"I do, too." Her smile is crooked. "She delivered all of us, right?"

"In this very bed." I take another deep breath through my nose. "Could you crack the window?"

"Won't you be cold?"

"Just open the damn window!"

Pearl scurries to pull aside the blanket. I feel bad, but then a contraction hits and I forget her until the pain subsides.

It is hard to concentrate on the story of the March sisters. Still, hearing Pearl read, not stumbling over the hard words, pleases me. I'll have to tell her, when this is done, if I remember.

Trudy returns and checks me again. "Still not there." She wipes her hands on my apron, which is wrapped around her substantial middle. "Your water should have broken by now."

"Get me up." This happened with Pearl, I remember—my waters didn't break and Mama made me walk until I sobbed with weariness. But the baby came quickly after that.

Leaning on Pearl and Trudy, I circle the bedroom. The draft makes my damp nightgown stick to my body, but I am so hot it feels good. "Again," I say when we have completed a few circuits. "I can feel him shifting."

It takes a while, but my waters break, soaking the rag rug at the side of the bed. "Now," Trudy says, "we are getting somewhere."

My body remembers what comes next, even if Mama isn't here to remind me. They get me to the bed and I shift until I'm firmly on top of the newspapers. There is a new tension in my body. My belly ripples as the baby works its way downward.

"Much better." Trudy's rough hand rests on my knee. "Soon, I think."

"I want to push." The urge comes on suddenly, the next contraction arriving with a lick of fire down my spine.

"Not yet." She looks around. "Pearl, is this all the towels? Get more, if you have them. If not, go next door and bring mine. Also, make sure the water is hot, and when you come back, bring the scissors."

I am grateful my daughter is gone for the worst part. I bite my lip as the contraction peaks. "Trudy—"

"Not to push yet." Her voice is firm. "Just breathe. Where are your beads?"

Finding them, I begin to murmur the familiar words, hoping they will bring me calm, but instead, with the pain comes fear. What if she can't bring the baby? What if it dies? What if I die? How will Daniel cope, with no job? I don't want Pearl to leave school—

I can't quiet my thoughts enough for the rosary to work its magic. "Does everything look right?" I ask. "There's nothing wrong down there?"

Trudy's face appears. "Nothing is wrong, my friend." She pats my shoulder. "Do not worry yourself."

"Don't touch me." I can't bear the idea of being touched. Being touched is what got me in this situation in the first place. Daniel and his damn touching. I forget how much I enjoy the touching. It's always the men who get women into this state and then go off somewhere so they don't have to witness what they've done.

The pain rolls over me. I wrap my fists in the covers and pull, every muscle in my body tensing along with the contraction. My eyes burn with sweat and I squeeze them shut, blocking out the dim room, Trudy's face, the cross on the wall—the same cross that says my role in life is to bring forth babies in blood and pain.

"This is bullshit," I say through clenched teeth. "I've had enough."

"Ha!" Trudy laughs. "When the mama starts to swear, it's time to push." Her hands are on my knees again, ignoring my order not to touch me. "Yes," she says. "I can see the head—the next pain, you push, my friend."

The next pain is not long in coming. I push, and a howl rips from my throat. A small part of me worries that they can hear next door, as we hear Trudy arguing with Hermann. Then I stop caring because I'm on fire. The flames are burning up the bed and my baby will have to pass through them to be born.

I tuck my chin to my chest and push again, giving it everything I have. Trudy has hold of my shins, pushing my feet back against my bottom. Another wrenching, tearing pain, and then a respite. I gasp for air, and try to steady my breathing so I can pant through the next one.

"Here are the towels!" Pearl hurtles through the door with an armload of linen and stops short at the sight of me. I imagine what she sees from that angle, but then another pain comes from the base of my spine and I stop caring. This is the one. If I can ride this to the end, I can get some rest.

I reach out, and Pearl grasps my hand. "Now," I say, "now he's coming." The pain goes on and on, and I no longer feel the baby, no longer feel the lower half of my body. The only thing left is the cold breeze from the window, keeping me from burning up.

I push and pant and cling to Pearl's hand.

"Yes!" Trudy cries, bending swiftly to catch the baby as it slithers from my body. "Beautiful, Ava!"

Pearl is sobbing, her face pressed to my shoulder. "You did so good, Mama," she says. "You did so good."

I fall back against the pillow. My hair is stuck to my forehead, and my own rank sweat, mixed with the other scents of childbirth, fills my nose. I wait while Trudy busies herself below my suddenly boneless knees. The shaking starts somewhere deep inside. Is it the afterbirth? Another contraction grips and I push, doubling over and refusing to take the baby from Pearl until it passes.

He is red and wrinkled and sticky, like all babies. He looks me full in the face, opens his mouth and roars, producing a sound quite unlike anything I've ever heard from an infant.

"Very good!" Trudy exclaims, from the end of the bed.

I unbutton my nightgown and settle the towel-wrapped baby against my breast. He is so warm and so new; I worry now about the draft, but Pearl has already shut the window.

"Teddy," I say. "We'll call him Teddy."

My muscles flutter and twitch. The trembling becomes so bad that I gesture for Pearl to take the baby. "What's wrong with me?" I hold out my hands.

"What, this?" Trudy slaps my fingers. "Baby shakes is all."

Pearl bundles Teddy in another layer of towel and sits on the stool beside the bed. "What are baby shakes?"

Trudy pulls the covers up to my chin. "Is like when you carry something heavy for long time," she explains, "and when you put it down, your arm shakes. Pushing out a baby is hard work, same as that." She pats my shoulder. "Is just your body recovering."

It makes sense, but I still worry. "It's never happened before."

My friend shrugs. "It happens, it doesn't happen. My daughter-in-law, twice it did, twice not." She lays a finger on Teddy's cheek. "I go down and bring tea. Everyone has worked hard tonight."

Claire

"Well," Irene says, settling into her chair near the fire, "that was a lovely dinner."

Harry makes a sound of agreement, looking lost without a newspaper to hide behind.

"I thought the Brussels sprouts were a bit overdone." The words emerge unbidden from my mouth.

Her plucked eyebrows raise. "That was my mother's recipe." Irene positions her gray suede pumps on the ottoman, crossing her legs neatly at the ankle. "And Mrs. Fell prepares them exactly right."

Reproved for having an opinion, I lean back and tuck my legs under me. Irene glances in my direction: shoes on the furniture! Defiantly, I slide one foot further.

"I wish Ava had a telephone," I say to Harry. "I'd love to hear how they're doing."

"I would, too," he says. "I enjoyed seeing them."

His words warm me more than my new bracelet. Concern about his reaction was one of the reasons I delayed visiting for so long. Ava is abrupt and Daniel silent more often than not, and children in large quantities are an unfamiliar experience for both of us.

"How many children do they have?" Irene asks fastidiously.

"Five." Deprived of his newspaper, Harry lights a cigarette.

"Possibly six by now," I remind him. "I hope Daniel remembers to send a telegram."

"I can't imagine." His mother shudders theatrically and settles an ivory cashmere cardigan around her shoulders. She is never averse to regaling us—discreetly—with tales of her suffering. "One nearly killed me."

"Good thing you got it right the first time," Harry quips.

Irene shudders again. "I think I'll take tea in my room and turn in early."

When the door closes, Harry moves to the sofa beside me. "Now," he says, removing his gold cufflinks and folding his sleeves once, to just above his wrists, "we have the place to ourselves."

"What about Mrs. Fell and her Brussels sprouts?" I lean into him. Wearing only his vest and shirt, he is nevertheless as warm as a radiator.

"They *were* overcooked. They've always been overcooked. It's a terrible recipe, and Mother will never hear otherwise."

I laugh and find myself on the verge of tears. "It's been a lovely day," I say. "I don't mean to sound ungrateful, but I wish we could have been in Scovill Run."

"I know." He strokes my hair. "Once the baby's born, why don't we give Ava a few weeks to recover and then drive up again? If you want a longer visit, you could stay at the hotel in town and I'd come back for you in a week or so."

"I'd love that." I imagine treating the girls to a night at the Mansion House—even Ava if she'd allow it. "I'm going to have to make more of an effort."

"She won't reach out on her own." Harry chuckles. "Your sister is proud."

"Don't I know it," I say. "I think that's why we grew apart—I felt funny going home, afraid she'd think I was showing off, but she was never going to be the one to reach out first."

Harry puts his arm around me. "Then we'll reach out to her. It doesn't have to be showing off; we can't help having money. And I would love to spend some of it on them, but I understand how she feels."

There must be a way. I can't rein in my impulse to care for her children, and if I hold back until next Christmas, the box will be too big to ship. I cuddle against him and stare into the fire, letting myself be hypnotized by its flickering. "I wonder if it will be a boy or a girl?"

"A girl, I hope," Harry says. "Dandy's already following in his father's footsteps but the young ones are bright kids for all that they act like hoodlums. They were asking all kinds of questions about the car when I had them clean it. The older one especially seems to have a real mechanical bent."

"I can't imagine going underground." I blanch at the thought of my small nephews trudging to work on the breaker. "There *must* be something else."

"There's nothing, and the company doesn't pay enough for people to leave." Harry tells me what I already know. "And you know many of them have no desire to change jobs—mining is in their blood. I made Daniel an offer and I don't think he even heard me."

"He wouldn't," I say. "Neither would Ava. She can't imagine living anywhere else." I lean back against him. "I think your mother had the right idea."

"Hmm?" He sounds sleepy; the fire is getting to him as well.

"Let's go to bed."

Pearl

December 31, 1931

I haven't had time to write. Daddy lost his job and Mama had the baby, both on Christmas. He's called Teddy, and Mrs. Metzger delivered him. Mama said I was too young to be there, but I saw most of it. I can't imagine going through that over and over.

I think something's wrong and they aren't telling us. I don't remember her staying in bed like this after Thelma was born, and neither does Dandy.

Since she won't come downstairs, I'm doing the cooking. And the laundry. Teddy's only tiny but he makes a lot of mess. I haven't even washed clothes, only sheets and diapers. The boys like being dirty, and I don't care enough to nag them. Daddy is quieter than ever, worrying about Mama and wondering where he can find work.

I should write down what we got for Christmas, so I can send Aunt Claire a thank you letter when I find a stamp, but I'm too tired. Gosh, she must have spent the bank.

I can't admit even to Dandy how scared I am. Mama's the glue that holds us together. If something happens to her, we'll come apart.

Part Two

January 1932 - November 1932

11

Claire

"It's a boy."

"What?" Harry looks up from his paper to the buff-colored slip in my hand. "Ava had the baby?"

"Yes." I look down at the telegram Katie has just given me. It reads, TEDDY KIMBER BORN CHRISTMAS DAY. ALL WELL.

Teddy is the name I would give my son, although I'm sure if I ever succeed in producing an heir, Irene will insist on saddling him with Harrison Edward Warriner, III. Harrison!

Ava's choice surprises me, though. With three boys, she's had ample opportunity to use it before, and I wonder now if Mama's policy of silence kept her from naming one of the others after the sweetest child in our family's sorry history.

Teddy was two years older than me, but people often assumed we were twins because we looked so much alike. He was bright, full of fun and trickery, a lot like Toby and George. Mama kept him from the breaker until he was nine, but she was eventually overruled—by Tata, and by Teddy himself. He was in a rush to be a man, but it was being a boy that killed him. Six months before our father's death, he chased a stray dog onto the culm pile near the mine. The pile was dangerous—all the boys knew it, and yet they still played there, searching for fragments of coal to bring home, or just being boys and pushing their luck.

My brother's luck ran out that day. He climbed higher and higher, chasing the dog, the other boys cheering him on, and then he slipped. Instead of sliding down the sulfurous, reeking pile, he slid *into* it. Struggling only made him sink deeper, and though some boys ran for help and others threw a rope, the pile kept moving, pulling Teddy under and flowing outward until the boys ran from the friend they were trying to rescue.

Two days later, when they brought him home, Tata roared that he'd brought it on himself—and that if any of the rest of us ever went near the pile, he'd beat us until we were in no better shape than Teddy. He was drunk, Mama said.

After the funeral, Teddy vanished from our lives. His clothes were swapped for garments that fit the rest of us, and his bed was given over to me and Ava. Jake took to sleeping downstairs, or on the back porch. Sometimes he didn't come home at all, and Tata would rage about that.

Our father wasn't a bad man, but his weakness for spirits made him short-tempered, and after Teddy died, he drank more and more. I don't know if he was drunk on the day of the cave-in, but he was probably hungover. Not that he could have done anything to stop the mountain from coming down on top of him.

That morning at breakfast, Jake was quiet. Sullen, Tata said, prodding him. When he failed to react, Tata blew up and knocked him across the kitchen. Mama got between them with an iron pan until they stopped fighting, and eventually, they went to work. In the late afternoon, as we waited by the mine entrance, I prayed that if the earth had swallowed anyone, it wouldn't be Jake.

It took hours for the rubble to be cleared, but my brother made it out with only a broken wrist and two cracked ribs to show for his ordeal. His mind suffered more than his body. Like Mama, he didn't talk about hard things, but he told me, one afternoon while he was still healing, that he saw the wall come down on Tata, and he was glad.

Ava

The blanket is pulled to one side, weak morning sun brightening the room. I focus on the sun, rather than the blanket. In the days of plenty, when Daniel worked steadily and my two eldest children were babies, I made crisp blue gingham curtains for the upstairs windows with the money I earned from cleaning houses for the mine managers' wives.

Four years ago, I cut those curtains up to make a dress for Pearl. Thelma will likely fit into it this spring. I'm sure she'll be pretty as a picture, but to me, it's a reminder of the things we don't have. It doesn't seem like much to ask, that my girls have nice things *and* my house has window curtains.

I glance at the baby in his cradle. Gerald Flannery made that cradle for a son he never knew. I wonder if he wasn't better off; he never had to work himself to death to support his baby or watch him grow up spindly because he couldn't provide for him.

It seems wrong to think this way, but I am too exhausted to work out why. I turn away again and close my eyes.

A wailing worms its way into my dreams and drags me from sleep. It's not the siren, it's the baby, producing a disproportionately large sound. "He's probably wet," I say to Pearl's unseen presence.

"No, he's hungry." She brings him to me. "You've been asleep for hours."

I thought I'd only just closed my eyes. "Give him here, then."

"What is it?" Pearl's eyes are on my face. "Is something wrong?"

"He's fine." The baby sucks well, but it doesn't feel like it did with my previous babies. "I'm just tired. I wonder if I can sleep while he nurses?"

I can and I do, waking only when Daniel comes up later with a plate and a cup of tea. "You must be starving," he says. "You and Teddy both. You've been asleep since three."

Yawning, I push myself up on my elbows and feel a dull ache below. It's not enough to stop me from sitting up; I just don't want to. "I'm not hungry."

His face creases. "You've hardly eaten. And Teddy needs a feed."

He puts the plate on the dresser and fetches the baby. I fasten him onto my nipple, feeling the tug of his tiny mouth. It *was* different before. The sensation of sucking always sent me deep inside myself, a flush of light surrounding both me and the baby. Nursing has always given me joy.

I feel no joy now. I feel no hunger, either, and not much of anything for the tall, stooped man who stands anxiously beside the bed. This is also wrong, but thinking about it takes too much effort.

"What is it?" He's wearing his Sunday shirt, and I want to tell him to change, but there's no point. He will, eventually.

"Nothing." I try to concentrate on the baby's mouth. It's easier if I close my eyes. "I'll put him in the cradle when he's done. You can go back down."

"I want to keep you company." He paces silently, wearing out his socks on the bare floor.

"I don't need company." I adjust the pillow behind my head without dislodging the baby. "I just want to sleep."

"You've done nothing *but* sleep." There's an edge to his voice. "Teddy's more than a week old, and you haven't been awake two hours straight since he was born."

"He nurses whether I'm awake or not." I shift him to my left breast. "See, he's figured it out already."

Daniel looks pinched. "What about the rest of us? Pearl is skipping school to run the house, and the little ones need you."

I want to see them, but they'll bring so much noise and energy into the room that it will wake me up. "Not yet," I say. "Pearl's a big girl. She'll manage. I just need..."

"Sleep. I know."

"Why are you angry?" I can see the plate on the dresser, but my appetite is as distant as the memory of childbirth. More than a week? How have I lost so much time?

"I'm not angry, Ava, I'm worried. You've always been yourself once the babies were born."

"I am myself." But I'm not. I can't remember who I was just a week ago.

The room is dark. A slight weight rests on the bed near my right foot. "Mama?"

I didn't raise you to lay down before trouble.

"But, Mama, I—"

The bed shifts. *It's time you got up.*

The next time I open my eyes, the blanket is pulled back and the room is empty. Perhaps it was always empty, but Mama's voice is clear in my head, and so is her direction. I reach for the robe draped over the footboard.

People are counting on me.

I feed the baby sitting on the edge of the bed, watching the snow drift past the window, and think about going downstairs. I can't stay in this room forever. I can't sleep forever, and I can't ignore the changes that have occurred since Christmas.

It's clear—Daniel will have to leave Scovill Run to find work. I'll have to remember how to mother an infant and keep track of the other kids. Pearl and Dandy, kids themselves, will have to carry more weight until things get back to normal.

What is normal? Will we be able to provide for the kids? Will Daniel be able to find work? How will we keep the rent paid so Mr. Henderson doesn't put us out? The fears arrive in a squall fiercer than the snow outside, almost enough to send me back to bed.

I resist, smoothing the sheets, bringing the quilts up, fluffing the pillow. Making the bed usually makes me feel accomplished: one small bit of order in the chaos of my life. Today I feel nothing. Picking up the baby, I look around. The bedroom is safe, while downstairs, although warmer, seems full of danger.

The creaking stairs give me away, and there is a rush as the children swarm around and escort me to the kitchen, glad to have me back where I belong. Thelma dogs my steps while Pearl seats me near the stove and dishes out tea and breakfast. Toby and George squat in a corner, arguing quietly over the wooden car their father gave them for Christmas, but they keep looking up as if to check if I'm still here.

Daniel leans against the back door, smoking. I'm sensitive to smoke when I'm pregnant, so no doubt he's happy to be able to smoke indoors again.

"Where's Dandy?"

"Work." Pearl slides a plate in front of me. A fried egg, toast with a scraping of butter. A jar of strawberry jam from Claire's Christmas parcel appears on the table. I spread some on my toast, anticipating the sweet taste of summer, but it tastes as gray as the weather. I take another bite, chew some more. "Does this taste right?"

"Yummy," Thelma says. "Pearl gave me the spoon."

I want it to taste good, but it's flat. "I guess I'm just not myself yet."

In a fog, I resume my daily activities. Every part of me is heavy. It takes effort to wash, to dress. To feed the baby. To feel connected to him. That's the thing that makes me cry whenever I'm alone. I *wanted* this baby. Named him after my brother, now that Mama can no longer be upset by it. But I don't feel anything but an exhausted sense of obligation.

And fear. Fear that I'll do something wrong, even though I can take care of a baby in my sleep. But what if I was wrong before, and just got lucky? What if this time, I trip up and something happens? Look at Thelma—she was perfect, but she grew up with those twisted legs. Was that my fault? What if I damage this one, too?

I should be over the moon with gratitude for my baby, for the rest of my healthy children, but my emotions are buried under a blanket; I know they're there, lost in the thick folds, but I can't reach them.

Pearl

January 9, 1932

We can't keep on like this. Mama got up a few days ago, but it's like she's sleepwalking. I haven't been to school for two weeks. I haven't been to church or to visit Granny, either. I say the rosary while I'm doing chores, but I don't think God is listening.

Toby and George finally understand something is wrong. They sit at Mama's feet while she ignores them and stares at the calendar on the wall, or out the window.

Another funny thing—she never calls Teddy by his name.

Early this morning I went down to stir up the stove and saw Daddy already on the back porch. I thought he was smoking but he was just standing there with his hands jammed in his pockets. It looked like he was crying.

12

Claire

The afternoon sun filters through the net curtains, falling on the patterned carpet just short of my feet. A copy of *The Good Earth* is open on my lap, its paper dust jacket carefully set aside. I am fascinated by the story, but I can't focus. It is too early to think of napping, but I haven't been sleeping well. We've heard nothing from Scovill Run since the telegram at the beginning of January. If anything happened, surely they would have let me know?

A clank echoes from the hall, followed by a muffled thud. I pop to my feet, sending Pearl Buck sprawling. *Mail!*

Katie is turning from the door as I emerge and holds out a lumpy envelope. "There's one for you, ma'am."

The envelope is addressed in painfully neat cursive. Pearl, not Ava.

"Could you bring tea, Katie?"

"Yes, ma'am." She smiles. "I hope it's good news."

I slit the envelope with a scimitar-shaped opener. Why hasn't Ava written herself?

> *Dear Aunt Claire,*
>
> *I'm writing for all of us to say thank you for the presents. Mama said you overdid it but really they were wonderful. Thelma sleeps with her doll every night, and I've been reading Little Women before bed.*
>
> *We have a new brother, I'm sure Daddy told you. He came on Christmas. His name is Teddy, and I saw him being born.*
>
> *Daddy lost his job. He says we will be fine, but Mama is worried I think, because she's real quiet. I miss Granny. She would know how to make it all right.*

Please write, Mama needs cheering up.

> *All our love,*
> *Pearl, Dandy, Toby, George*
> *Thelma and Teddy*

P.S. Dandy tried out the camera on Christmas but there is nowhere to get the film developed and he asks could you please, and send the pictures?

I let the paper slip from my fingers. A new baby, Daniel unemployed, and my sister in need of cheer. Ava has little patience with those who need cheering, so this is perhaps the most worrying part of the letter.

The door opens and Katie brings in the tray. "Good news, I hope?"

"It's from my niece," I say, focusing on the positive. "Telling me about her new brother."

She puts the cup and saucer in front of me. "Well, that is good news."

"I wish you'd bring a cup for yourself." She is the only person in the house I feel close to, besides Harry.

Katie makes a face that isn't quite laughing at me. "And the other Mrs. Warriner would say what, if she caught you having tea with your colored maid?"

She would say a great many things, none of them kind or nice, and all of which would make me cry. "She's out," I say weakly.

Katie joined the household during one of Irene's rare absences. I should have arranged for a temporary girl, but instead, I put notices in several of the nicer shops and Katie Hedges appeared the next day. In her late teens, with rich brown skin, a soothing voice, and better manners than my mother-in-law, she was unlike anyone I had ever met.

"My husband's mother deals with the staff," I warned her. "Mrs. Warriner can be...brisk."

"I've got a thick skin," Katie said cheerfully. "I'm sure I've met worse."

When Irene returned and confronted me about our new maid, I was again reminded that I was not mistress of my own home.

"I find it difficult to believe you would have taken on that girl in my absence. I have always been in charge of the servants." Even Irene's impeccably-arranged hair seemed annoyed.

"Well," I said, "I wasn't the one who got Phyllis in the family way and made her leave. Katie's a hard worker and I like her."

"She makes me uncomfortable." Irene played with her gloves, not meeting my eyes.

"Because she's a Negro?"

She gave every appearance of being offended. "We'll see how it goes. I'll have my eye on her."

She never actually answered my question, but two years later, Katie is still with us—my one friend in the house, and my sole victory over my mother-in-law.

"Mrs. Fell is here." Katie inches the saucer closer. "Tell me the rest of your news. You don't look like it's all sunshine and babies."

I glance at the letter again. "It's not." I sip the tea and smile in spite of myself. Katie makes it strong and sweet, the way I like it. Indian, not China, another mark against me in Irene's endless ledger. *Nice people* drink China tea. I am not nice people.

"My sister's husband lost his job."

"Oh, that's too bad. Coal miner, isn't he?"

"Yes, he is. Was." I think of him as a miner, the way I think of Ava as a mother. "I don't know how they'll manage."

I will write to them tonight. Harry offered Daniel a job before; there's no reason now not to take him up on it. Maybe they could all come to Philadelphia—Ava, the children, little Teddy... Is he blond or dark, my nephew? Blue eyes or brown? I want to see him. I want to see all my family.

If I can't have babies, I will care for Ava's, if she will let me.

Ava

"We need to get Teddy baptized." Daniel drops a load of wood in the box, and I flinch at the noise.

"It hasn't been that long." The weather has been cold and gray since the birth, with frequent snow. "Taking him out would be dangerous."

"It's been three weeks." He hangs his coat and scarf by the back door before clipping his knitted gloves to the line stretched over the stove. "We've never waited this long before."

In the other rooms, the windows are etched with frost, but the kitchen is almost warm. I shift closer to the stove, wrapping the baby in the folds of my woolen shawl. He mustn't get a chill. "I think we should wait."

"We had George baptized the first Sunday after he was born." Daniel pours a cup of coffee and drinks it standing up.

"Maybe the weather was better."

"It's his birthday today, so it's not likely."

How have I failed to remember George's birthday? Letting my mind drift is just easier, and Pearl undoubtedly has everything under control. "We wanted Harry and Claire as godparents."

"Have you asked them?"

I'd started a letter last week, but got no further than "Dear sister," before putting it down, knowing there was no point. After finding my sister again and hearing her story, I can imagine no one else as my son's godmother, but winter is no time for travel.

Daniel picks up the broom and brushes debris from beneath my chair. "Why are you so afraid for Teddy? You weren't like this with the others."

"I just am."

"Pick your feet up." My husband is capable of far more than cleaning the house. He is a painstaking worker—that's why the company kept him on, even after the union mess. "I'm going out again."

"Where to?" He is dressed in heavy pants, two shirts buttoned over his long underwear. More clothes than he needs just to bring in wood.

"Walk down to the store, see if anyone's looking for day labor." He opens the door and sweeps the dirt carefully onto the porch.

The wind enters like a knife and I curl around the baby. "You just want out of the house."

"Idleness doesn't suit me," he agrees. "And there might be something, even if it's just helping Callum unload. He'll give me a sack of potatoes for saving his rheumatism."

As far as I'm concerned, Callum is the source of our current problem. Him and that radio. I haven't let them switch it on since I came downstairs. "I can't imagine he'll be getting anything today."

"You haven't been to St. Stan's since Teddy was born, either." Daniel squats and takes my hands, looking into my face as if he's trying to recognize me. "You never miss mass."

Selfishly, my regular attendance is not just because I'm Catholic. I revel in that hour each week when fear of God keeps my kids quiet, if not completely still. Now that I am surrounded by silence, I don't need to leave home to find it. I miss going to church; I miss the feeling of being renewed after communion, but I just…can't.

"I'm still recovering." The tension between us stretches, elastic. "I don't know why it's so important to you."

He drops my hands. "You're always the one who wants them baptized before they're dry. What would happen to Teddy if—"

"Exactly," I interrupt, my fear of disaster looming larger than the risk to my son's unbaptized soul. "What if something happens? It's safer to keep him at home."

He hitches a chair close to mine. "What are you afraid of, Ava?"

The question goes to the heart of what is plaguing me. Why *am* I so afraid? I wasn't like this before, not even with Dandy. He never felt like my *first*, because I had mothered Claire and Teddy and innumerable neighbor babies on my way to actual motherhood. I'd never had this sensation that the world was full of terrors aimed directly at my baby.

"I don't know," I say at last. "I just am." Tears overflow and I swipe at them roughly, embarrassed to cry in front of my husband.

"Oh, sweetheart." He leans forward and puts his arms around me, rounding his back to make room for the baby between us. "I wish I knew how to help."

"So do I."

His grip grows more purposeful. "He'll be baptized this Sunday."

"But—"

"We are taking this baby to church." His tone brooks no argument. "We'll wrap him in every blanket in the house if it makes you feel better."

"What about godparents?"

"Pearl and Dandy are old enough."

"But he's their brother." They have enough adult responsibilities without the added burden of their brother's spiritual wellbeing.

"Lillie would want him baptized."

It isn't fair to use Mama against me. I look down at the downy blond head nestled under my chin. "Fine."

That I've given in shows how upside down we are. Normally decisions like this are left to me, but my certainty disappeared with my sense of safety. It feels like the floor could open in front of me at any time.

But the floor is already open. It opened on Christmas when Daniel came home without a job. He won't be out of work forever, but there's not much likelihood of finding real work in the depths of winter. We'll be relying on Dandy's income for months.

"I'm off, then."

I blink, and realize he's still there, watching me. "Yes."

"I'll let Father Dennis know about Sunday." He runs a finger along the baby's cheek. "Is he nursing well?"

He sucks fine, but I don't feel like I have enough milk. It's probably my imagination again, dreaming up things that can go wrong. "Be home in time for supper."

Daniel tucks the ends of his scarf inside his coat. "If I'm going to be late, I'll send word."

I am filled with sudden, irrational rage. "You know how hard it is to try to feed you all on next to nothing—you can't even say you'll be home on time?" My voice shakes.

"Jesus, Ava." He reaches for his gloves, flaps the stiffness out of the dry wool. "I don't want to fight over whose life is harder."

I turn away, my shoulders straight with the effort of holding back more tears. This isn't who I want to be with Daniel. I'm always frightened, always exhausted, always resentful. It's poisoning everything.

"Ava." His lips brush my neck. "I'm sorry. I wish I could do better for you and the kids."

All he has to do is get close and I turn to jelly. It's been that way since he was skinny Danny Kimber, the neighbor boy. At first, there was just a bone-deep knowing between us, but by the time we were fourteen, we were shirking chores to lose ourselves in kissing, hiding away down at the creek, in my brothers' deserted treehouse, and once, memorably, in the church, pulling apart with a hunger deeper than when we began. I suspected that the desperation in my body could be cured by the desperation in his, but I would not know for certain until our wedding night.

Twisting away, I say, "Enough of that, or we'll have another one to worry about." On cue, the baby gurgles and pulls away from my breast. I quickly cover myself.

Daniel's expression changes. "Fine," he says, tugging on his gloves. "You stay here and save the world on your own."

Pearl

January 15, 1932

Mama and Daddy had an argument today. I couldn't hear all of it, but it had to do with Teddy. When he came home for supper, he told us Teddy would be baptized on Sunday, and Dandy and I are godparents. Mama said Aunt Claire and Uncle Harry are also his godparents, but they can't come.

Uncle Harry isn't Catholic, so I wonder if he actually can be Teddy's godfather if he can't bring him up in the church? Not that Dandy and I are much use at our age.

Claire

I pick up Dandy's film while I'm out doing errands. On a whim, I had asked for two sets of prints, and as I walk through Rittenhouse Square, I open the packet and flip through the photos. Their contents make me drop onto a bench, suddenly breathless.

The first photo is a family grouping, Daniel standing in the back, the children—minus the photographer—clustered around a still-pregnant Ava. Everyone is smiling except for my sister, who looks impatient and uncomfortable.

There are several pictures of the little boys. Harry will be pleased with the success of his cowboy and Indian suits. Thelma poses with her doll, looking as much like a doll herself as a child can manage. Another photo features Thelma in a chair, with Pearl leaning alongside, a baby in her arms.

Teddy!

A smile rises to my lips as I see his tiny face, the tuft of pale hair sticking straight up. He is beautiful.

I skim the rest of the photos. Although there are a few more of Teddy and the rest of the children, there are no other photos of Ava. She gave birth but seems to have disappeared from her family's life afterward.

13

Ava

Father Dennis stands before us in his green vestments—ordinary time, he once confided to Mama, was his favorite time of year because the color of his vestments reminded him of Ireland. "What name have you given this child?"

"Teddy," Daniel says when I fail to speak. "His name is Teddy."

I take a breath to clear my head; I can't look as fog-brained as I feel. Daniel was right—I've always insisted on baptizing my babies as soon as possible, and it is as much for the naming as for their membership in the life of the church.

"And what do you ask from God's Church for Teddy?"

"Baptism," I say. The word comes out clearly; it is only my son's name I have trouble saying.

When I was small, the priest had explained the importance of names, and it stuck with me. When Adam named the animals in the garden, it gave him dominion over those creatures. When I name my children and bring them into the church, they are fully *mine*, even as I also give them over to God.

Perhaps this is what I need, to bring me closer to my son.

"You have asked to have your child baptized. In doing so you are accepting the responsibility of training him in the practice of the faith." Father Dennis looks at us both. "It will be your duty to bring him up to keep God's commandments as Christ taught us, by loving God and our neighbor. Do you clearly understand what you are undertaking?"

"We do."

He turns to Pearl and Dandy, stiff and self-important as parents themselves. "Are you ready to help the parents of this child as Christian parents?"

"We are." Dandy's voice is too loud, while Pearl's is just a whisper.

It is the right thing to do—for Teddy, and for my family. Mama is beside me, her love and pride filling me. How she wanted to be here for this last grandchild.

The priest signs a cross on the baby's forehead, and we follow suit. I close my eyes for the intercessions and invocation of the saints, murmuring, "Lord, hear our prayer" and "Pray for us" as required. The comfort of faith fills me—how can anything go wrong, when we have asked not only God and Jesus Christ, but Mary and St. John the Baptist and St. Joseph and all the rest to pray for this tiny child. My Teddy.

I give him over into Pearl's arms for the application of the fragrant chrism, and we move to the font, where Father Dennis questions us and asks for our profession of faith.

"Do you believe in God, the Father almighty, creator of heaven and earth?"

"I do." Daniel's fingers touch mine.

"Do you believe in Jesus Christ, his only Son, our Lord, who was born of the Virgin Mary, was crucified, died, and was buried, rose from the dead, and is now seated at the right hand of the Father?"

"I do." I curl my fingers through his and squeeze.

"Do you believe in the Holy Spirit, the Holy Catholic Church, the communion of saints, the forgiveness of sins, the resurrection of the body, and life everlasting?"

"I do." Daniel's thumb caresses the back of my hand. It will be all right.

Teddy howls beautifully when the water touches his forehead. Pearl and Dandy hold him, looking so adult that I have a momentary sense of unreality. How have my children grown up so quickly?

Afterward, Pearl insists on carrying the baby home through the light, spitting snow, and I give in, feeling light for the first time since his birth. It's not cold enough for the snow to stick, but I still want to get back inside. You can't be too careful with a baby.

When Daniel opens the door, I step around him and unexpected heat touches my face like a summer breeze. I slip the coat from my shoulders. "What—?"

"I did a couple extra hours," Dandy explains with a sheepish grin. "I wanted it to be a party. For Teddy, and for you, Ma…because you're up again."

There are more practical uses for his money, but I love him for wanting to give us a proper celebration instead of huddling in the kitchen like we do every other day. "Thank you." I pull him to me and kiss his cheek. "What a lovely idea."

We listen to a music program while we drink tea and eat the small cake Pearl made, which she serves on Mama's flowered china plate. This adds to the festive atmosphere, and I realize that between birth and the fog of sadness afterward, I missed Christmas entirely.

"What did they have you doing?" Daniel asks abruptly.

Dandy blinks. "Where?"

"At work."

"Just work." He shifts in his seat. "You know."

Daniel lights a cigarette, and in the flicker of the match, his eyes are dark. "What I *know* is there's no overtime right now."

Our son shrugs. "There was a little, and the guys knew I wanted to do something for Teddy, so they let me have it."

"They're too broke to be generous." He exhales a plume of smoke. "But there's another place you could have gotten it."

Dandy glances at the coal bin. "I don't know what you mean."

I look from one to the other. There isn't much work, but why couldn't Dandy have done a little extra? There is something they're not saying.

"I think you do." There's an edge to Daniel's voice now. "I've seen you come home dirty when you're not working."

There *are* times when he comes in with his hands black, his pants and shirt stiff with coal dust, but I honestly haven't paid much mind. It's just laundry, and it never ends.

He shrugs. "I was out with my friends. Sometimes we get dirty."

"Toby and George get dirty," Daniel says. "You've been messing with something that's not yours."

My chest tightens, and the heaviness of the last weeks presses on me. It's been such a good morning—why must they spoil it by fighting?

"Fine," Dandy says, his head lowered. "Me and some of the boys, we've been working a little side job."

"You're bootlegging."

"Bootlegging?" I look at my son incredulously. We've tried so hard to keep talk of liquor away from the kids. I can't believe Dandy would do that, even for money.

He shakes his head. "No, Ma. We're just—"

"You're stealing coal." Daniel rakes his fingers through his hair.

The kids watch the back-and-forth, the remnants of the cake forgotten. Even Teddy is round-eyed, feeling the tension thick as the shawl Pearl has wrapped around him.

"If they find out, you could end up in jail." Daniel's hands are knotted on his thighs. "Or worse."

I know what 'or worse' is, and it turns me cold inside.

"And we could lose the house." That is what worries him most, I know: not the illegality of whatever our son is doing, but the house. Though we try not to think about it, it belongs to the company and could be taken away at any time.

Dandy's brows draw together, the sharp line between them a mirror of his father's expression. "You care more about them than us. After everything they've done—after firing you on Christmas." He appeals to me. "They'll never miss what we take. We're not selling it, just bringing it home." A glance at the coal bin. "Haven't you noticed it never really empties?"

"I have," Pearl says. "I wondered."

Daniel stands. "I won't have a thief in this house."

"I'm just doing what needs to be done." Dandy's lip trembles. "You can't make me stop."

"We'll manage." I put a restraining hand on his arm. "Your father's worried, the same as I would have been if I'd known what you were up to."

He twists away, his face contorted. "How are we managing?" he spits. "Not with the money *he's* bringing in."

I close my eyes against the explosion that is sure to follow.

"You're not a man," Daniel says slowly, "only a boy with a jumped-up idea of what manhood means." He glances at me, tempering his words. "I could put you over my knee right now. I won't, because I don't want to upset your mother. But you're done with all that."

"I'll stop when things are better." Dandy is on his feet, moving around the room with his father's nervous energy. "For now, I'm going to contribute any way I can."

"Things won't be better if you end up dead." I barely recognize my husband; the fury on his face is something I've only seen directed at the mine owners.

"They won't catch me." He kicks at the coal bin. "Someone needs to work."

The words strike Daniel like a blow; he nearly staggers. "I'm the man of this house. You'll obey me." He towers over Dandy, but my boy has learned fearlessness in the mines.

"Are you?" He straightens and meets his father's eyes. "Then why am I the only one with a job?"

Time stops as my husband's hand flashes out. Dandy rocks backward, hitting the edge of the stove before he falls. He scrambles up, and I spring to my feet and get between them.

"Stop it!"

"Keep out of this." Hot tears flood my eyes. Daniel has never shouted at me before.

"Leave her alone, you bastard!" Dandy reaches around me and his father shoves him again.

All the air has gone out of the room. I stand between the two people I love most on earth and feel the ground beneath my feet fall away even further.

"Get out," he says. "I won't have a thief under my roof."

"Daniel!"

"I mean it." He grabs his coat. "When I come back, you'll either apologize—and quit bootlegging—or you'll be gone." He is out the door before anyone can stop him. No one tries.

Pearl buries her face in Teddy's wrappings. Thelma looks at her and begins to wail. Confused, the little boys move closer to their sisters.

"I'll talk to him," I say weakly. I don't know what I'll say, but I'll find the words somehow. I can't lose my son.

Dandy rubs Pearl's back. "Don't worry," he says. "I won't go far."

"You're not going anywhere." I gather Thelma onto my lap and try to quell her sobs. "He's not leaving, baby."

"I'm not staying, Ma, not after that."

I leave Thelma to Pearl and follow as he sprints up the stairs. "Let me talk to him, Dandy."

"Don't make excuses for him." His face is red with the effort of holding back tears.

"I'm not." Striking Dandy is inexcusable, and his words even more so. "Just try to see it through his eyes."

He yanks open a drawer and pulls out his work pants and an extra shirt. "Why? So I can be like him?"

"He's ashamed," I say softly.

"Then he should find work." My son gives no quarter. "Do you have a bag, Ma?"

"He didn't want to leave you and Pearl to watch over me." I curl my fingers around his bicep and feel my boy's wiry strength. "Don't do this," I plead. "I'll make him see sense."

Dandy strips the case from his pillow and shoves his clothes inside. "I can't stay here. If he shouts at you again, I'll kill him."

I swallow hard, pushing my tears down. Using guilt will only backfire—he is not ready to apologize, and Daniel is not in any state to have a rational conversation. "He loves you."

"Not right now, he doesn't." Dandy looks at me with his father's eyes. "And I don't love him, either." He puts his arms around me. "Some of my friends room at Mrs. Nordstrom's. That's where I'll be if you need me."

"I need you here." I clutch him to me. "*We* need you here."

He pulls free, looking ready to cry himself. "My salary will still be banked at the store. You won't go without."

"I'm not worried about that." My baby is standing before me with all his possessions in a pillowcase. "Dandy—"

"You should be."

Claire

We drive back from church in a gentle drift of snow. Irene frets as if the sky were falling, but I can't wait to get out and feel the air on my face. After Baxter drops us at the door, Harry retreats to his office. I am officially at loose ends. Again.

I wander up to our bedroom and sit at the dressing table. The vanity tray sparkles with cut-glass bottles, and I lift one idly and sniff the stopper, closing my eyes to take in the heady scents of rose and jasmine, the underlying note of vanilla: Shalimar, my current favorite. I dab my wrists; Irene discourages perfume on Sundays as inappropriate, though her hair was freshly waved and a touch of lipstick brightened her tight mouth.

It is only me that does not know, after all this time, what is and is not done in Irene's world—although I suspect her standards vary, to make certain I never meet them.

Thoughts like this will drive me mad. I retrieve my address book and hurry downstairs to the telephone alcove. There is a separate line in Harry's office; this is the one for household use. I dial quickly, before I lose my nerve.

Marie Whittle is one of the wives in our group; on a recent evening, after I responded under my breath to one of Irene's pronouncements, she made a point of speaking to me, and I understood that I was not alone in my thoughts, only in speaking them aloud.

I listen to her high-pitched greeting and the sounds of children in the background. "Can you sneak out this afternoon? *Mata Hari* closes this week and I still haven't seen it. You know I'm a fiend for Garbo."

There is a moment's pause. "I'll get the maid to watch the boys. It's her afternoon off, but I'm sure she won't mind."

I spare a thought for the maid, who most certainly *will* mind. "Can't your husband watch them?"

Her laughter fills my ears like the tinkling of a chandelier. "Purvis made them, darling, and he pays for them. You can't expect him to spend time with them, as well!"

As I change out of my church clothes and walk to meet Marie on Walnut Street, I wonder about Harry, and how he would behave if we had children. Would he be a proper father, or just a checkbook, like Marie's husband?

I want to believe he would love a child, but if he can't—if he is Purvis Whittle and a hundred other men of our acquaintance—I will make up for it.

If I get pregnant, and *if* I carry the baby to term.

If is the cruelest word in the English language.

Ava

Supper is over before Daniel returns. When he comes in, we're sitting in the front room. Not listening to the radio, not doing anything. Just sitting.

He looks around. "Is he gone?"

"Yes." I lift Teddy to my shoulder. "Daniel—"

"No." He goes upstairs and we can hear him pace overhead as he tries to work out his anger.

There is a loud sniff. When I turn to look, four pairs of tearless blue eyes stare back at me. Pearl jerks her head toward the stairs. "Can you talk to him, Mama?"

"Tomorrow." I'll get nowhere when he's like this. "When he's calmer."

She looks skeptical. To keep her from attempting to speak to him—the worst thing right now would be for another kid to question his judgment—I ask her to read from *Little Women*. "There's no point in wasting the heat."

"Not with what it's cost us." Pearl fetches the book and settles Thelma against her.

I tilt my head back and let the words flow over me, but my mind is busy trying to find a solution to our shattered household. I know Daniel sees our son's actions as a betrayal of the way he's been brought up, but how can he not also see that Dandy is following in his footsteps, doing whatever he can to serve his family? He wasn't careful in how he spoke, but he's a boy, and can't be expected to always govern his words.

Thelma interrupts the reading. "Does Daddy hate Dandy now?"

"Of course not, baby." My stomach twists at the fear in her eyes. "He's just mad."

"But what if he gets mad at us?" George's voice trembles. "Will he make us leave?"

"No," I promise, looking from child to child. Teddy's hair tickles my chin. "He won't. And Dandy will be home before you know it."

Pearl

January 17, 1932

Today was the worst day ever. Worse than even Granny dying. It started out good, with Teddy's baptism. Dandy and I were godparents. Mama was acting more like herself, and it felt good to be a family again.

Then we went home and everything fell apart. Daddy blew up at Dandy because he's been digging coal somewhere. Dandy wouldn't back down, and he hit him and told him to get out. Mama begged him not to go, but he did.

Daddy came home hours later. Mama tried to talk to him but he went upstairs and I read *Little Women* until bedtime. I love that book so much, but now all I can think is that my brother is gone and the littles are scared of Daddy.

I'm scared of him, too. When he hit Dandy, I didn't recognize him.

14

Ava

My husband won't talk to me. Not about Dandy, not about anything. He's not a talker at the best of times—people sometimes take his lack of conversation as sullenness, but I've always been able to read him, the same way I can read my kids. This silence is different.

Dandy will be fine. I know that. Nordstrom's is one of the better houses for single men, much nicer than where Daniel lived before we married. But for all his attempts at manliness, he's just thirteen. And because Becky Nordstrom's mouth runs like a duck's ass, everyone will soon know my son has left home, and why.

I don't care about that.

What I care about is how Dandy feels, and that I was unable to protect him from his father's anger. There have been spankings before, of course, when the boys got out of hand, but Daniel and I grew up with too much casual violence to use it in our own home. That he could so easily find it in himself to strike Dandy is shocking to me.

I have discovered more about my son's activities, and the bootleg mine the boys have started somewhere on the mountain. It doesn't surprise me that Daniel is upset. He's more letter-of-the-law than I am, despite his history. I supported his efforts when they tried to organize the Gracie in 1926, even after the Coal and Iron Police left him bloodied on the porch. The mines *weren't* safe, the owners *were* greedy and careless, and men should have the means to protect themselves.

A flaming bottle through the front window changed all that. Toby got cut up pretty bad—the scar is still visible when he gets his summer haircut—and the scorch took a week to scrub off the walls.

Next time I went to the company store, Mr. Henderson, the agent, smirked at me. "Heard you had a little fire, Miz Kimber. Better tell your man to be careful. Damaging company property will get you put out on the road."

My fury boiled up, but I simply nodded and said we'd be more careful in the future. Then I went home and told Daniel he was done with the union, or he'd have to find someplace else to live. I knew what the CIP was capable of. They're gone now, but the mine owners still have ways of dealing with rule-breakers, Pinkertons or some other private goon squad.

I shiver at the thought of them targeting my son.

We've been lying side by side for the better part of an hour, our bodies not quite touching beneath the piled quilts. Daniel's breathing tells me he is still awake.

"Al Denning got a letter from his brother."

"And?" My patience is wearing thin. After days of rebuffing any attempt at conversation, he decides to talk now.

"There's a warehouse going up in Scranton, near the rail yard. They're looking for men."

"Then you should go."

He shifts, and I can just make out his profile against the pillow. "I'm worried about you."

"I'm fine." I know what he means, but the fog that enveloped me after Teddy's birth has dissipated, driven away by Dandy's banishment. "You should go."

His fingers touch mine under the covers. "Do you want me to leave?"

"It might be best, for a while."

The hand retreats. "What do you mean?"

"Until things calm down." There's no point in not being truthful. "Have you noticed how quiet the kids are? They're afraid to put a foot wrong in case you throw them out."

"Jesus." There are tears in his voice. "I hope you told them—"

"They don't believe me," I say flatly. "I couldn't protect Dandy, so why should they be any different? It has to come from you—and you have to show them, not just say the words."

He is quiet for a long time. "I didn't mean to be so hard on him."

110

His breath is warm on my cheek. I nuzzle him, trying to connect in the way that has never failed. "I know."

"I was angry," he says. "I still am. He supports this family better than I do."

"It's only temporary." I stroke his cheek with my free hand. "Even if the mine doesn't call you back, you'll find something. This job, it might turn into regular work."

"But it's not here."

"We'll manage, me and Pearl. Dandy will come around for the heavy work, even if he's at Nordstrom's." I wait for him to say Dandy can come home, but instead, he puts his arm around me and pulls me close.

One step at a time.

I snuggle into the curve of his body and try to sleep.

Claire

"Letter for you." Harry stands in the doorway, already changed for dinner. "It was mixed in with mine."

The envelope is from Scovill Run, postmarked three days ago. The handwriting is large and unformed: another one of the children. Ava hasn't responded to my last three letters.

What is going on?

There's no time to read it now. I finish my hair and screw on earrings that match my Christmas bracelet as Harry watches. He likes to see me well turned out, and I enjoy dressing up for him. I apply a fresh coat of lipstick and slide the envelope under the vanity tray to read when I am alone.

Irene is insufferable all through the meal. The soup is too hot and the roast is undercooked. I'm starving and don't care about the soup; I'd already downed several spoonsful before she began her litany of complaints. The redness in the beef looks delicious, and I let Harry carve two slices for me before it is sent back to the kitchen.

"You shouldn't encourage Mrs. Fell by eating whatever swill she sends up." Irene's hands rest primly on either side of her empty plate.

"I'm not." I cut into the beef with gusto. "I like my meat pink."

She sniffs. "That's not pink, that's raw. That beef could get up and walk around the dining room if it were any rarer."

I snort, imagining a black and white cow ambling around on her precious Aubusson. "I'd like to see that," I say. "Could you pass the potatoes, Harry?"

When we have finished, we relocate to the living room. I wait until Harry and his mother are settled with coffee and excuse myself. I have to get away before Irene makes me angrier, and I want to hear the news from home, though it nagged me all through dinner that—again—Ava wasn't the one to write. She promised, but there has been nothing but a note in mid-December, acknowledging the gift box and scolding me for spending too much money.

Opening the envelope, I unfold a single sheet, marred by black fingerprints. Daniel, then, not one of the children.

Claire,

> *Would you and Harry take the baby? He is a fine boy but small and Ava has little milk. She is better now but at first cried all the time and stayed in bed. I have to look for work and she will be alone with the kids.*
>
> *If you will, write like it's your idea. She won't agree if I suggest it.*

Daniel

I sit back, fanning myself with the letter. When has Ava ever been unable to cope? This sounds worse than Pearl's assessment of the situation.

And take Teddy? How can Daniel even ask that? My sister would never permit it, and as much as I want a child, I want *my own child.* I want the emptiness in my marriage filled with a life I have produced from my own body, from my union with Harry.

These last few days, I've begun to hope again. I've been lightheaded in the mornings, but there's been no nausea—not yet. My breasts are tender, but that could be my monthly, which is a few days late.

I will not think about this astonishing request until I know for certain. If there's a chance I'm starting another baby, I want to put every ounce of strength and attention toward that. It has to happen eventually; I've prayed so long and so hard God has to have heard me.

Opening the box where I keep my stationery, I slide the letter inside. I will write to Ava again tomorrow, inquiring about everyone's health, and see if she responds. Daniel is probably panicking; men often do, where babies are concerned. For all his restraint, Harry is always distraught when I miscarry, having found something he and his money cannot control.

Ava

Ten men decide to try for the jobs in Scranton. They leave from the store on Saturday morning, crammed into the back of a battered Ford truck, and we wave them off and walk home in the gray slush. The boys dart off and I settle Teddy in his basket and tell Pearl to read to Thelma while I start on the baking.

For the moment, the house is quiet and my mind opens to embrace the peace. Now that I feel more like myself, I can start sewing again. When Daniel returns, perhaps he will have come to his senses and let Dandy move home.

In the meantime, there is the never-ending worry about money.

"I'm not sure what to do." Trudy, whose brother has also gone to Scranton, joins me for tea while the bread rises. "The kids are always hungry. There aren't enough potatoes in the world to fill the boys' bellies." I think of my garden, the chickens—how in summer, it feels like plenty, and then in the winter, no matter how much food I put up, we run low. "Even with Daniel and Dandy gone, there's not enough."

"I know," she says heavily. "It is the same with us. With my Karl gone, and now Hermann, it is me alone with the babies. We are already behind one month on the rent until they send money."

"How long will they let you go?" We too are behind on the rent, and Mr. Henderson is less patient these days since many of the tenants no longer work in the mine.

"I know not." Her face creases with worry.

"Mama would have found a way." I voice my darkest fear, that I will not be able to handle hardship as well as my mother. "She always did, even after Tata died."

Trudy stares into her cup, rubbing at the faded design until I think she'll rub it clean off. "You don't want to do everything she did."

"What do you mean?" Perhaps Trudy remembers some trick I've forgotten.

"She was desperate," she says. "You understand."

Those were dark days. "I'm not going to judge her. I'm hoping for ideas."

"She did things for Mr. Tradd." Trudy bites her lip and fiddles with the flowered scarf covering her pin curls. "Special things. When the rent came due."

"When the..." Mr. Tradd was Mr. Henderson's predecessor, but they are cut from the same cloth. Finicky men, not likely to grant favors. Except Mr. Tradd, on a few occasions, had done just that. He'd given Mama an extension after Tata died, and again after Jake left.

Another time he sent men out to repair the roof, and I still remember his gruff, "No charge, Mrs. K," as he chewed his cigar and thrust his hands into his baggy trousers. "Mr. Tradd has no bottom," Claire had whispered, but I wouldn't giggle because very little was funny anymore.

I choose to ignore Trudy's words and look around the kitchen. It is not large, but Mama, Pearl, and I managed to work there well enough. An idea dawns, and I speak quickly, pushing away thoughts of what my mother may have done. "What would you say to moving in? I can sleep with the children, and you can have the front bedroom with Fritz and Hetty. When Karl comes back, we'll make room for him, as well."

"Really?" She folds her hands, raw and pink from hanging out laundry in the cold. "Will Daniel not mind?"

"We've rented rooms before, to his friends." I grow excited. "I never like it, because of the girls, but this is the perfect solution. Besides, Daniel's not here."

"Then I drink to our partnership." Trudy clinks her cup against mine. "When times are hard, we women find a way to survive."

The next morning, I send Pearl for Dandy. He and another boy help Trudy move her furniture and a few boxes to our side of the wall. Rather than give up the house, she rents it to two recently-evicted families. "So it doesn't go back to them," she says, making the face we all make when referring to the company. "Soon maybe we'll be able to move back when our men come home and bring money."

"From your mouth to God's ears." I carry my things into the smaller bedroom, where I will share a bed with my daughters. "I don't care if they have to rob a bank."

That's the difference between Daniel and me: at this point, I wouldn't care if Al Capone waltzed into my thin-walled house, so long as he brought a bag of cash. My husband is upright, and upright people go hungry.

I don't mind being hungry. That's what I tell myself when I have bread dipped in coffee for supper and watch the kids eat. Under the dirt and scabs of little boyhood, George and Toby are scrawny, all elbows and knees, while Pearl has the sharp cheekbones of an older girl; she gives the best of her plate to Thelma, who will never get stronger if she's undernourished.

Teddy squalls because I don't have enough milk, but if I eat enough to feed him, another child will go hungry. It is on me to solve this problem, and I don't know where to start.

15

Pearl

February 20, 1932

The house is crowded since the Metzgers moved in. There's nowhere to hide my diary except under the mattress. There's no peace at all. I knew from babysitting that Hetty Metzger was awful, but now she's in the front bedroom and Mama sleeps with us girls, and the boys are on the other side of the curtain.

Daddy's not back, so I guess he found work. He hasn't sent any money, but we got a couple of sewing jobs so we were able to put a little on the rent.

Now that Mama is feeling better, she brought out the fabric that Aunt Claire sent in the Christmas box and is going to make dresses for Thelma and me. This cloth is so new it feels crunchy, and Mama made me wash it before she cut it up, so it doesn't shrink after. It felt like a crime to take the shine off Thelma's pink striped cotton, and nearly as bad to see my blue flowers flapping on the line next to it.

I've never had anything brand new before, it's always been hand-me-downs picked up at the church swap, dresses I've seen on my friends' older sisters.

There was fabric for Mama, but she hasn't cut into it. She said her best is good enough, once she can fit into it again. Her best is older than me, and even though it looks nice, you can see from the seams that it used to be a different color.

It feels silly to be so excited over a dress. Frivolous. That's a word I read recently and looked up in the dictionary at school. I feel like Meg March when she got dressed up for the ball, a sow's ear into a silk purse for sure.

Claire

"Good God," Harry says from behind his newspaper.

"What is it?" I put down the piece of toast I've been nibbling and try to ignore the smell of his coffee, which makes me queasy even as I celebrate the cause.

He tilts the paper my way. "Colonel Lindbergh's baby has been kidnapped."

"What?" I've already been sick in the privacy of our bathroom, but his words make my stomach turn over again.

The newspaper shows a photo of Anne Lindbergh holding her infant, and another of a group of women with a slightly older child. The headline reads *"Lindbergh Baby Kidnapped in his Sleep from Nursery in Home at Hopewell, N.J."*

"Who would do such a thing?" Irene dabs her lips with a napkin.

Harry reads further, the paper trembling in hands suddenly unsteady. "Someone climbed through the window and took him from his bedroom."

We met the Lindberghs a few months after their son was born, at a party given by the mayor. Colonel Lindbergh and I exchanged pleasantries, but I felt a real connection to his wife, who, when asked about her baby, said she would rather be at home with him than socializing.

"That's ridiculous." Irene's cup pauses in mid-air. "People don't just go around climbing through windows."

Harry sighs and drains his coffee. "There's a ransom demand."

"I hope they pay it." I would do anything to get my baby back.

Leaning down, he drops a kiss on my hair. "Even if they do, there's a chance this won't end well."

After he leaves, I take up the paper, looking at photos that show the house and note which window was used to extract the child. There is a heaviness in my chest. How must Mrs. Lindbergh feel? It is the worst thing I can imagine, to have a much-wanted baby, to have money and status and everything necessary to raise that child in health and safety, and then to have him stolen in the night.

"That poor woman."

"One can't worry about strangers," Irene says. "Hand me the society page. I want to see if Ellen Simpson has returned from London."

I can't stop thinking about the Lindbergh baby. I listen to the radio news, and after Harry leaves for the office, I pore over every inch of the *Inquirer*. He and Irene both think my preoccupation isn't healthy. They are right, but I can't stop myself.

There is no real news, but each new piece of speculation, rumor, and conspiracy is illustrated with photos of that precious boy. I should think about something else—my own child, for example. According to the doctor's calculations, I'm nearing my third month, almost far enough along to feel safe.

But I don't feel safe. I *never* feel safe. Working on the nursery feels like a jinx—will I be lucky enough to have a baby by late summer? Everything is tied to the missing child. So long as he is alive, my pregnancy will continue.

I am afraid of what will happen if they find him dead.

Pearl

March 3, 1932

I visited Dandy at Mrs. Nordstrom's after school and read a newspaper left on her porch. Mr. Lindbergh, who crossed the ocean almost five years ago, has had his baby stolen. It's terrible. I came straight home and cuddled Teddy like mad, and when I told her, Mama just shook her head.

Last night after the littles were asleep and Mama was knitting, I turned the pages of Granny's Bible, trying to find her again. Some days I hear her voice so clear, but on days like today, she's just a photograph in my head. It hurts to think of her like that, she boiled with life like a kettle.

But anyway, I found four dollars hidden in the Bible, their edges stuck down with flour paste. She must have been saving them for something special. I haven't given them to Mama yet. I'm not sure why.

Ava

Once the Metzgers are moved in, life settles into a new rhythm. Spring is coming: there is always housework and sewing and eternal laundry, but it is also time to turn over the garden and start seeds indoors by the stove. Peas and beans first—in April they will be transplanted into the warming soil and will be established by the time we set out the less hardy plants.

My partnership with Trudy was a good idea. We work well together, in the kitchen and out. Her grandson, Fritz, a quiet boy of nine, goes to school and counts the days until he can enter the breaker. Hetty is seven, a pert child who follows Pearl everywhere. One day my daughter snaps and makes her cry.

"What got into you?" I ask as we walk to the store together. It isn't like Pearl to lose her temper.

"I'm sorry." Pearl plods along, pulling the wagon Daniel made for the children when they were small. "She was teasing Thelma."

That sallow-faced little brat teases my Thelma? I've never seen it, but I don't doubt Pearl is telling the truth. "What did she do?"

"She was imitating her walk," Pearl says, pain in her eyes. "And the other day she tore Thelma's doll dress, the blue one."

At the store, I give Teddy to Pearl and hand over an envelope of cash for Mr. Henderson. With the little that remains, I buy lamp oil, potatoes, and a sack of flour. Mr. Callum loads it into the wagon, his ears pricked for gossip. "Heard from Dan?"

"Not recently." We haven't heard anything in two weeks, but one of the other women got a card and told me the men are staying together at the building site.

The storekeeper's mouth twists under his mustache. "I'm surprised. Didn't think he'd be one of those fellas to just do a bunk."

"He'll be back," I say with a glance at Pearl. "He's working."

"I hope you're right, Miz Kimber." His chins wobble over his tight collar. "These Depression divorces, as the papers are calling them, seem right unfair to you womenfolk." He waves us off and goes back inside his warm shop.

"Why does he think Daddy would leave?" Pearl asks, tugging her hat down over her reddened ears.

"Some men do, I guess." My girl doesn't miss much. "But some men shirk their responsibilities. That's not who your daddy is."

She tucks her chin and considers, pulling hard on the wagon. "But he wasn't himself," she counters. "Not when he left, anyway."

"No," I hand her the baby and take my turn with the wagon. "But he's proud, your dad. And not working makes him feel like less of a man. That's why he got so angry at Dandy."

She chews her bottom lip. "Do you think he'll come home?"

"Of course he will." I hope I'm right. Daniel wouldn't leave on his own, but anything can happen in a city, and we wouldn't hear about it for weeks.

We walk in silence and then Pearl asks, "Was that all the rent?"

"Half." I stop for a moment to adjust my scarf. "I should be able to manage the rest when Mrs. Brown pays for her coat, and if Trudy keeps contributing toward the food. When your dad comes home, we might even be a little ahead."

It's all castles in the air. For all I know, Daniel will come home with nothing but lint in his pockets. We're two months behind, Geneva Brown shows no sign of paying for her coat, and Trudy might leave if I complain about Hetty.

"Mama," Pearl says, "I think Granny knew something like this might happen."

16

Claire

The headline reads *"Hope Fades for Safe Recovery of Lindbergh Baby."* I scan the article, my fingertip racing along the lines of text, hoping for any scrap of good news. There is none, and I sag in my chair.

"You're going to lose your baby if you don't stop worrying about other people's problems." Irene's pronouncement comes from across the breakfast table.

I put the paper down. "Don't be horrible."

"It's the truth." She cuts her scrambled egg with precise movements. "You're working yourself into a state. Where will you be if you lose this one?"

It is silly and superstitious that I've hung the success of my pregnancy on the safety of Charles and Anne Lindbergh's son. I know it, but I can't seem to stop—thoughts of my baby and little Charles Augustus Lindbergh run on parallel tracks. They did not ask my permission.

"I'll try." My voice is weak. I pick up the heavy silver and make an attempt at my food. Every morning, Irene orders a full breakfast, and every morning I rearrange it on my plate and consume nothing but toast and tea.

"It's the least you can do."

"What?" I put the fork down before I throw it.

"It's the least you can do." She raises her voice so her dense daughter-in-law can understand. "Give my son a son of his own. Give *me* a grandchild. I didn't expect much, but I thought you were at least capable of that."

The buttered toast turns into a boulder and I swallow hard to get it down. I've never been strong enough to stand up to Irene. Tears form in the corners of my eyes and run down my cheeks.

Harry never told me his mother's reaction when he announced our engagement, but it was obvious I would not have been not her first—or her fiftieth—choice for her darling son. My assumed fertility was the only thing she ever approved of, and since I have failed repeatedly in that regard, I am nothing more than a source of disappointment. Sometimes I wonder if I'm not a disappointment to Harry, as well. A man wants sons, and a man in his position can afford them.

I think of Ava, with all those children, and Daniel constantly at risk of losing his job. No, that isn't right; he's already lost his job. I've somehow managed to put his letter out of my mind. Pregnancy makes my brain foggy, though Irene would say that's nothing new.

I should write to Ava again. Distract her. Women sometimes get the blues after a baby is born, but that doesn't seem like something my sister would be afflicted with, especially after this many children. Nothing stops Ava.

"You're woolgathering."

Are even my thoughts policed?

"I was thinking about Ava." I lay my knife and fork across the plate. I can't eat another bite, no matter what Irene says. "She's not doing well after this last baby."

"I'm not surprised." She purses her mouth; it pleases me to see lipstick has feathered into the vertical creases of her upper lip. "With that many children, a woman's body breaks down. She'll be lucky if she sees them graduate from high school, if indeed any of them even attend school."

"They all go to school, except the eldest boy." What would happen if I flung my tea in her face? Her powder would run, and her hair—those perfect, steel-gray waves—would collapse in such a way that even her maid couldn't repair it.

I feel about my mother-in-law's maid the way I feel about most things having to do with her. Evans is slight and narrow-shouldered, with a pointed nose that makes her look like a rodent. She acts like a rat, too, sniffing out improprieties that she murmurs into Irene's ear as she dresses her for dinner or sets her hair into those immaculate waves.

"I assume he's in the mines with the father?" Her distaste is apparent. "I can't imagine allowing my child to do that. It's unfathomable."

"It's completely fathomable." My tears are gone, replaced with something I recognize as anger. "If you're poor, that is. They don't want their children to work, but they also don't want their children to starve."

"Hmph." She folds her napkin and takes a small sip of water. "There are charities to take care of people who can't manage their funds."

"What funds?" I laugh in her face. "You make it sound as if they've made a few bad investments. It's not a matter of charity, it's a matter of opportunity, and there are none. Everyone is at the mercy of the mining companies. If they shut down or cut shifts, people go hungry."

Irene pushes back her chair. "It doesn't bear thinking about," she says. "Happy thoughts, Claire, happy thoughts. If you want this baby, you must stop dwelling on things that upset you."

I've been staying close to home, but traveling upstate by car should be safe enough. When Harry comes home, I'll suggest a quick weekend trip. I need to check on my sister without the filter of the postal service, and I have to get away before I brain Irene with a frying pan.

The seamstress is coming later to adjust a few of my dresses, which are growing snug in the waist. There are pregnancy girdles, but the idea of compressing my baby is repulsive to me. I remember Ava's enormous belly; with my smaller frame, I will look ridiculous. I am looking forward to it.

I shift in my seat, adjusting the cushion behind my low back, which has been aching since I got up; perhaps I slept wrong or strained it somehow when I was rearranging the contents of the nursery closet yesterday.

A cup of tea will put me to rights. I ring for Katie, and as I lean back, I feel the dull ache in my back again, and also a familiar tugging sensation, low in my belly.

No.

I bolt from my seat, not waiting for Katie to come, and run for the bathroom, one hand on my stomach, the other holding tight to the railing. The bathroom seems miles away. When the door finally clicks shut, I hike up my skirt and see the bright flare of blood on my ivory silk pants. I sink to my knees on the bathmat, all my strength gone.

Katie knocks lightly. "Ma'am, are you all right? Do you want your tea in your room?"

I don't respond. The white hex tiles are cold under my cheek, but the rest of me is boiling.

She knocks again, louder, and I know the racket will annoy Irene. "Go away," I call. "I'm fine."

"I'm coming in." She gasps when she sees the blood on my skirt and the fluffy blue bathmat. "You stay right there, ma'am, I'll get help."

"Just get me up." My legs don't seem to be cooperating. "I've done this before."

"You're bleeding bad." Katie pulls a towel off the rail and folds it, pressing it between my legs. "You hold that tight, I'll be right back."

Men come, and an ambulance, and I lose track of myself. Later, at the hospital, Harry rushes into my room on the doctor's heels.

"It happened again." I meet his eyes over the white-clad shoulder of the man who could not save our baby.

"So long as you're safe, darling," Harry says. "That's what matters."

The doctor looks up. "I'm going to ask you to wait outside, sir, while I examine your wife."

Harry objects, but one nurse manhandles him out of the room while another stands at my shoulder. I close my eyes, not caring what happens.

I have failed. Again.

While I wait for the painkillers to take effect, the sounds around me begin to filter into my consciousness. Babies: crying, howling, wailing. Babies everywhere, except in my small white-painted room which looks out into the top of a barren and leafless tree.

It makes sense that I was brought to the Women's Building at Pennsylvania Hospital, but it is the last place I want to be. I press my lips together and pray for oblivion.

In the afternoon, an unfamiliar doctor comes in to see me. He is younger, with slicked-back hair and an energetic manner. "How are we feeling, Mrs. Warriner?"

"Empty." My mouth is dry, my head hurts, and I am still fuzzy from the drugs.

The doctor pats my arm. "These things happen, my dear. Better luck next time."

His comforting words feel like a punch to the stomach. When I can speak, I say, "Have you looked at my history?"

Female patients, especially married female patients, aren't supposed to take that tone. His eyebrows raise, and he takes my chart off the foot of the bed and scans it. "Hmm. Not our first miscarriage, I see."

"Not 'ours,'" I say. "Mine. And it's my sixth."

"I'm sorry for your losses, Mrs. Warriner." He comes closer, the chart still in his hand. "But motherhood isn't for everyone. Or at least not every *body*."

"I'm beginning to believe that." I feel slightly more charitable; it must be the medication. "I can't do this again."

"Understood." He folds his hands over a belly that resembles a five-month pregnancy. "Shall I have that conversation with your husband for you?"

"Why?"

With a tight, uncomfortable smile, he says, "Husbands don't always understand..."

I blow out a breath, almost laughing. "Doctor, my husband understands how babies are made, and so do I. But I can't do this again."

"There are methods of prevention, of course." His red cheeks make him look younger. "Sheaths, for example. Or you could be fitted for a pessary."

"I'm Catholic." It isn't that contraception hasn't crossed my mind during my years-long journey to this hospital bed, but I've never been comfortable with the idea—until now. But those methods still fail; Marie Whittle's second son was born after she started using a pessary.

I rest my hand on the rail that prevents me from climbing out of bed and going home. "What about a hysterectomy?" Irene had such a surgery years ago, claiming that Harry's birth had damaged her. I often felt sorry for the father-in-law I never met; I was certain his access to Irene's bed was restricted after Harry was born.

"We prefer to do that only when it's necessary."

"It *is* necessary." I know in my heart that if I have to endure this one more time, Harry will be visiting me at the Byberry Asylum.

Again the condescending eyebrow. "There are standards which must be met, Mrs. Warriner, that's all I mean."

"Then how do we meet them?" I fold my hands on my own deflated stomach.

The doctor backs slowly away. "Is your husband coming in later today?"

"He is," I say. "He should be here soon. What difference does that make?"

"I'll need to speak to him first."

As he ducks neatly out the door, I consider ringing for a nurse and having the doctor brought back to explain himself. He won't, though, no matter what kind of scene I make. He'll wait for Harry because as a woman I'm not expected to understand big words or make decisions about my own body.

Harry arrives within the hour, straight from his office. He puts his case on the floor and kisses me thoroughly. "You look better." His fingers lightly tweak my chin. "There's more color in your cheeks."

"I feel a bit better," I tell him. "Though the color is probably from wanting to throttle my doctor."

He drags a chair over so he can sit with me. "What's Lyle done?"

"Not Dr. Lyle. Another doctor, a younger one. He's waiting to speak to you."

"Why?"

I watch his face carefully. "I asked if there was anything they could do, medically, to keep me from getting pregnant again."

He takes my hands and brings them to his lips. "Oh, darling. I know it's been hard."

"Giving birth is hard." I want him to understand that I'm not afraid of pain. "It's this I can't do again, Harry."

"Well, there are ways—"

"I know there are." I think of those sad rubber sheaths we tried when I was under orders not to get pregnant for six months. "As a Catholic, I shouldn't be in favor of anything that limits my ability to bear children, but I want to be your wife more than I want to be a mother or a Catholic."

This is the conversation the young doctor wants to have with Harry. He wants to warn him off me, to tell him that continued relations would risk my health. Is it unladylike to imply that the idea of a marriage as barren as I am, a marriage without intimacy, is not what I want? I love what Harry and I do in bed. It was a revelation on our wedding night, discovering that what I had experienced at fifteen could, with the right man, be something quite different, and eventually wonderful.

"Let me talk to him," Harry says. "I'll see if I can hunt up Lyle, as well, just to get everyone in on this."

"Do let me know what you all decide," I call after him. "It's only my body..."

The light fades while I wait, and eventually, I switch on the bedside lamp. There are a few magazines, but they don't draw my interest. Film stars in fancy dresses don't seem important when my future is being decided without my input.

When Harry returns, he has both Dr. Lyle and the young doctor, whose name tag reads Dr. Benedict, with him.

"Well? What's the verdict, gentlemen?" My tone is more flippant than I intend.

"Verdict?" Dr. Lyle comes forward and takes my hand, checking my pulse and smiling down at me. I don't dislike him, but we have never met under good circumstances.

"Did you talk about my request?"

Dr. Benedict glances from me to my silent husband. "There might be something..."

"What?" I sit up too quickly and subside against the pillows, wincing.

"Salpingectomy." He lets the unfamiliar word hang in the air before continuing, "Otherwise known as tubal ligation. It's a relatively new procedure. I'm surprised you've heard of it."

I didn't know there was a specific procedure; I assumed with all the advances in medical science, if they couldn't let me keep a baby, there had to be a way to prevent me from continually falling pregnant.

"Is it safe?" Harry speaks for the first time.

"It's quite simple." Dr. Lyle explains the procedure, finishing with, "It would be less uncomfortable for you than...well, the reason you're here today."

Dr. Benedict joins the conversation. "I'm sure this is something you two will need to discuss."

I want to climb out of bed and slap his smug face, but I can't, because I have been given hope, however slim, that my persistent failures are at an end; it would not do to injure him. "Harry?"

He looks between the two white-coated men. "This is my wife's decision. I trust her to know what is best."

Smiling apologetically, Dr. Lyle says, "I'm sorry, Mr. Warriner, but hospital policy requires *your* consent for any such procedure."

"Then you have it," he says, and I recognize from the way he articulates his words that he is furious. "Fully."

"You must understand, Mrs. Warriner, once this is done, you won't be able to change your mind."

Dr. Benedict is determined to annoy me. "I think I know my own mind," I say crisply. "Dr. Lyle, is this something that can be done while I'm here, or would I need to come back?" Now that I know this procedure exists, I want it done as soon as possible.

"I would recommend a brief delay," he says, more comfortable with this line of conversation. "Before undergoing another procedure, no matter how minor, you should take a few weeks to build up your strength. You lost a significant amount of blood. When you return, you'll only be here for a night or two, so you can be monitored afterward."

There is more, but I stop listening. I can make this painful cycle stop. It will take another stay in the hospital, but I've had plenty of those. One more, and my uncooperative body will no longer be in control of my life.

The doctors leave when my dinner arrives. Harry returns to his chair, looking at the unappetizing contents of my tray. "I should have brought something from home. I'm sorry."

"It's all right."

"Are you sure, Claire?" He is not asking about the food.

"I've never been so sure of anything." I take his hand, find his palm unexpectedly sweaty. "Harry, I can't do this again without going crazy. The hope and the failure, again and again and again."

Pushing the table aside, Harry sits on the edge of the bed and gently puts his arms around me. "I know," he says, as I bury my face against his neck. "I know, darling."

I wipe tears with my free hand. "I'm sorry I'm such a disappointment—"

He blots my face with his handkerchief. "I am disappointed," he says, "but not in you. Just in the situation. I don't want to risk your health."

When my tears subside, I eat my unappealing dinner before it gets cold: sliced chicken with gravy, mashed potatoes, and peas that are more gray than green. "Mrs. Fell could learn something from them about overcooking vegetables. Do you want the cake?"

"You should eat it."

"I'm more tired than hungry."

"Then I'll let you get some rest." He gathers up his coat and case, and puts his hat on at a rakish angle to make me laugh. "I'll be back first thing in the morning. We'll get you home, and as soon as we can, we'll arrange for the operation."

"Thank you." The words are insufficient to express the gratitude I feel for his acceptance of my failure, for loving me anyway, for standing up to the doctors and letting them know my decision is his decision.

When the orderly comes to take my tray, I rally myself. "Could you have someone bring pen and paper? I need to write to my sister."

17

Ava

The men return in early April, the building in Scranton far enough along that only those capable of finish carpentry are asked to stay on. Daniel looks tired, but some of the darkness has cleared from his eyes—work will do that for a man. When I ask how it went, he proudly hands over almost fifty dollars. It is not enough to cover what we owe, but seeing my husband restored to something resembling his former self is beyond price.

"At least we can breathe for a while," Daniel says. "I was going to head up to the store later. Want me to pick anything up?"

"No, but you can drop off the back rent and clear most of our tab." I want Mr. Callum's insinuations refuted by Daniel's presence.

He shakes his head in disbelief. "I thought we'd be ahead. Hasn't Dandy been contributing?"

"We can't rely on his income," I remind him. "He needs money for his room, and he's only just started making a full salary." I play my trump card. "You can't expect him to support us unless you let him come home."

I do not mention—yet—what has been on my mind more and more since he left for Scranton. Is it selfish of us as parents to stay here, to let Dandy work in the mine, to force Pearl to carry the worries and responsibilities of a grown woman when there is an alternative?

Claire and Harry are more than willing to help us. If Daniel took that job from Harry, we wouldn't have to accept their charity for long. I want the kids to be tough, to grow up knowing how to take care of themselves, but how much of that is already in their character? Do we need to inflict unnecessary suffering on them, just to make them better people?

"We'll figure out something." He ignores my mention of Dandy, focusing his displeasure on Trudy and her grandchildren. "At least Hermann stayed in Scranton. It's too crowded in this house."

While he was away, we enjoyed being all in one room, but Daniel likes privacy, so I have him haul Mama's bed upstairs and re-hang the curtain between us and the kids. Pearl is out with a friend, but Thelma dogs his every step, and he stops every so often to ruffle her hair and grin down at her.

"Trudy's been a huge help," I tell him. "I got a few dress orders, so she's been doing all the cooking while Pearl and I sew. If we finish while it's still light, we don't have to waste lamp oil."

Daniel nods, looking around as if the house has become unfamiliar to him in this short time. "Where are the boys?"

I shrug. "They cleaned up the garden for me this morning, so I gave them the afternoon to run." I lift Teddy from his basket by the stove. "This one doesn't get too far from his mama, at least not yet."

"He's grown some." Daniel takes the baby from me and tucks him against his shoulder, dropping into the swaying movement of an experienced parent. "Is he feeding better?"

"I think so." I'm not sure. He sucks down whatever I can give him, but whether that's enough, I have no idea. "If you walk down to the store, can you bring home a sack of potatoes? And there's a dance at the hall tonight if you're not too tired."

"I'm not," he says, pulling me to him. Teddy makes a small noise of protest and then settles in between us. "God, I've missed you."

It had been peaceful without him, but there had also been an emptiness—in the house and in myself. I wrap my arms around his middle. "I missed you, too."

Having him gone allowed me to calm the kids and work on a plan to reunite my family. Daniel and I have always been on the same page when it comes to the important things, and being angry with him felt unnatural—but no more unnatural than watching him force Dandy out of the house. It would take careful handling to bring him around.

"Are you okay?" He pulls back to look at me.

"You mean, am I better than I was after Teddy was born?"

"I was worried."

"I know." I lean my head on his shoulder. "I'm better. I don't know what happened, but it's faded." The shadows are still lurking,

131

and on the rare occasions when I am alone, I give way to tears, but he doesn't need to know that.

"Off to the store, you." I move away reluctantly. "I'll never finish this if we spend all day canoodling."

He kisses me again. "I missed canoodling, too."

A quick storm blows up while he is out. It slacks off, but it's still raining when I hear the kitchen door bang open. "The potatoes are on the back step," he calls. "I didn't want to drip through the house." But drip he does, heading to the stove to dry off, shedding cap and jacket onto the nearest chair.

Shaking my head, I pick them up and hang them to dry properly. "Tea?"

"Please."

The kettle is hot. I pour a cup and hand it to him, smiling as he first uses it to warm his hands. Putting the cup down, he reaches for his jacket, rummaging in the inside pocket. "Letter from Claire," he says. "Wonder how they're doing?"

"Fine, I'm sure." I slip the envelope—white, rather than her usual pale blue—into my apron pocket. I've been meaning to write to her for weeks, but I never seem to have the energy. So much for my promise to be a better sister. At some point, she'll give up on me again, and it will be my fault. "Are you still up for the dance?"

By way of answer, he reaches out and grabs my waist, swinging me around the kitchen. "A little rain doesn't stop a Kimber from dancing with a pretty woman."

I let him waltz me around the table. "What about your wife?"

"She can't stop me, either." He spins me with a flourish, dropping into a chair and pulling me onto his knee. "Not when my wife's the prettiest woman in Scovill Run."

There is a squeak behind us. Toby and George are framed in the doorway, their expressions somewhere between shock and horror.

"This will be you soon enough," Daniel says and kisses me soundly. The boys flee, their socked feet thundering up the stairs, and we collapse into laughter.

"Go to sleep now." I watch the boys as they squirm and shove, unable to keep still even under the covers. "You think you'd be exhausted from acting like hooligans all evening."

"I've got them, Mama." Pearl begins to murmur a story, and they immediately fall silent. What would I do without her?

Listening to the rise and fall of her voice, I sit on the edge of the bed and take off my shoes, rubbing my sore feet. I wonder if there's any wool felt in the sewing box to cut down for liners; the cardboard isn't enough to keep me from feeling every pebble.

Slowly, I remove my dress, smooth its wrinkles, and hang it on a hook by the window. Despite my dancing, it will have to serve another wearing before it is washed. I pull my nightgown over my head, then remove my underthings, as Mama taught me, and as I've taught the girls.

It's then that I see the letter on the dresser, where I'd tossed it earlier in my haste to go out. It may not be her usual stationery, but it bears that lovely penmanship our teachers tried to beat into us. In Claire's case, it stuck.

Dear Sister,

I hope this finds you recovered and in good spirits. It has been far too long since I have heard from you. I hope Daniel has found employment and your worries are eased.

Harry and I are both well, though we were recently disappointed again in our hopes for a little one. The doctors have advised that continuing to try would be dangerous. We have not yet determined our course: Harry wants a son and I would love a dear girl to pet and play with, but I do not wish to bring a child into this world a half-orphan and leave my husband to raise her alone, nor do I want him to find another wife for the purpose. And Harry does not wish to adopt the offspring of strangers.

How is this fair? You have an abundance of children, with insufficient means to support them, and we, who could give a child every advantage, have been deprived of the blessing of children.

I have not put this suggestion to Harry and am only setting it on paper now because you would never agree, but my dear sister, would it not be wonderful if we were to adopt a child—

from you? Think of the advantages we could bestow. The older children are far too attached and can be a help to you in such difficult times, but little Teddy is young enough that he would adjust easily to the change. While we would make sure he never forgot you, I'm certain he would quickly learn to love us.

What do you think, Ava? Is it a mad idea? And does its madness preclude you from doing it? Please write and share your thoughts. I have enclosed a stamp to speed your reply.

Your loving sister,
Claire

I drop onto the bed, the letter crumpled in my hand. Her request would be laughable, except I remember our conversation the night we sat with Mama. I know how it is with her—this request, however shocking, is heartfelt and made in all seriousness. Turning the lamp low, I sit in the near-dark, blood singing in my ears, until I am in a state where I can face Daniel.

How can she even ask such a thing?

Because she always has. Claire asks, and Claire receives. She's been the golden child her entire life, our father's pet, as much as he had one, and the only child Mama allowed to finish school. Then, instead of helping to support the family, she ran off and found a job and a husband and left us behind.

Claire gets everything she wants without trying.

Except this.

Under the anger and horror I feel at her suggestion, there is a small vein of joy that I can do something she cannot. I don't like that I feel this way, but there it is. I can have babies with the ease that other children can run, while Claire is like…Thelma.

The house is quiet now, all of the kids asleep. Teddy is sprawled in his cradle, the covers already at his feet. I straighten them and lay my hand on his forehead. It is warm, the curls sticking to his skin. Teddy boils with life, even as he sleeps.

How can I consider Claire's request?

How can I not?

Daniel is on the davenport, the radio turned low. His head is tilted back, listening to the music.

"They're out."

He opens his eyes. "Did you knock the boys over the head? Where do they get the energy?"

"You tell me. You were the same." I sit in the chair opposite him. "I worry about them."

He stretches his arms over his head, and his bad shoulder pops, making me flinch. "You worry too much."

My face warms. "What else can I do? We're only two steps from losing this place." It isn't the right time for this conversation, but the letter has me stirred up. I take a breath. "I'm worried, Dan. I can only do so much, and there's still nothing here for you. What happens if Dandy loses his job?"

"He hasn't yet." He turns the radio up a notch and jazz floods the room. "Best deal I ever made," he says. "I could listen to this all night."

I reach over and snap it off. "I wish you'd never gotten the thing."

"You listen to it, too. It's not just me."

The chair screeches as I shove it back. We're close to arguing, and he's only just returned. "Do you want tea?"

I stare into the darkness while the kettle heats, and am startled when something moves in front of the window. Dandy opens the back door a moment later.

"Hi, Ma." It is obvious he didn't expect to find me there.

"It's after eleven." He's cleaned himself at the pump; his hair is damp and his hands cleaner than his wrists, but his shirt is streaked with black and one knee is out of his trousers. "Why weren't you at the dance? And what are you doing out this late?"

"Nothing." His expression tells me differently. "I just stopped to check the woodpile."

"Your father's home," I warn. It's been a long day already, and seeing his son covered in coal dust won't put Daniel in a forgiving frame of mind.

"I'll go, then." He reaches around me to grab an apple from the counter and replaces it with two cans of condensed milk. "See you around, Ma."

The kettle boils. Instead of taking the cups to the front room, I sit at the table with my head in my hands. After a few minutes, Daniel joins me. He takes a sip of scalding tea and says, "What's got you so upset?"

Wordlessly, I push the letter toward him. He moves closer to the lamp, his finger moving slowly across the paper as he reads.

"Your sister's got brass," he says, shaking his head.

"How could she?"

"We have an abundance of children," he says mockingly, "with insufficient means to support them. Does she expect us to just hand one over? They're not a litter of puppies."

"As if we would even consider it." I think again of the sadness behind those written words, and stiffen my spine, finding Mama's voice. "Family stays together."

"She really can't have her own?" Now Daniel looks out the window. I hope Dandy is well away.

"No, she can't, but that's beside the point." I curl my fingers around the cup. "She's asking for our baby."

"Well, he'd be the logical one," he says. "She's not wrong—at his age, he'll love whoever feeds him. And they can do that better than we can."

Within three months of Teddy's birth, my milk has begun to dry, probably because the kids get the bulk of my food. The knowledge that they're still hungry most of the time claws at me. We've failed them, and there's not a damn thing we can do about it. If I eat any less myself, Teddy will starve, and I already half-wonder if that's why Thelma is the way she is.

"A child belongs with its parents."

"Don't bite my head off." He looks at me, his brown eyes serious. "Maybe a child belongs where it can have the best life." He puts a hand over mine, his hard palm comforting as a shield. "He's either going to grow up wild like George and Toby or skinny and sickly like Thelma. The older two are only sturdy because we could afford to feed them when they were little."

I put my head on my folded arms, unwilling to let him see my tears. "I've only ever wanted the best for them," I say when I can trust my voice not to shake. "That's all."

"Maybe this is what's best, for Teddy." He draws me to my feet and I lean against his chest. "Come to bed. We don't have to decide anything right now."

18

Pearl

April 14, 1932

Something's going on. Daddy came home, so Mr. Callum was wrong, but Mama's all buttoned up and Daddy can barely keep in the house. I know she still gets sad sometimes, but she's not in bed or crying, so I don't think it's that. It must be bad, or they'd talk to us.

I think it's more than money. They're always worried about that. I tried to tell Mama I could quit school and get a job cleaning rooms at the hotel and she near took my head off. But we can't keep counting on Dandy. He's only a kid, no matter what he thinks. At least if I got a job, there'd be two of us earning besides what Mama brings in.

If she won't let me leave school, I'll just do more sewing with her. She and Granny taught me everything they know, and if I work at it, I'll get faster.

Maybe that will be enough?

Claire

It's been weeks since my letter to Ava and I haven't heard a word. I could blame the drugs, but it was selfishness and desperation that made me write. She'll probably never speak to me again.

I've been home from the hospital for two days, but my husband and maid conspire to keep me horizontal, if not actually in bed. The late afternoon sun slants through the sitting room window, brightening the delicate blue and gold oriental carpet in front of the loveseat. The combination of colors makes me smile, even when there is nothing to smile about.

The room originally belonged to the housekeeper, but shortly after my arrival, I turned it into my private retreat. I chose the paint, the fabrics, the delicate dark furniture, transforming it from a flavorless servant's room to the place where I am happiest. There is a profusion of slipper satin cushions on every surface, and the pale yellow walls are ornamented with paintings bought on our trips to Paris. It is the one place in the house, even including our bedroom, that is wholly mine.

When Irene first saw it, she raised a judgmental eyebrow. "That is a poor person's idea of a rich person's room."

In those early days, such a pronouncement could flatten me for weeks, but since no one would ever see this room unless I invited them in, I disregarded her for once.

There is a soft knock, and Katie enters with the tray. "How are you feeling?"

"Tired of being waited on?" I sit up and she slides a stool under my feet. "Katie, I can get up."

"Mr. Warriner told me to keep an eye on you."

I take a deep breath. "You're doing an excellent job." I sink back, deciding not to argue the point. "Was there any mail?"

Katie shakes her head. "You know I would have brought it right in if there was." She pours the tea and places the saucer within my reach. "Now drink up."

"Yes, mother," I mutter, making her laugh. I will not ask again if she will join; Katie's standards of propriety are higher than my own.

I laid in a supply of books ahead of the surgery, but the pile is already dwindling. While I can't see the tiny ormolu clock on my desk, it should be almost time for Harry to come home. Then I will be sprung from my cushioned prison, to sit at the dining table, and then sit, again, in the living room, before going to lie down in my bed. I had never imagined a trip to the bathroom would feel like a luxury.

Putting my book aside, I sit up straight, feeling only the slightest discomfort. Dr. Lyle was as good as his word; this procedure was less painful, and certainly less traumatic, than any of my miscarriages.

Before they rolled me away for the operation, Harry leaned over the gurney and took my hand. "Are you sure, Claire?"

It was a question with many meanings. In the weeks leading up to the operation, he said over and over that he wanted me to be happy. I didn't know how to say I wasn't sure I could be, without a baby. I could, at least, stop living in fear of the inevitable loss, but it wasn't the same.

"I'm sure," I said, closing my eyes. The anesthesia took it all away for a while, and when I woke up, it was done.

The decision to have the surgery felt like the first independent choice I had made since leaving Scovill Run to seek my fortune in Scranton. Even getting married hadn't really been my idea. Once Harry proposed, saying no was impossible.

The front door closes, and his footsteps echo on the marble floor. "In here," I call.

"Stay put," he responds. "I'll be right there."

I hear him talking to Katie, her high laugh, and then the door opens.

"How are—"

"I'm fine," I interrupt. "If someone asks me how I am one more time, I'm going to run around the block, just to prove that I'm able."

"Please don't do that." There is laughter in his voice. "I have something here that might convince you to stay indoors." He holds out a pink box from my favorite French milliner.

How is a hat going to keep me indoors?

He puts the box on the tea table and it shifts, seeming to weigh more than a normal hat. Waving a hand over the lid, he says, "Go ahead."

Hats are one of my weaknesses. I can't help myself—I snatch off the lid, expecting to see feathers or flowers. Instead, I am met with brown and white fur and a pair of shining black eyes.

The puppy stretches and shakes itself. Its ears, which are nearly as wide as the box, flap wildly, and I giggle helplessly.

"Harry?"

He lifts the tiny creature out and places it on my lap. "I know it doesn't take the place of a baby," he says, his words tumbling over each other, "but I thought it might cheer you up."

Did he think I could be placated with a puppy? "I don't see how—" I break off as the puppy stands on its hind legs and begins to wash my face.

"It's a *papillon*," he says. "Because of the ears."

It has been some time since I've used my French, but I know the word. The puppy's ears *do* resemble butterfly wings; it is a perfect name. "I don't know..."

"You wanted a dog before." He looks stricken. "I thought it would take your mind off things."

I have always wanted a dog, but Irene refuses to allow animals in the house—even her bridge friends have to leave their miniature poodles at home when they come to call. Early on, when I was so totally alone, a dog would have made a difference. Now, I'm not so sure. He licks my chin, and I melt, just a bit.

"He's very sweet," I say, thinking of Irene's reaction. "Does he have a name?"

Harry beams. "Not until you give him one."

The puppy turns around several times and settles in a tight circle on my lap. I lean over and kiss my husband. "I'll think of something that suits him."

Ava

There is no escaping Claire's letter and its painful question. I stop at the church, hoping Father Dennis will be able to help. There is no one else I can talk to: Daniel has already given me his thoughts; I can't tell the kids, not yet; and Trudy is my friend, but she is not *family*.

I catch the priest at the altar rail with a rag and a can of Brasso, whistling.

"Why don't you get someone else to do that?" I stand well back from the ammonia reek.

"The ladies are all too busy." He rubs energetically at a spot on the brass.

"And Father Anton?"

He straightens, one hand going to his low back. "I sent the young man out visiting. It's time he gets to know his parishioners."

"And who's been stopping him?" I smile, to take the sting from my words. Father Dennis does not share his parish willingly or well, but he needs help. "I thought you might want to take a break and give me tea."

The priest's office is a cramped room to the side of St. Barbara's shrine. One narrow window lets in a sliver of light, which dies immediately upon entering the untidy space. Despite lamps on either side of the desk, the room has a twilight feel, and a hint of liniment lingers in the corners.

Father Dennis produces a tin thermos. "What's on your mind? You're not often one to come to me with troubles."

"I try to handle my own, Father." I take a chipped cup from the shelf and let him pour. "But this is beyond me. Things are bad right now."

"Because Daniel is out of work? Him and many others." He must hear stories like mine a dozen times a week.

"I got a letter from Claire." The tea is strong, and none too warm.

"How is your sister?" He takes a sip and grimaces. "Sugar. I forgot sugar." He rummages in a drawer and brings out a small tin. "I was glad to see her at Lillie's funeral."

"So was I." I take a spoonful of sugar, feeling indulgent. "I've missed her. But her letter, Father—she had an unusual request." My hands are clasped, the knuckles white. I shake them out and rest them on my thighs. It does not do to appear this upset, even in front of Father Dennis. He will know anyway. "Claire and her husband have no children."

"That is a shame," says Father Dennis. "Children are a blessing in a marriage."

I raise a brow. "As I should well know. But Claire can't *have* children."

His forehead creases. "I am sorry to hear that. Tell her I'll pray for her."

"She's asked for more than prayers." I swallow the lump in my throat. "She's asked for Teddy."

Father Dennis blinks. "Teddy?"

I'm obscurely pleased that this has shocked him. "She makes a good case, Father. She and Harry could give him everything he needs."

"I can see that." He turns the cup on his desk, spreading dampness on a layer of papers. "She's always been baby mad, your sister."

"It's not that we don't love him." My eyes are burning, and I squeeze them shut until the urge to cry passes. "I don't want you to think that. But we've got five—six—mouths to feed, and I don't know how we're going to feed them." I run my fingers over my hair in frustration, shoving in an errant pin. "Daniel is more in favor of it than I am. As he would be, I suppose. He feels guilty he can't support us."

"He's proud," Father Dennis says. "As you are. I don't know a woman in town who does more."

"I wish Mama was still with us." I didn't realize how much I leaned on her until she was gone. "She would have found a way."

"You remind me more of her each day."

I take comfort in that, but then I think of the lengths Mama went to in order to protect us. It feels obscene, to ask the priest if my mother traded herself to pay the rent, and I end up dancing around it, asking whether or not Mama had ever come to him at her wits' end.

"Of course," he says. "But she always knew what had to be done. She just wanted it confirmed."

"Was she... was she ever ashamed of anything she had to do?"

"Why would you ask that?" His already pink face flushes. "I won't break the seal of the confessional, Ava, not even after her death."

"I wouldn't want you to," I say hastily. "I'm sorry, Father, I'm not even sure what I was asking."

"Well, then." He looks uncomfortable, turning the cup round and round in his big hands. "And anyway, Lillie never told me what she was confessing to."

"How do you confess something but not say what it is?"

"Your mother was a hardheaded woman. I knew my limits." He looks down at the floor. "She came in one morning, a few months after your father died, and said she had something to get off her chest." Shaking his head, he adds, "But then she wouldn't tell me what it was."

"Was she upset?"

"Upset with herself. She'd let herself down, she said." Father Dennis tips back in his chair. "She talked around it for about a quarter hour, much the way you talked around asking your question, and then demanded penance. I said I couldn't give her penance if I didn't know the sin. She gave me that look, you know the one—"

I did.

"She said it wasn't a mortal sin. She hadn't stolen anything, and she hadn't done murder."

It is enough. What does it matter, anyway? Mr. Henderson isn't knocking on my door, asking for favors, and it wouldn't solve this particular problem if he was.

"Do you feel giving Teddy to your sister would guarantee at least one child getting through these hard times unscathed?"

"Yes." He's hit the nail on the head. "There's that, and there's also… maybe it's a silly notion, but I wonder if Thelma isn't the way she is because of me. Because of something I did wrong." My heart thumps, and I take a deep breath, let it out. "Teddy is so young. He's the one who will be hurt most by the lack of food, or, God forbid, if we have to leave."

"It hasn't come to that?"

"Not yet," I tell him, "but it's never far from my mind."

Father Dennis shakes his head. "A union would guarantee your boy a proper wage, and Daniel might still be working himself."

I've heard enough of unions and what they can or can't do for my family. I focus on what *is* now. "Pearl wants to leave school, but I won't let her. She can go all the way, like Claire did." And a rich man won't swoop down and carry her off, leaving us all in the dust. "I won't risk that, either."

He puts his hands over mine on the desk and bows his head. "Let's pray on it, shall we?"

His hands are warm, larger even than Daniel's, though without his leathery palms and cracked knuckles. I let their comfort seep into me, and pray, not to God, but to my mother.

We gather in the kitchen before mass on Sunday—all of us, even Dandy, who has been invited specially. Claire's letter weighs on me, and I've told Daniel that the entire family needs to vote on the matter. Once breakfast is finished, Pearl clears away the dishes and I look around the table.

"We have something extra to pray over today," I tell them. "I want you all to listen to me and your daddy."

Toby pokes his brother and Daniel smacks the back of his head. "Listen to your mama now," he says. "This is no time for your foolishness."

"You all know your Aunt Claire doesn't have any kids," I begin. "Well, she and your uncle have been to a bunch of doctors in Philadelphia, and they say she can't have them. Ever."

"That's so sad," Pearl says. "Aunt Claire loves babies."

Daniel nods slowly. "That's it," he says. "Your aunt wrote us a letter, asking for a favor. A big favor."

"What does she want?" Dandy stands at the counter, scraping the last of the oatmeal from the pot with a wooden spoon. Unlike the others, he isn't wearing church clothes. "One of us?"

I look at my husband uncertainly. I hadn't anticipated anyone would guess before we could explain. "Well, yes."

"She wants to adopt Teddy," Daniel says bluntly. "She can't have babies, and they can give Teddy a better life than we can."

"No, they can't!" Pearl looks close to tears, Teddy nestled in her arms. "We love him."

"Your aunt will love him just as much," I say. "She's been married for as long as you've been alive, Pearl."

"Let her adopt someone else's baby." Dandy sits and puts an arm around Pearl. "Why take one of us?"

Daniel flattens his hands on the tabletop. "Because whatever baby they get will have a good life, and a good education. And if someone is going to benefit, they feel it should be family."

"But why Teddy?" Pearl leans her chin on his head and he smiles widely at us, his family. At his mother, who is about to betray him.

"Because he's young." I try not to look at his toothless grin. "Can you imagine how hard it would be for any of you to leave home?"

"I'm not goin' nowhere!" George says and kicks Toby. "She can take *him*."

"You stinker!" Toby elbows his brother in the ribs. "Let her have George!"

Daniel reaches across and gently knocks their heads together. "I wouldn't do that to her. She'd send you back, with a bill for damages."

The sound of bells drifts in through the window, open to the soft April air. "Eight o'clock, time to go." I reach for Teddy, but Pearl turns away with him still in her arms. "Your father and I have talked this over, but we want you to be part of the decision. I'd like you to pray on it. Ask God what's best—for Teddy, not for us." I look at Dandy. "Won't you come with us?"

He shakes his head. "I can pray just as well in the woods, and I don't have to put on a monkey suit to do it."

Walking the twenty minutes to St. Stanislaus, I ponder the reaction of my two eldest. I expected Pearl to object, but I never know what Dandy's thinking these days. Ahead of us, Pearl herds the younger boys, but she finally gives up and lets them run. "Wait for us on the steps," she calls. "Or I'll clock you." She drops back beside me and Thelma, shifting Teddy to her other shoulder. "Do we have to give him away?"

"We don't have to," I say, "but you're old enough to know how bad it is right now."

Thelma tugs at my skirt. "I can eat less."

"Sweetie, if you eat any less, you'll blow away." I ruffle her hair. "You don't cost us a penny."

"I could get a job," Pearl says again. "After school, if you won't let me quit."

"You've got a job—helping me and keeping your brothers from killing each other so I don't have to." It feels like I am talking to another adult. Pearl is growing up as fast as I did. "Besides, I doubt you could find anything that would pay as much as we'd lose on the sewing."

"I could do what Aunt Claire did, get a job outside."

She's stubborn; I like that. "You could, but you're not going to. And anyway, she waited until she finished school. I couldn't, because Granny needed help, but I want better for you. We want all of you to have better lives than we've had, and getting an education is the only way."

"I read just fine."

"You read better than any of us, but there's more to it than that. Someday this bad spell will be over, and the world will be different. I won't be able to teach you how to get by in that world, because I won't know. All I can teach you is how to be good at being poor."

"You've taught me how to be a mother," she says. "I see that every day."

"And someday, you'll put those lessons to use," I tell her, "but not too soon. That's another thing I don't want for you—too many children, too fast."

My daughter ducks her head. Her light brown hair swings forward to cover her face. "Do you regret having us?"

I look down to see if Thelma is listening, but she is focused on setting her feet just right on the road, which is cracked and rutted from the winter. "Not a single one of you," I say. "Even Toby and George. But there's not much choice once you're married. Babies come, and they keep on coming.

"For some women, like your aunt, they don't come at all, or they can't carry them. Remember a few years ago, when Thelma was just little? I lost a baby then, and it made me and your daddy sad, but it was the only time. Your aunt has lost *six* babies."

Pearl's face closes over "Maybe there's a reason God won't give her one."

"Maybe the reason is she's supposed to have Teddy."

19

Claire

We are at breakfast when the doorbell chimes. It's too early for company. Seated at the table with Harry, Pixie curled on my feet, I listen for Katie's light step in the hall, the murmur of her voice. Moments later she appears in the dining room with a yellow envelope.

"Telegram."

I expect it to be for Harry, some bit of business that couldn't wait until office hours, but she hands it to me. The envelope is addressed to "Mrs. Claire Warriner," and I know immediately what it contains. My hands shake as I put it to one side, wishing I hadn't eaten those poached eggs with my toast.

"What is it?" Harry folds his napkin. "Are you all right?"

Nodding, I say, "It's from Ava."

"Aren't you going to open it?"

"I'm afraid to." It's time to be honest with my husband. "I asked for something. This is her answer."

He looks puzzled. "What did you ask for?"

I take a sip of tea, wishing it was something stronger. "Teddy."

Harry chokes on his coffee. He wipes his mouth, puts his napkin down again, and asks, precisely, "You did what?"

A wave of heat floods my face. Ava's telegram will call me twelve kinds of stupid, and she will warn me never to come near her children again. Harry will agree with her. Why had I ever followed Daniel's ridiculous suggestion?

"I asked if we could adopt Teddy," I say. "I wrote from the hospital, after the…last time." Despite the warmth in my face, my hands are freezing and I rub them together under the table. I should have told him about Daniel's letter. It is too late now.

"Adopt him."

I hang my head. "I know you don't want to adopt. I thought maybe if it was my sister's child, it might be different. He's so young—it wouldn't be a hardship on him, the way it would with an older child."

"You've thought about this, haven't you?" Harry pushes back his chair and holds out his hand. "Let's take this into my office. We can talk, and Katie can clear up."

His office is sacrosanct; I can count on one hand the times I have been in there for more than a few moments. Pixie and I follow, and I stand just inside the door, hands clasped behind me.

"You look like a schoolgirl waiting for a reprimand." Instead of sitting at his desk, he pauses by one of the button-back chairs in front of the fireplace and waits until I join him.

"I am." I rub my palms on my thighs, creasing my pale blue crepe dress. "Harry…did I do the wrong thing?"

"I don't know." He laughs, almost unwillingly. "Why don't you open it? There's no point worrying until you know what she's said."

The envelope seems to pulse with a life of its own. "I'm afraid to," I admit. "Ava's got an awful temper." I think back to when I'd written the letter; it feels like a dream. "I think the medicine made me brave. Or stupid. I just remember thinking it wasn't fair that they have so many children, and we can't have any."

Tears, always close when I think about my lost babies, slip down my cheeks. Pixie whines, and puts a paw on my knee.

"I'm useless," I say. "I'm like a shiny object you saw in a store window, something you had to have but now that you've got it, you realize it has no purpose. And the best thing you can do is put it away in a cupboard and look for a new shiny object that can do more than just be decorative."

Harry stares at me. "Darling, I didn't marry you for the children you'd give me—I married you because you were the most beautiful girl I'd ever seen, because I fell in love with you and couldn't imagine letting you go."

"You didn't get your money's worth." I glance down at my hands, with their expensive rings, their lacquered nails. Hands that haven't done anything useful since our marriage. "When you acquire a wife, you expect her to be able to do all the normal wifely things. I can't be your hostess, and you don't need me to cook or clean house, but I can't do anything else."

He kneels in front of me, displacing Pixie, and takes my hands. "You talk about yourself as if you're a bad investment. When I met you, I had more money than I knew what to do with, but I wasn't happy. You make me happy—that's your value, Claire. It doesn't decrease because you can't have children."

I look at his dear face, furrowed with worry, and feel sillier than ever. Poor man, cursed with an infertile wife with a head full of feathers. "Let's just see how Ava phrased her refusal," I say. "Then you can go to work, and I can go do something useful, like buy a new hat."

He hands me a silver paper knife and I slit the envelope, unfolding the telegram slowly, putting off the inevitable even though it is in my hands.

SEND THE PAPERS. I'LL BRING HIM IN MAY. DO NOT THANK ME. IT'S NOT FOR YOU.

The words are so clearly Ava's that I can hear her voice, but it takes a moment for their meaning to sink in.

"Harry." My voice trembles as I hold out the telegram. "We're having a baby."

Pearl

April 26, 1932

I'm sick. They said we could vote, but they'd already decided. Dandy and I said no, of course, and George and Toby said they didn't care. Thelma was crying so hard they couldn't understand what she was saying, so they decided she meant yes. I cried more than Thelma then, and I haven't spoken to anybody for two days. Daddy tried to talk to me, and Mama told him to leave me be. They say it's best for Teddy, but I can't believe anything can be better for him than being with us.

I like Aunt Claire, but she's NOT his mother. And I don't care how much money they have, he'll be lonely without any brothers and sisters.

Claire

After Harry finally leaves for work, after we have laughed and cried, reading the telegram again and again, I venture into the room next to our bedroom, whose door I haven't opened since my last miscarriage.

The first time I got pregnant, it was within six months of our wedding. I started to prepare the nursery then, adding to it every time I was given another chance at motherhood. The nursery will be occupied at last. Not by the baby I wanted, but by the baby I can have. Teddy Kimber, named for my lost brother, will come, in time, to replace my lost children.

What should we feed a baby his age? Excluding mother's milk, I have no idea. Isn't there some sort of powdered formula these days? I will have to investigate. I am glad, now, that Ava is waiting a few weeks; it will give me time to read up on modern motherhood and buy more things for Teddy's room.

The nursery is bright, its two windows, curtained in dotted swiss, facing north. Perhaps not the most masculine choice of fabric, but they will do for the time being. The cheery yellow walls make me smile—a safe color, suitable for a boy or girl. The cradle is already in place, its bedding stored in boxes in the attic; I will have Katie bring it all down.

A rocking horse! He'll need one, sooner or later, and I wonder if perhaps that perfect horse I'd seen at Wanamaker's is still available. Ava would have skinned me alive if I'd bought it for *her* son, but as ours, Teddy can have it and be welcome to it.

I'm singing as I circle the room, touching the furniture that has held so much promise and even more heartbreak. The dresser, which will hold his tiny clothes. The handsomely carved cradle, sturdy as the boy who will sleep in it. The wide rocker near the window, intended for me to sit in while I nursed.

I drop into it now, pushing myself slowly back and forth, smiling as I make plans. A stray thought enters my mind, and I stop rocking.

Irene!

In all our excitement, we never discussed how to break the news to his mother. I will bear the brunt of her reaction—Harry rarely sees her displeasure, as she prefers to air her grievances after he goes to the office. She will have much to say about Teddy.

Not ready for that conversation, I avoid her by going shopping. Baxter could deliver me to Wanamaker's, but I have grown less appreciative of his silent efficiency over time. I decide to walk.

It is a cool spring day, and the daffodils have erupted into bloom in Rittenhouse Square. I stop for a moment to admire them. Daffodils are the most spring-like of flowers; they even grew in Scovill Run, where their brilliant yellow was soon dusted with black.

Through the park and onto Walnut Street, then over to Chestnut. I regret my impetuous decision as I see the increasing changes the Depression has wrought on the city. Men linger on corners, aimless as young boys, passing stubs of cigarettes, sometimes whistling at girls as they trot briskly past. Their rowdy laughter feels menacing, and I cross the street to avoid them, exhaling when the monolith of the department store rises before me.

Inside, an oasis of moneyed calm. I should feel guilty, but I do not. I will take a taxi home.

The rocking horse is, by some miracle, still available. The toy department clerk remembers me from Christmas. "I thought you'd be back," he says.

"The situation has changed," I tell him. "Please don't have it delivered until tomorrow. I want it to be a surprise."

The horse can't arrive before we've told Irene, though a rocking horse the size of a live pony would be quite the announcement, I think, smiling to myself. Perhaps a tag that reads, "Congratulations, you're going to be a grandma."

After I complete the purchase of the rocking horse, I treat myself and take the elevator up one floor to the Crystal Tea Room. As a girl, if I'd been asked to describe a fancy department store restaurant, I would have described the pillars and marble floors and expensive linens, but I might not have thought of the smart little tables, intimate for two, perfect for a woman dining alone. Miniature vases of pale pink roses dot each table, and the chandeliers for which the restaurant is named reflect off the vaulted ceiling. Not many things live up to childhood fantasies, but this place does.

A plate of tea sandwiches arrives, looking like a dolls' tea party. I select a crustless triangle and allow myself to dream of incipient motherhood, smiling faintly at the organ music drifting up from the main store.

Katie is clearing the dining room when I arrive home. "I'm sorry," I say. "I got held up. I hope Mrs. Warriner didn't wait."

"No, ma'am. She went to her room to write letters."

In Irene's coded language, that means she is napping. "I'll be quiet as a mouse," I say with a smile. "Could you bring a few boxes down from the attic tomorrow?"

"Of course, ma'am. Which ones?"

I try to hold back a grin and fail utterly. "The ones in the back marked 'baby.'"

My maid's embrace knocks me breathless. "Oh, I'm so happy for you!" She jumps back, one hand flying to her mouth. "I'm sorry, ma'am, I don't know what came over me."

"I do," I say. "The same feeling I had. I'm walking on air right now." I lower my voice, not wanting Irene to come and investigate. "We haven't told Mrs. Warriner yet—we'll do it after dinner."

"Is there anything special you'd like?" Katie beams at me again. "Any little thing Mrs. Fell could make that might tempt you?"

"No, I'm fine." She knows I've had surgery, but not the reason: best to clarify things before her misunderstanding grows. "We're adopting my sister's baby, so you won't have to deal with looking after me. He'll be five months old by the time he arrives."

Ava

It's done. I sent the telegram myself, leaving before breakfast to walk the three miles to the next town. I don't want Mr. Callum to know any more of our business than he already does. Daniel offered to accompany me, but I shook my head. "I need to go alone."

Perhaps I am being cruel. He feels this impending loss as much as I do—it is his joblessness that has brought us to the point of giving Teddy away—but I am selfish with my pain. I do not want to share it, not yet.

The kids will adjust, eventually. Pearl is glaring at me like I've killed someone, and I haven't seen Dandy since he made his opinion known. Thelma looks like a rag doll with half her stuffing out; I didn't think she was so attached to the idea of no longer being the baby. She is too young to understand what we've done. Or is she?

I try to imagine Claire's reaction when she receives the telegram. I was curt, perhaps, but words cost money and I don't waste them even when they don't. I've never been so glad not to have a telephone, else she'd be ringing it off the wall before I'm even home.

As I follow the road back into town, I see a group of boys climbing along the edge of the pile and circling around the back of the Gracie's works. It's broad daylight—brazen behavior if they're off to the bootleg mine. I stop and watch, and two men emerge from behind the breaker and follow them.

Company men? Or men like Daniel, in need of work?

I shake my head and continue on. It's none of my business.

Claire

"I had a letter from my sister today."

Harry pauses, a forkful of Lady Baltimore cake halfway to his lips. "How is Aunt Nora?"

"Very well," Irene says, "though of course she's worn out from dealing with John's estate. She's asked me to stay with her for the summer."

My ears perk up. A nice long visit with Aunt Honora is just what Irene needs, or at least what I need for her. "Do you think you will?"

Irene purses her lips. "You know I'm not one for traveling."

"But the heat and humidity bother you so." It would be lovely to have her out of the house while Harry and I become accustomed to parenthood.

"Traveling is just as unpleasant—the trains are so uncomfortable these days." She picks at the cake with her fork. "Mrs. Fell is losing her touch. This icing tastes strongly of vanilla."

"I didn't notice." Harry takes a breath. "Speaking of sisters, Claire's sister is coming to visit next month." We didn't have time before dinner to discuss how we were going to broach the subject, and I am happy he jumped in when he saw an opening.

"I'm surprised they can afford the train fare."

"She'll manage." I imagine Irene with vanilla frosting all over her face and put my fork out of reach.

"I'm going to send tickets," Harry says. "It's the least we can do. She's bringing us a very special gift."

Irene looks over her spectacles. "What could that possibly be?"

"Her son." A smile breaks across Harry's face. "We're going to adopt her youngest boy, Teddy."

I resist looking at her and reach for Harry's hand instead. "Isn't it wonderful? We'll have a baby at last."

"What's wrong with him?"

We both blink at her. "What do you mean? He's perfect." I want to run and get Dandy's photographs to prove it; I'd been looking at them again before dinner, admiring his fat cheeks and curly hair.

"Why would you say that, Mother?" Harry's fingers squeeze mine. "Ava's doing us an enormous favor by letting us adopt her son."

Irene shakes her head slightly, a tremor of disapproval. "What kind of woman gives up a child unless it's defective?" she asks. "I only met her at your wedding, but she didn't seem the type to be handing out children, willy-nilly, no matter how many of them she has."

"There's nothing will-nilly about Ava," Harry agrees. "I don't imagine this was done lightly. But times are hard, Mother, much harder for them than for us. Ava and Daniel know we've been trying for a child of our own, and now that's out of the picture, this arrangement fills a need for both of us."

There it is again, his business language. I wouldn't have used words as impersonal as filling a need, but perhaps it is the best approach with Irene, who doesn't respond well to emotional appeals.

"It is very good of them," I say. "And they know he'll get the best of everything with us."

"Leaving the rest of that tribe of wild Indians to fend for themselves?" she asks. "What good is giving away one when you still have so many mouths to feed?" Irene looks at her son. "I do hope you're not overpaying for this, Harry."

Something flickers behind his carefully expressionless face. "We don't discuss financial matters at mealtimes, Mother, hasn't that always been your rule? Besides, whatever arrangements I've made with the Kimbers are between them and us."

He never talks back to her; this, more than anything else, shows me how much he wants this child.

"We haven't discussed money," I say, not wanting Irene to think Ava had sold Teddy to us. "She just wants what's best for him."

"What is best for a child is to be with its parents." She rises, brushing her plum-colored skirt with more vigor than the task requires. "I will retire now, and write a letter to my sister. By tomorrow morning, I hope you both will have come to your senses."

"Tomorrow morning, our attorney will be drawing up the adoption papers." Harry's chin has a defiant tilt.

"Have you spoken to him?" I ask when the door closes behind her. "Will it be difficult?"

"Less difficult than this," Harry says, with a small smile. "I spoke to Burt this afternoon. He and I will meet first thing to finalize the paperwork. If you write to Ava tomorrow, we can enclose the papers with your letter."

I push my plate away, no longer interested in dessert. "Harry, would it be inappropriate to have some champagne? Just the two of us?"

He scoops me up. "This deserves a celebration."

"It does, doesn't it?" I'm goosebumps all over, thinking about it. "Harry, I'm going to be a mother."

20

Pearl

April 28, 1932

Mama started talking as we did laundry today. She said she knew I was mad and didn't want to talk, but she's mad, too. The world is an awful place, and giving up Teddy is saving him from suffering. He's so tiny, she's afraid something could happen to him. She looked at Thelma when she said it, and that scared me.

So I still hate everything, but I'm not mad at Mama anymore. I didn't like being mad at her.

Ava

Claire and Harry waste no time. Within days, we receive a thick wedge of paper with lines down either side, written in language neither Daniel nor I can understand. What it boils down to is that our child will become their child as soon as we put our names on the document.

I sign before I can change my mind, and Daniel does the same. He's been in favor of this exchange from the beginning, but it's worn on him. When I shove the contract across the table to him, he blinks away tears.

"Well, that's done." He slides the papers back into the envelope. "Are you okay?"

"Yes." I am not okay. I am far from okay, but I am not going to think about that. Other things come first: getting the other kids through this without upsetting them, finishing my sewing so I can be away for a week without losing money or dumping everything on Pearl. Keeping Daniel from feeling guilty. "I'm fine."

The envelope holds more than the contract and a letter which I cannot bring myself to read. "They've sent two tickets," I say, holding them up. "Surely Teddy doesn't need his own?"

"They probably think you'll need company on the journey," Daniel says. "Can you handle him by yourself?"

"I can, but..." Daniel can't go; one parent needs to stay home. Pearl can't miss the end of the school year, and that would put responsibility for my family on Trudy, who has her own younglings to look after. Toby and George can't be separated for that long. I would like to take Dandy, but we can't afford to lose his income.

"Take Thelma," Pearl suggests.

Daniel looks skeptical. "It would be hard on her."

"It's a train, she wouldn't have to walk. And she could help with Teddy." Knowing she can't go, Pearl advocates for her sister.

"I could." Thelma speaks up. "I can hold him on my lap as good as anybody."

"Would you like to visit your aunt?" I am embarrassed that I hadn't considered her. Thelma's face lights up, and the decision is made.

Pearl

May 10, 1932

Mama looks sad, but she says she's fine. She always says that, like she's not supposed to have feelings. When I have kids, I won't hide stuff from them.

I'm not upset about Teddy anymore. I can see it's right. What I am is jealous. It's hard to admit that because I love Thelma more than anybody, but if she goes with Mama and Teddy, I have a week on my own with Daddy and the boys. A week of cooking and cleaning and breaking up fights. I'm exhausted and it hasn't even happened yet. And I feel terrible wishing I could be the one to go instead.

Ava

I wondered why Harry, with his bottomless supply of money, hadn't sent first class tickets, but I understand when I board the train with Thelma and Teddy. Third class is uncomfortable enough. First would have been unbearable.

"People are looking, Mama," Thelma whispers, ruining my illusion that kids don't notice things. She smooths her too-short skirt over her thin legs and centers Teddy on her lap. "We look poor."

"We are poor," I say quietly, wishing I'd let her wear her pink-and-white dress on the train. "But just because they have money doesn't mean they're better than us. You remember that."

She leans her head against my shoulder and sings softly to her brother. Teddy is simply himself, a babbling, cooing boy capable of charming anyone. The conductor, taking our tickets, pauses to tickle him and praise his beauty, and the woman across the aisle, with an enormous wicker basket of food for just herself and her husband, smiles kindly at him.

We left on the early train. I made Daniel find a ride to Scranton, reminding him, when he questioned me, that leaving from Scovill Run would only cause gossip, and I wouldn't be there for a week to cope with it. It is easier to leave unobserved, and saves him and Pearl from having to explain anything.

Let them talk. I can barely justify this to myself; I'm not likely to discuss it with the neighbors, other than Trudy, who cried so loudly I almost lost my composure. When people ask, I will say Teddy has gone to stay with my sister and imply it is for his health—which it is. Evaporated milk isn't as expensive as powdered formula, but it still cuts deep into our food budget; Claire will be able to afford formula and premade baby food after that.

It is for the best. So why do I still hate myself so much for doing it?

The train slows into another coal town. No one gets on, but we linger for twenty minutes as coal cars are hooked on behind the passenger cars. Even going to Philadelphia, we cannot escape coal.

At noon, I open the sack lunch Pearl has prepared: two sandwiches—more bread than meat, two apples, and a small slice of cake from Trudy. I take Teddy onto my lap and pass Thelma a sandwich.

The view has changed from squalid coal towns to long expanses of trees with scattered villages. It is surprising to see a life so different, yet so close to home. Scranton was intimidating, and Philadelphia will be far larger. The week ahead looms endless.

The train slows again, stopping at a platform on the edge of a field with two people waiting to board. They settle into our car, and when the conductor passes again, I flag him down.

"How long until Philadelphia?"

He checks his watch. "Another ninety minutes, ma'am, if everything runs on time."

Ninety minutes. An hour and a half before I put Teddy into Claire's arms. I give my half-eaten sandwich to Thelma, who swallows it whole, and lay Teddy against my chest. He is warm and accommodating, always ready for a cuddle. Thelma was the same, but George had never cuddled—he screamed and thrashed until he was fed and put in the cradle next to Toby. Pearl had been a good baby, placid but independent.

Stop thinking of them as babies. They are children, growing more quickly than I would like. Casting back to their diaper days will just make me sad. Teddy is my last, I'm sure, which makes giving him up even harder. I want to watch him grow into a sturdy, scabby-kneed little boy, his curls standing up around his head like a halo.

I close my eyes. Teddy growing up in my sight means Teddy following his father into the mine.

It's bad enough Dandy is there. I still have to figure out how to prevent Toby and George from joining him. The only good thing I can think of about the Depression is that it might save my sons from a life underground.

Thelma is asleep, an apple core in her lap and crumbs freckling her chin. I want to brush them off but she is sleeping so sweetly, that I let her be. Better she misses the ride, along with the opportunity to watch me regret every choice I've made in the last fifteen years.

That's an exaggeration, but the hypnotic rhythm of the train and the monotony of the trees are strangely conducive to self-reflection. I don't have much time for it normally, and that suits me fine. I try to remember the last time I sat still for this long, with nothing in my hands and no one needing anything from me, and I can't.

As we grow closer to Philadelphia, the view becomes more built-up. Along the tracks, I see men trudging along, looking to jump the train. There are tents and shacks outside of the rail yards, with more men standing around. Is the whole country out of work? I think of Daniel in a place like that, and I'm glad he came back from Scranton. Nothing good can come of these camps full of desperate men.

Soon we draw up on an enormous hulk of a building, a whirl of construction activity taking place. *Someone* is hiring. The conductor, noting my interest, says, "That's the new Philadelphia station. It should open up sometime next year."

"Are we there?" Thelma brushes herself off and stows the apple core away.

"Almost, little lady." He rests his hand on her seat back and points out the window. "Once we cross the river, then we'll be at the station."

When the train stops, people surge toward the doors. We move more slowly, and I stop on the platform, one hand on Thelma's shoulder, to let them get ahead. The conductor told us to go through the doors and follow the signs to reach the street level waiting room.

I look at the steep flight of stairs and sigh. I can't carry her; I already have Teddy and our cardboard suitcase. "Take your time, baby."

Broad Street Station feels simultaneously crowded and empty because there is so much echoing space above our heads. Fifty different conversations flow past, overlaid with a rhythmic clacking sound.

"Where are they, Mama?"

I peer through the crowd. I've never been among this many people before; it makes the skin crawl on the back of my neck. I locate the source of the sound: a flipboard, announcing arrivals and departures. Along the walls, men in suits hide behind newspapers in elevated, throne-like chairs, while shoeshine boys kneel at their feet. Other young boys brandish cones of paper-wrapped flowers. Still more hawk newspapers.

The Lindbergh baby is on the front page again. I can't make out the headline before my view is blocked.

Through the crowd, a woman's cry reaches me. I turn toward it and see Claire, clutching a crumpled newspaper, Harry frantically trying to calm her. I push my way toward them, using my suitcase as a battering ram, hoping Thelma can keep up. In the midst of the din, Teddy starts to wail.

"What's wrong?"

Claire looks up from Harry's gray flannel shoulder. "The baby's dead!" she explains, wiping her eyes with a gloved hand.

"What baby?" I shift Teddy from one hip to the other.

"The Lindbergh baby." Her tears begin afresh. "He's dead."

I catch myself before I roll my eyes; she seems truly undone by the news, which anyone with a brain had to expect after such a long time. I can control my face, but not my tongue. "If you don't get yourself together this minute, I'll get on the next train and take this baby home again." I tilt my chin. "Claire?"

She stops mid-sob and reaches for Teddy. He is a warm and solid bulk in my arms, flailing in his upset, with a thoroughly sodden diaper. I kiss the top of his head and hand him to her. He continues to cry for a moment, then realizes he is being held by someone new and takes a breath, reaching out and patting her wet face.

Another tear starts down her cheek, this time for the baby she is holding. She nuzzles his neck, blowing on his sweaty creases, and my own eyes begin to fill, watching them. Just in time, Harry says, "The car is right outside. You must be exhausted." He picked up our suitcase. "Is this everything?"

"Not a lot to bring." I cup my daughter's head; she is nearly as sweaty as the baby. "Thelma's been a big help."

"I'm sure." Harry scoops her up with his free arm. "Let's get you back to the house. We can have a bite to eat and then you can nap if you want."

"Your room is all ready," Claire says, tearing herself away from Teddy. "And the nursery is all set up."

"Can I sleep in with Teddy, Aunt Claire?" Thelma asks. "Just for now?"

Before I can agree that he'll settle more quickly with her familiar presence, Claire nods and says, "I'll have a bed moved in for you. That's a very good idea."

I let Harry get ahead and watch my sister. Claire holds Teddy as if he's always been hers; I swallow hard and begin the process of letting go.

21

Claire

We spin through the revolving doors and emerge onto Market Street. I point across toward the ornate wedding cake of City Hall. "That's where Harry worked when he was on city council."

Ava dismisses it with barely a glance. "You could fit all of Scovill Run in that building."

Traffic is light and the trip to the house is accomplished in minutes. Teddy remains quiet; like Thelma, his gaze is fixed on the sights slipping by the car windows. When we pull to the curb on Delancey Place, my sister closes her eyes as if in pain.

I lead them up to the dark green front door with its stone columns and the iron-and-glass lantern overhead. After so many years, it is simply *home*, but I see Ava's expression as she takes in the long, quiet block of brick and brownstone buildings and the tidy flower beds on either side of the steps, and remember my first terrifying glimpse of the house.

Katie opens the door and jumps back so everyone can enter. Without looking, I know she has an enormous smile for the children. "Everyone, this is Katie. Katie, this is my sister, Ava Kimber, and her daughter, Thelma." I turn so she can see the baby. "And this is Teddy."

She bobs and says, "It's a pleasure to meet you all." Laying a brown finger on Teddy's chubby fist, she says, "And it's a special pleasure to meet you, Master Teddy."

The baby gurgles and everyone laughs. The tension is broken for now. "Let's get you upstairs," I say. "I'm sure you'd like to change, and if anyone wants a bath, Katie will be happy to run it for you."

Ava raises an eyebrow. "Unless they've invented something new, I think I'm capable of turning a faucet." She gestures at her dress, a faded gray-and-white floral that has seen better days. "There's not much to change into. I hope I'll do."

Of course. How stupid, to assume Ava would arrive with clothes for every occasion; that tiny cardboard case holds a week's worth of clothing for herself and Thelma, and whatever she thought necessary for Teddy. I wonder if her pride will permit me to buy a few new things for them during their stay.

Sudden shrill barking makes us whirl, and the sound of toenails sliding on marble heralds Pixie's arrival.

"I'm sorry, ma'am, I had him shut in the kitchen." Katie bends to pick up the dog but Thelma is there first, crouched on the floor, having her face washed by the ecstatic puppy. "Let me get him—"

"Please," Thelma says, around the dog's tongue, "please, aunt, what's his name?"

"That's Pixie," I tell her. "If you don't mind him licking you, he'll be your friend forever."

She sits on the entry floor and takes Pixie into her arms. "I've always wanted a dog." She looks up at her mother. "Haven't I?"

Ava's smile doesn't reach her eyes. "You know why we can't."

She nods, burying her face in Pixie's fur. "But I can still *want* one."

"He's yours, while you're here," I say. "He'll even sleep on your bed."

The girl looks up, her face split by an enormous smile. "I'd like that, Aunt Claire. I'd like that a lot."

Ava

We are ushered upstairs, and everyone disperses: Claire to change Teddy's diaper and give him a bottle, and Thelma with them, unwilling to be parted from that damned dog. I fend off the maid, who offers to unpack for me; I am embarrassed to have anyone see how shabby my things are, much less this smiling colored girl who is wearing a dress nicer than anything I have brought with me.

The room itself is the size of our entire first floor. There is a wide bed with a pink quilted spread, and I bounce experimentally on the edge to see what a proper mattress feels like. Bedside tables are adorned with fresh flowers and small lamps with pink silk shades. The windows are draped in enough fabric to clothe me and my daughters, and the figured carpet is plush under my feet.

Claire suggested a bath, and although I look at the tub with longing, I decide against it. I will be here for a week; there will be plenty of time for that. I emerge from the bathroom, face and hands clean and my hair re-pinned, and go in search of my children.

The long hall has a patterned runner and white-painted doors at regular intervals. All the doors are closed, giving no hint of what lies behind their blank faces. Turning toward the front of the house, I open a door and find myself in the master bedroom. Three large windows, shrouded in misty lace and swagged with ice-blue curtains, overlook the street.

There are two beds with matching silver-blue spreads, with a table in between. An alcove holds Claire's dressing table, covered in bottles and jars, a fluffy, feminine scene that announces my sister's presence as clearly as the blue silk robe folded over the bench.

An open door beckons and I find the nursery. Teddy lies in the cradle, flat on his back, arms flung over his head. Thelma is curled on a small bed nearby, the dog nestled against her. All are solidly asleep.

There is an enormous rocking horse in one corner, large enough for Thelma. Is the beautiful cradle borrowed, as Claire claims, or is this yellow-painted room where my sister's hopes have lived—and died—all these years?

Pearl

May 13, 1932

It's not fair. I can say that here because no one will ever read this. It's not fair Thelma gets to see Aunt Claire. It's not fair that I have to stay home and take care of Daddy and the house and the boys.

I can hear Granny saying nobody likes a begrudger, but I can't help it. Right this moment I'm jealous of my crippled sister. I love Thelma more than anyone, but just once I would like to feel like somebody's first choice.

Ava

After an uncomfortable supper, I excuse myself and go outside to clear my head. Even though the windows are open to the spring air, the house feels oddly closed in—I think it's all the layers of curtains. I stand on the front step, taking in the sounds, glad there are at least trees on the street, with birds singing their familiar evening songs. I decide to walk to the end of the block, explore just a bit of my sister's world.

It is strange that rich people choose to live like this, all their houses running together down the length of the street, with no room for a garden or a front porch worthy of the name. I come to the corner and turn onto Nineteenth Street, walk a short stretch to a narrow street called Cypress, and follow it back to Eighteenth, where I am confronted by a brick mansion that takes up half the block and makes the Warriner home look like a tenement.

When I pass the mansion, with a tiny, tidy garden enclosed by spiked iron fencing, I turn again and follow the brick sidewalk back to Claire's, strangely pleased that I haven't gotten lost.

When I let myself in, I look from the marble entry into the living room. Harry is alone, a newspaper folded on his lap.

"Can I offer you a drink?" He gestures toward a stocked liquor cabinet, and I remember the whiskey he brought to Mama's funeral. Prohibition doesn't exist in this world.

"No, thank you. Where's Claire?"

"I sent her up to bed," he says. "She was worn out."

"I think we all are." His mother is nowhere to be seen and I am relieved; the old woman said little at supper, but her disapproval—of me, and my children, and quite possibly our arrangement—was clear. It's almost enough to make me approve of the situation, but not quite.

He puts the paper aside. Light reflects off his spectacles, making it impossible for me to see his eyes. "I didn't know Claire wrote to you until your telegram arrived. She didn't think you would agree."

I sink into a chair. It feels luxurious, not having springs poke my backside when I sit. "I nearly put her letter in the stove."

"What stopped you?" He sounds genuinely interested.

"Practicality," I say. "Things are bad right now." They don't appear to be improving, but I don't bother to say that. "I worry about all the kids, but especially Teddy."

Harry nods. "Because he would be the one most easily harmed."

"He's not thriving. My milk—" I look away, embarrassed to discuss such things. "We can't afford the powdered stuff, so we've been feeding him condensed. It's not good enough, though."

"Things *will* get better." Harry moves to the chair next to mine and takes a cigarette case from his inside pocket. "This is an aberration, what's happened to the world. None of this could have been predicted." He pauses. "Well, some of it was—but no one expected everything to go wrong at once."

"I don't mind being poor," I tell him. "It's all I've ever known. And I've known since I was Thelma's age that I would marry Daniel and repeat my mother's life." I wipe away unexpected tears. "But this is different. I don't mind working hard. Neither does he. But when no one wants your work, what do you do?"

He lights a cigarette and offers it. Though I constantly beg Daniel not to smoke because of his lungs, I take it and inhale. It's calming. Maybe that's why the men won't give it up, even though they have to scavenge butts from the ground.

"I was shocked that you agreed." He brings his cigarette to his lips. "It seemed wrong to even ask."

"A man wants his own child." I watch the smoke curl in front of my face. "I understand."

Harry's hands rest on his knees, but there is tension there, like he wants to spring up and stride around the room. "That won't happen. Claire lost another baby since we saw you last."

"She mentioned it in her letter."

"It's too much," Harry says, and his voice cracks. "Every time Claire falls pregnant, I'm as helpless as she is. I can buy anything, pay for any doctor, but I could do nothing to stop her from losing those babies."

He covers his face with one hand, and I realize, horrified, that he is crying. I touch his arm. "Men are always helpless where birthing is concerned. It's been women's work since the dawn of time."

"It is work she has failed at, and I can't bear that, either." Unfurling a monogrammed handkerchief, he explains Claire had some kind of operation after the last miscarriage. "She worries about my feelings. If you can find a way to let her know Teddy is enough, I will be forever in your debt."

The conversation over Mama's body rings in my ears. *What if he leaves me? What if he finds a woman who can give him children?"* With all those fears, she still made certain she couldn't get pregnant again. How much worse was the pain than her fear?

"You wouldn't leave her?"

"Good God, no." Harry looks appalled. "But I want her to be happy, and she hasn't been, not for a long time." He puts his hand over mine on the arm of the chair. "She needs Teddy more than you know."

Claire

I only sleep for an hour. When I wake, I'm no longer physically tired, but a deep core of emotional exhaustion keeps me from dressing and joining Harry and Ava, whose voices drift faintly from downstairs. Instead, I pad softly to the nursery door, where the glow of the night light shows both children fast asleep. Thelma has indeed taken Pixie to bed. At the sound of my footsteps, the dog's ridiculous ears perk and flutter.

"Shhh," I say. "Stay." Pixie obeys, snuggling into the curve of Thelma's knee.

I lean over to look at Teddy. I can't believe he is here, in this cradle that has been empty for so long. When Ava handed him to me in the train station, I hadn't expected the immediate impact of holding him. Warm and solid as a small animal, helpless. Mine. I wanted to wrap myself around him and never move again.

It was bad luck that she caught me crying—her judgment at my public loss of composure was plain on her face—but when I read the headline, *"Lindbergh Baby Found Murdered in Woods Near Hopewell Home,"* the station went strangely quiet. I thought he'd be safe, alive because my baby was not. The two had become so conflated in my mind that I couldn't believe my child hadn't paid the price for little Charles Lindbergh.

There was no way to explain that to Ava. My sister is all impatience where emotions are concerned, and a train journey with two small children would do nothing to increase her tolerance.

Despite my tears, she gave me Teddy. Holding him opened up something inside. I love babies, but I haven't held one in years, not since Thelma was tiny. Most of the people we socialize with have children, but they also have nannies who keep them out of sight during cocktails and dinner, so avoidance hasn't been difficult.

Teddy will not have a nanny, I vow. Katie will be more than enough help.

As soon as I can find a way to distract Ava, I will take him to the doctor. I don't want her to think I question their care of him; I just want to do whatever is necessary to make him grow and thrive in his new life.

He kicks his legs, and I rest my palm on his stomach. He is smaller than I expected but looks healthy. Ava emphasized the need for formula, and he took a full bottle before his bath, and another before he slept. I do not like thinking he's been hungry, and I forgive my sister's moodiness because it is rooted in worry.

She has agreed to stay for a week, while Teddy settles in. I cannot imagine how we will fill her days. Ava needs occupation in the way I need to feel useful; we just go about it differently.

My sewing machine is in my sitting room, covered by a cloth. I wonder if she would like to try it out, and if that will occupy her sufficiently during her stay. I can show it to her after breakfast, and judge her reaction. It might work.

22

Ava

"Do you mind if we go to the park?" Claire holds Teddy on her hip, smiling as he plays with her hair. He is dressed in an impractical white sailor suit and looks like a baby from a magazine advertisement. "Just for a little—I've got a coach for Teddy, and Thelma and I will walk very slowly. I'll even leave Pixie home."

"I don't want Thelma wearing herself out." I am the one who is worn out: it is after nine, and they have already eaten breakfast.

Thelma had been leaning against me, but she detaches and goes to Claire. "Aunt says it's not far, Mama."

I kneel in front of her, thinking of uneven sidewalks and stray dogs and busy streets, all the dangers that can befall my slow-moving little girl. "Are you sure? Things are further in the city than they look."

"We'll be careful," Claire says, her free hand tangling in Thelma's curls. "I'd like to take them out for a while, just us together."

Pretending at motherhood, I think. When we were girls, pretend was putting on Mama's good hat and swanning around, playing at being a lady. Well, she's a lady sure enough now, so maybe all that pretending got her somewhere.

"You have fun," I tell them. "I've got a headache. Once I finish my coffee, I'm going to take advantage of that big bathtub and then put my feet up until you get back."

I am happy to have time to myself; despite ten hours of sleep, I am exhausted. The train journey, the agony of handing over Teddy, the endless supper with its rich food, Irene Warriner staring at me like I was a hobo who had wandered in off the street. Coming upstairs after speaking with Harry to hear Claire singing Irish lullabies to my baby. *Her baby.*

It is too much.

Claire pops back in to ask if I'd like to try out her sewing machine later in the day, and I jump at the offer, embarrassing myself in my eagerness to see her magical machine.

After they leave, I follow the siren call of the bathtub. I will disturb no one, I have learned: Claire and Harry have their own bathroom, as does Irene. The luxury of having three indoor bathrooms! This, more than anything, brings home the vast difference in our situations.

A flowered robe is folded on the bench at the foot of the bed. I undress and put it on, and venture down the hall. In addition to a white pedestal sink and a flush toilet, there is an enormous claw-foot tub. I wonder if sinking into it will wash away not only the ingrained dirt of Scovill Run, but all the sorrow, exhaustion, and worry in my head.

Turning on the hot water—hot water on demand!—I inspect the array of bottles and jars at the side of the tub and choose lilac bath salts because they remind me of Mama. The bottle doesn't say how much to use. I pour some in and watch it foam. I add a little more, waiting impatiently until the water is high enough for me to skin out of the robe and drop it over the side. As I settle into the tub, the water rises to my collarbones, and I drop my head back and sigh. Would anyone notice if I spend the rest of my visit in the bath? Everything feels very far away, submerged as I am in scented bubbles.

I have never felt like such a country mouse in my life. At home, it doesn't matter if the furniture is shabby—it's no different for our neighbors. During the week, the kids do as they please, but on Sundays, their clothes are clean and pressed, and those dirty children have been scrubbed within an inch of their lives.

Claire's house is like a movie set. I can picture Greta Garbo or Norma Shearer gliding through her rooms, drinking from those short, fancy glasses Harry favors, dropping their furs on the green brocade sofa in the living room after they come in from a glamorous evening with Douglas Fairbanks, Jr. People who live in rooms like this don't get dirty or go hungry.

This place has so much to offer Teddy, things we could never give him. Here he can grow up to be a smart, strong boy who will take his place in the world that will come after the Depression; he will be a man like Harry, with a secure office job, coming home in the evenings to a pretty wife, drinking cocktails before supper—although he will call it dinner—then going out to the symphony or to see a play.

I will miss my happy baby. I shut my eyes against sudden tears. And what about the other kids? Pearl isn't happy with our choice, but she'll cope. She takes what comes and makes the best of it, like me.

But Dandy dotes on his brothers, and as the only employed male in the family, he takes it personally that he isn't earning enough. It hurts to see my son full of pain he doesn't know how to articulate.

I worry that, after spending time here, Thelma will be jealous of Teddy's luck, but she is such a sweet child that it might not occur to her to be envious. I am more concerned Claire will turn her head and she'll spend the next year begging for a puppy.

As always, Daniel is my main concern. He saw the sense of Claire's proposal before I did, but he hates it. His inability to find work shames him, as if unemployment were a character flaw. I miss the Daniel I have known all my life, but men are men, and there is no plumbing their depths.

I would rather put my head down and get on with it. If I don't have to worry about extra milk and baby food for Teddy, our money will stretch a little further toward the back rent. Mr. Henderson is kind, as agents go, but he won't let us slide indefinitely, even if no one is clamoring to rent the house.

It could be worse. After Tata died, the agent dropped by the house constantly, and now I know why. Mama scolded me and Claire if we were rude to him, but she disliked being in a position where he had the right to ask us for money. When we were finally caught up, she made us go with her to his office to drop the limp, folded bills on his desk and ask for a signed receipt.

The water is beginning to cool. I drain the tub and towel myself dry, shrugging back into the robe. The house is quiet, and I sink into the fat chair in my room. Just a few more minutes of peace, while the others are out. I know nothing more until Claire speaks at my shoulder, startling me awake.

"Is everything all right?" I sit up and she pushes me back.

"Everything is fine." She is as delighted as a schoolgirl. "I gave Teddy a bottle and put him down for a nap, and Thelma is looking at picture books."

"Did she manage the walk?" I don't want her visit ruined with memories of being unable to keep up.

"No problem at all." Claire bounces off the bed and looks in the mirror, fluffing her hair. "We walked very slowly and rested on a park bench. She liked the pigeons."

"She likes all creatures." Much of her time is spent at the kitchen window or on the back porch, watching the rabbits eat my garden. "She always has."

"Ava…about Thelma. Has she ever been examined by a doctor?" Claire picks at a loose thread on her hem, but every line of her vibrates with tension.

"Of course." Does she think we decided to ignore the problem and hope she would get better on her own? "Back when she first started walking, Dr. Kerr looked at her." It had been awful, watching him run his hands over Thelma's curved legs. "He said she was a cripple, and we would have to learn to accept it."

The sewing machine lives in Claire's sitting room. Why does she need a separate sitting room, I wonder, when they have that spacious living room with its marble fireplace? I've learned some questions aren't worth asking and turn to the machine instead, running my hands over the glossy black arm, admiring its gold paintwork and the way it folds out of the wooden table. What I could accomplish with this!

"It's too good for me," she says, echoing my unspoken thought. "If you had electric, I'd send it home with you."

"I'd love to try it out properly." I've stitched some scraps together to get the feel of it, but I itch to run real fabric under its shining silver foot. "Don't you need a new dress?"

Claire laughs. "Not if you ask Harry. I exceed my dress allowance every month."

"Let me make one for you." I puzzle over the mystifying concept of a dress allowance. "It will give me something to do and make me feel less beholden."

She puts the marvelous machine away. "You're my sister, I don't want to hear any of this nonsense about being beholden."

I appeal to her sense of guilt. "I need something to do, Claire, or I'll climb the walls."

She gives in after more protest. "We can go to the shops tomorrow morning. Now I feel less guilty—Harry and I have a dinner tonight we can't get out of, and I didn't want to leave you here on your own."

"I'll be fine," I tell her, though I dread eating supper with just Irene for company. "I'm a big girl."

Her nose still crinkles when she smiles. "But you're stubborn as a child. You have to let me buy some fabric for you, that way you don't have to worry about changing for dinner."

Is it obvious to everyone that I'm uncomfortable wearing the same dress at every meal? "Fine," I say in return. "But nothing fancy. Something I can wear at home without feeling ridiculous."

Claire

I knock smartly on the closed door of Harry's office. When I hear his faint response, I lean in. "Would you mind if I ask Max Byrne to dinner on Monday?"

Harry blinks, pulled willingly out of his paperwork, but slow to catch up. "Not at all."

"I know it's rather sudden." I fuss with my bracelets, knowing what Ava would say about my interfering.

"If he's available, why not?" He lights a cigarette and drops the match in a bronze ashtray. "Will your sister be up for strangers?"

"I don't know," I say. "But I'd like him to meet Thelma."

His brow furrows. "What have you got in mind?"

I perch on the arm of his chair. "I asked Ava if anyone had ever looked at Thelma and she nearly took my head off." I imagine discovering something is wrong with my child and not having the resources to deal with it. It explains much of my sister's simmering anger. "The company doctors never try very hard, unless it's putting a miner back together so he can work again. Ava and Daniel don't have money for tests, even if they'd been suggested."

After the last several years, I know how many tests medical science can come up with if there is a question to be answered or a puzzle to be solved. "I thought perhaps Max could look at her...and see."

"That's a fine idea," Harry says. "I'll call him myself if you like. It's been too long since he and I have had a chance to catch up."

"Thank you, darling."

I close the door and lean against it, trying very hard to keep from smiling. What if I am interfering? Thelma is a precious child—as precious as Teddy—and if something can be done to help her, is it wrong to try?

A faint cry reaches my ears, and I hasten up the steps to reach the nursery before Ava or Katie. Teddy is a sweet boy, he stops crying as soon as anyone picks him up, and that makes it hard for me to put him down again and focus on anything, but once he settles, I do just that.

Planning a dinner party is proof that I am not focused on my baby to the exclusion of the rest of the world.

Ava

After Claire and Harry leave, I suffer through an uncomfortable meal with Irene. My only consolation is that she finds it as unpleasant as I do, and as soon as our dessert plates are cleared, she excuses herself and returns to her own rooms.

At Katie's suggestion, I take tea in the living room, where she has lit a small fire. It is a treat to have a fire in May, but this large house holds a chill. I sit in the closest chair and slip off my shoes to toast my toes, thinking of the conversation I'd had earlier with Claire when she dragged me to her closet to help choose a dress for the evening.

It is closer to a room than a closet, stuffed with more dresses than she'll ever have occasion to wear. When she sees my expression, she looks abashed. "Harry likes to buy me things."

"I can see that." I sit on the vanity bench as she paws through one shining dress after another. "What do you do with yourself?"

"Do?" She pauses, hanger in hand, her pretty face scrunched as she tries to parse the question. "What do you mean?"

"I'm just curious." I fold my arms. "You don't have kids. You don't work. What do you do with your time?"

Claire smooths her hair. "We traveled quite a lot before the Crash," she says. "Our last trip was to Paris, two years ago. It's my favorite place."

Paris. What must that be like? "That's you and Harry," I say. "What do *you* do?"

"I read. I go to the movies." She pushes at her cuticles. I remember the gesture; she's unsure of herself. "We go to the theater, the orchestra. I'm on a few charity committees. I shop—as you see."

"You shop." I push back the bench, abruptly sickened by what she's become. "Have you done nothing useful in twelve years?"

She does not speak and when I turn to look, tears are running down her shell-pink cheeks. "I was never useful," she chokes. "Not like you or Mama. I was always this... pretty thing. No one expected me to be useful."

Claire

As he said he would, Harry ran for city council after the war, but his political career was blessedly brief. Campaigning was easy, once I realized my sole function was to hang on his arm and look pretty. Being the wife of an elected official was different; I was forced to stand back as Irene played hostess for my husband. She said my inexperience would cause embarrassment, but she never made any attempt to teach me.

Not long after our wedding, she told me that young wives needed to be seen and not heard. If I'd been Ava, I might have spoken up for myself, but I've never been as strong as my sister. It would likely have made no difference. Irene would just have gotten her teeth into another portion of me and worried it, like a dog with a bone, until I was in shreds.

It made me uncomfortable in both my home and my marriage, and it hurt that Harry—so good in every other way—failed to notice how often his mother criticized me.

What he did notice was that he and his political friends weren't often on the same page and he decided, before his first term was half over, not to run for re-election. "I'm going to leave while I still have friends and some chance of influence."

"Can't you influence them from the council?"

He lit a cigarette, fumbling with the match. "Not in the way I expected. You can't do *anything* directly. Politics is a web of nepotism and favors that go back decades—and nothing ever benefits the people who need help most. I've suggested veterans' programs multiple times, because so many of them have had trouble getting jobs, and every single proposal has been shot down. I'm banging my head against a stone wall."

My husband was disillusioned, but all I felt was relief.

He tried to accomplish things on his own, with some success, but other times he needed input or funds from his former colleagues, and that meant we still socialized with them regularly.

With society parties, unpleasant as they are, talk runs along superficial lines and it is easier to play along. I've never been comfortable with Harry's political friends, men who act surprised when I open my mouth and actual words come out. Am I supposed to purr like a kitten? Or maybe just squeak, like a doll with a faulty voice box?

I am very tired of being a doll.

This dinner has been agony, the wives silent, examining their nails while their husbands hold forth on the current economic climate. I want to be with Teddy but I am stuck in a hard chair, wearing a dress that is just slightly more than the occasion warrants because I was so upset by Ava's question that I grabbed the first thing that came to hand. She exposed me as a silly, brainless bunny who has spent a dozen years—how long it sounds, said that way!—ornamenting myself and looking at paintings and buying frivolous hats.

No one knows your weak points like a sister.

After dinner, the men go off to have their brandy and cigars while the women gossip, judge each other's clothes, and complain about servants. Philadelphia society is like an English novel, without the accents or the dreary weather. I want to scream, but I'm already enough of an oddity; screaming would only confirm their suspicions.

When the party reunites in the drawing room, the mayor is holding forth on a proposed bill to deal with poverty in the city. He is against it, as are most of the men in attendance.

"I don't see why we have to foot the bill for these migrants." Alexander Larsen gestures with his glass. "They just stop here to take from us before moving on."

"Leeches," someone says. "I walked past that soup kitchen on Walnut Street the other day. The sheer number of men in that line—it's like they aren't even trying."

"Some men just don't want to work," the mayor agrees.

I experience a moment of lightheadedness as I hear my own voice. "Doesn't everyone deserve to eat?"

The room falls silent as those in attendance listen to the novelty of a woman with an opinion.

"What an impertinent question." Larsen's naturally flushed face has taken on an aggrieved reddish hue.

"Now, now." The mayor lays a moist hand on my shoulder, "Questions are not so impertinent when asked by a pretty woman."

Would I get in trouble for slapping a public official? Probably. "You're describing my sister's family," I say, not caring that I am admitting to a background I prefer to keep hidden. "Is she—are her children—less worthy because they're poor?" All the resentment that has built up over years of listening to these conversations comes spilling out. "What happens to the family who saved for a rainy day and still finds themselves drowning? Who should they rely upon, if not the government, at least in the short term?"

There is a sharp, surprised female sound: I've shocked the wives, as well.

"What have you been letting her read, Harry?" the mayor asks. "She'll be turning communist next."

"I don't know about communism," I say. "But I do know it's unfair that people like us are prospering because we're cushioned by the wealth we knew how to invest wisely before the Crash. The fortunate shouldn't begrudge help to those who need it."

Harry puts a hand on my elbow, but it feels like fellowship, not a warning. "I don't monitor what my wife reads," he says. "She thinks for herself. It saves me the trouble of thinking for both of us."

The men laugh, somewhat uncomfortably, and I feel a rush of love for my husband, who has certainly evolved from the starchy man I married. Perhaps I've had some influence after all.

23

Claire

On Sunday, Harry takes Irene to church while Ava and I walk to St. Patrick's with Thelma. I haven't been there in years, other than for a few weddings, but I sink easily into the religion of my youth. When we exchange the kiss of peace, I want to gather Ava into my arms but hold back—she has been quiet all morning, and I fear a return of her spikiness if I am overly affectionate.

Afterward, we ride the streetcar to Fourth Street where the fabric merchants gather, rows of small Jewish-owned shops and pushcart vendors, open on Sunday because most are shut for their Sabbath the day before. It is a wonderland for Ava, and I believe she could have spent the entire day wandering through the shops.

I point to a few stores I've patronized before, but she drags me into each one on the row, asking questions that make the clerks re-evaluate her and answer in detail.

Our search ends at Mendel's, an unfamiliar shop with a dark green awning jutting over the sidewalk. It looks half-closed, and the bolts of fabric displayed are not particularly appealing. But Ava's nose twitches like a bloodhound's, and she hauls me through the glass door. A bell jangles warning of our intrusion. The shop smells of trapped heat, and I linger near the door, hoping for a breeze, but my sister plows on, searching for something only she can see.

I try to rein her in. "Look at this one." I point to a roll of ice blue taffeta already spread on the cutting table. It shimmers under the hanging lights, looking like the surface of a half-frozen stream.

"No," Ava says decisively. "This is it." She yanks a bolt of dark blue satin from a shelf, unfurling it over the taffeta before anyone can stop her. It looks like ink spilled across the table or a midnight sky with no stars. It is beautiful, but a little severe.

"I like the pale blue." I push the satin aside to compare them.

"It's a little girl's color." Ava holds the satin up against me. "This is who you are, you just can't see it." She turns to the shop assistant. "Do you have patterns? I'm looking for—"

I will not argue. She won't listen, and her instincts about clothing are usually correct. If the dress is awful, I can put it in the closet and forget about it. It's the gesture that is important, both the making and the receiving.

Ava

I could have found something in the very first shop, but Fourth Street was the kind of heaven I've only dreamed of, each store a treasure trove of color and texture and potential and, selfishly, I wanted to see it all.

The midnight blue satin is the last thing my sister would choose for herself, but it is exactly right. There are depths in Claire which are invisible to her—whether she's forgotten them, or allowed them to be squashed down, or maybe she never knew they were there.

I think Harry knows. And if he can just step out of the shadow of that dragon he calls a mother, he will make a fine husband for that sister of mine.

We head back uptown, and because I stubbornly did not allow Claire to spend money on me, she drags me into a store called Bonwit Teller and she and a frightening saleswoman in a black smock manhandle me into a fitting room and force me to try on dresses.

"You should have just let me buy fabric." Her voice drifts through the curtain, followed by a braceleted arm holding two more hangers. "We're not leaving until you make a decision."

I yank off the blue dress—what is it with Claire and that color?—and address her disembodied voice. "I don't want you to spend money on me. This store even smells expensive!"

The curtain rattles open and I flinch back, not wanting to show my safety-pinned slip to the saleswoman.

"We're on the least expensive floor," Claire tells me airily. "And I think *this* one is just right."

I open my mouth to object and then look at the dress. It's something I could wear to church without looking overdone. The print calls to me. Leaf green, brown, and ivory in a geometric pattern, it should be loud but somehow manages to be pleasing. I touch the fabric, admire its faint sheen. "Rayon?"

"How would I know?"

"It is rayon, madam," the saleswoman confirms from just beyond the curtain. "One of our newest arrivals."

I try it on, waiting for the side zip to strain over my baby weight, waiting for the neck, with its pristine collar, to gape. Waiting to *hate* it.

But I don't. The dress falls smoothly from my hips to flare around my lower legs. The print disguises the softness of my middle. The collar brightens my face.

"Well?"

Silence. The curtain rattles open again and Claire joins me. "We're buying this dress," she says.

I meet her eyes in the mirror. "*You're* buying this dress."

Though I dislike the flaunting of Prohibition, I appreciate the Warriners' habit of gathering in the living room before the evening meal. Harry and Claire have their drinks, of course, but Katie brings me tea, and I sit on the davenport with Thelma while my sister cuddles Teddy on her lap.

"We're having company for dinner," Claire says, over his head. "I hope you don't mind—he's a friend and was at loose ends this evening."

"It's all right with me." I can hardly object. "I hope I'm decent enough for company."

Katie has pressed my new dress and my feet are squeezed into shoes which Claire also insisted on buying. They will be comfortable, eventually, but right now I would prefer to be barefoot on this soft carpet.

"Of course you are," Harry says from behind one of his everlasting newspapers. "And besides, Max isn't the type to notice. He's only interested in golf and his patients."

The bell rings shortly after, and Claire returns with a stocky, rumpled man with sandy hair and a suit that belongs in a vaudeville act. "Max Byrne, this is my sister, Ava Kimber. Ava, Dr. Max Byrne."

I shake Dr. Byrne's hand. Despite his lamentable taste in clothing, he has a nice face. "It's very nice to meet you, doctor."

"Call me Max," he says, barely giving me a cursory glance before he squats in front of the davenport. "What's your name, young lady?"

"I'm Thelma." She gives a most angelic smile. "That's my mama."

"Very nice to meet you, Miss Thelma." He shakes her hand, then gestures toward the window. "I rode my bicycle over here, would you like to see it?"

Holding his hand, Thelma limps over to the window and giggles as he whispers to her.

I looked from Max to Claire, light dawning. "What kind of doctor is he?"

"He's a research physician at the Children's Hospital," Harry says quietly. "We thought he might like to meet Thelma."

Typical Claire, pushing in where she isn't needed. Dr. Kerr already told us that nothing could be done for Thelma, and all this Dr. Byrne will do is get her hopes up. We don't need that—none of us, not Thelma, not Daniel, not me.

In the beginning, Thelma was like any other toddler, pulling herself up on a chair and falling on her bottom, over and over, but it took ages before she could stand on her own. Her legs were curved, and even when she was three and could walk, her movements were slow and jerky, not like the other kids, who went from crawling to running in what felt like days. George especially. He and Toby were close in age, and George couldn't stand his brother doing something he couldn't.

I push these unhelpful thoughts away. "Isn't dinner ready?"

"Katie will let us know." Claire sits beside me. "All he's doing is talking to her. Is there a problem?"

"The problem," I say, keeping my voice low, "is you. You never let things go."

My sister's mouth drops open and she takes a deep breath. "You're right," she says at last. "I don't. And sometimes that's a good thing. Let's not ruin the evening."

There is a squeal, and Max Byrne skips across the room, followed by Thelma. Pixie, barking excitedly, runs between their feet. Max turns quickly and watches Thelma, and there is something appraising in his expression, despite his laughter. "You caught me!" he cries, and scoots away again, my child hot on his heels.

I slump back. Thelma doesn't like strangers, and yet this man has her *running* in the house. There is a magic at work here I don't understand.

Katie enters silently to stand at Claire's side. "Dinner in ten minutes, ma'am."

My sister looks from me to my daughter. "Thelma, would you like to have dinner in the nursery with Katie? You can read her one of your storybooks after you're done eating."

"Yes, please!" Thelma holds out her hand. "I'm hungry!"

Claire takes the kids away, and Max drops down next to me. "Your children are beautiful," he says, straightening his tie. "The baby's a fine boy if ever I've seen one."

"Thelma's a fine girl," I say, defensive of my darling. "Just as fine as Teddy."

"Of course, she is," Harry agrees. "No one said otherwise."

Max's eyes are light hazel, with green flecks. He focuses them on me. "You've obviously seen through me," he says. "I'm here at Harry's request, to take a look at your little girl."

I take a breath, hold it before answering. "She's fine."

"No one has said otherwise." He holds my gaze. "Would you mind answering a few questions?"

"That depends." *Let's not ruin the evening.* Claire's words echo like one of Mama's sayings. "What do you want to know?"

"When you were carrying Thelma, did you have an easy pregnancy?" His gaze rests on me with an almost physical weight.

The question throws me. "Not particularly," I say, wondering what he is after. "My early pregnancies were easier."

"They're usually more difficult." Max leans forward, elbows on his knees. "What happened with Thelma?"

"She was a twin." The words are out before I can stop them. "The other one was born dead."

Harry's newspaper gives a sharp crack, but he leaves us to our conversation.

"I'm sorry."

"Thelma was puny, and always colicky. She didn't develop as quickly as the others. I always wonder if the second baby stole her strength." I look down at my hands. "I never told anyone about him, not even my husband. Only my mother knew because she delivered them."

Max is silent for a moment, while I deal with the fact that I've spoken about David. Even Mama didn't know I'd given him a name.

He nods, returning to the topic of Thelma. "What time of year was she born?"

"Early April," I say. "Why?"

"Just curious." Pixie hops up on his lap and he fondles the dog's feathery ears. "Did you spend much of that pregnancy indoors?"

"How did you know that?" Claire couldn't have told him; there was no way she could have known. "We had an ice storm and I fell, at about five months. I had some…" I glance over, but Harry is absorbed in the financial section. "I had some bleeding, and my mother and the doctor thought I shouldn't risk another fall."

"A logical response."

"But?"

"It's just a thought," he says. "Would you mind if I ran a couple of tests?"

I shake my head. "Thelma's already been looked at by our local doctor. We can't get her hopes up."

Max nods. "I just think your doctor might have been wrong."

"What do you mean?"

He pauses. "I think Thelma has rickets."

I think of newspaper photographs of poor, half-starved children, with their bowed legs and gaunt faces. "Thelma doesn't look like that."

He puts his hands on his tweed-covered knees. His fingers are blunt, with ragged nails. "You're right, she doesn't. You're thinking of children who developed rickets after they were born. I think Thelma may have been born with a vitamin deficiency, and her bones grew improperly because of it."

I look at him, eyes narrowed. "What would have caused this deficiency? And why doesn't Teddy have it? We've got less now than we had when she was born."

"He's what, six months old?"

"Almost. He was born on Christmas day."

Max nods so enthusiastically his curly hair flops forward; he is no more a fan of pomade than he is of dignified clothing. "So you were up and about in nicer weather during his pregnancy. Among other things, vitamin D deficiency is caused by a lack of sunlight. It's not just the children. If you were suffering a severe deficiency yourself during the pregnancy—which is likely, if you spent months indoors—it could have been passed on to Thelma."

It is a lot to take in. I remember months trapped in the cold house, the near-constant sleet keeping me from any attempt at escape. Using a chamber pot because I was afraid of falling on the ice on my way to the outhouse. Relying on Mama and Daniel for everything. "So it's my fault?"

"No," he says quickly and reaches for my hands. "Sometimes things just happen. But if that's the case—and I should be able to tell when I test Thelma's blood—there's a very good chance she can be helped. She's young enough, her bones are still malleable."

I pull my hands free. "She'd be able to walk like a normal child?" I don't want to imagine it, in case it can't be done.

He exhales. "I don't want to promise you the moon, Mrs. Kimber, but if that is the cause, we can give her a course of vitamins and exercises, and most likely braces for her legs. They might not be completely straight, but she'll walk better than she does now, and with less pain when she gets older." He clasps my hand again. "Isn't that worth looking into?"

Claire

We drop the subject of Thelma over dinner, Max and Harry discussing the situation in the city while Ava and I eat quietly and avoid each other's eyes.

"I know the mayor's a friend of yours, but he's a damned idiot." Max spears a piece of steak with his fork. "No one is starving in Philadelphia? He hasn't been to some of the places I've been!"

"I know." Harry looks somber. The mayor doesn't consider him such a good friend these days because he's brought up some of the same points, and that was before my performance the other night. "To make it worse, the Council is in near-full agreement. It doesn't exist, because they don't want to see it. The way things are going in the poor areas of the city, starvation may not be what kills the people."

I pass a bowl of potatoes hashed in cream to Max, who is looking at his plate as if wondering where the first serving had gone. He scoops a pile into an empty spot and continues, waving the spoon at Harry for emphasis. "No, they'll be dying from other diseases they providentially contracted because they're poor!"

His face is flushed. He is a charming man, if only someone would make him cut his hair, shave properly, and take him shopping for quieter suits.

I'd missed something by going upstairs with the children, but Harry will fill me in later. Ava wouldn't have been as open with Max if I was in the room. She is sitting opposite him now, but her eyes are fixed on the yellow damask wallpaper. I wonder if she is considering Max's suggestion. It would be wonderful if something could be done for Thelma.

Again, I have an idea I haven't mentioned to Harry, but I think he will agree. We both feel guilty about Teddy, and helping his sister would go a long way toward alleviating that guilt, in addition to doing something for Ava and Daniel that they can't do themselves.

Growing up poor is enough of a burden, but I'd escaped the future Scovill Run planned for me because I was pretty and ambitious—and mobile. Growing up poor and crippled isn't a death sentence, but Thelma's life would be that of a maiden aunt to her siblings' children, at best, a woman useful to everyone, having nothing of her own. I want more for her. I want more for all my nieces and nephews, but Ava is so determined to do everything on her own that I know better than to try. At least all at once.

My sister's pride has always been a sticking point, but it's gotten worse over the years, as their situation has gotten worse. There is nothing wrong with accepting help, especially from family, but Ava is determined to manage, no matter the cost. She can't cure the Depression on her own, though—men smarter than Harry don't understand what happened, much less how to fix it.

"Harry, could I send a telegram after supper?" Ava's eyes are bright now, alert; she has come to some decision. "I'd like to stay a few more days so Dr. Byrne can take a look at Thelma."

Ava

I escape up the stairs while Harry and Claire say goodnight to Max on the front step. Irene follows more slowly, her arthritic knuckles gripping the rail. "Dr. Byrne is always so entertaining," she says. "Don't you agree?"

185

"He is." And enlightening, but I don't want to think about that now, or discuss it with her; Irene came down with Claire, and therefore missed my discussion with Max.

"Very different, I'm sure, from dinner conversation at your house."

Is the old woman offensive or just clueless? "Not very," I say. "Daniel gets together every week with his gentleman friends and they discuss the issues of the day." I pause at the landing. "Of course, for them it's not the stock market, it's more about whether or not they can afford to feed their children, but it's all the same, isn't it?"

All I want is the peace of my bedroom, but I go to check on the children first. Leaving the door ajar so the hall light filters in, I look first at Teddy. He is on his back in the center of his cradle, snoring, a tiny copy of his father but for his pale hair. I cover him and turn to the narrow bed where Thelma lies awake.

"I waited up, Mama."

"You shouldn't have, but I'm glad you did." I sit on the edge of the bed. "Did you have a nice dinner with Katie?"

"It was yummy." She yawns and snuggles against my hip. "I'm sleepy now."

"Did you like walking with your auntie the other day?"

"Hmm."

It sounds like a yes. "Thel, baby, did you like Dr. Max?"

"Yes." She perks up at the mention of his name. "He plays like he's my age."

Is it wrong to get her hopes up, as well as my own? "Dr. Max told me there's a chance he could make you walk better. Would you like that?"

Thelma sits straight up and throws her arms around me. "Yes!"

"Shhh." I check, but Teddy is still asleep. Wrapping my arms around her slight body, I say, "It might not work, baby. He said it might not."

"But it might?"

"Yes."

"Can we do it?"

I sigh. "There's one thing. You might have to stay here for a while—without me."

"It's nice here." She doesn't sound quite as certain.

The length of our separation is what keeps me from giving in at this point—that, and Daniel's reaction to my making such a decision without him. I wish we were on the telephone so we could discuss it. "It might be months."

When Thelma speaks, her voice quivers. "But I might be able to walk, Mama." She sniffs. "And I would be company for Teddy, while he got used to being here."

"That would be a very brave thing to do." I hold back my tears at her courage, more than I have at this moment. "Do you think you could stay with your aunt and uncle for that long, without me?"

She nods, her hair falling in her face. "I'd miss you and Pearl and Dandy and Daddy." After a pause, she adds, "And maybe Toby and George. A little."

"I won't tell them. It'll be our secret."

"You have the perfect bosom for this." I stand back and look critically at the way the satin drapes over my sister's form. "You really do."

"Your bust is larger than mine." Claire has always been self-conscious of her small breasts, sewing ruffles onto her corset cover to pad her figure as soon as she was old enough. Without such undergarments, it's more difficult to give the appearance of curves that don't exist in nature.

"Size isn't everything," I assure her. "Mine are like this because they've fed half a dozen babies. They certainly don't stand up on their own anymore." I smooth the fabric where it clings to Claire's midsection. "And my stomach is not to be discussed."

"You're not fat!"

I have to laugh. "I'm not thin, either. And stretch marks are the price of motherhood."

Daniel likes to run his fingers over my stretch marks. He says they're like rings in a tree, except they show how many saplings I've made. It's a shame the planter of all those saplings doesn't show as much wear and tear, but he's always been lean, even in times of plenty.

As I wait for him to respond to my telegram, I busy myself with Claire's gown; it gives me something to do with my mind and my hands. I am not good at waiting. I feel guilty about making a decision without talking to him first, but Thelma deserves this chance, and I would say as much even if he disagreed with me. I have to be here for the testing, to make sure she and I are comfortable with Max's treatment plan.

I worry about what Daniel is thinking, and how Pearl is coping with the boys. Even with Trudy in the house, the brunt of dealing with Toby and George will fall on her. Dandy promised to check in on them; those two can get into mischief in minutes, much less two weeks without me to derail their plans.

In the end, my telegram said only that I would be delayed for a week because a doctor was going to look at Thelma. I want to explain about Max Byrne and his ideas, but he can't see her until later in the week and I want to know something before I put it in writing. I wish Daniel would call; Harry wouldn't care about the cost, and I'd feel better if I could just hear his voice.

24

Pearl

May 18, 1932

We got a telegram yesterday. Daddy swore and threw it at the stove. He missed, or else I'd probably never know they're staying another week. Teddy's settling in fine, Mama says, but there's a doctor who wants to look at Thelma.

I've prayed so hard for God to straighten her legs that I shouldn't be mad—maybe this doctor is God answering my prayers. But I miss her. I hate sleeping without her, and I hate not having her and Mama to talk to. Mrs. Metzger helps with the laundry and the cooking, but only Mama can make the boys do things around the house. With me, they just laugh and run away. And I still want to drop Hetty in the outhouse.

Ava

Shortly after noon, Baxter deposits us at the front door of Children's Hospital. The ride is so short that I tell him we will walk back. I hope I'm right; I have no idea what Max Byrne's exam will entail.

Nor will I find out. After sitting with us in a bland outer office, asking questions and writing copious, illegible notes, Max swings Thelma up in his arms. "You can amuse yourself with a magazine," he says, gesturing to a selection on a nearby table. "Thelma and I will be back soon."

"I should be there."

"Thelma's a big girl, she'll manage just fine."

His expression brooks no opposition, and Thelma, who always wants to be with me, shakes her head. "I'm okay, Mama. Dr. Max will take care of me."

When the door closes, I am reduced to paging through a movie magazine and listening to the faint piping of my daughter's voice. There is a squeal, once, and I jump to my feet, but then she laughs and I sit down again, feeling foolish.

After the longest hour of my life, Thelma reappears, smiling from ear to ear. There is a small white bandage on her arm, but she pays less attention to it than I do.

"All done," Max proclaims. "For now, anyway—I don't want to put her through too much at once. I'll get the results of her blood test back in a few days."

I expect him to show us out, but he surprises me by snatching his hat from the rack and following us onto Nineteenth Street.

"Don't you have work to do?" Max reminds me of Claire's dog, constantly at our heels, wagging in a manner alternately annoying and endearing. He would beg for treats if encouraged.

"I did it." He smiles again and offers his arm. I take it and watch as he links hands with Thelma on the other side. "Now it's time for ice cream."

"That's not necessary." There is no point in my daughter getting used to such luxuries, even if she does end up staying here for a while. It will hurt all the more when she has to leave them behind.

"But he promised!" Thelma objects. "When he was taking my blood out, he said I could have ice cream if I didn't cry."

"And she only made one little squeak, which barely counts, so that means two scoops for Miss Thelma." He looks down. "What kind will it be?"

"I don't know," she says, swinging his hand. "I've only ever had ice cream once, and then it was chocolate."

Max bends down to her level. "Did you like it?"

She nods, her curls bouncing. Claire has outfitted her with a pink bow to match her candy-striped dress, and set her hair in pin curls for today, decking her out for a party rather than a doctor's appointment.

"Then we'll have to try all the other flavors until you find your favorite." Instead of offering his arm again, he takes my hand along with Thelma's and swings us both along as if we're the same age.

Karen Heenan

He irritates me, taking liberties left and right just because he can grant favors. I don't want to make a scene in front of my daughter, so once the ice cream is achieved, I will make sure to keep my cone in whatever hand is nearest to Dr. Max Byrne. We turn onto Walnut Street, and I realize we are across from Rittenhouse Square. I know how to get back to Delancey Place from here, and I feel a little more in control.

"Here we are." He leads us under a green-and-white awning to the ice cream parlor. Plate glass windows with fanciful painted illustrations look out onto the park, and inside, tables and chairs of twisted metal are scattered across a bright tile floor. Most are occupied on such a warm afternoon.

Thelma makes her way to the chrome and glass case where the ice cream is displayed. She read off the names slowly but correctly, and I am proud of her. "Vanilla, chocolate, strawberry, pis...pistachio. Rum raisin. Nee-a-polly-tan." She screws up her face. "What's that, Dr. Max?"

"Neapolitan," he repeats. "That's vanilla, chocolate and strawberry together, see?" He turns to me. "What will you have?"

"I don't need ice cream."

"I don't care if you *need* it," he says. "It's a beautiful afternoon, and I've skipped out on my job to spend time with two lovely ladies. I want to eat ice cream."

Then eat your damn ice cream. I swallow the thought. "Chocolate, then." I've never had chocolate, only vanilla; Thelma and I are opposites. "Thank you."

"My pleasure." He doesn't just smile with his mouth or even his eyes. It comes from someplace deep inside, and it is very hard to resist.

"Stop trying to charm me." My irritation rises up. "I'm not a child, and I'm not one of your patients."

"I'm not trying to charm you. I'm charming. There's a difference." Tweaking Thelma's bow, he asks, "What's it going to be, my girl?"

"Neapolitan," she says. "All the flavors!"

Max places the order and finds a window table for us. On the way, he pulls a children's magazine off the rack and hands it to Thelma. She takes it but turns to look out the window, where two poodles, their leashes tied to a lamp post, yap noisily.

I wait until she is occupied before saying, "I don't see much of a difference."

"That's because you're trying too hard to resist."

"I don't need to resist one more person trying to fix my life," I say. "One is already too many. Harry means well, but all I hear is 'you should do this, you should do that, maybe you wouldn't be in this situation if you had done the other.' I'm sick of all you rich men who know best."

"You think I'm rich?" Max tilts his chair back.

"You're a doctor." I tuck my feet under my chair, hiding the shoes which are the clearest evidence of my poverty. The new shoes are safe in their box, where they won't hurt my feet.

"That doesn't mean I'm rich. The University of Pennsylvania Medical School is as immune to my charm as you are. They expected me to pay for my education. My parents are dead, so I worked my way through college and medical school, and if you must know, the reason I didn't let you past the waiting room earlier is because I'm sleeping in my office right now."

The counter girl brings three dishes of ice cream, and for a moment there is silence as we all dig into the cold sweetness. Chocolate ice cream is a revelation; I want Max Byrne to disappear so I can enjoy it in peace, but I also can't let go of his last statement. "You're sleeping in your office?"

"I am." A smear of pale green decorates his upper lip. "Would you like to know why?"

"Do I need to?" The man doesn't know when to give up.

"I think so. What are you doing tomorrow evening? After dinner?"

"Getting ready to go home." Back to a place where I understand how people behave.

"I'll have you back before bedtime, I promise," he says. "I go out on Friday evenings with a doctor friend. You should come along."

"What, to one of your speakeasies?" I ask. "Or have they passed the repeal? Either way, I don't drink."

"I don't go to speakeasies," he says. "And no, we're still dry. Technically."

"But you drink, I saw you with Harry."

"I'll take a drink if it's offered by a friend," Max agrees, "but that's the extent of it. I have a friend in the coroner's office. Did you know Philadelphia averages ten deaths per day because of Prohibition?"

I glance up. "Prohibition was supposed to stop all that."

"Well, it didn't. People who don't know how to make liquor kill themselves, and others, with alarming regularity." He scoops up another spoonful of his pistachio ice cream. "And we won't discuss the criminal gangs. It was safer for everyone before they tried to fix it."

"Wherever you want to go, I'm not going." Infuriating man. As if I want to go out with him—all I want, at this point, is to make sure Thelma is safe and to get home to Daniel and the kids.

"It's not a bar," he says, a touch of irritation in his voice. "It's the furthest thing from a bar. You'll find it enlightening. At least, it might enlighten you a little bit about me."

"I don't need to understand you." Thelma won't notice my rudeness; she is licking the empty bowl. "You're treating my daughter. My sister is paying. I'm grateful to you both. I'm not sure what else is required."

"*This* is required." Max smiles, but it isn't his usual smile. "This is required, or I won't treat Thelma. How's that for a deal?"

"What?"

"I'm doing it as a favor to Harry," he says, "and because she's a sweet kid who I think I can help. But I'm honestly sick of your behavior, and this is how you pay for it."

I stare at him. "And what have I done?"

"You're angry at the world. I'm happy to treat your daughter, but I wasn't put on this earth to be your punching bag." Max raises an eyebrow. "So you'll be ready on Friday. I'll pick you up at six."

There is a sting of truth in his criticism. "What are we doing?"

"You'll find out then. Wear comfortable shoes."

Pearl

May 20, 1932

Daddy yelled at Mrs. Metzger this morning. She only asked him to pick something up at the store, but he said last he knew, she wasn't his wife and he didn't have to fetch and carry for her. Mrs. M's voice shook, but she said since she was putting money into this house and cooking for his children, he should respect her. And then she said if he wouldn't, she'd wait until Dandy stopped past.

I ran in from the porch then, but it was too late. He told Mrs. M to go back to her own house. And she's going. She's crying and (I think) swearing in German, and she asked me to find Dandy to help move her furniture back. I'm afraid to have him in the house because mentioning him made Daddy blow up, so maybe I can find a neighbor boy to help.

How are we going to manage without Mrs. M's money? And what will Mama say when she gets home? She likes having Mrs. M here.

Claire

I accompany Thelma for her second round of tests on Friday. When we arrive, Max ushers us into his outer office, looking past me into the hallway.

"It's just me today." I smile at how obviously he is looking for my sister. "Ava thought since I'll be doing her future appointments, we should do a test run."

He nods and brings us back to the exam room. It is scrupulously clean, but still somehow untidy, and for some reason, there is a feather pillow in one corner. "That doesn't sound like your sister."

"What do you mean?" I help Thelma up onto the table, where she sits, swinging her feet.

"She's not the type to hand over control before she has to." Max reaches for his pen. "Now, Miss Thelma, how are you today?"

"Good." She gives him a smile that would light a room. "Are you going to take more of my blood?"

"No," he tells her. "I got enough already. Today we're going to measure you, and take pictures of your bones!"

"Oh." Her face falls. "I thought maybe…"

"You thought more blood meant more ice cream?" Max guesses. Her cheeks turn pink. "Yes."

"Well, maybe your aunt will take you for some after we're done."

"But I want *you* to come again," she says. "I liked having you there."

It could be a trick of the light, but I swear he blushes. "I didn't know you were with them yesterday."

"A post-exam treat," he explains. "I do it for all my prettiest patients."

"And the prettiest mothers," I say to his turned back. Max goes very still, and I feel bad. In all the years of our acquaintance, I've never known him to date. I once asked Harry if Max perhaps didn't like women, but he assured me that he did, and made an oblique reference to a failed engagement.

Perhaps she was a difficult woman. Like my sister.

After a moment, Max turns back and opens a folder on the exam table next to Thelma. "As I suspected," he says, "the blood results confirm that Thelma had rickets as a very young child. It probably stems, at least in part, from a vitamin D deficiency she inherited from her mother."

Harry had repeated their conversation. I was shocked Ava had spoken so personally to Max, and I cried when I found out about the stillbirth. Thelma's survival would have done nothing to reduce the pain of that lost baby.

"How are you going to treat her?"

Max stands in front of Thelma. "Stick your legs straight out, my girl."

She giggles. "You know they don't go straight!" Brought up to hip level, her legs are considerably bowed.

"Rickets means that Thelma's bones were softer than usual when she was born, from that vitamin deficiency, but also possibly from a lack of calcium. She's still undersized, and Ava said she grew slower than the other children. Once she started walking, those soft bones weren't up to the challenge of bearing her weight, and that's why they're misshapen." He puts a gentle hand on the curve of Thelma's leg. "I'm going to speak to a few friends to see if they have any ideas, but I would start with a change in her diet—plenty of calcium, irradiated milk, lots of sunlight." Max tilts Thelma's chin with a fingertip. "You're going to spend a lot of time playing outdoors this summer, Miss Thelma."

She giggles again. "Can I take Pixie to the park, Aunt Claire?"

"Not on your own," I say. "But Katie or I will go with you every day."

Max swings her off the table and reaches in his pocket for a peppermint. "Once we're done with the x-rays," he says, "I'm going to measure her for braces, to start the process of straightening her legs. I hoped her mother would be here to discuss that."

"Come to dinner tonight, if you'd like," I tell him. "It might be easier to talk to her outside the office."

"Most of my patients' families prefer their consultations *in* the office. But no," he says, "I'm seeing your sister tonight, anyway. I invited her to come out with me and John Spencer."

I blink. "To one of those camps?"

He snaps the folder shut and spins it onto his desk. "Yes."

"But that's—"

"Have you been to one?"

"No. Harry says they're awful."

"They are." He drops down to Thelma's height. "Missy, I need to talk to your aunt. Can you sit outside and look at the magazines for a moment?"

"What are you doing?" I ask when Thelma has gone. "My sister came in yesterday madder than a wet hen. She didn't even mention you'd taken them for ice cream."

"Your sister," Max says, "has a chip on her shoulder the size of Plymouth Rock. She doesn't like anyone to do anything for her, even if it's something she needs."

"Tell me something I don't know. She's always been that way." I fiddle with my gloves; it feels disloyal to discuss Ava with him. "She's proud, and she's poor. It's a bad combination."

"It's probably what's kept them going." He bunches his fingers in his hair, making his unruly curls worse. "But she's under the misconception that no one else has it bad. I want her to see that hard times are everywhere."

"So you're going to take her to a Hooverville?" I don't like the sound of that. Those camps sound like free-wheeling Wild West towns, full of desperate men.

"John and I go out most Fridays," he says. "The men there are no different than me or Harry—or Ava's husband, I'm sure. Just fallen on times harder than they could conceive, doing what they can to survive." He cocks his head, and gives me a look I can't decipher. "I think it will do your sister a world of good."

25

Ava

When the bell rings, I am waiting. I motion for Katie to stay back and open the door myself. Max Byrne leans on the iron rail, clad in another one of his dreadful suits—this one is a gray and blue check with a very definite thread of *orange*. "All ready?"

I look at him. "No, I thought I'd stay in."

Unfazed, he waves me toward the car. I slide in, and as he introduces me to his friend, Dr. Spencer, my hip bumps into a large wicker hamper. A second one sits alongside. "What is all this?"

Max looks over the seat. "Sandwiches, mostly."

"Every week, he browbeats restaurants into donating them," Dr. Spencer says. "I don't know how he does it."

I know very well how he does it.

Before I can inquire about our destination, the two men start discussing one of Spencer's patients. The city rolls by on the other side of the glass, and when we turn up a wide street, I glimpse an ornate, sand-colored building ahead of us. With its low-pitched roof and numerous columns, it looks like a temple from a silent movie. "Is that where we're going?"

"Almost."

The car circles around the building, which turns out to be an art museum, surrounded by well-kept landscaping and graceful trees. One more turn, however, and we are in a different world.

The museum is set on a steep hill, and the back of that hill has been dug out to provide shelter, while the grassy area on either side of the road is littered with tents and wooden shacks. "A Hooverville?" I ask. "Here?"

"Why not here?" Max pulls out one of the hampers, stacks his black doctor's bag on top of it, and staggers toward the nearest shanty, calling over his shoulder, "You're in charge of food."

I don't have to ask what he means because a line has formed before the hampers hit the ground. For the next hour, I pass out sandwiches, pour cold tea, and speak to a wide variety of the men living on the art museum's hillside—for it is almost exclusively a men's settlement. They seem surprised to see a woman with the doctors.

Max and Dr. Spencer set up nearby, and soon another line of ragged men stretches beyond my view. As I hand out sandwiches, I watch the doctors work and am surprised by the familiarity and laughter; they are providing charity, but there is no air of false piety about them. They treat each one of these dirty, defeated men as equals.

As I give out the food, I force myself to echo their attitude. Each one of these men, in their dirt-stiffened clothing, waiting for a handout, could be my husband.

When the last sandwich is gone, I join Max. "What can I do?"

He doesn't look up. "Cut me off a strip of bandage about three feet long." To the man in front of him, he says, "This is going to hurt."

"No worse than when it happened." The man's face is hidden by a battered felt hat but the flatness of his tone is pure coal country. "Do what you need to, doc. It won't heal itself, else it would have by now."

Tearing off a strip of bandage, I watch while Max examines a gash that runs the length of the man's forearm. The edges of the wound are red and angry, and yellow pus is visible in the open areas. I sniff discreetly; it's nasty, but it hasn't festered.

Max cleans the wound thoroughly and, anticipating his next move, I thread a needle and have it waiting. He looks up, surprised, then turns back to the arm and adds a neat row of black stitches, finally covering the area with rusty-red mercurochrome. "Can you wrap it?" He is already looking ahead to the next patient.

The man follows me to one side, where I make swift work of bandaging his arm. The entire procedure is carried out without either of us making eye contact, but when I finish, I touch his wrist. "It should heal just fine."

"Ava?" His eyes are gray-blue, like mine. Deep wrinkles fan out from their corners—a man who, despite his deprivations, has smiled more often than not. Under the weathering of hard living and more than a little grime, ghosts of freckles spatter his cheeks.

"Jake?"

As the car pulls away from the camp, I turn to Max. "Did you think I would fall apart?"

He shrugs. "I wasn't sure."

"I don't do that."

"You don't fall apart?" He settles himself and removes his hat. "Ever?"

"No." I look back at a knot of men standing by the road. Some wave, others just stand, shoulders slumped. Jake is not among them.

"How are you comfortable with such things?" Dr. Spencer asks from the front seat. "I was impressed with your bandaging skills after Max stitched that cut."

"I have three sons," I tell him. "My stitches may not be as neat as Dr. Byrne's, but I can clean a wound and pour whiskey on it as well as any physician."

Stifling a laugh, Max says, "So there is drink to be had where you come from—you just keep it in the medicine chest."

"It never stopped being available for medical purposes, as you well know." I don't mention that the bottle is hidden deep in my dressmaking supplies where it won't be found by a curious boy or a despondent husband.

The car noses around the museum and turns back down the parkway toward City Hall. I am drawn to the museum and wish there was time to visit. I will ask Claire to take Thelma during her stay; one of us should experience the art. Better that it be my daughter.

"Isn't it tiring to be strong all the time?" Max asks, his voice soft.

My mind snaps away from thoughts of great paintings. "Can't you ever just be nice?"

He turns toward me, putting his bag on the floor. "I think we continually get off on the wrong foot."

"What do you mean?" The car is warm. I can smell soap and the wilting starch of his collar.

"You seem to think I brought you out here to upset you."

"Was there another purpose?" I am upset, but not in the way he thinks.

He closes his eyes. "You act as though only your part of the world is suffering. I wanted you to see that it's everywhere, that people other than your family, through no fault of their own, are in places they couldn't have imagined even a year ago." He takes my hand, and this time I do not object, because it feels impersonal, doctor-like. "I also wanted you to see that the person caring for your daughter isn't doing it out of some misplaced desire to impress her mother."

His earnestness makes me smile even as I pull my hand away. Max has an odd boyish quality that both intrigues and irritates, but I do not doubt he is serious about helping those suffering men—and my daughter. "I don't need to be impressed," I say, letting warmth seep into my voice. "It's enough that you can help her."

"I'm glad I can." One corner of his mouth turns up. "And I don't mind if I impress her mother just the slightest."

We stop at a light and I turn to the window and gasp. A fountain, lit by the fading lavender sky, is right beside the car. Encircled in shrubbery and flowers, its water spout showers down on three enormous reclining figures. It is the most beautiful thing I have ever seen. "What is that?"

"The Swann Fountain," Dr. Spencer says over his shoulder. "Named after a doctor who put drinking fountains in poor neighborhoods all around the city."

"The night it opened, we took the streetcar down after my shift at the hospital." Max smiles reminiscently. "There was a band, and we danced the tango."

The light turns green, and the car begins to move; soon the fountain will be gone.

"Can we stop?" There is something about it that calls to me. "I'd like to see it."

"John, can you keep my bag until the morning?" Max asks. "I'm going to take Mrs. Kimber sightseeing."

He pulls obligingly to the curb. "At nine o'clock?"

"At whatever time the lady likes," he says. "As that's the time, then, yes, we're going sightseeing at nine o'clock."

And just like that, I am alone with Max Byrne—by choice! It unsettles me, and I am already unsettled. I have no idea how far we are from Claire's house, and despite his boyishness, there is something about Max that makes me wary.

Crossing the street toward the fountain, I wonder what it would be like to live in a place like this. Despite the hour, the square is full of people, sitting and walking about, their conversations carrying on the evening air, which is soft and does not smell like despairing men and infected wounds.

I wonder what I am doing here.

"The figures represent local Indian tribes and the rivers named after them," Max says, pointing out the two female and one male figure. "The Delaware is the largest, then the Schuylkill and the Wissahickon."

"Schuylkill," I repeat. "What a strange word."

"That's the river behind the museum. It's not an Indian word, despite how it sounds," he explains. "It's from the Dutch settlers. It means 'hidden river'."

"You're just a fountain of information."

Max yelps with laughter. "I didn't know you made jokes."

I cock my head. "I can, if the occasion warrants."

He nods sagely. "If the moon is in the correct phase, and the shadows fall just right on a sundial only you can see."

I know it is no more than a return joke, but it makes me sound hard and unable to enjoy myself. Is that how everyone sees me, or just this strange man Claire has flung into our lives?

"Shall we?" He gestures to the broad rim of the fountain. "Rest your feet for a moment, you're not used to all this city walking."

Sitting a few inches away from him, I gaze over the dancing water. In addition to the Indian figures and their accompanying swans, there are frogs and turtles spraying jets back toward the center. Dabbling my fingers in the water, I wonder if living here, even for a short time, will change Thelma. Being surrounded by beauty has to change a person—look what it's done to Claire.

"I don't mean to push." Max looks down at his scuffed brogues; one of the laces is untied. "I hope you'll forgive me."

"It's hard enough accepting help from my sister," I say, "but then you pop up out of nowhere and tell me you can fix Thelma, when we thought she was beyond help, and that everything wrong with her is because of me." My eyes are treacherously moist, and I blink hard. "It's a lot to take in."

"None of it was your fault," he says. "It was just something that happened, like this whole damned economic collapse. None of it is the fault of the people who are most affected."

He distracts himself, and I speak again, more comfortable with these larger issues. "I'm good at being poor. I'm an excellent poor person. But there was always something to stretch before, and even if Daniel wasn't working full-time, we had something. Now…" Restless, I get up and begin to walk.

"You don't have to do it all yourself," he says, following me. "Isn't there anyone you can count on?"

"My husband." How did we end up talking about my life? "But I'm used to dealing with things on my own. He used to work nights, and now, if he's working at all, it's away from home. Problems can't always wait. And sometimes"—I hesitate, offering a piece of myself I barely acknowledge—"sometimes I don't tell him because then I would just have to worry about his reaction. It's easier to do it myself."

"That's understandable."

Several other couples are seated on the edge of the fountain. Most are holding hands or talking quietly. None of them look like they are discussing the meaning of life. "No, it's not," I say. "I'm a wife who lies to her husband to make her own life easier."

"It sounds as if you need it made easier." He takes my arm, turning me back toward the fountain.

At his touch, I buckle and put my hands over my face, crying as thoroughly and uncontrollably as a child. The long week of strangeness and worry and fear—for Teddy, for Thelma, for Daniel—washes over me like a wave, and I go under. Max blocks me from view and lets me cry, standing close without actually touching me. In the dim light, we must look like a courting couple.

Ivory soap. He smells of Ivory soap. How is that even possible after several hours of working in the heat in that stinking camp?

"I'm sorry." I wipe my eyes with my fingers. "I don't know what came over me."

Max passes me a handkerchief with a flourish and watches as I blot my eyes and blow my nose.

"I don't *do* this." I am angry at my loss of control. "We should go back now." He turns agreeably and offers his arm again. I hesitate and then take it, letting him match his step to mine.

"Maybe you just needed a stranger to talk to," he says, as we cross the parkway. "Someone who doesn't know that you don't do that."

My tears leave me feeling like I've run a race, and leaning on his arm is a comfort. We walk in silence for several blocks. I'm not sure how far we are from Claire's house. Nothing looks familiar. The streets are emptier, but there are still lights burning in windows. At home, most houses would be dark by this time, to save on lamp oil, and because everyone gets up at dawn. My steps begin to drag, and he slows to accommodate me.

"I don't know if I could get used to this."

"Crying in public, you mean?" He bumps my shoulder with his to let me know he is joking. "Or something more mundane?"

"Everything." I let out a breath, not quite laughing.

Rittenhouse Square comes into sight, and I sigh with relief. He is right; my feet aren't accustomed to hard sidewalks, and my thin soles find every stone and bump.

"Would you like to sit?" he asks. "You've had a long night."

"This week has been a month long." I turn toward the nearest bench, bathed in the golden glow of a lamp. "Just for a moment. Claire must be concerned."

"She knows you're with me."

"Exactly."

It is after eleven when Max deposits me on the doorstep. He departs with a jaunty wave, and it strikes me that he is walking back to his office to sleep. It feels odd, having any kind of concern for him; his plan to expose me to the hardships of the world has worked, in a backhanded way.

The door is unlocked, and Baxter appears from somewhere to lock up behind me. "I'm sorry, did you stay up on my account?" I hadn't thought about the servants.

"It's no matter," he says and bids me goodnight.

A cup of tea would be lovely, but I'm not going to risk waking either Katie or the frightening Mrs. Fell. It can wait until morning. I don't want to see anyone else tonight except my kids.

When I reach the second floor, the nursery door opens and Claire slips out to join me. "You're back late."

I glance past her at Teddy and Thelma—both sleeping—and let her into my room. "You're as bad as Baxter, waiting up for me."

Claire shrugs. "I had words with Irene earlier. I'm still too keyed up to sleep." She sits on the bench at the foot of the bed, her aqua silk kimono reflecting light from the bedside lamp. "Besides, I was worried. I told Max it wasn't a good idea, taking you to that camp."

"Why?" My scalp aches from the weight of my hair and I remove pins and rub my temples. "It was fine."

"Let me." Claire pulls the brush through my hair. "I don't think I could have done it. That kind of men...they make me nervous."

"That feels nice." I close my eyes. "They're just men. It wasn't that different from being at home." It was, perhaps, the most at home I'd felt since getting on the train.

"Children I can manage," she says. "And women. The women are usually grateful, especially if you help their children. But sometimes they're like you. Angry. I don't always know what to say to them then."

Ouch. I start to deny it, but what's the point? Claire, for all the flaws I've assigned her, knows me too well. "You just have to let us work through it," I say at last. "It's not directed at anyone in particular." It is more a sense of betrayal than anger. Life, already difficult, has decided to become worse.

I meet her eyes in the mirror and am tempted to tell her about Jake. Instead, I say, "You should understand—we've been through the same losses. We're never safe. Whatever we have, it can vanish in a heartbeat."

My conversation with Max has made me careless; this is something I've never said aloud. I wait for her reaction.

"That's not how I see it," she says, her lower lip between her teeth. "But I don't think there's a right or a wrong way. You grew up fast because Mama needed you, but I was trapped in childhood—it felt like you two against the world, and all I did was get in the way." She sees my expression and holds up her hands. "Our lives would be completely different if either of them had lived."

"Mine would be the same." I had known, long before Tata's death, what my life would be.

"You would still be married to Daniel," she agrees, "but maybe you would be a little softer, and more trusting."

I raise my eyebrows. "And who would you be?"

"I might be more like you," she says. "Tata always made such a fuss over me, I don't know if I could have brought myself to leave if he hadn't died."

He had fussed over her, that much was true, but he had also made her cry. I learned from Mama how to deal with him, to skip out of his way when he was violent and seal my ears to his drunken words, but Claire was too young to acquire the knack. I can't imagine she would have stayed because of him.

"I hated what it did to us," I say quietly. "I hated worrying about Mama. I wasn't done growing up, and I felt like her mother half the time."

She puts down the brush and rests her hands on my shoulders. "I never saw her cry."

Neither did I. And I never talked about them, afraid it would hurt her. I wonder now if that silence hurt all of us.

"How did we get here?" Claire whips my hair into a neat braid. "I was worried about the camp, and here we are rehashing our childhood."

I drop my head forward, trying to loosen the tightness from my neck. "That's why I worry so much about the kids," I tell her. "We never lose our childhood. I wonder how much of this they're going to carry with them forever."

"Hopefully they'll carry knowledge that their parents love them and are doing the best they can." She squeezes my shoulders again. "Get yourself to bed now."

Leaving Teddy with her is for the best. No one watching Claire and Harry with him would think otherwise. But the other kids—how will losing their baby brother affect them later? That's the worry that keeps me up at night, a worry that I haven't shared with Daniel or my sister.

"I know you don't want to hear it," Claire says, blocking my path, "but thank you, from the bottom of my heart. I don't know what I'd do without Teddy."

"You'd manage," I say, not unkindly. "As we all do."

I shut the bathroom door and lean against it, hoping she takes the hint and leaves me alone. I have sustained more shocks this evening than I can handle, and I need peace. From the sheer volume of need in the city to my unsettling conversation with Max—much less the reappearance of my lost brother—I am exhausted.

Jake didn't hug me when I reached for him. He glanced down at his filthy overalls and took a step back. "I recognized your voice," he said. "Not you, so much as the sound of home."

I heard the same thing in his voice. "Where have you been all this time?"

He shrugged. "Here and there. I found work after I left, did really well for a while. And then"—he shrugged again—"Now nobody is doing well. How about you? Do you live here?"

"I'm visiting." It was easier not to tell him about Teddy. "Claire lives here."

A smile split his face. "Clairy is here?"

I explained her marriage and a bit about her life. "Her husband is one of the ones still doing well."

"I can't see her, then." His expression darkened. "I don't want to embarrass her."

"You wouldn't embarrass her." Seeing Jake would make her so happy. "She copes with me. I'm a little cleaner, but she never liked me as much."

"It's enough to know she's okay." He shoved his hat back on his head. "I got to go, sister."

As he walked away, I shouted Claire's address after him. "Go see her. She needs you." All I got in return is a raised hand before he disappeared into the crowd of men.

After I wash my face and clean my teeth, I listen at the door before opening it. Claire is gone, hopefully to bed. I resist checking the nursery, climbing straight into bed to wallow in silence until I fall asleep. All this constant talking, Claire and Harry and especially Max, is exhausting.

Claire's chatter is as constant as the hum of the city, and as unnatural, while Max confuses me. He is as disarming as a child, but he tricked me into opening myself in a way that made me vulnerable.

I want to go home to my silent husband, who loves me without making a song and dance of it. With Dan, everything too revealing is left unsaid. He knows me and I know him, and we don't have to have the kind of conversations that make me feel exposed.

26

Pearl

May 23, 1932

We have new boarders to replace Mrs. M. They're friends of Daddy's from the Gracie. One is Mr. Leckner, whose wife died last month. He's sad and very quiet. The other is Mr. Nolan. He's not sad or quiet. He used to live at Mrs. Zielinski's rooming house but he says he left because I'm a better cook.

They share the front bedroom, and the boys are in with Daddy. I asked if I could have Granny's bed back in the front room, with a screen pulled around it, because I don't want to sleep on the same floor as all those snoring men. I don't know how it's going to work when Mama and Thelma come home. Whenever that is.

Ava

My train leaves in the morning. This is my last chance to spend time with Thelma for months, and with Teddy forever—at least as his mother. There is a bruised feeling deep inside when I think about my baby.

"But this dinner is in your honor," Claire says. "You can't stay home."

"Why can't we just eat here? I don't want to go to some fancy place." I don't know how to behave in the kind of places they frequent.

"It's just Bookbinders," she insists. "It's a fish house."

She flits around my room, touching everything, and I put a hand on her arm. "Don't you remember what it was like when you first came here?" I ask. "All this is strange to me."

She stops short, abashed, and her eyes fill with easy tears.

"I didn't think," she says. "We don't have to go out. I just wanted to do something special before you left." Her smile is tremulous. "It's been so good having you here. Having my sister back." Her voice cracks and a few tears slip down her cheeks.

I try to reconcile Claire's neediness with her good fortune. How can a woman with so much be so unhappy? Is it the way Irene treats her—or the way Harry doesn't see it? Or is it because she hasn't had the one thing she wants? It makes our difficult decision just the tiniest bit easier to live with, and again I think I will take my hard life over my sister's plenty.

And Thelma, as much as it hurts to leave her behind, will ease Teddy's entry into the household, and give Claire another focus for her abundant affections. By the time she comes home—hopefully, in time to start school—my sister will be firmly established as Teddy's mother.

"Are you sure it's not fancy?" I can wear the green and brown dress again, Katie pressed it and hung it back in the closet. I don't like the idea of servants, but I could get used to someone else doing the ironing.

"Your new dress will be fine," she assures me, pleased that I have given in. "I'm paying Katie extra tonight to stay with the children. It'll be just the four of us."

I pull out the stockings Claire purchased and inspect my shoes. Perhaps I will ask Katie for polish, rather than wear my new ones, which pinch. "You, me, Harry, and Irene?" I imagine her staring at me while I figure out the forks and almost change my mind.

"Lord no." Her nose wrinkles. "This is a party, not a trial. No, Harry invited Max." She holds up a hand before I can frame an objection. "I know, but you have to admit, he's good fun. And he's going to be spending so much time with Thelma, I thought it would be helpful if you got to know him a little better."

Max Byrne is a good doctor, which is all I need to know about him. He is also, as Claire says, good fun—if only those qualities weren't outweighed by his ability to irritate me to distraction. I can't back out or ask Harry to uninvite him.

"Fine," I say, not bothering to hide my feelings. "What time are we leaving? I want to spend some time with the kids and have a bath beforehand."

Claire claps her hands at her easy victory. "Our reservation is for seven. Max will meet us there."

It is a warm evening. A breeze from the river carries with it the scent of fish and, very faintly, garbage. This part of the city seems older than Rittenhouse Square, the buildings shorter and more utilitarian. Despite some shops with large windows and colorful signs, it feels down-at-the heel, a bit shabby. I ask if I am correct.

"It's much older," Claire confirms as we walk toward the restaurant. "Independence Hall is just a few blocks away." Her cheeks turn pink. "I'm not much of a Philadelphian. All these years, I've never actually gone there."

History was my favorite subject in school. A lot of it has gone out of my head over the years, but I still remembered reading about the hot summer of 1776 and how the men in Independence Hall kept the windows closed because there was a livery stable across the street, and the heat and the flies nearly drove them mad. I would have liked to have seen it, but it's too late now.

Just inside the restaurant's glass doors, its black and white tile floor is the setting for numerous tables, each with a starched white cloth and folded napkins and a mystifying array of silverware and glasses. Why can't people just use one of everything? Is it too much to ask?

"We're waiting for a fourth," Harry advises the waiter, as if we have all the time in the world. "We'll order when he arrives."

"Very good, sir." He presents us with menus and disappears after filling our water glasses.

The menu is huge. I take a deep breath and decide to conquer it in sections. Every problem can be solved if you start somewhere.

Appetizers. I know from listening to Irene that these are the small plates that precede the actual meal. Jumbo shrimp cocktail, crab meat cocktail, lobster cocktail. I wrinkle my nose. "Cocktail?"

"It's because they're served in a glass," Claire whispers. "It's not a drink."

I have never encountered shrimp, crab, or lobster, in or out of a glass, except in books. The next section is no better. *Oysters and clams,* followed by words that make no sense: littleneck, cherrystone, blue point.

Soup. At last, something I recognize. I have never tasted snapper soup or clam chowder, but I know how to eat soup.

There is a stir, and I look up in time to see Max Byrne weave his way through the tables. He drops heavily into the chair next to me and smiles an apology. "I was over at the day nursery on Arch Street, and realized when they started putting the young ones to bed that I was running late."

"Day nursery?" He always manages to say something that requires an explanation.

"It's a place where working parents can leave kids who are too young to stay home alone. I stop in once in a while to look them over. The director is a friend."

I'm not going to be able to get away with just having soup, so I retreat behind the menu again and soldier on. I'm not afraid of trying new foods, just of making a fool of myself by not knowing how to eat what I've ordered.

Max leans back and peers around his menu. "I love this place. When Harry said dinner was on him, I made sure I was available."

"And here I thought it was me." This place is putting me out of joint; I almost sound pleasant.

"If I said that, you'd start hurling silverware at me." His smile is disarming. "Have you decided what you're getting?

"Claire calls this a fish house," I say, shaking my head, "but in my world, fish comes out of a river. I don't know what any of this stuff is."

"Ah." He stares critically at the stiff card. "Well, they have more than seafood, you know. You could get a steak."

"That feels like cheating."

He is quiet, deciding on his order, and then he reaches across and points to the bottom of the menu. "Try one of the samplers. You won't have to commit to a whole plate of something you might not like."

I read the descriptions, listening to Claire and Harry talking quietly across from us. The five-star platter consists of fresh fish, deviled clams, deviled crab, fried oysters, fried scallops, potatoes, coleslaw, and a salad. It amazes me that this is intended for one person.

"I give up." Max is annoying, but I would rather embarrass myself in front of him than allow my sister to see how bothered I am by a simple menu, which is not simple at all, but a symbol of everything unnatural that has occurred in the last two weeks. "What does deviled mean?"

"Have you ever eaten deviled eggs? It's the same idea, but with crab meat."

With everything I've been through over these last two weeks, why is a menu the thing that threatens to drive me to tears? "Food isn't this complicated at home," I manage to say. "Other than having enough of it."

"I imagine this is a bit different." Sensing my discomfort, Max aims to distract me. He gestures toward the doors. "When this place opened, back in the nineties, Sam Bookbinder bought his seafood right off the pier down the street. Back then, his customers were sailors and stevedores." Winking, he adds, "The rich folk discovered him later."

"Does most of this come from the ocean?" Transporting fish from far away seems like an extravagant waste of time and money, but wasting money is what city people do best.

"Most of it," he says. "It's not that far."

"What?"

"We're closer to the New Jersey shore than to your hometown."

If only I'd known! Claire had suggested day trips to amuse us, but I turned her down. Would I have accepted, if she'd told me the ocean was so close?

The waiter returns, pad in hand. Harry orders for himself and Claire: snapper soup, shrimp cocktail, a half dozen oysters for him, followed by salmon, and broiled scallops for her.

"Shall I order for you?" Max asks.

I nod, afraid I will misspeak and order something even more mystifying than what I've chosen.

"New England clam chowder for both of us," he says, "and a shrimp cocktail to share. The lady will have the five-star platter, and I'll have the deviled crab."

"Very good, sir."

"You didn't order the lobster thermidor," Harry says. "Getting conservative with my money?"

"I thought I'd leave you some," Max replies, grinning. "That way I can weasel it out of you for one of my causes."

I watch their easy banter. Claire chips in occasionally, but it is mostly the men trading barbs, thoroughly enjoying themselves. Harry's hands look empty without a newspaper or a drink, but he makes do with a tall glass of iced tea.

In a few minutes, the waiter returns with a tray of steaming bowls. I watch as Claire selects a spoon and dips it into her soup.

The chowder is rich and creamy. Potatoes and celery add a familiar note, but the interesting, chewy bits must be the clams. "This is good."

Max beams. "I can't cook, but I know how to eat."

"Well, I can cook," I tell him, "but I wouldn't know where to start with this."

"A recipe book," he says wryly and spoons up more chowder. "I'm sure a woman like you can follow a recipe."

The worrisome cocktail turns out to be a half-dozen pink, finger-like creatures curled over a glass with some red sauce and a slice of lemon.

"Dig in." Max squeezes lemon over the shrimp and picks one up by its tail, dipping it into the sauce. It disappears in two bites and he deposits the empty shell on a small plate.

I follow his lead, viewing the shrimp with skepticism. Dip, bite, chew. The flavor is different from the clams, sweeter, with a meaty texture, but I don't like it as much. I finish the shrimp, leaving a bit more meat in the tail than he did.

"What do you think?"

I raise my shoulders slightly. "Not as good as the chowder."

"They're an acquired taste." He devours two more and looks questioningly in my direction.

"Go ahead. I'm sure there'll be more than enough food on this platter you've ordered." Much of my discomfort during this whole visit, I've realized, has been unaccustomed fullness.

When the platter arrives, I think it is a mistake. Surely something this large is meant to be shared. "I can't eat all this," I whisper to Max.

"You don't have to," he returns. "I know for a fact that the kitchen gives the leftovers to a soup kitchen."

This comforts me. Having watched Max select the inside fork to attack his deviled crab, I pick up the same one and dig into my dinner, choosing to disregard the conversation between Max and Harry until it becomes impossible to ignore.

"Rugged individualism my"—Max breaks off and looks at me and Claire—"foot. The man wouldn't know a rugged individual if one walked into the White House and bit him on the posterior. We can't afford his moralizing right now. People need help."

Each time I decide to dislike Max Byrne, he says something that echoes my thoughts, albeit more colorfully and with bigger words.

"Do you think Smith or Roosevelt has a better chance at winning the nomination?" Claire asks. I am impressed that she participates in their conversation; at home, even though some women vote, we don't talk politics. "Roosevelt's just another rich man."

"Not all rich men are the devil," Harry says with a laugh. "You married one."

She smiles sweetly. "And it was the best decision I ever made, darling. But you know what I mean—most rich men in American politics treat the poor as if they're the ones who brought on the Depression."

I stop chewing.

"Roosevelt's for the common man," Max says earnestly. "He can't help that he's rich. He understands the plight of those struggling, and he wants to make it better." He stabs the baked potato with his fork. "He'll choose the right people to bring this damnable Depression to an end."

"What about Al Smith?" Claire asks again. "He was governor of New York, same as Roosevelt."

Harry shakes his head. "He was fine for New York, but he's Catholic—I doubt the rest of the country will be as sold on him."

I take a swallow of iced tea, overtaken by momentary dizziness. None of the people at this table doubt that their vote—or their opinion—matters. What must that be like?

Claire

Max keeps up a constant stream of chat, amusing us all with his stories. I debated inviting him because he annoys Ava, but with her departure looming, the distraction of his presence seemed like a good idea.

The two weeks of her visit have flown by. I have been glad of her company as I get used to having two children in the house but selfishly, I am ready for her to leave so I can spend more time with Teddy. I haven't inhaled him the way I want to for fear of rubbing her nose in my good fortune.

Thelma is a lovely bonus to the arrangement. Knowing we can help, and return her to her parents healthy and whole, makes me feel less guilty. She is a sweet-tempered child, as pretty as she is clever, and well-spoken for her years. It must be because she is surrounded by older people all the time; I was the same way, and it took starting school to interact with children my age.

If Thelma stays into the fall, she will be ready for school. I picture myself pushing Teddy in his carriage and walking with her, and make a mental note to research schools near the house.

The waiter clears and comes back to take our dessert order. We order coffee, and Harry, as always, chooses rice pudding. "What kind of pie do you have?" I ask.

"Cherry, strawberry, chocolate cream, and lemon meringue," the waiter says. "We also have strawberry shortcake this evening, and three flavors of ice cream."

"Let me guess. Chocolate, vanilla, and strawberry?" Max looks at Ava. "Shame Thelma isn't here."

My sister actually smiles. "Tempting as that is, I think I'll try the lemon pie."

I order shortcake, and after a moment of wavering, Max joins me. "I can never resist an opportunity for whipped cream. Or strawberries."

"I've never tried making meringue," Ava says. "I understand how it's made, but it's wasteful, all those egg whites."

Waste is one of the harshest words in my sister's vocabulary. In her house, as in our mother's, nothing goes to waste. Not worrying about discarding a ruined blouse for fear that a child will go without, or being told sternly that a little embroidery will cover the stain and make it even prettier, was one of the happiest discoveries in my new life as a married woman.

Does that make me superficial? Perhaps, but more people would be like me if they didn't have to work so hard at being poor. That's what it is, work. People act like the poor are lazy, sitting in their falling-down houses and waiting for charity to come along, but I've never seen anyone work as hard as my parents did, or Ava and Daniel.

They have insisted that Teddy is a gift and they want nothing in exchange. I know it came about because of their financial situation and the low period Ava suffered after his birth, which she still has not mentioned, but it occurs to me now that he might have been offered up pre-emptively, as they live in a tied house with no source

214

of income other than what Ava and Pearl can bring in with their sewing. What if they lose their home?

It will make her angry, but I'm going to talk to Harry about wiring money to the agent, enough to give them some breathing room but not enough to be insulting.

It is a very fine line, managing Ava. I think I'm getting better at it.

Ava

Claire has gone upstairs to check on the kids while I go into the living room with Harry, resisting the urge to follow her. They will be her sole responsibility soon enough. "What exactly," I ask, "is a lesser Biddle?"

He barks a laugh. "You've been listening to Max."

Max is a terrible gossip, regaling me with indiscreet stories about people I will never meet, and throwing in a few jabs at Irene Warriner, who is one of few people he seems to genuinely dislike.

"It's all you need to know to understand my mother," he says. "The Biddles are an old Philadelphia family. Most of them were quite wealthy. My mother's branch was a bit down on its luck when she married my father, but a lesser Biddle still believes they are superior to ninety percent of the population."

"I see."

Harry fiddles with his cigarette case. "In other words, Mother married Father for the same reason Claire married me."

"Claire married you because she loved you."

"She married me to escape Scovill Run," Harry says flatly, then he softens. "I am fortunate she has come to love me."

I lean back in the chair and wiggle my toes in my tight shoes. "Our mother always said it was easy to fall in love with a good man," I tell him. "I don't know what she felt at the time, but she loves you now."

"I know we're not supposed to thank you," Harry says, "but I was afraid for Claire—before."

"I didn't do it for her. Teddy needs more than we can give him. God only knows when Daniel will have work again, and you can't tell a child to stop being hungry." I meet Harry's concerned gaze. He's a good man; he can't help being rich and a bit stiff. "Don't go offering me money. It's enough—more than enough—that you're helping Thelma. Buy my train ticket home, and that will be the end of it."

"As you wish." He exhales a plume of smoke. "Would Daniel ever consider taking a job here, do you think? I could find a place for him in one of the mills, or perhaps a factory job."

"I doubt it." It would mean moving, and neither of us has ever lived anywhere else. I close my mind to the fact that if we're put out, we'll have to go somewhere. "He just wants to do the job he's always done." The likelihood of this happening anytime soon is depressing. "But I'll try."

"Thank you." He smiles broadly. "There, I got to say it after all."

27

Claire

Ava will not allow us to drive her to the station. "It's easier if we don't do a big farewell scene."

She is right, but I don't like it. "What if we just—"

"No." She will not look at me. "It will upset me to have them there, do you understand? I'd rather say goodbye here and have Baxter drop me off."

Ava gets her way, and we wave her off from the front step. As the Packard glides away, I can see her, square-shouldered, in the back seat. She doesn't turn around.

Beside me, Thelma is quiet. She cried earlier, when she spent a few minutes in my sitting room with her mother, but she's decided to be brave. If a five-year-old child can get through this without tears, so can I.

Ava also asked for time alone with Teddy. I acquiesced but was hurt when she shut the door in my face. They were only in there for a few minutes, but when she opened the door, I could see that a line had been crossed; she had made whatever mental separation was necessary. She kissed him on the forehead and handed him to me, and this time, there was no hesitation.

"I'm going to miss Mama." Thelma leans against me. "Won't you, Aunt Claire?"

"Of course," I say. "We all will. But you'll see Dr. Max tomorrow, and that's something to look forward to."

Harry bends down and lifts Thelma onto his hip. "Tomorrow's Friday. If Saturday is a nice day, what would you say to a trip to the zoo?"

I take Teddy back upstairs and then pop into the guest room. Although Katie has not yet turned out the room, there is no sign that Ava has ever been there—the bed is neatly made and all the surfaces are clean. On a whim, I open the closet and see the dress from

Bonwit's on its hanger. On the floor are the shoes I bought for her, with her stockings rolled neatly inside.

Ava

The train winds through the upstate Pennsylvania hills, passing through small, pretty towns with white church steeples, patches of forest, green scrub woods, and coal towns, where nothing is white, not even the steeples. The hills grow higher as the train enters the Northern Coal Field.

We stop in Scranton, but Scranton no longer interests me. I've seen—and survived—Philadelphia, all I want is to go home. To spite me, the train makes a long stop, passengers getting on and off, cars being coupled and uncoupled. Finally, it begins to move, slowly now, with empty cars that will be shunted off at Scovill Run.

The hills stay green for the first few miles out of Scranton, but as we draw closer to my home, the ugliness makes itself apparent: broken trees, raw earth clawed from the hillsides, equipment scattered about in varying stages of use or decay. The mines look busy, despite what Harry says, and I hope they will make a turn and call Daniel back to work.

Harry bought a first-class ticket this time, but I changed it after Baxter left and pocketed the difference. How I travel isn't important; my mind is busy working out how to explain Thelma's absence to Daniel and the kids. Saying it's for her own good sounds too much like how we explained Teddy's adoption.

I think again of Claire and Harry with their elegant shoes and evening cocktails, their ordered life that seems to exist outside the Depression. I'm not angry with them. They aren't the people who say the poor are lazy, or men just don't want to work, and yet I still can't entirely forgive them for never having to worry about their next meal, or whether their children will have shoes in the cold weather.

Teddy will be so much better off than the rest of my kids. It is unfair to them, to let him escape to a better life when they will have to live, possibly for always, as the poor. Even if they make it out, they will be marked by poverty. As I am. Daniel is. We don't know how to be anything but what we've always been.

The wheels slow as we go into the final curve, and the first houses lurch into view. These are the old houses, original to the town, which house the mine managers and their families. When coal was discovered, the company came and bought up all the existing buildings and constructed whatever else was needed: a company store, a hotel, the town hall.

It is an ugly place. I've never really thought about it before, because it is my home, and its beauty or lack thereof has no importance, but I allow myself a momentary thought of that glorious fountain before I shut Philadelphia away behind a door in my mind.

The station comes before the mine; the empty cars will be uncoupled here and taken on a separate track to the Gracie. As the train shudders to a stop, I reach for my suitcase. It is heavier now, thanks to Claire's generosity, but I am coming home without two of my children. The thought of facing my family makes it hard to breathe.

Only one other person gets off at Scovill Run, a man in a gray suit and a bowler. No one who lives in town would wear such a hat, so he must have something to do with the mine. I follow him across the platform and look around.

"Mama!" They are waiting just off the platform, at the side of the street. My heart lifts when I see Dandy with them, though he stands far away from his father. Toby and George launch themselves at me, rocking me on my feet. I squat down and hug them, gratified to see such emotion from my normally unaffectionate pair.

Pearl speaks over their heads. "Mama, where's Thelma?"

I hand my suitcase to Dandy. He takes it and waits, with his sister, for my response.

"She's with your Aunt Claire."

"You left her there?"

Everyone starts talking at once and my first impulse is to get back on the train and disappear. I hold up my hand for silence, and eventually, they stop talking and look at me.

"I left Thelma with Harry and Claire," I say, "because they know a doctor who can help her."

"And how do we pay for that?" Daniel asks. He looks exhausted, whether from keeping the house running without me or from low spirits and unemployment.

"Harry and Claire are paying." I shrug off my guilt. "They want to."

"What did you give them, a two-for-one deal?" His eyes are dark, almost black; he's in that unreachable place already.

"She'll be back." Why is he being so obtuse? "But for now, she's staying on so they can help her."

He turns abruptly and the rest of us follow. I lengthen my stride to catch up and grab his arm. "What's wrong? Don't you want her to walk better?"

"I thought you'd check with me before giving up another kid," he says, shaking me off. "That's all."

I should have been more explicit in my telegram. But he should have responded—called or wired back to say he didn't favor the plan. "I'm sorry, okay? But it's such a good opportunity for her."

"Like giving away Teddy was a good opportunity for him?" He walks so quickly that dust swirls around his legs.

"You were the first one to say we should do it." I am stung by his anger. "Don't change your tune now."

His head whips around and there are tears in his eyes. "I'm not changing my tune, but I'd like to know what music you're listening to. You left here not even wanting to give up Teddy. Now you're back without Thelma, looking like you've had a fine vacation, while the rest of us have been stuck in this shithole town."

I back away. Daniel rarely gets angry, but when it happens, as with Dandy, it is best to give him time to cool down.

Falling into step beside Pearl, I ask, "How has it been?"

"Fine." Pearl's head is down, her hair hiding most of her face.

"The boys all right?"

"Fine."

I look over my shoulder. "Dandy?"

He shakes his head, looking just like his father. "What do you want me to say, Mama?"

Rebuffed by everyone, I wait for Toby and George, who, now that the novelty of my return has passed, are scuffling and darting around like bees. "Slow down," I say. "I haven't seen you in weeks, tell me what's been going on."

"Toby tore his pants," George tells me, "so he couldn't go to school until Pearl mended them."

"I don't imagine you minded." I cup the back of Toby's stubbly head. Someone—Pearl or Trudy—has given them their summer haircuts already.

"I didn't have no pants." His tone is aggrieved. "I couldn't go outside unless I wore a *skirt.*"

"It didn't kill you, I see." How long did it take for Pearl to get around to stitching his pants? "What about you, George?"

"I caught a bunch of frogs," he offers. "And Pearl, she made us help in the garden."

"I don't like planting." Toby spins in a circle and collapses into his brother. "It's dumb."

"You won't think it's dumb when you want to eat." Pearl shakes him, none too gently. "Food doesn't grow in the kitchen."

She walks close to me, stubbornly silent but supporting me in a way that my menfolk are unable to do. I know what that posture means; I looked much the same at her age when I was upset. "Honey, she'll be home in a few months. Maybe by the time school starts. This doctor is going to put braces on her legs and help her walk. I didn't want to leave her behind, but it would have been selfish to say no."

Finally, she says, "Is she happy there?"

"Yes," I say, not wanting to tell her just how easily my little girl fitted into that household. "Claire has a dog."

Pearl smiles shakily. "That'll do it." She watches her feet for a long stretch of the road. "Can they make her better?"

"Dr. Max—Max Byrne, he's a friend of Harry's—he seems to think so. At least better than she is now." I explain that as Thelma gets older, her crooked legs will cause her more discomfort. "Really, anything he can do to keep her from being in pain..."

"I hadn't thought of that." Tears roll down her cheeks. "I thought she'd limp, but not hurt. I just miss her. I hate being the only girl in the house."

"What about Trudy?" Daniel is nearly out of sight.

"She's a grownup." Pearl lets me take her hand. "And she's gone back next door, anyway."

I stumble, bruising my foot on a stone in the road. Maybe I should have brought those new shoes. "Why?"

"Daddy made her leave." She sighs. "I think he felt like she was bossing him, but she wasn't. Not really."

It is my turn to sigh. I know Trudy, and I know Daniel's sensitivity to being managed by anyone but me. "So we'll need to find new boarders, if I can't convince her to come back."

"Daddy already did," she says. "Mr. Leckner and Mr. Nolan."

I can't put faces to the names. "What are they like?"

"All right." She shrugs. "Daddy's mad all the time lately."

"Mad how?" I want to ask about Trudy, but this is more important. "At you?"

"At everyone," she says. "Or everything. The dinner's not right, the boys are too loud, the lamp smokes too much." She squeezes my fingers. "I know why, but it's so tiring."

I hug her to me, sorry to my core that she's had to deal with such adult matters. "I shouldn't have left you on your own for so long. And we didn't celebrate your birthday."

"Twelve isn't any different than eleven." She wipes her face with her sleeve. "And it's okay about Thelma. I don't want to be selfish. I want to be like you."

Pearl

May 27, 1932

Mama's home, but Thelma's not. There's a doctor in Philadelphia who thinks he can fix her legs, so she stayed with Aunt Claire. I miss her. We all miss her.

Daddy is taking it real bad, though. It reminds me of when he fought with Dandy. He didn't say anything at first, just walked away and left us to go home alone. Later he and Mama went for a walk. When they came back, I could see she'd been crying. Mama never cries.

Claire

All of my fears while waiting for each pregnancy to stabilize or depart my unwilling body are doubled—trebled—when there is an actual baby in my care. When Teddy cries, is he hungry? Angry? Wet? Does he miss his real mother? Will I ever be enough?

I find it difficult to be away from him. Despite Katie's repeated offers to watch him while I accompany Thelma to her appointments with Max, I prefer pushing him in his coach. It slows my pace so my niece can keep up, and it keeps my baby under my gaze.

When he takes his first staggering steps, I will be a wreck. When he progresses to running, I will exhaust myself trying to protect him from all the dangers of the outside world. Even now, when he only crawls about on his mat or sits in his crib, happily playing with his teething ring or waving his legs at the toys hanging overhead, I fret.

"He's a fine, healthy boy," Harry tells me repeatedly. "Max said so, and the pediatric doctor confirmed it. You're wearing yourself out for no reason."

"I just want everything to be perfect," I say. "What if *his* legs are crooked?"

"Then we'll have them straightened," he says easily. "There's nothing wrong with Teddy's legs, Claire. He's crawling already."

He is, at barely six months, and I can see him looking at the bars of his crib, trying to work out how to pull himself up.

Irene, of all people, supports me. "You can't make up for those early months of deprivation," she says. "Who knows what lasting effects they had? Look at the girl."

The girl, as my mother-in-law consistently calls Thelma, is thriving. If it weren't for her legs, she would look like every other girl her age. Harry thinks I'm overreacting, but I can't find a way to be objective about Teddy.

Only Irene, who has never been on my side, indulges my nerves.

When Thelma picks Teddy up one evening to cart him off to bed, I trip over the ottoman in my attempt to help her. "Let me do it, sweetheart," I say. "You're not strong enough to carry him."

Thelma turns, and in her elfin face, I see the shadow of my sister. "But Aunt Claire," she says, "I used to put him to bed all the time at home. Why can't I do it here?"

"Because she's worried about you dropping him," Irene says sharply. "Don't talk back to your elders."

"I'm not going to drop him."

Is it possible to be shamed by a little girl? I swallow my fear. I *am* being ridiculous, and I don't want to make Thelma fearful, too. "You go ahead. Be careful on the steps, that's all I meant. I'll be up in a few minutes." I resume my seat and listen to her halting footsteps climbing the stairs.

"We made it," she calls down, and then the nursery door shuts.

Exhaling, I tip my head back. "Why can't I just trust that everything is going to be okay?"

"It takes time," Harry tells me. "It took a lot to get here, be patient with yourself."

Irene fusses with her stick before pushing herself upright. "Claire may be right to worry," she says. "There may be something wrong with that boy you can't even imagine yet."

Harry's face darkens. "That's enough, Mother," he says. "There's nothing wrong with Teddy." He turns to me. "Let's go up and watch Thelma get him ready for bed. That way we can both be sure she's comfortable doing it."

I take his hand and we leave Irene standing before the cold fireplace, her plans thwarted. She is playing on my fears for her purposes, but I can't imagine what they are.

Pearl

May 31, 1932

There's not enough sewing to keep me busy, so I found a job. Daddy told me I didn't have to work yet, but I don't think he understands Dandy and I aren't kids anymore.

It's just cleaning and helping Mrs. Zielinski with the laundry. She has ten men in her rooming house. They're all on day shift, so they're not around when I work. I know how to get coal dust out of everything by now. Mrs. Z. was impressed.

Ava

The weather continues to warm. School ends just after I return and George and Toby disappear into the woods for days on end, coming home only for meals. Daniel picks up a few odd jobs and spends much of his time enlarging the garden, filling the stove box, and doing things that keep him outside and away from me.

Dandy appears in the kitchen one afternoon, shortly after Daniel has gone out. Does he watch the house, waiting for his father to leave?

"All right," he says. "Tell me about this doctor, and what he can do for Thelma."

"Are you ready to listen?" I reach for mugs, but he shakes his head.

"I'm here, ain't I?" He hooks an ankle around the chair leg and drags it out from the table.

"You're just like your father." Except that his father has barely spoken to me, much less apologized. "He doesn't talk sense when he's mad, either."

"I'm not like him." Dandy squirms in his seat. "But tell me what the doctor says."

We're still not right with each other, Daniel and I, and I don't know when it will get better. The day I came home, he made me so angry that I cried, and ever since, our connection seems to be gone. When I roll against him in bed, he takes what is offered but there is no longer the same joy for either of us. I lay rigid, praying this brief moment of pleasure won't result in another baby. He suspects, and it makes him rough. Part of me likes it and part of me is sickened that we have come to this.

The new boarders are another sore point. I am upset that he evicted Trudy and her grandchildren—not only is Trudy my friend, but she helped us in the dark days while Daniel was in Scranton. Still, I can't accuse him of acting without asking my opinion, for fear of what he'll say.

Mr. Leckner is all right, but I don't much like Tom Nolan. There are times I think I smell liquor on his breath, but he pays the rent promptly, eats what he's given, and is gone most of the time, so I learn to ignore him.

Weeks pass before I manage to catch Daniel alone during the day. Every time the kids are gone, he finds a reason to be out of the house himself, but I ask over breakfast if he will repair the table leg broken by the rough-housing boys, and he agrees.

After Pearl goes to work and the boys head off to the woods, I follow the sound of hammering and swearing to the kitchen and find the table overturned on the floor. A cigarette smolders unattended in a saucer as Daniel glares down at the table.

I lean on the back of a chair. "How's it going?"

"It's going." He reaches around me for the cigarette.

"I didn't mean the table."

"I know."

Blowing out an exasperated breath, I say, "Daniel, are we ever going to talk?"

"Nothing to say." He stubs out the cigarette. "You've gone and sold our children to the highest bidder."

"Don't make it sound like I did this on my own." I am done coddling his anger. Even after the blow-up with Dandy, I had been able to get through to him sooner than this. "You signed the adoption papers yourself."

"Harry paid our back rent." Daniel drops the hammer with a bang, making me jump. "When I went to the store yesterday, Henderson was there. He congratulated me—in front of everyone—for getting caught up. How do you think that made me feel?"

It doesn't surprise me. "I told him we didn't want money for Teddy, especially since they're paying for Thelma's treatment."

"Well," Daniel says, "he paid anyway, so your useless husband doesn't have to earn his keep."

"You're not useless." Harry's generosity gives us some breathing space, no matter how it makes Daniel feel. "And there's not much work to be had, or you'd have found it." I think about Harry's offer. Would Daniel be interested, or would he see it as Harry trying to control us? I'll test the waters later when things are a bit calmer.

"Thelma will be back." I pour a cup of lukewarm tea and fold myself into the nearest chair. "I wouldn't let them keep her."

"Wouldn't you?" he flares. "We're down to three kids. How do you think Lillie would feel about that?"

"It's not all my fault." I blink hard to stave off tears. Why can't women get angry without crying? "You threw Dandy out and scared the skin off the rest of them. They're still scared of you."

He goes quiet, the anger that boils inside coming close to the surface. I draw back. Provoking him isn't going to help matters. If I want him to ever allow Dandy back in the house, I have to stay calm and do a better job of managing him.

"I know you're upset," I say carefully. "I know you hate not working, but don't take it out on the people who love you." I put my hand over his. "Karl Metzger is thinking about going to look for work again. We can manage if you want to go with him."

"So now you want *me* gone." He pulls his hand away.

"Oh, for God's sake." I get up, banging my knee on the table. Pain surges up my leg. "Can I say anything you won't take the wrong way?"

Daniel picks up the hammer. "Just let me finish this."

Unwelcome in my own kitchen, I get no further than the front room before I have to stop. Leaning against the Singer's wooden cover, I cover my face with my hands and allow myself a moment of despair. Before Philadelphia, we were happy, most of the time. Daniel always had his moods—and unemployment made them worse—but I barely recognize the man in the kitchen and wonder if this is who my husband is now.

28

Pearl

June 8, 1932

I wish Daddy and Mrs. M could have gotten along until Mama came home. I don't like Mr. Nolan. He smiles at me, but not when anyone is looking. Yesterday he said I was going to be real pretty when I grew up, he could tell. Girls are supposed to like compliments, but I got all sweaty and scared inside when he said it, and he saw that and he laughed and laughed.

Claire

When Harry reminds me there is a dinner dance at the Bellevue Stratford on Saturday to raise funds for unemployment relief, my only thought is whether it will be fancy enough to wear my new dress. Thelma and I went to Lit Brothers last weekend, ostensibly to buy clothes for her, but before going home we ended up in the ladies' department. Not only did I purchase a ridiculously beautiful dress, but I was also extravagant and had shoes dyed to match.

Thelma's enthusiasm was contagious: she squealed and clapped at every dress I tried on, but when I came out in the silver taffeta with its satin shoulder drape, her mouth fell open. "That's the one, Auntie!"

Harry likes to see me in nice things, so I bought it. Even if the party turns out to be a waste of time, Thelma and I will have had a good time getting ready.

But these are the parties I enjoy, where if I end up talking to someone who makes me feel like an imposter, I can excuse myself to get a cup of punch and find more congenial companions elsewhere.

It is a surprise, as I stand chatting with the wives of two councilmen, to see Max Byrne cutting a path through the ballroom. He greets both women by name and deposits a smacking kiss on my cheek. "I have someone you should meet," he says, tucking my arm through his. "You don't mind if I steal her, do you, ladies?"

They smile indulgently as he tows me away. "You are incorrigible," I say. "No wonder my sister was so exasperated by you."

"Was she?" Max is decently clad for once, unable to get away with wearing one of his terrible suits to a formal gathering. His tuxedo is clearly borrowed, but his shirt is white, his studs are polished, and his bow tie is only slightly askew. "Why is that, do you think?"

"She has sons. She prefers her men adult, and well-behaved."

He stops. "My behavior is exemplary, and I know the most interesting people." He continues his forward path, stopping to exchange greetings with several high-profile men. "Do you know Prue Foster?"

"Yes." I blanch. Mrs. Foster scares me witless. She is one of those women who can see through anything; born to wealth, she nevertheless married up and is one of the doyennes of Philadelphia society. We have met on innumerable occasions, but I'm not sure she knows my name.

"She's looking for a few ladies to help with a pet project, and of course, I thought of you." Max turns that smile on me, and unless Mrs. Foster's pet project is white slavery or torturing kittens, I know I'll have a new pursuit before the evening is out. Maybe it will be something that can be solved by the writing of a large check; I am most comfortable with that kind of charity.

Prudence Foster is at the center of a group of elegantly-dressed men and women, talking with great animation. In her mid-forties, she has smoothly waved dark red hair and small, gold-rimmed spectacles. When Max and I join them, she swings around and greets him with affection. "Max, darling!"

"Prudence, darling!" They exchange kisses with gusto. "I heard you were recruiting for one of your excellent schemes, and I've brought my dear friend Mrs. Warriner to be one of your victims—I mean, one of your recruits."

"Some of my recruits do feel like victims," Mrs. Foster says, "but I hope you're not one of them, Mrs. Warriner. I asked Max to introduce us; I have a feeling about you."

"I'm sure I'll enjoy being involved." I swear silently as Max bows and vanishes into the throng—off, I am sure, to corral some other helpless—or hapless—person into doing his bidding. How does he do it? "What do you have in mind?"

"Let's not talk now." Mrs. Foster puts a light hand on my arm. "I can barely hear myself think in this place. Won't you have lunch with me on Monday? I'd much prefer to talk"—she gestures at the din around us—"without all this nonsense going on."

Harry claims me for the next dance. "I didn't know you were friendly with Al Foster's wife." He swings me around so my taffeta skirt rustles.

"I'm not," I say. "Max set me up. We're having lunch on Monday, so I'll find out then what she wants from me."

"I do wish people would stop leaving bequests to orphanages." Mrs. Foster waves her fork for emphasis.

"You do?" I am dizzied by the speed and vehemence of my hostess's discourse, which has bounced from her disapproval of the mayor to Bonwit's latest fashions to her opinion on the color of Jean Harlow's hair. I focus on the plate of sole and asparagus in front of me and hope I can keep up.

"I want their money, of course," she declares, "I just wish they'd let go of it while they're still alive. We need money now, not when they pass on—with some of these biddies, it could be decades!"

My mother-in-law has a portion of her estate earmarked for a children's home, and I wonder if she is one of the "biddies" Mrs. Foster has in mind. "Biddy" is a rather tame word for Irene, but perhaps they aren't well acquainted.

"Max Byrne said you were looking for recruits." Since the table is being cleared, I should find out the purpose of my visit before I am handed my hat. "What exactly are you recruiting *for*?"

"Come into my parlor," Mrs. Foster says. "Edna, we'll take tea in ten minutes."

While the dining room is designed to impress, with a glittering chandelier and swagged velvet draperies that nearly overwhelm the polished mahogany furniture, Prudence Foster's parlor is a sunny room with white filet net curtains and light bamboo furnishings. It looks like it could be anywhere but Philadelphia. Spiky plants in split reed baskets heighten the sensation that I have wandered onto the set of some tropical film. "It's lovely," I say inadequately.

"I have to keep up appearances in the rest of the house, but this is my nest."

In addition to a desk that would not have looked out of place in a tea planter's office, her nest contains a tea table and two chairs set between the windows, a chaise with a variety of pillows in shades of tan and leaf green, and a large carved Buddha. I admire the statue while we wait for tea. Prudence Foster will not speak until we are equipped with cups.

Once seated, with the smoky scent of lapsang souchong filling the air, she says, "I'm organizing an event for Christmas, and I need every pair of hands I can get."

That doesn't sound specific; I hope I can fade into the background. Mrs. Foster is not as terrifying as I thought, but she *is* exhausting. "What do you have in mind?"

"You know I'm on the board of the Presbyterian Orphans' Home?" Not waiting for a reply, she plows on. "Joe Moore's administration has failed the children of this city, and while I've been able to raise quite a bit to keep the orphanage going—it's difficult to say no to me, you may have noticed—the generosity of my set only goes so far.

"Just because children are without families for whatever reason does not mean they don't deserve Christmas. And I want to organize an enormous Christmas gala for them—not just the Presbyterian Home, but the Home for Friendless Children, and the St. Vincent's Home, as well."

It is a worthy if ambitious plan. "Where do I fit in?"

"I thought of you straight away. When I heard you had adopted that dear little boy, I knew you wouldn't have the same distaste, shall we say, that some of the other ladies have."

"Teddy is my nephew." She needs to know he isn't just some random orphan, yet I want to defend those other children, as well. "My sister's boy."

"He's lovely," Mrs. Foster says. "Although I thought you had a girl with you, too—I saw you on Walnut Street a week or so ago. Lame, is she?"

"Thelma." I smile. "She's also my sister's, though she's only with us because Max is treating her."

"Dear Max," Mrs. Foster says. "He can't see a problem without trying to fix it. Which is a very good thing for me."

"He's been a great help," I agree. "The doctor who first examined Thelma said there was nothing to be done. Either he didn't know, or he didn't care to waste his time treating a poor child."

"That's terrible." Mrs. Foster's face is all concern. "Where was she seen?"

I throw caution to the wind. "Scovill Run. It's a mining town upstate. I grew up there."

"Well, we all have to come from somewhere." She refills our cups, spooning sugar into mine without asking. "It's where we end up that matters. And you have ended up in proximity to me, which means I shall find ways to make use of you. May I call you Claire? If we're to work together, all this formality will only get in the way."

"Certainly." I wonder if I have the nerve to call this force of nature by her first name.

"You must call me Prue—that's what all my friends call me." She reaches for a small notebook and pencil. "Now, let's get down to business."

Her driver drops me off after five, and I encounter Harry in the hall, surrendering his hat and case to Katie. "Where have you been?" He kisses me in greeting. "You look a bit...dazed."

"I was caught in a hurricane named Prudence." I smile faintly. "You're looking at one of the organizers of the Orphans Christmas Gala of 1932."

He bursts into laughter and hugs me to him. "My poor darling. What does that entail?"

I snuggle against him for a moment, breathing in the comforting scent of bay rum. "I'm still not quite sure."

Pearl

June 18, 1932

Today Mr. Nolan came out of the outhouse while I was working in the garden. He tried to pat my bottom and when I pulled away he got mad and said I should be grateful that a man wanted to touch me, a girl with a face like a bucket. If I'm as ugly as all that, why does he keep after me?

Ava

Claire has written again, three chatty pages, enclosing a drawing and a painstakingly printed note from Thelma, and a lengthy report from Max. I read the letter out after supper when we are waiting for a radio program to start. "It sounds like everyone's doing well." Thelma's picture makes my chest hurt. "Doesn't it?"

"Mmm." George is playing on the floor and doesn't look up. Toby is on the davenport, swinging his legs, rhythmically kicking his younger brother.

"Stop it." Pearl gets between them. "What does the doctor say?"

I read Max's words over again. "That he's fitted her for braces to straighten her bones, and she's doing exercises to make her muscles stronger. Max will re-fit the braces in a few months, once he starts to see progress."

"Do they hurt?" Pearl's eyes are full of concern. She has been quiet all day—missing her sister, no doubt.

"Max says no," I tell her. "They're heavy, but not painful. Just uncomfortable sometimes."

"Who's Max?" Toby fiddles with the dial, getting the program to come in more clearly.

"Thelma's doctor." I shouldn't have used his first name. "Dr. Byrne."

"Why do you call him Max?"

I shrug, putting the envelope to one side. "Because I met him as a friend of your aunt's before I knew he was a doctor. Thelma calls him Dr. Max."

Jack Benny's voice fills the room. I close my ears, imagining what Thelma and Teddy are doing. It's after six; supper will be over. If it's a nice night, Claire might take them to the park. I remember the ice cream parlor and wonder if Thelma has tried any more flavors.

Daniel pushes himself up and opens the front door. I follow him outside and watch as he lights a cigarette. "What is it?"

"Nothing." He exhales, and the smoke lingers in the still air. "They can do so much for her that we can't."

At least his hostility has faded. I sit on the step and pat the space beside me. When he sits, I lean against his shoulder. "They're good people, Dan."

He nods. "It's just hard."

I didn't read the postscript of Claire's letter aloud. "There's another thing," I say. "Harry's offered you a job if you want it."

The expression on Daniel's face, when he turns toward me, is a mix of hope and fear. "Move to the city, you mean? Work for him there?"

"Well, yes."

"We can't afford to move." His fingers tighten on the cigarette, and he stubs it out on the step and drops it into his shirt pocket for later.

I put my hand on his knee. "You could go on your own first," I suggest. "Since the rent's paid up here, Pearl and I could organize things and follow with the rest of the kids once you're settled."

He shakes his head. "Not without Dandy."

"If we moved, he'd come along."

"I'm not so sure."

I kiss his jaw and direct my words toward his ear. "You leave Dandy to me."

"I don't know." Daniel stretches and cracks his knuckles. "I've been thinking about going to Washington. There's talk of our war bonus being paid early. That could save us."

Five years after the war ended, Congress had promised the soldiers a bonus for their service, but it wasn't due to be paid until 1945. In these times, with so many men out of work, asking for what is owed doesn't seem unreasonable. What I don't understand is my husband wanting to go to Washington. After he got back from France, he swore he would never leave Scovill Run again—that was another reason why I'd been hesitant to mention Harry's offer.

"If they pay it." I'm not counting chickens before the eggs are laid, much less hatched.

"They promised." He shifts on the step. "There are men— veterans like me—going to petition the government."

His sense of justice is strong; it's what got him involved with the union years ago, an unfortunate move that dogs us to this day. The government has the money, I am sure of that; maybe they will agree to pay up and he will come home feeling less helpless and angry. "Why don't you wait a bit, see what's happening?"

"Maybe." He bumps his shoulder against mine and stares out into the warm evening. "Maybe."

Pearl

June 25, 1932

Jacky Polikoff asked if he could walk me home when I left Mrs. Z's this afternoon. I said I couldn't stop him, but I ran inside as soon as we got home. He's nice, but I'm not going to be like Mama, liking boys at my age. And right now, I can't even think about them, because of what's happening with Mr. Nolan.

He came out of his room as I was coming up the stairs. He said he saw me flirting with Jack, and called me a name I don't even want to write. Then he pushed me up against the wall. Mama was in the kitchen, talking to Toby, I could hear them, but I couldn't scream. He got his hand up my skirt and into my drawers before I could get loose.

I threw up in the chamber pot and had to sneak downstairs to empty it without anybody seeing. He was gone by then.

Claire

"Katie is going to have to go if she can't control the children." Irene is ensconced in her high-backed chair with her feet up on the ottoman. "I could hear them all through the house today."

"Katie has duties beyond the children." I wish Harry wouldn't leave me to make conversation with his mother. "They can't have been that loud."

Irene snorts. "Mrs. Jennings, Mrs. Battle, and Miss Caldwell were over for cards, and they were shrieking and the girl's braces were thumping up and down."

Thelma's braces did thump, but the nursery is nowhere near Irene's rooms. "If you had a card party, then Katie was either in the kitchen or with you. They're children, they have to play."

"You're just making excuses," she says sharply. "It's obvious your sister never disciplined them."

The newspaper crackles, but Harry remains hidden. I take a deep breath. "My sister is a good mother, but *they are children*. They make noise when they play. I'm sorry if it bothers you. Perhaps you should play cards at Mrs. Battle's until they're old enough to be in school." I take a large sip of sherry, wondering where my bravery has come from.

She reaches for her cane. "I may have been mistaken about your sister," she says. "Perhaps it's *your* influence." She puts her hand on the back of Harry's chair. "I'll say goodnight now."

Harry folds the paper and stands, kissing his mother's cheek. "Good night, Mother. Sleep well."

Her footsteps retreat up the stairs. I stare at the glass in my hand; it is trembling. *I* am trembling. "You could speak up sometimes when she's like that."

He looks baffled. "She's always like that. What would be the point?"

"The point," I say, taking another gulp of sherry, "is that she treats me like an unwelcome houseguest, even after all these years. I thought she would be nicer, once we adopted Teddy, but apparently, he's not good enough either."

"Darling—"

"I mean it!" I am on the verge of tears. If I make Harry angry, then so be it. "I will not allow your mother to treat them the way she's treated me. I'd rather send them back to Ava than have them feel unwanted."

The bed springs creak under Harry's weight. "Are you awake?"

"Yes." The clock's faint green glow shows it is ten past midnight. I tried to sleep, but I've done nothing but go over what I said to Irene and then to Harry, still unbelieving. Have I finally reached a breaking point? It doesn't matter; either way, tomorrow will be impossible.

Harry is very still. "I'm sorry," he says at last. "I've tuned out her bitterness for so long, I never thought about its effect on you." His hand reaches under the sheet, and I cling to it. "I'll talk to her. I won't have her upsetting the children—or you—any longer."

"I should have said something sooner, instead of blowing up like a geyser." His fingers curl between mine, and I scoot over in the narrow bed to make room for him.

"Perhaps," he says, and there is laughter in his voice. "But I should have spoken to her myself, long ago."

I turn onto my side and Harry puts one arm over me. I relax into the curve of his body. Suddenly sleep no longer seems impossible.

In the morning, I take my breakfast in the nursery, allowing Harry time alone with Irene. He pops in before leaving for work. "The dragon has been bearded in her den," he says. "Care should be taken with your approach, but I've put out the fire."

I can't imagine what it took to confront his mother, and I am grateful. "I will tread lightly," I promise.

"Uncle!" Thelma calls, and Harry drops everything to pick her up and spin her around. The weight of her braces makes her swing wider, and he steps back before they crack him in the shins.

"I do believe you're growing." He kneels in front of Teddy, who is crawling determinedly through a block castle Thelma has built on the carpet. "And you, Master Ted, are a destroyer of worlds." Teddy crashes through another tower of wooden blocks before stopping to smile up at him.

"Da." He grabs a block and offers it.

Through the haze of my tears, I see Harry's face. "That's right, Ted," I say, "that's your Daddy."

Harry's eyes glisten behind his glasses. "I wish I didn't have a meeting this morning," he says. "I'd like to spend the day building castles with these two."

"Tonight?" Thelma begins to rebuild the tower her brother just toppled. "Can we build a castle before dinner?"

"That sounds like a fine idea," he agrees. "I'll try to come home early, let's see how much we get done before Katie rings the dinner bell."

I do not venture downstairs until after ten, hoping to avoid Irene, but I am not that lucky. She is on the telephone and stops speaking when I approach. I pass her with a nod and go down to the kitchen.

Mrs. Fell is stirring a large pot on the stove. "What can I do for you, Mrs. Warriner?"

"Nothing right now," I say, "but Mrs. Foster and Mrs. Good are coming for luncheon on Thursday. I wanted to give you more notice because of the holiday. Fish for the main, I think. The rest I'll leave to you."

"Yes, Mrs. Warriner. The fishmonger calls on Tuesday. I'll find something nice for you."

Irene is waiting in the hall. "I was just speaking to Mrs. Ramsay."

"How is Aunt Honora?" Harry's aunt is down-to-earth and has a sense of fun that is absent in her sister.

"Very well, but sorely in need of company since her husband's death. I've agreed to spend the rest of the summer with her." Irene smiles triumphantly, and I know I am supposed to be upset that she is being driven from the house because of my tantrums. Somehow I'm not bothered at all.

"How lovely for both of you," I say. "Do you need Katie to help you pack?"

"Evans will manage. We'll be at Mrs. Ramsay's home in Cape May until September. If I extend my stay, I'll send for my fall wardrobe."

Tap dancing on the marble floor would be inappropriate and would undo much of Harry's good work. "When are you leaving?" I will happily reschedule my luncheon to get her out of the house.

"My plans aren't finalized," she says. "Evans will need time to pack. I'm going to pay a few quick calls this afternoon." She looks up as Katie comes in, having finished sweeping the front steps. "Katie, tell Mrs. Fell I will take my dinner on a tray this evening."

"Yes, ma'am." She ducks her head and sidles past.

"I still don't like that girl," she says. "Sneaky."

"She's an absolute jewel." Katie is my ally in this house, even more so than Harry. The other servants are all Irene's creatures. "And the children love her."

"Well, I won't have her helping Evans with my things. Who knows what would be missing when they were unpacked?"

It is pointless to argue with her. "I'm going to take Thelma to see Dr. Byrne now." I slip on my cloche. "We'll be back by noon. Are you lunching in or out?"

"Out, I think." She pats her hair before the mirror and draws on her gloves. "You needn't wait for me."

Good. That means I can treat Thelma to lunch in the dining room, with flowers and linen napkins and the best dishes. After being poked and prodded and having her braces adjusted, she'll deserve that, and more.

Pearl

July 1, 1932

I wish someone would notice what he's doing. But they're too tired, or too busy talking about Daddy going to Washington. Maybe I'm making something out of nothing, like he says. Maybe a girl like me should be flattered by the attention, but I still want to throw up whenever he looks at me. And I'm scared of what will happen if Daddy goes away because Mama can't protect me.

29

Ava

The fireworks at the end of the company picnic are the highlight for the children, but if I am honest, my favorite part is eating a meal I do not have to cook myself.

There was fried chicken, corn on the cob, and enough lemonade to sate even my bottomless children. They should be full enough that they don't have the strength to run around, however, Pearl is the only one in sight, sitting one blanket over, talking to a school friend. Toby and George are racing around the picnic grounds like wild Indians. Possibly pretending to *be* wild Indians. They will return when they want more food.

I lie back on the picnic blanket, my head in Daniel's lap, and watch the fireworks sizzle and scream above our heads.

"Happy?" Daniel's arm rests across my stomach.

"Yes." For the moment, it is true. Sometimes I just have to let my mind rest and enjoy the moment. Tomorrow my husband will still be out of work, my kids will be hungry again, and our home will still be at risk, but today is a holiday, and I will celebrate by giving myself a day's respite from worry.

"Thelma loves fireworks."

"I'm sure they have them in Philadelphia."

"I know." A rocket explodes overhead into an enormous red chrysanthemum. "I miss her, that's all."

"So do I." I reach for his hand. "I just keep reminding myself she'll be better when she comes home."

"There was nothing wrong with her, to begin with," Daniel says stubbornly. "One of us is always there to help her."

The fireworks mount to a crescendo, fountains of color painting the sky over the ball field. It sounds like a battle, but it's so beautiful. I close my eyes. Why can't he see that she doesn't want help?

"What if they're just getting her hopes up?"

"They're not," I say. "Max told her there was a chance it wouldn't help, and she said so long as she didn't get any worse, she wanted to try."

There is an emptiness where my little girl belongs and I can't wait for it to be filled again. She is so brave. At her age, I'm not certain I would have had the courage to stay away from my family for months on end, no matter what the promised outcome.

Daniel's words are almost lost in the final explosions. "Well, if *Max* says so."

I sit up, rub his arm briskly to cover my annoyance; I must remember to call him Dr. Byrne. "I'll write to Claire tomorrow. Maybe they can visit before the end of summer."

It is dark now, and my ears ring with the sudden silence. Pearl gets to her feet, yanking her skirt down toward her knees. "Should I look for the boys, Mama? It'll be time to go soon."

"Round them up if you can." She probably heard the whole conversation.

He waits until she leaves to say, "Don't ask them. I don't want to see Thelma like that."

Claire

"Wake up, ma'am. Please, wake up." Katie is hovering by my pillow.

"What is it?" When Harry got up at six-thirty, I felt the start of a headache and decided to stay in bed a little longer.

"It's the other Mrs. Warriner, ma'am. She's gone."

Damn it! I should have gotten up, just to see her off and out of my hair for the rest of the summer. It's a snub she won't likely forget. "Well, it can't be helped now," I say, settling back against the pillows. "I'll have breakfast here in half an hour, and then I'll get dressed. The ladies are coming for lunch today."

Katie bit her lip. "It's not just her that's gone, ma'am."

"Of course not." I close my eyes and wait for her to leave. "She took Evans."

"It's not just Evans, either. She took everyone."

"Everyone?"

"Mrs. Fell and Baxter."

241

"What?" I scramble out of bed and Katie hands me my peignoir. "He would have just driven her to the station."

She shakes her head. "He said to tell Mr. Warriner the Packard would be in the parking lot, at the east end."

"But…Mrs. Foster is coming for luncheon today. They can't be gone." Blood rushes from my head. Irene is punishing me for the children, for being obstinate about Katie, as if I am myself a child in need of correction.

Katie opens a drawer and hands me fresh underthings and a slip, and I go to my dressing room to change. "The blue and white one, Katie, if you don't mind." I take the dress and emerge moments later, doing up its tiny white buttons. "I'm sorry, I shouldn't be asking you to help. You're not my maid."

"I don't mind, ma'am. I'll do what I can—I just don't think I can manage this whole place on my own."

Ava couldn't manage this place on her own, and I have the utmost faith in my sister's managerial skills. "Of course you can't. It's not meant to be cared for by one person." I take a deep breath. One thing at a time. "My luncheon today—I can't put it off, so we'll have to cope with that."

Katie gives me a crooked smile. "I can cook, ma'am—my mama taught me—but I can't cook fancy, like Mrs. Fell."

"I don't need fancy, I never did." I take her arm. "Let's see if they left anything in the kitchen before they abandoned ship." Pushing open the door, I survey the well-lit, rear-facing room with gratitude. "At least she did the dishes."

"I did them." Katie gestures to the few plates drying on a rack near the sink. "They left everything as it was."

Anger surges. How dare Irene crook her finger and make the servants abandon us? "Do they realize Harry pays their salaries?"

Katie giggles. "They will." She opens the refrigerator. "They left the food, anyway."

"Small mercies." The cool air lowers my temperature, if not my temper. There is a paper-wrapped package from the fishmonger on the top shelf; that is my lunch for Prue and the others. I rummage and find fresh green beans which can be steamed while the fish cooks. "I can manage trout and string beans," I say. "I was a decent cook, once upon a time."

"You can't do your own cooking." Katie looks scandalized. "What will people think?"

Worrying what people think has been my main occupation until now. "I don't have time for that," I tell her. "I'm going to start on lunch, you're going to get the dining room and my sitting room tidied up, and then I'll write an advertisement for a new cook and house man and you can post it for me."

Katie vanishes upstairs with polish and rags, while I lean against the big wooden table and gather my wits. I can cook lunch, but what about dinner? And what about next week, when Harry has his business associates over? How long will it take to find a capable cook? I can't prepare dinner and play hostess—another position Irene left open, expecting me to fail.

Knives are missing from the rack, and there are two conspicuously open spots on the wall where the pots are hung, but otherwise the kitchen is untouched. I've never liked Mrs. Fell, and good riddance to her, but I thought Baxter at least was loyal to Harry.

Thelma is set to watch over Teddy, and I have finished topping the beans and am looking for the ingredients to make a sauce when Katie returns. "Ma'am, I think I know where you can get a new cook."

I spin around. "Where?"

"My parents got let go last year. They're staying with my brother." Katie looks at the floor. "My daddy, he works some, but it's not steady, and my mama hasn't found a new place."

"She's a good cook?" My mind is already made up. "What about your father? Does he drive?"

"Yes, ma'am, she's a fine cook, and my daddy, he drives, he repairs cars. He does a lot with his hands." A blush tints her dark cheeks. "They could even share my room, if it's not too much trouble. My brother needs the space—he's got three boys and his wife's mother living with him already."

"Can you call them?"

"No, ma'am—they live in South Philadelphia, in the colored section. There aren't any telephones there, except in a few stores." Katie's hands knot together under her apron. "I could maybe go get them later."

"Or you could get them now." Turning away from my preparations, I tow her toward the hall. "Why don't we try it for a week?" I ask. "I'll pay them, whether or not they stay on, and they can sleep in Mrs. Fell's room. If they're anything like you, I'm sure they'll be fine."

Katie's eyes widen. "But ma'am, you haven't met them."

"I don't need to. You're their reference."

"You mean she just up and left?" Prue hoots with laughter. "Irene flew the coop?"

I join in her merriment. "Not only that," I admit, "she took the servants with her, all but Katie."

That silences them. Interfering with servants is serious business. "However will you manage?" Stella Good asks. "I wouldn't know where to start."

"Your lunch will be cooked by my own two hands," I tell them. "Fresh trout with a butter and herb sauce, green beans, and for dessert...a pie from Mackie's." I shrug. "I left it too late and ran around to South Street."

Prue gives me a considering glance. "I didn't know you were such a resourceful creature, Claire. Vanquishing a mother-in-law and whipping up lunch, all in one day." She removes her gloves, one finger at a time. "Perhaps I should let you off the hook with the Christmas gala and put you in charge of writing a pamphlet to teach us all to do the same."

"The cooking part or the mother-in-law removal?"

The ladies burst into laughter. "The mother-in-law, definitely," Stella says. "Mine doesn't live with us, but her visits tend to linger."

"Like the smell of fish," Prue says. "I can't believe Irene stole your cook. How does she expect you to survive?"

"For today, at least, Katie cleaned and kept an eye on Teddy and Thelma," I say, "while I started on lunch. She's gone now to get her parents—the mother cooks and the father can drive—and Teddy is down for a nap. Thelma has been bribed with ice cream if she keeps him quiet while we're eating." I am quite proud of my organization. "But I will have to leave you for a few moments because the fish won't cook itself."

"Oh, let us come with you!" Stella drops her gloves on the hall table. "I loved playing in the kitchen when I was little."

Their interest does not extend to helping; I leave them at the table with tiny glasses of white wine and put the trout fillets into a pan with butter. The room immediately fills with their scent, and my guests exclaim as though they have never smelled food before.

Perhaps rich people have come too far from the kitchen if this is how they respond to food that can be cooked over any campfire. I take a smaller pan and put it on to heat, adding butter, a slosh of wine, some chopped shallots, and a squirt from a wedge of lemon, the rest of which can be used later for our tea. I let the mixture reduce and carefully add cream, not letting it get too hot.

I move the fish to one side, off the heat. "Prue, can you hand me those plates?"

Three plates are lined up next to the stove, and I remove the fish, placing a fillet neatly in the center of each. I pour the herbed cream sauce over it and add a pile of green beans alongside. Waving my hand over the plates, I proclaim, "Luncheon is served, ladies. Shall we take it upstairs, or eat down here?"

Ava

Tom Nolan breezes past while I'm working in the front room, wishing me a good morning, and is out the door before I can say more than hello. I can't warm to him, though I like his money well enough.

A few minutes later, after I've shifted from the machine to the window to finish some hand stitching, Pearl comes slowly down the steps. She's been furtive and jumpy lately, very unlike my smiling girl—and I don't think it's just missing Thelma.

"Everything okay, baby?" I wish she would tell me what's on her mind. "Did you finish the beds?"

"Yes, Mama." Her voice is low, and she ducks into the kitchen. I look from her to the door which Tom Nolan just bounded through with his merry smile, and a dark fear enters my heart.

When he returns in the late afternoon, Pearl is safe at her job, and Daniel is at the store, talking about the veterans gathering in Washington. The boys are wherever they go all day.

"Mrs. Kimber." He greets me and spins his cap through the air. It lands neatly on the hook. "Something smells delicious, as always."

"You can take your meal now, if you like," I tell him, "and then pack your things. We need the room back."

"What?" He stops, and his expression undergoes a subtle change. He's wary of me.

"We need the room," I repeat.

"I don't think Dan will be happy that you're throwing me out." He folds his arms. "Have you asked him?"

I'm right. I *know* I'm right.

"I run this house," I tell him. "Daniel let you move in while I was away, but I want to offer the space back to the Metzgers. Mr. Leckner has already found a room elsewhere."

He leans against the door frame. "And where am I supposed to go?"

I meet his gaze without flinching. "I don't care."

"This isn't just about wanting the Germans back in here." His mouth curls. "Little bitch ran to mama, didn't she? Well, I didn't do anything she didn't beg me to do."

My sewing shears are in my lap, under my apron. I want to jam them into his chest for even thinking about my Pearl. I will find out what he *has* done after he's out of the house. "You will leave now, or Daniel will know the reason why. And he won't take it as calmly as I am."

Nolan's face contorts, and there is a long moment when I wonder if he's going to come at me. I steel myself to use the shears—I will kill him rather than let him touch me—but he turns and runs lightly up the stairs. Drawers bang and in a few minutes he is back, a sack thrown over his shoulder.

"I'll go," he says, his eyes glinting. "For now. But you haven't seen the last of me, Ava Kimber."

When the door slams, I fold in my seat, dropping my head into my hands. It's not until he's gone that I realize how scared I have been—and still am, with that parting threat.

I take a deep breath, straighten myself. I won't think about that now. For the moment, his departure is enough, and later I will figure out how to explain it to Daniel. If I tell him the bastard has interfered with Pearl, he might kill him. That would be a fine solution to the problem, but I'm already worried about how we'll manage—a jail sentence would take him from us for much longer than a trip to Washington.

When Daniel comes home and finds the men gone, there's a bit of a scene, but by suppertime, I have convinced him it's for the best. Across the table, I see Pearl's eyes shine, and the tension slip from her shoulders.

Should I ask what he's done, or let her come to me? I don't think it's gone as far as I feared—Pearl couldn't hide a rape—but she will be embarrassed if I ask straight out if he's touched her. I know he has, and now he will not.

Unless he comes back.

His threat keeps me up at night, worrying about a repetition of what happened to Claire. Nolan isn't CIP, but he works for the company and there would be no recourse if something happened— any more than there was recourse for Claire when I found her in the woods behind our back garden, frantically trying to clean the blood from her thighs and tidy her hair before Mama came home.

There's been enough abuse of the women in this family. If Nolan comes back, I will deal with him.

Pearl

July 7, 1932

He's gone. I don't know what happened, but he's gone. So is Mr. Leckner, though I didn't mind him. Mama told me to clean the front room because she's going to ask the Metzgers back. If they won't come, she says, we'll move the big bed in there. She's done with men in the house.

She's acting funny. Probably she's mad about losing the rent money. I went out back to throw out the scrub water from the floor and cried over the basin, I was so relieved.

Claire

I attempt cleaning up before Harry arrives. Katie isn't back and I hope that means she has convinced her parents, and they are on their way. Thelma proves unexpectedly helpful, standing on a crate to do the dishes. Teddy prattles in his high chair while I rummage in the pantry to see what we have in the way of dinner fixings.

I hear the distant closing of the front door. "Stay with Teddy," I say, and throw off my apron.

"How was your day?" I kiss Harry's lips and relax against him for a moment.

"Like any other day." He sighs. "Everyone wants to work, no one wants to pay their bills. What's for dinner?"

"Well," I say, leading him into the living room, "there's breakfast, or we could go out for dinner. Have a drink."

"What are you talking about?"

I hand him a glass. Despite the wine with lunch, I feel the need for an additional cocktail, and the news of Irene's shenanigans will be more palatable washed down with gin. As we drink, I regale him with my day and watch his face as he understands what she has done.

"Does she understand," he asks, downing the last of his martini, "that she's only responsible for Evans's salary? Mrs. Fell and Baxter are paid from the household account—or at least they were."

"She'll realize." I laugh. Gin or spite? I don't care. "And so will they."

"In the meantime, what are we supposed to do?"

I drain my glass. "You did say everyone is looking for a job."

"I did," he agrees. "But not everyone is suitable. You've never interviewed staff, other than Katie—although she was a gift from above."

"I'm hoping the gift keeps on giving." I tell him about her family, and that I've offered them a week's trial, sight unseen. I'm suddenly anxious that I've overstepped. "Katie's mother is a cook, and her father can drive and fix cars. He sounds at least as useful as Baxter."

Harry paces, empty glass in his hand. "What happens when they all return in September?"

"I don't know." I press my lips together, then tell the truth. "I don't care, really."

"Mother has always demanded loyalty from the servants." He kicks at a non-existent wrinkle in the carpet. "That's her issue with Katie."

I resist rolling my eyes. "That, and the fact that she's a Negro."

"I don't like to think that," he says, with a raised eyebrow, "but you're probably right. So she may well come home to a house full of Negro servants."

"She may well." And it will serve her right. "If they're as good as Katie, she can give Mrs. Fell and Baxter a reference, because I won't." Steps drag in the hall, and Thelma appears in the doorway, holding a squirming Teddy.

"I finished the dishes, Aunt Claire," she says, turning toward me. "And I looked, there are eggs and sausages in the icebox. We could make breakfast."

Harry bounces Teddy on his knee, making him squeal. "You two seem to have it all under control," he says. "If you like Katie's parents, I'll abide by your decision."

I have lost the knack for domesticity. The back door opens as I bring the dishes down from the dining room and my first thought is to chuck them out into the alley.

"What's all that, ma'am?" Katie rushes to take them from me.

"We had sausage and eggs for dinner," I say. "I might remember how to cook, but I'm rubbish at more than one meal a day."

"I'll take it from here." She snatches her apron from its hook and drops it over her head. "Ma'am, these are my parents, Esther and Mason Hedges. Mama, Daddy, this is Mrs. Warriner."

Esther Hedges steps forward. She is a small woman, of a lighter complexion than her daughter, with graying hair skinned back into a tight knot. "Pleased to meet you, ma'am." Her smile is very like Katie's. "My daughter has talked so much about you."

I shake her hand. "She must have said something nice, else you wouldn't be here."

Mason Hedges hangs back, and I turn to him. "Mr. Hedges, I want to thank you and your wife for coming on such short notice. Did Katie tell you what happened?"

"Yes, ma'am." His voice is deep and resonant, with a touch of the South. "That your mother-in-law done run off with your help."

"Daddy!"

"That's about the size of it." I offer them seats at the kitchen table. "And I don't expect them back until September. Truthfully, I'm not sure if I want them back, though I don't have any say about Mrs. Warriner."

"You can't choose family," Mrs. Hedges says with a tight-lipped smile, and I remember they have been living with their son and his mother-in-law.

"Katie, why don't you check on the state of Mrs. Fell's room? I can finish up here. Your parents are going to need somewhere to sleep, and your room isn't big enough for three."

"Don't you even want to try out my cooking, ma'am?" Mrs. Hedges ties on my discarded apron and edges toward the sink.

"I'd be happy to," I say. "We breakfast at seven-thirty on weekdays. My husband likes his eggs over easy and the children like them scrambled. I don't care, so long as I don't have to cook them." I gesture at the plates in the white enamel sink. "I grew up cooking, but I never enjoyed it."

"I've cooked since I was your little girl's age," Esther Hedges tells me. "It's not so much a pleasure as a habit. I don't think I'd know what to do if I couldn't." She meets my eyes squarely. "If what Katie says is true, then Mason—Mr. Hedges—and I will stay for the week. After that, you can let us know if you're happy."

Mr. Hedges has found a rag and is wiping the table. Competence rolls off them in calming waves. It is going to be all right. The household will not fall to pieces. Irene can return in September and see that her treachery has made no difference at all.

"I'm already happy," I say. "I'm over the moon."

30

Ava

Hermann's cast-off newspaper becomes a daily bone of contention as Daniel follows the progress of the Bonus Army and I try to throw cold water on the idea of him joining what I consider to be a mad and pointless effort.

"It's a matter of principle," he says, draining his tea. "We're *owed* that money."

I look over his shoulder at the *Times-Tribune*. A grainy photograph shows a sea of tents with the familiar buildings of the nation's capital behind them. The article says thousands of veterans have already gathered.

"They marched on the Capitol?" I put a hand on his shoulder and lean closer. "Isn't that dangerous?"

"Why shouldn't we ask for what we're owed?" He drags his fingers through his hair. "I'm still tempted to join them."

"I thought you wanted nothing to do with the army, ever again?"

He'd gone to war a boy and he'd come back a man, and a changed one. Two inches taller, more taciturn than ever, prone to nightmares and flinching at loud noises. I didn't care. I had my husband back, and my son had his father. Everything else would come in time.

And it had. Father and son learned together to sleep through the night, and once Daniel was back underground, he became himself again. Mining made him who he was. Even I did not complete him the same way.

"It's the principle," he repeats, his jaw set. He looks no older than Toby. "This money could save us."

"Is it worth the risk?" The newspapers make it seem like a grand adventure, but nothing is simple when ordinary people step up and ask for what they deserve. "You went to war without expectation of this bonus."

"So what?"

"What was it President Coolidge said at the time... patriotism isn't patriotism if it's bought-and-paid-for?" I smooth the dish towels and fold them away into a drawer.

"Some garbage like that," he says. "What did he know anyway?"

Men don't get to be president without some knowledge, even if we don't agree with how they apply it. I open my mouth and shut it again. He's in no state to listen to reason.

"Ava, this could set us up for the next few years, even carry us until I can get back in the mine."

"How much would it be?" He isn't going to be deterred, so I might as well start making plans.

"I've been trying to reckon it out," he says, pulling a scrap of paper from his pocket. "There's two different payment levels."

I never understood the idea behind the bonus. What was the point of promising to pay something twenty years on, anyway? The way the world is going, half the veterans will be dead of starvation by then.

"See here?" The paper is covered on both sides with figures. "It's supposed to be a dollar a day before we shipped out, and a dollar and a quarter for each day of overseas service."

I do my own calculations. "But you joined up in June of 1917, and didn't come home for almost two years." His excitement begins to make more sense. "That's over five hundred days right there."

"Exactly." He slams his fist on the table. "If they pay out, it's over seven hundred fifty dollars."

What could we do with that much money? More to the point, what couldn't we do? I would feel as rich as Harry Warriner with seven hundred fifty dollars.

Visions fill my brain: bills marked *paid*, shoes for all the kids. Maybe even one of those wringer washing machines... though that would mean electricity, which doesn't exist anywhere in Scovill Run but the mine officials' houses. Still, if I'm going to fantasize, why not a fully electrified house? And a sewing machine like Claire's. Books for Pearl. Film for Dandy's camera. Dance lessons for a miraculously straight-legged Thelma. I stall at the boys. What would they want?

"What's the first thing you would do?" I ask. "What's the first thing you would do with the money?"

Daniel smiles, the open-hearted boyish smile I see far too rarely these days. "I would buy you a proper diamond ring."

I look down at my hands. They are raw and red, the knuckles swollen. The cheap wedding band he gave me in 1916 is dark, most of the silver worn away. "I don't need a new ring."

"You asked what I would do," he says. "Do you know what I feel like, not being able to give you what you need?"

"I have what I need." I take his hand across the table. "There are things I want, but they aren't necessary. Everything I need, you've given me."

"Don't try to make me feel better." He gets up to pour more tea, ducking the lines of wet clothes that stretch across the kitchen. "You work like a drudge, taking care of me and the kids, keeping this place up. You deserve a life like Claire's."

"I don't want a life like Claire's," I say, appalled. "Sitting on my behind all day, deciding what to wear. Wondering if my hair is blonde enough. Painting my nails." I laugh, but there is an edge to it. "Can you imagine?"

"I can." He sits back down, staring into his cup. "You're as pretty as she is."

What nonsense. I touch his cheek with my fingertips. "I just worry about this Washington idea, that's all. Mama always said the meek would inherit the earth," I remind him.

"She just said that to keep us in line," he says, raising his brows, "or maybe to keep us from getting our hopes up. From where I stand, the meek will get trampled on by the people who already own the earth and everything on it, same as they always have."

I know when I've been bested. "I'd prefer you not go alone." Too many bad things can happen on the road. According to the newspaper, some men have brought their families, but it would be impossible for us to go. "Maybe Frank would go? He was in the war."

"Maybe." He shoves the chair back, more bounce in his step than I've seen in weeks. "I'll hitch over and talk to him today, see what he thinks." He looks down again at his calculations, our discussion at an end. He will go to Washington.

I hope to God he gets what he's owed because I'm not sure how much more disappointment he can stand.

Claire

I arrive home to the miracle of a letter from Ava on the hall table. I follow Thelma's slow progress to the nursery, Teddy high on my shoulder. "Your mama sent a letter," I tell her, and she turns on the stairs, her face brightening.

"Will you read it to me?"

"Of course." Portions of it, anyway. "Let's get Teddy settled and then we'll open it."

Teething is a painful time, and Teddy appears surprised by his own crankiness. I look at his mouth; his gums are red and swollen. "Poor little man," I croon, and he smiles briefly at my tone before whimpering again. "Reach me the Paregoric, Thelma?"

She brings the brown bottle and I smear a few drops onto Teddy's gums. He continues to cry for a few minutes, until the numbing takes effect, and then he relaxes against my chest. I lower him into the cradle, watching as he reaches for his favorite bear. Soon he is dozing, and I retreat to the rocker with Ava's letter, keeping an eye on Thelma as she dresses her new doll—I couldn't bear the thought of her being deprived—and explains that they must play very quietly.

Pushing the chair back and forth with my foot, I absorb my sister's unsatisfactory words. She thanks me for the photographs of Thelma and Teddy, then goes on to relate that Daniel is considering going to Washington with the Bonus Army. She sets down the facts, not telling me how she feels about them, but I'm almost certain she's not in favor of something so risky.

"Pearl has a job," I tell Thelma. "Cleaning at one of the boarding houses." School is done, so it won't interfere with her studies. "And your mama says they missed you at the picnic."

Thelma puts the doll down and comes to sit on my lap. "I miss Mama," she says, a quiver in her voice. "And Daddy."

I wrap my arms around her. "I know." I have suggested to Ava that we bring Thelma for a visit, but there was no mention of that in her letter. "Dr. Max says maybe you could go home in September, though you'd have to come back to get your braces adjusted. Would you like that?"

Her finger retreats to her mouth as she considers. "I can't walk to school in braces," she says at last. "It's too far."

The school is a mile from the house; there is no way she could manage the walk. "I'm sure your mama will find a way."

She shakes her head, curls bouncing. "I'm not going in the wheelbarrow."

Laughing, I draw her closer. "We'll see about you starting school here, then," I say. "And maybe we'll drive up to visit before then, so everyone can see how well you're doing. Would you like that?"

Ava

Dandy's boarding house is only a fifteen-minute walk, but it is on the edge of town, where the company pays even less mind, if that is possible. At this time of year, the unpaved road is baked hard, but in winter and spring, it will be a sea of mud. My hem is covered in clinging dust before I reach the house.

Rebecca Nordstrom is sweeping the porch, a futile task at the best of times. She leans on her broom, glad of the distraction, and I pass the time of day with her before asking for Dandy.

"He's round back with the other boys," she says. "I got some extra sugar, so I put them to work in the garden in exchange for a cake this weekend."

Asking adolescent boys to work for food is a sound plan. I miss Dandy's help in my garden, but I've seen less and less of him since my return from the city. That is about to change. I'm not going home without an agreement from my boy that things will soon be different.

When I come around the side of the house, Dandy and three others are sitting on the back step, smoking. There is a small pile of weeds on the ground between them, evidence they'd started with good intentions. I wait until one boy sees me.

"Dan, it's yer ma."

Dandy carefully stubs out his cigarette and puts the butt into the front pocket of his overalls. "Hey, ma." He lopes over to kiss my cheek. "Everything okay?"

"Sure. I just like to see my son once in a while." I link my arm through his. "Take a walk with me. I won't take you away from your work for too long."

"Sure." He calls over his shoulder, "Do my part, Nat? I'll catch you up next time."

I steer him away from the house, filling him in on his brothers' latest exploits until we are out of Becky Nordstrom's hearing. "We'd like to see more of you."

He ducks his head. "I know. I feel bad."

"Then come home. Pearl and I miss you. The boys are running wild without you to crack down on them."

He scuffs his bare feet in the dust. "Dad has plenty of time for them since he's not doing anything else."

"They need their brother. And I need my son." I hadn't expected him to be so bitter about the fight with his father all those months ago. "Come home."

"No."

I let out a breath. "You're only fourteen."

"I'm working, which is more than *he* can say." His jaw clenches, stubborn as the man he maligns.

"That's not his fault. You cost them less than a man, it's the only reason they keep you on." I squeeze his arm to temper my words. "He didn't mean it. He was upset about that bootleg mine. So was I."

"Well, you didn't call me a thief."

"I mind my tongue better than he does," I tell him. "But it's not safe. You could get hurt."

"We're careful," he says earnestly. "It's not just us now—there are men there, too. They have more experience and better tools. We were just trying to dig coal for our families, but they want to make money at it."

I'm not sure that is an improvement. "Well, we still don't like it, but you're right—you're near grown, and we can't stop you. Come for dinner Sunday night."

Dandy considers the invitation. "If he starts in on me again, Ma—"

"He won't." How I will keep that promise, with Daniel's moods, remains to be seen. "He's been low since I got back from Claire's, worse than before. Now he's got this idea that he wants to go to Washington."

"With the bonus men? I read about them in Missus Nordstrom's paper," Dandy says. "A lot of people are going."

"We can't go, not and keep the house. Would you go with him?" I lean against him. "It would be good for your dad to have company."

"What about Uncle Frank?"

"He hasn't made up his mind yet, but it's not the same as having his son by his side, you know that. Think of the adventures you two could have." I appeal to the boy inside the working man. "Riding the train, camping in Washington."

His eyes light up. "We could hobo down."

"Or you could take the train," I say. "We have a bit of money put aside."

"Save it. I know how to catch a train without being caught. We do it most weekends, hop an early freight and go to the movies in Scranton. One time we went to a baseball game. It was swell."

I visualize my son jumping onto a moving train and my stomach turns over. "Well, dinner with your family isn't that exciting, but we'll expect you nonetheless."

"I'll be there." He kisses my cheek. "And I won't start anything."

Neither will Daniel, I vow. A man needs many things, his son foremost among them. Daniel will have his son if I have to beat them both to accomplish it.

Walking home, I stop at St. Stanislaus and slip into a pew. Prayer is a default, and as I sit with my head bowed, my thoughts begin to clear. What I want is also clear—for Daniel to give up his foolish notion of traveling to Washington—but that is an argument I won't win. Convincing him to allow Dandy to go along will have to do.

And maybe it will all come to something, but I don't expect it to. No one in Washington is looking out for us—that's nothing new, even to my idealistic husband. Pearl and I will continue to sew and clean and take in laundry, and Dandy will continue to work at the bootleg mine. Daniel will be shamed and he will be angry, and that too is nothing new.

It's no different than Harry paying the rent. Daniel might call it blood money, but I don't agree. Those who have means should use them. I think of Max Byrne and his constant attempts to get the wealthy of Philadelphia to do their share, and wonder if Jake is still at the camp near the art museum.

Claire

"You really should learn to drive," Prue says, as we climb into her sporty little roadster. "It's such a feeling of independence."

"I already come and go as I please." I take a moment to admire Prue's mannish charcoal suit, topped with a miniature fedora. Next to her, in a flowered dress and pale straw hat, I feel about as businesslike as a kitten. "Baxter was always able to drive me, and now we have Hedges."

She pulls away from the curb in a screech of rubber against cobblestones. "True, but you're still being *driven*. You're not driving yourself."

What's wrong with being driven? This whole independent woman thing takes a lot of getting used to. I mull over the idea as we cross the South Street bridge over the Schuylkill. On the other side, the houses start out as grand as those in Rittenhouse Square, but as we continue heading southwest, they become smaller and packed more tightly together. Children play ball in the street, while men sit on front stoops or congregate on the corners. There are few women.

"Here we are."

Our destination is a large brick building wrapped by an iron fence. It looks like a school, but with a less welcoming aspect. There must be close to a hundred children in the yard, boys and girls, toddlers to sturdy adolescents. Though there are organized games going on, many of the children are just sitting, hands in their laps, staring through the fence.

We pass through the gate and the unlocked front door. I look back, waiting for one of the children to make eye contact. No one does.

The inside of the building resembles the outside. It is clean enough, with green distemper on the walls and a faint scent of cabbage, but it looks like a safe place, though not necessarily a pleasant one. Certainly not a *home*.

"Mrs. Foster, so good to see you again." A man emerges from a door off the front hall. He is short, middle aged, and his suit has seen better days. He smiles questioningly at me.

"Mr. Carson." Prue offers her hand. "This is Mrs. Warriner. She's helping me organize the Christmas party."

He shakes my hand a little too heartily and leads us into his office, which has clearly been cut from a larger room—the dentil molding around the ceiling is interrupted by a plain wall, and one window edges uncomfortably close to a corner. The desk is covered with folders, and a dented metal ashtray holds down one corner.

"Thank you," he says after we seat ourselves on plain wooden chairs. "We do as much as we can, given our budgetary constraints, but this is the kind of shindig we just can't afford, and that they frankly deserve."

"Why are there so many of them?" This is far from the only orphanage in the city. Are they all this crowded?

"It's this damn Depression," Carson says. "Excuse my language, ladies. We're about twenty percent above our normal numbers, and the city has withdrawn most of our funding in the last year."

"That makes no sense." The window behind his desk overlooks the play yard and its lackluster children. "Why?"

"Why are there more children, or why has the city pulled our funds?" He polishes his glasses with his tie and slides them back on his nose. "I can answer one question, but not the other. The numbers have increased because there are so many desperate families, both in Philadelphia and traveling through."

Prue leans forward. "Has it slowed down at all?"

He shakes his head. "We got four more only yesterday, a brother and sister, an older girl, and an infant."

"Someone surrendered an infant?"

"Someone dropped off an infant," he clarifies. "In a box, on the step. They rang the bell and disappeared before we could answer the door."

"That's terrible." I imagine how desperate and fearful the mother must have been to leave her baby at an orphanage. Then I think of Ava. What had it cost her to give up Teddy?

"It may be," Carson says, "but it's not uncommon. For a family on the road, babies are the ones most likely to suffer."

I am not going to cry in front of this strange man. *I am not.* But more than anything I want to run home, wrap myself around Teddy, and kiss him all over. And then I want to talk to Ava, to find out, honestly, how she is.

"How many of these children will find homes, do you think?"

Carson considers Prue's question, folding his hands under his chin. "Not many," he says. "Which might benefit them, in a way. If times improve, and their parents return, they could be reunited."

Prue nods slowly. "But we all know how likely that is to happen." She crosses her legs, one foot beginning to wag. "These children will be here until they're old enough to work and start lives of their own."

"Just like their parents." The children outside are, but for the grace of God, Ava's children. "What can be done for them?"

"Right now, we just want to give them Christmas, to remind them they're children and there's still some magic in the world." Prue folds her hands in her smooth serge lap. "Once we've achieved that, we'll have to discuss it."

It isn't enough. This is a huge problem, and smarter people than me haven't found a solution. But nothing can be accomplished without starting somewhere. I remember vividly how certain childhood memories stand out, even when surrounded by hardship or sadness.

I will find some way to improve their lives, but first I will make sure that Christmas, 1932 is something they will remember forever. "Prue, who do you know at City Hall who can put pressure on the mayor to reinstate their funding?" Planning a party is all well and good, but they need to keep the lights on and the kitchen running.

"Albert and I have some small influence." She looks at Carson. "I'll make a few calls, see if we can at least get the council to take it up again."

He exhales. "That would be most appreciated. I can't say I understand his attitude. For someone who proclaims his Christian values so loudly, it seems most un-Christian to pretend that orphans don't exist."

Carson hands us off to a young woman named Abigail, who gives us a tour of the place: the kitchen, the dining hall, the dormitory-style bedrooms—three for boys, three for girls—and a rudimentary washroom.

"This is the nursery." Abigail gestures at a closed door. "We've got seven babies at present, though the number changes often."

"Do they die?" I want to see the nursery and flee the building, in equal measure.

"No." She smiles. "People always want babies. And they'll grow up not knowing, so perhaps it's for the best. The older children will remember they had another family, once."

I close my eyes. Will Teddy remember that he had another family? He has only the one, really, but with two mothers and two fathers. It will be confusing for him, later. As much as I consider him my child, I can never forget that Ava is his mother. We will tell him the truth, as soon as he's old enough to understand. Harry and I have discussed it, but we haven't come to a decision as to when or how.

"The poor little things." Prue looks from me to the closed door. "If you don't mind, I don't think I'm up for a room full of tinies."

A wave of relief washes over me. I'm trembling at the thought of seeing seven unwanted infants. "Maybe next time."

Carson rejoins us in the downstairs hall. As he ushers us toward the exit, the door swings open and Max Byrne dashes in, his bag under his arm.

"Carson," he says, pushing the hair out of his eyes, "sorry I'm late again. I had a patient who—" He notices us and stops short. "Sometimes it pays to be less than punctual if the reward is such a lovely sight. Prue, how are you? How is Albert?"

"He's just fine." She kisses him on both cheeks, and I wonder why upper-crust Philadelphians insist on behaving as if they're French. "What a rascal you are. Everywhere I go, I run into you."

"Dr. Byrne volunteers his services." Carson pulls his watch from his vest pocket. "Not a lot for you today, Max. A few new ones, but they look to be in fine fettle, just a bit underweight."

"Good." Max turns and kisses my cheek, once, and properly. "How is Teddy? I've been meaning to call in."

"Teething," I tell him. "But growing like a weed all the same. Come to dinner—come home with Thelma after her treatment, we'd love to see more of you."

"I'll do that," he says. "How's your sister?"

"I had a letter, but she didn't say anything." I raise a shoulder. "It's infuriating."

Max smiles broadly. "That seems a most appropriate word. Next time you write, please send her my best." He puts a hand on Carson's shoulder. "Lead on, *mon general*. Take me to your new recruits."

The car is stuffy from sitting in the sun, and we roll down the windows. "I don't know how Max gets by," Prue says. "These places pay for his medical supplies, but he donates his time."

I wonder if he is still stopping by the camp near the museum. Ava described the condition of the men and the way Max and his friend just charged in, speaking to everyone and treating injuries, sores, and illnesses that were not part of their regular medical practices.

Like the children at the orphanage, the men are there because of the damn Depression—to use Carson's words. Why are most soup kitchens run by churches and charities, with little to no contribution from our local government, when we are one of the largest cities in the country? It feels like the poor are being punished for being poor.

How many of these questions would I be asking if I'd had a different upbringing or a different sister? Every time I see a ramshackle truck crammed with children, furniture—sometimes even animals—I think of Ava.

31

Ava

It is warm to have the stove lit for so long, but this dinner has to be perfect. As perfect as we can manage, anyway. We sacrificed one of our oldest hens to the pot, and she has been joined by an onion, a handful of carrots, and a few stalks of celery from the garden. Because boys are boys, and bottomless, there is also a pot of potatoes on the back burner.

"Killing the fatted calf?" Daniel removes the lid and the rich smell of stewed chicken fills the air.

"I would, if we had a calf," I tell him. "Olivia will have to do. She went broody all the time anyway."

"So we're having chicken Olivia for dinner. What else?"

"Dumplings," I say stolidly, not rising to his bait. Daniel is nervous about seeing Dandy, but he won't say so; that would be too straightforward. "And unless you want to help make them, you'll get out from under my feet."

"Yes, ma'am." He pats my bottom before skinning past, and the door bangs behind him.

I shake my head. Men are just large children sometimes.

The flour bin is nearly empty. I dump the remainder into a chipped yellow bowl, add salt, baking powder, and a bit of fat. Dumplings were Tata's favorite, and I can make them in my sleep. A small jug of milk stands close by, and I pour a bit into the bowl.

"Can I help, Mama?" Pearl comes in with the laundry basket balanced on her hip. "Mm, Olivia smells good."

"Better than she did in life, that's for sure." I finish the dough and turn it out on the board. "I'm good here. When you put that away, maybe give the front room a quick sweep?"

"Dandy's not company." Pearl swings past the table but grabs the broom on the way out.

He isn't. He's my son, and if I have my way, he'll be living in this house again by nightfall.

By the time he arrives at the back door, I have dismantled Olivia onto a platter and am waiting for the dumplings to finish cooking in the rich brown broth.

"Hi, Ma." He knocks the dirt off his shoes before coming in.

I raise my wooden spoon. "Is that the best you've got, kid?"

He hugs me tightly, dipping me until I lose my balance. "Better?"

Upright again, I whack him with the spoon. "From one extreme to another." The dumplings are floating. I scrape the chicken back in, covering it to keep warm. "You can call the others."

He hesitates at the door. "Is it okay?"

"We've talked about it," I tell him. "If he says anything, hold your tongue and I'll head him off." I touch his shoulder. "He's nervous, too."

His cheeks redden. "It's stupid, being scared to see your own father."

"No, it's not." I move past him. "You set the table, then. I'll call everyone."

Nothing remains of Olivia but bones and dirty dishes, which can wait until morning for once. We shift to the front room, and Daniel switches on the radio.

"Mrs. Nordstrom's got nothing on you, Ma," Dandy says. "That was good."

"Your mother can make a meal out of nothing. She's a wizard."

"Witch, if you're being accurate." I lean against Daniel's shoulder. "And this kitchen witch is going to need more flour. I used the last of it for the dumplings."

He puts his arm around me. "I'll get it tomorrow."

"I can pick it up," Dandy offers. "On my way home."

I am filled with love for my son. "You do that."

The little boys go out back until the light fades, and Pearl and I enjoy the music while Daniel and Dandy smoke on the porch. Through the open window, we hear them discussing the situation in Washington.

"Do you think they'll go?"

"I don't know," I say. "But if they do, at least they'll be together." The program switches to a commercial, and I turn the volume down, but their voices are too quiet now for me to make them out.

"It feels funny, not having anything to do." Pearl is as bad as me, always needing something in her hands. But there are no sewing jobs, the mending is done, and neither of us can bear the idea of knitting in this heat. "Are you sure I can't do the dishes?"

"You can read," I suggest. "I'd rather listen to you than the radio."

We are almost done with *Little Women*. I know the boys don't care how the story turns out, so I hand the book to Pearl and stretch out on the davenport with my feet propped on the arm. Leisure is a strange feeling.

Claire

Thelma has undergone another round of x-rays, something which always earns her a dish of ice cream and thus makes her happy. I have asked her to look at movie magazines in the waiting room while I have a word with Max, but when I sit across from him, I am unsure where to start.

"What is it?" he asks. "Thelma looks to be improving, but I'll know more in a day or so when I review her films."

My fingernails dig into my palms. "This is by way of a consultation," I say, trying to maintain an even expression. "For myself."

His eyes widen, just for a moment, and then he sinks back into his usual loose-limbed pose. "What is it?"

The office is clean but bleak. It bothers me that Max spends so much time here and then goes to worse places, like orphanages and homeless encampments, in his free time. What does he do for pleasure? We must have him over soon. That would be sufficient reward for surviving my first foray as Harry's official hostess and spending an evening with three stuffy businessmen and their cardboard wives, and Max needs to be distracted from all those depressing better angels he spends time with.

"You know I had an operation a few months ago?"

He nods. "Harry mentioned it, but nothing specific."

"They called it a tubal ligation." I close my eyes, seeing in my head a black-and-white movie cartoon with tubes waving wildly, then being tied together. "So I can't become pregnant again."

"A salpingectomy." Max looks intrigued. "How was your recovery?"

His professional interest makes it easier to respond. "Almost painless, especially when compared to the miscarriages I've had."

"Of course." He switches instantly from professional to personal. Picking up a pen, he passes it absently between his fingers, like a magician doing a coin trick. "How can I help?"

"I want to know…" I bite my lip, then tell him the truth. "I was raped when I was fifteen. Do you think that's why I lost so many babies?"

Max's eyes fill with quick, shocked tears. "Gynecology is not my area of expertise," he says gently. "Did you ask Lyle?"

I shake my head. "He would have told Harry."

"What you tell your physician is confidential." He's too kind to ask why I haven't told Harry.

"They always tell the husbands. They're the ones paying the bills." Max is naive where women's lives are concerned. "And I never told Harry because it was in the past, and I want to leave it behind. But I can't, until I know…"

"I *can't* tell you," he said slowly, staring down at his hands, the wandering pen still. "Not with any certainty. Every human body is different. I assume you had no medical care at the time?"

"Only Ava."

He brings his lips together before he says anything about my sister. "It could be. That's all I can tell you, Claire. There could have been an internal injury that's prevented you from carrying a pregnancy to term." His fists clench, whether in anger on my behalf or, more likely, at the injustices of the world in general.

"So I'll never know." It doesn't matter; now that pregnancy is no longer an issue, I feel a spreading calm in the place where the frantic knot of worry existed. But it would have been good to have an answer, once and for all.

"I'm sorry." He picks up the pen again, but it slips through his fingers. "Does it matter, now that you have Teddy?"

"Not in the way it did," I say, closing my eyes. "I would have liked to know if my body was to blame, or…him."

"He was to blame," Max says harshly. "Even if what he did had nothing to do with your inability to carry a child. You've carried *him* in your head all these years, it must have been like having a tumor."

That's it, exactly. I stare at Max and wonder how this scatty man with his millions of projects can diagnose my problem with such precision. I've carried the CIP officer in my body for fifteen years, like a filthy, toxic growth, and when the doctors opened my body, they cut him out. All I have left is the recovery.

I can do this.

I lean across the desk and take one of Max's strong, square hands. "Thank you. Now tell me you'll come to dinner tonight."

Pearl

July 18, 1932

Dandy is home! I don't know how Mama did it, but she did. She asked me which of the hens was laying worst, because we needed a chicken for Sunday dinner. Olivia was my favorite, but she was broody, second time this year, and I caught her eating one of Mabel's eggs, so she had to go.

So we had Olivia and dumplings and Dandy and Daddy sat across from each other, both of them twitchy as cats in a room full of rockers. But nobody said anything stupid, and by the end, they were making plans to go to Washington and Mama was nearly crying from relief.

If Thelma was here, it would be perfect.

Ava

"It's not a pleasure trip." Daniel pushes the suitcase back across the bed toward me, rumpling the sheet.

"Maybe not," I say, automatically checking to make sure the case hasn't caught on the center seam, which already needs mending. "But you have to take something with you."

"Not much, not the way we're going."

I puff out a breath. The bedroom is sticky, and I haven't been sleeping well. "I still don't like it." I shove the suitcase back under the bed. "There's money for tickets. Frank's taking the train."

"That's Frank," Daniel says. "Dandy and I, we'll hobo down."

When I suggested this expedition to bring father and son together, I hadn't counted on Daniel taking to Dandy's suggestion with such enthusiasm. The idea of them sneaking onto a train, or jumping off one, is enough to give me nightmares—and has, for the last several nights.

But they are excited, and I can't ruin it by showing my worry. "Fine," I say. "Have your adventure. Try not to get arrested."

"We can run pretty fast." He grins like a boy and swings me around. His hands are firm around my waist, and I wish that time would stop for a while so we could have a proper parting. "We're not going to need you to wire bail money."

He folds his clothes, almost neatly, into a canvas pack. It doesn't seem enough for such a trek, but he has nothing else besides his suit and his heavy coat, both of which have been brushed and packed away for the warmer months.

Downstairs, I have sandwiches, apples, and a thermos of tea to start them on the journey. I will slip some money to Dandy for future food purchases. They might be riding the trains illegally, but I won't have them begging door-to-door like real hobos.

"Can we at least come and see you off?"

"And where would you like to do that?" Daniel's exasperation shows. "Are you going to come to the bend and wave to us as we jump on board? That'll be a good way to make sure no one notices."

"Fine," I say again, not feeling fine at all. "I'll stay here with the kids. Today, *and* while you two are off seeing the world."

He rummages in a drawer, coming up with his winter socks and shoving them into the bag. "They're too hot, but we'll be walking a lot, and they're more comfortable with my old boots."

They were recently darned; I doubled the toes and heels because he is so hard on them. "I wish I had time to knit you an extra pair."

Daniel gives me a crooked smile. "It's mostly men. I don't think anyone will care if my feet smell."

His socks come off stiff enough to walk to the washtub. "It'll just be one large cloud of man-stink over Washington."

I look through the pack while he watches me, sighing theatrically: pants, both his shirts, clean underwear. No spare shoes because there are none. Hopefully, the cardboard liners in his boots will hold.

"I put a few stamps in with the food. Let me know you get there."

"Dandy will do it," he says. "You know how much I like to write."

Even as a new bridegroom away at war, his letters were painfully short and infrequent. "Make sure he does, then." I wrap my arms around him and press my face to his shoulder. "Be careful, both of you. Don't do anything stupid."

"Woman," he says, "that is an ass-backward way of saying you'll miss me. Can't you just say it straight out?"

"I'll miss you." I tilt my face up to his. "Is that good enough? I'll miss you every day, and I'll miss you even more at night."

"I'll see you in your dreams, then." His arms come around me tightly and he kisses me in a way that will keep me up thinking about it. "This will be good, Ava, I promise. This many people, the government can't see us and not recognize what we've done. They can't *not* give us our pensions."

I hope he's right, but I don't have his faith in government. Or in most things, for that matter.

"When I come home with the bonus, we'll be able to set things to rights. Pay Harry back, first of all. Maybe move to Philadelphia, who knows? Maybe working with Harry—for Harry—wouldn't be so bad."

"We'll see." It's not the right time for that discussion. "We'll talk about it when you get home."

Dandy's voice echoes up the narrow stairs. "Dad, we need to get moving. We have to be in place before the train leaves the station."

He slings the pack over his shoulder and jams his hat on, clattering down the steps as if he and Dandy are the same age. I give the food parcel to Dandy, who carries a pack similar to his father's, and explain about the stamps. I also slip him two dollars while Daniel is calling for Pearl. "You watch out for each other."

"We will, Ma." His cap is pushed to the back of his head and his black curls, freshly dipped in the creek, spring ebullient from their confinement. He needs a haircut, but he looks so much like Daniel that I don't have the heart to tell him.

"Be careful," I say again. Toby and George said their goodbyes at breakfast and disappeared into the woods, but Pearl joins us from the kitchen.

"Goodbye, Princess Pearl." Daniel catches her up and she flings her arms around his neck. "Keep the boys in line."

"Yes, Daddy." She swipes at her eyes. "Have a safe trip."

I let Daniel pull me into another embrace, although part of me is already working out how things will run with the two of them gone. There will be less cooking and less laundry; if I can find any sewing, I can make back that two dollars before they even reach Washington.

As my menfolk disappear down the road, Mama's words, the benediction she said every morning over Tata and the boys, come unbidden to my lips. "Keep them safe and bring them home."

"What's that, Mama?" Pearl blots her tears with a corner of her apron.

"Nothing," I say. "Just a silly superstition."

32

Pearl

July 24, 1932

Dandy sent us a card on July 22, and we got it today. They got there ok on the boxcars, and now they're camping in a place called Anacostia Flats. He must have copied that off a sign, he could never spell Anacostia on his own. He says Daddy met a man he knew in France, so I guess he's enjoying himself. They're going to the Capitol soon for the vote.

Ava

When I come out of the store, maneuvering the heavy basket around the screen door, Nolan is on the porch. For a moment, it is almost a relief: I've spent days waiting for him to appear. Then fear reasserts itself.

"Afternoon, Mrs. Kimber. No one around to help you today?" He looks like a fox watching a rabbit.

My heart is in my throat, but I speak calmly. "Not today, Mr. Nolan."

He throws his cigarette down, grinds it under his heel. "I guess they're all at home. How's that sweet daughter of yours?"

I swallow hard. "You stay away from Pearl."

"She didn't fight me," he says with a lazy smile. "The plain girls, they always want it."

"Stay away from my family." I can barely manage the words.

The door opens. "Don't you have a home to go to, Nolan?" Mr. Callum looks between us. "Do something useful, carry Mrs. Kimber's basket."

"I can manage." It is too public. If I make a scene, it will be all over town before I'm even home. "I've carried worse."

Nolan takes the basket, and the touch of his fingers makes my skin crawl. "I was just making the same offer, Callum. Mrs. Kimber gave me a home—for a while, anyway. The least I can do is carry her groceries."

"It's not necessary," I say stiffly, but he's already off the porch and heading down the road with my family's food. I trot after him, wondering how to get rid of him before we reach the house. Pearl can't see us together.

I'm not used to being scared of men, but Nolan terrifies me. Not only is he a threat, but he is a threat to *my daughter*. I think of Claire, and the information we withheld from Mama for this very reason—because her protective rage would have made her do something that might have taken her from us, and we had already lost enough.

He walks easily, swinging the basket in one hand, the other in his pocket. "Daniel still in Washington?"

I shake my head and lie to him. "He's on his way home. He may be there already."

"Fool's errand, if you ask me." Nolan nods to a pair of men in work clothes, heading in the direction of the breaker. "He's as likely to get money from the government as he is to get his job back at the Gracie."

That is my fear, but hearing it from Tom Nolan's mouth makes me feel shaky and disloyal. "You can't know that." I reach for the basket. "I'll take it now. Thank you for carrying it this far."

"I'm always willing to help." He transfers it into his other hand. "I'd be pleased to pay a visit, maybe say hello to young Pearl."

Before I have formed the thought, I snatch a large can of peaches from the basket and swing for his head. It makes a satisfying crack against his forehead and he staggers, dropping the basket.

"You bitch!" Blood wells from a cut over his left eye. "Wait until I—"

Nolan staggers closer. I swing again and hear the crunch as the can breaks his nose. He doubles over, howling, and I grab the basket and run for home.

Father Dennis arrives within the hour, summoned by Toby.

"I need your help," I say without preamble. "If it's possible."

"With God, all things are possible." He winks. "And if I can lighten His load, I'd be happy to do it. What do you need, Ava?"

I slide a cup of tea toward him. "It's Tom Nolan. He's become a problem."

"Friend of Daniel's, isn't he?"

"He wouldn't be, if he knew," I say bitterly. I tell him my suspicions, and that Nolan has confirmed them with his comments about Pearl. "I'm afraid of him. I haven't felt like this since I was a girl."

Father Dennis nods. "There was that one CIP agent, Luther, he was a man like that. Trifled with more than one girl in this town."

"I know." My voice is barely audible. "He died."

"Even his horse didn't care for him," he says. "Threw him so he broke his neck."

This is the most I've thought of Luther in twenty years. "I remember you wouldn't bury him."

"Neither would the Methodists." His heavy shoulders lift in a shrug. "God may forgive, but man doesn't have to—though he should try, in most cases."

I cover my face with my hands. "Nolan threatened Pearl. I'm sorry, Father, I'll make a full confession for this, but I hit him with a can of peaches."

"You did what?"

"Hit him with a can of peaches," I say through my hands. "I think I broke his nose."

Father Dennis's mouth quivers. "So he'll not be feeling friendly right about now."

I shake my head. "He wasn't friendly before I hit him."

"True enough." He sips his tea. "Don't you worry, Ava. I'll see that he leaves you be."

A shudder runs through me. "Does the church have power over a man like that?"

"Likely not." He flexes his big hands. "But Father Anton boxed in the seminary, and I'm not dead yet myself. Put your trust in the church."

Claire

Harry is distracted at dinner, speaking little and only responding when I ask a second time. "What *is* it? Is something wrong?"

"It's nothing," he says, laying his knife and fork precisely across the plate. "I might have to go to New York on Monday, that's all."

"You like New York." He hasn't traveled in months, now that I think of it. I often accompanied him when he went to the city, but traveling with the children would be inconvenient, and I do not want to leave them for more than a few hours.

"I do," he agrees, taking a sip of wine. "But I wouldn't be home until Thursday night. I'm concerned about leaving you alone for that long."

"I wouldn't be alone." Instead of panic, I feel a rush of excitement. Irene's absence makes me more comfortable in the house, not less. "I have the children."

"That's what I mean. It's a lot for you to manage."

I sip my wine, crafting my response. "You have to let me grow up sometime, Harry."

He laughs at that. "If you're certain."

I blow a kiss the length of the table. "Just don't fall in love with the front desk clerk, that's all I ask."

"Why would I do that? Everything I want is here."

Two days later, Hedges drives him to the station. I offer to come along, but Harry chooses to make his farewell in the downstairs hall. "It's easier for me to say goodbye here," he says. "I miss traveling together."

"So do I." I particularly miss our long trips. It's been more than two years, and I don't imagine we'll get away any time soon, and not just because of the children. Before the Crash, we would have traveled without a second thought, but now it feels like flaunting the wealth we were lucky enough not to lose. "Maybe next time."

He gives me a lingering kiss. "What are you going to get up to while I'm gone?"

I look around. An idea occurred to me over breakfast, but I don't yet know if I have the nerve to carry it out. "Take the children to the park," I say, shrugging. "And Thelma to her appointment, of course.

And I might"—I close my eyes—"do a little shopping, if you don't mind."

"When have I ever complained about your shopping?" He claps on his fedora, embraces me quickly, and is gone before I can explain that I was thinking of a more significant purchase than a new dress.

In the previous day's *Inquirer*, I noticed an ad for bedroom suites with two-day guaranteed delivery. It has always bothered me that we sleep in a room decorated by my mother-in-law, and sleeping apart has only grown more painful over time. Many couples do—often when I leave my coat in our hostess's bedroom, I notice separate beds—but I also notice that those couples seem to have a distance between them.

With Teddy in the nursery and pregnancy off the table at last, I want to rebuild the intimacy Harry and I once had, before every act of love became fraught with such importance that I could no longer enjoy myself. It is time for a new bed.

Ava

The sound of Toby and George shouting reaches me before they tumble through the kitchen door. I raise a hand, waiting for them to fall silent. "One at a time. Toby?"

"It's Mr. Nolan," he gasps. "Did you hear?"

"Hear what?" My heart turns over. I step away from the vegetables I am cutting. "George?"

"They found him," George pipes up. "By the crick."

"All beat up," his brother adds, catching his breath. "And it wasn't *by* the crick. It was under the trestle."

"Who found him?" I pour them each a glass of water, trying not to sound too eager.

"Tommy Bosko," he says. "He was going fishing and he found him"—he glares at his brother—"over by the trestle."

"Was he badly hurt?" The boys are unaware of the ill will I harbor toward our former boarder, so I try to sound concerned rather than jubilant. "Did you see him?"

"No." George looks disappointed. "They said he was all bloody."

"His face was smashed," Toby says ghoulishly, throwing himself into a chair. "His teeth were gone and his eyes were black and they broke all his bones."

"Really?" Just how good a boxer had Father Anton been before he got the call? "Try that again."

Toby's lip juts out. "Well, his eyes *were* black, Tommy said. And he might have lost a tooth."

I raise an eyebrow. "He was missing one already. Anything else?"

"Dr. Kerr looked at him," Toby says. "That's all I know."

"And the train," George interrupts. "Don't forget to tell about the train."

"What about the train?" I return to the potatoes, watching the boys out of the corner of my eye.

"Let me tell it, George. You'll only get it backward." Toby puts his younger brother in a genial headlock and continues, "Father Dennis came and put him on the train."

"Going where?" The blade nicks my thumb and I press hard with my index finger to stem any bleeding.

They shrug as one. "Dunno."

In times of trouble, put your trust in the Lord. That was what Mama would have said. Maybe Claire and I had been wrong not to tell her about Luther; maybe a way could have been found to handle him. I think Mama would have approved of this solution, especially since it had the church's blessing.

Claire

The arrival of the furniture makes me feel in possession of some portion of my home, and I joyfully direct Hedges in placing the new pieces and moving the art and ornaments so they better suit the room. I fluff the new ice blue satin bedspread and have the Renoir hung so I can see it from my pillow. The colors pulse gently in the indirect light and I smile, suddenly knowing what my next bit of husbandless amusement will be.

I'm not certain Thelma is up to it, and when I explain to her the amount of walking involved, she makes a face. "Can I stay home with Teddy and Katie?"

"Of course," I tell her, surprisingly excited to be without the children for an afternoon.

Hedges drives me to Merion and parks outside the Barnes Foundation. The beautifully landscaped gardens—Mrs. Barnes is constructing an arboretum—are almost enough to tempt me to stay outdoors, but it has been too long since I have seen the collection, and something in my tired soul needs those paintings.

"I don't know how long I'll be." I'd never felt any concern for Baxter, but I don't want Hedges to be bored.

"Don't you worry, ma'am," he says. "Mrs. Hedges packed me a thermos and a sandwich. I'll stay right here and read my paper until you're ready to go."

Given permission to enjoy myself, I nearly sprint up the steps to the entrance. Albert Barnes has been collecting French paintings for nearly twenty years, but the museum—set alongside his suburban home—has been open for less than ten. He's an odd man, a scientist who sold his chemical company just before the Crash, but my interest in him stems from his unconventional taste in art.

I met him at a party several years ago, recognizing his name from a snide story in the newspaper—the Impressionists were still not *quite* acceptable to highbrow Philadelphia—and introduced myself. He was polite, judging me to be another society wife, but when I mentioned we had purchased a Renoir on our most recent trip to Paris, something flickered behind his eyes.

"Only one?" he asked. "I come home laden like a child let loose in a candy store."

I smiled at him. "You, sir, have a museum, while I only have a house." And a mother-in-law who controlled what was displayed on its walls, but I didn't mention that.

"I do not like to think of it as a museum." He tugged fretfully at his tuxedo jacket. "The classes are what is important, showing the people how to see art."

"But it *is* open to the public?" I asked. "I was told you permit visitors." If he did not, I would find a way to charm him into allowing me inside.

"Two days a week," he said. "That is as much as I can bear. My students must not be exposed to members of the public wandering about, voicing their idiotic opinions. For all the respect they give to the art, they might as well be at the zoo."

I raised my eyebrows. "I thought you believed in educating the public? How are they to get beyond their idiotic ideas if they are not exposed to painters like Renoir and Picasso?" I looked around, knowing that people would begin to wonder at our conversation. "Do you have any Van Gogh?"

His stern expression lapsed into an impish smile. "Not nearly as many as I would like." He patted my arm. "And you may make an appointment to visit them. My associate, Violette de Mazia, would be happy to take you through the collection. I will tell her you are not a zoo-goer."

I took him up on that invitation and found in Miss de Mazia a kindred spirit in both the love of art and the French language. She had, she told me, taught French to the workers in Dr. Barnes's factory before becoming employed at his enterprise in Merion.

For two hours, I wander in utter peace, soaking in the colors. I could have stayed longer, but I do not wish to wear out my welcome. The paintings I most wished to see today—the Cezannes and the Degas ballerinas—soothe me, and then Picasso and Chagall make me feel as if I have been put into a cocktail shaker. I emerge into sunlight which seems somehow less bright than what I have just experienced indoors.

Ava

The air is heavy with the scent of honeysuckle. It hangs from the trees and trails over a tumbledown farmhouse wall. I walk through the dappled sunlight, finding my footing carefully on the rough ground, ears pricked for my sons' voices.

It is cooler in the woods, the scent of damp rising from the earth, blocking out the reek of the town. The leaves are every shade of green, and a multitude of birds sing high in the trees. Growing up, I spent a lot of time in these woods, but I'd nearly forgotten what it felt like. I thoroughly understand why the boys disappear to this place at every opportunity.

I stop to take it in, and fish Dandy's note from my pocket, to read it for what seems the hundredth time.

> *Dear Ma. You seen the papers I guess. We're leaving today (July 28). Home for supper on the 30th, unless we hop an express.*

Dandy had reluctantly given me the location of their hideout, making me promise not to go there for ordinary, motherly reasons, but only for emergencies. When I reach the stream, I follow it to the fishing hole. There I find a small shelter knocked together out of scrap lumber, and George seated on a crate, skinning a rabbit. He looks up. "Hi, Mama."

I blink at his industry. George is the least likely of my children to volunteer for any unpleasant task. "I came to get you," I say. "It's almost three. Your dad and your brother should be home tonight."

"I know." He slits the rabbit carefully down the center and peels the pelt back from its belly. "Me and Toby, we been getting ready." Unfolding himself from the crate, he wipes his knife on a handful of leaves and abandons the half-skinned rabbit, leading me down to the water's edge.

Submerged in the deep end is a net with a half-dozen glinting, silver-brown trout. "I've got one more rabbit yet to skin."

"What is all this?"

"It's a celebration dinner." The 'what else?' is implied, though he is kind enough to keep it to himself.

"How did you catch the rabbits?"

"Snares," he says proudly. "Dandy showed us in the spring, but it took a while to get the hang of it."

I put a hand on his shoulder. "This is wonderful."

He grins. "Toby says we have to earn our keep until we can get real jobs."

"Where is your brother, anyway?"

He cups his hands around his mouth and hoots like an owl in the direction of upstream. After a moment, an answering call comes and his older brother crashes through the brush, barefoot and holding another fish.

"Hey, Ma," he says, sounding very much like Dandy. "Why are you here?"

"She come to fetch us."

Toby kneels and drops the fish into the net. "We were about ready," he tells me. "Or we will be, once George finishes cleaning these rabbits."

"I distracted him," I say. "Why don't I take the fish back, and Pearl and I can get started cleaning them, while you finish the rabbits together?"

They shake their heads. "I do fish, and he does rabbits," Toby explains. "We already divided up the work."

"You're also going to need a bath." I look them up and down. "You're filthy, both of you."

Toby notes with evident surprise the mud plastered all over his lower half. "No problem." He plunges into the fishing hole, spraying water everywhere. When he climbs out, he is wetter than before, but more or less clean.

I look at George. "That'll do for you as well," I say, "before you come home. Make sure you rinse the blood off."

My damp skirt clings to my legs as I walk back. I will brush off any mud when I get home, but it's due for a wash tomorrow anyway. Maybe I should pull some honeysuckle to put in a vase. It's not proper flowers, but the scent is better than anything except lilacs, to my mind. I want the house to look as festive as possible, to convince Daniel that the failure of the Bonus Army is not his failure.

33

Ava

When the boys got home, I started the stew, and the rabbits, still young, cooked up quickly. When the long whistle of the six o'clock train cuts through the stillness, I put the pot back on the heat while Pearl sets the table, and we all move out to the porch to wait.

We are still waiting, thirty minutes later, but the road is empty.

"Should I go and look, Mama?" Toby asks.

"Go ahead." George follows, and I catch hold of his shirt. "Not both of you."

"Aww, Ma."

"Stay put. I might need you here."

Toby soon returns, out of breath from his run to the station and back. "I saw a man who got off at the bend," he pants. "He said they wasn't with him."

I try not to think about the newspaper photos.

"When's the next train?" Pearl asks.

"Nine-thirty," Toby and George answer in unison. "Are we going to wait until then to eat?"

I wanted Daniel to come home to some kind of a welcome, but there is no point in everyone going hungry or letting the trout spoil. "We'll eat the fish," I tell them. "The stew will keep."

What if they don't come then? The unspoken question hangs in the air.

The meal is silent, all of us listening for footsteps. When we finish, Pearl retrieves the basin from its resting place in the oven. "I'll do the dishes, Mama," she says. "Why don't you go listen to the radio with the boys?"

For once, the boys turn the radio low instead of trying to break my eardrums, and I work on a dress for Pearl while I listen. She's grown so quickly in the last months, the only dress that fits her properly is the one I made from the fabric in Claire's Christmas box.

There is no new fabric to be had, so I have picked apart her plaid school dress to add an insert of dark green at the waist, lengthening the skirt and keeping the original hem intact. I attempt to make it look deliberate by cutting a new collar and cuffs in green—the color nearly matches the line in the plaid, so I hope she won't look like a badly pieced quilt. She will, at least, be decently covered.

By nine, the boys are dozing on the floor in front of the Philco, which has been switched off. Pearl is reading, and I have my feet up, the dress in my lap. We are all waiting for that final train.

"Is it done, Mama?"

I hold it up carefully; the basting stitches will be reinforced by machine in the morning. "What do you think?"

"It's pretty." She cocks her head. "Where did you get the green cloth?"

"Just something I had." It's not a lie.

She strokes the inset fabric. "This is from your good dress, isn't it?"

"I haven't worn it in ages," I tell her. "And I've remade it at least three times since I wore it to your aunt's wedding."

Pearl's eyes are bright. "But it was your best dress!"

I fold it and put it on the sewing machine table. "And now it's yours. I'm never going to fit into it again anyway." I think of the dress I left in Philadelphia, because I am proud and stupid. "I only used the bottom, so there's enough left to make you a whole other dress, if we're careful."

At last the whistle comes, this one deeper than the earlier shrieking tone. In the silence that follows comes the chuff of the locomotive and the faint clank of empty cars that will be dropped off in town. "Let's give them a half hour," I say quietly. "If they're not here by ten, we should put the boys to bed and turn in."

"Do you think something's wrong?"

Speaking my fear makes it more real. "Maybe they did a little sightseeing before they left."

"I read the newspapers," Pearl says. "I don't imagine Daddy was up for seeing the sights."

It's hard to know when to protect my children and when to let them experience life and its perils. My daughter is growing up, whether I like it or not—and much faster than I would have liked.

By ten-thirty, it is obvious they aren't coming. Pearl ushers the boys upstairs while I go out to the porch one last time. Few houses show any light, but the darkness is not absolute; clouds streak overhead, playing hide-and-seek with the fading moon. A light breeze stirs the flyaway hair around my face.

Digging my nails into the soft wood of the porch rail, I say a quick prayer, one that has no relation to the prayers I will say before bed. This is informal, and far more direct. *I've put my husband and son into Your hands, Lord, and if it isn't too much bother, I'd like them back now.*

Above me, Pearl is chivvying the boys into bed, her voice rising and falling.

There's a limit to what a man can take, I continue. *He's good, and he's strong, but You've been testing him. Let him come home and rest.*

A moment longer, looking down the road, hoping to see two figures emerge from the darkness. Nothing.

I turn the lamp low and leave it in the window, just in case.

Claire

It is the first of August before I am brave enough to wear the dress Ava made for me. I haven't even tried it on; what I saw in the mirror during the final fitting surprised and disturbed me enough that I put it in the back of the closet. But this is a special evening, and Prue Foster will be there, which makes me feel a bit braver.

For someone so buttoned up herself, Ava has created a dress far more daring than anything I have ever worn. The navy satin is staid enough, but stitched on the bias, it flows over my curves like paint. It is cut nearly to the small of my back, but in the front, a simple drape at the neck offers only a shadow of cleavage.

I look at myself in the three-way mirror, trying to decide if it will cause a scandal.

"My God." Already in his tuxedo, Harry stands in the doorway. He takes off his glasses and peers at me.

A blush climbs from the drape all the way to my hairline. "Is it too much?"

He gives a tiny, stunned shake of his head. "You look amazing."

"Ava made it when she was here." I turn in a small circle. "I haven't had the nerve before now."

"She should visit more often." Harry slides a hand down my satin hip. "I don't know if I want to show you off or keep you to myself."

I smile at him. "You lucky man, you get to do both."

At the party, a lot of the men look at me the way Harry did. I try not to mind; I've always had my fair share of attention, but I am nearly dizzy with self-consciousness this time.

Prue sails up early on. "Darling, where did you get it?"

"Get what?"

"That divine gown. I'm just dying of envy."

"My sister made it."

"Does she have a shop? I'd like one in emerald," Prue says. "Or is that too expected for a redhead? Aubergine, that's it."

I'm not certain Ava would know what color aubergine is, but I am pretty sure she would tell Prue it wouldn't suit her. "I'll send her your way the next time I can tempt her to visit."

"Tell her if she can make me look like you, I'll throw money at her."

Ava

By the first of August, I am near frantic with worry. Every time I hear the train, I want to clap my hands over my ears to drown out the hopes that will soon be dashed.

That evening, we eat the last of the rabbit stew. "I set the snares again today," George says. "I'll bring home more tomorrow."

We haven't eaten this much meat in ages. It sits heavy on my stomach, mixing badly with the anxiety already residing there. Pearl looks to feel the same, her freckles standing out like a sprinkling of cinnamon on her pale skin.

It is hot and muggy, so we move our chairs to the porch while Toby and George kick a ball around with the other boys. "Do you want to read?"

"Not really." Pearl settles herself on a straight chair. "I can't think straight."

I reach across and take her hand. "Me either."

"Is it always hard, Mama?"

"Is what hard?" Pearl's hand rests easily in mine, but I can feel the nervous energy pulsing through her like electricity.

"Loving."

I tip my head back and notice a bird's nest in the rafters. "Yes."

The sound of the door jerks me awake. Grabbing my robe from the foot of the bed, I hurtle downstairs to find my missing menfolk in the front room. I'd left the lamp burning for the third night in a row, but I can see little beyond their familiar outlines.

It is enough.

"Daniel?"

He turns. Even in the dim light, I can see the bruises on his face. "What happened?"

"Nothing." His voice is brusque.

I turn the lamp higher. "It doesn't look like nothing." Not only is he bruised, but his coat and shirt are black with what looks like soot. Dandy is in a similar state.

"I'm going to bed." He hasn't even looked at me.

I reach for him. "Are you hungry?"

"I'm tired." He shakes off my hand and hauls himself upstairs, leaning on the rail.

Dandy stares at his feet, but feeling my gaze, he looks up. "Let him go," he says. "It was a long trip."

"Aren't you tired, too?" His bruises are a few days old, by the look of them. Coming closer, I can smell scorch—it *is* soot on their clothing. "Was there a fire? Are you burned?"

He holds out his hands, displaying a few areas of peeling skin, and a larger red patch that disappears up his sleeve. "Not too bad. We got food from a lady last night, and she gave us butter for the burns." Ducking past me into the kitchen, he says, "That was the last time we ate."

I follow with the lamp. How have they come home in such a state, and fed on some other woman's charity? "What happened?"

"We lost our stuff," Dandy says. "All of it."

"Come out back with me." It isn't a request. I cut a slab of bread and smear some butter across the rough surface. That and some water is the best I can offer at this hour. I don't want to wake the children if Daniel needs peace.

In the glow of the lamp, I watch him devour the bread with the appetite of any adolescent boy. When he finishes, he turns to me. "I'll tell you whatever you want," he says, "if I know it myself."

"How did you get hurt?" I ask. "The burns, the bruises?"

He closes his eyes. "At the camp. Did you see the papers?"

"Yes. But they were confusing." Confusing and terrifying. "The army didn't shoot at people, did they?" It is inconceivable that they could turn on their own.

"The shooting was earlier in the day." He leans back against the post. "That was the police, and the people who got shot were up closer to the Capitol. We weren't there, we were back at the big camp by then. Dad found a few of his buddies from the war, and he wanted to say goodbye."

"Did you stay in the camp the whole time?"

"Pretty much. We found a shack near the far end, a family that went home early. Smart people, them." He rubs his eyes. "The camp was good, though. It was like here, everybody sharing food and watching over the kids. There was an old guy with a fiddle, and a few of the vets had mouth organs. At night, they'd play and we'd sing."

He paints a picture of the camp by firelight, the hastily constructed shacks, the tents, the crowds of men, tired out from their days of walking down to the Capitol to sing and chant and ask for their due. A sense of community, of family.

During the day, the camp belonged to the women and children. Laundry flapped in the lanes between tents while children darted beneath, playing soldiers or cowboys and Indians.

"It was good," Dandy repeats. "Dad was happy. He felt like they were listening."

"But they weren't." I remember the hope on Daniel's face when he left.

"No." His silence grows longer. "When they didn't pass the bonus, I thought there'd be trouble. Dad sent me back to the camp, but when he came later, he said it was quiet. The next day, people started going home."

"But you didn't?"

"I think he felt like he fit there. It was the happiest I've seen him in ages."

"What happened next? "

"Like I said, the shooting was early in the day. Somebody said a brick got thrown and the cops shot into the crowd. When the army came, people cheered. They thought the soldiers had come out to support them, but then they started riding their horses into the crowd and throwing tear gas bombs. They cleared out the camp near the Capitol, but it looked like they were going to leave us alone.

"Later that night, maybe around ten, I was sitting on the side of the street, waiting for Dad and listening to Pete, the old guy with the fiddle. All of a sudden we heard something, it started to drown out the music."

"What was it?"

"Cavalry." His voice thickens. "And tanks."

We sit, listening to the peepers. I cannot conceive of what he's saying.

When he speaks again, he sounds like a much younger version of himself. "It was dark and there was lots of smoke in the air and my eyes were burning. I couldn't find Dad. I tried to get to where I'd last seen him, but I got hit by a soldier on a horse. I don't even think he saw me." He pulls the neck of his shirt to one side. Even in the dark, I can see the bruises on his pale skin, spreading from collarbone to shoulder. "Nothing's broken," he assures me.

"When I got up, they'd moved on. I went back to our shack, figuring Dad would look for me there. He found me, but then the soldiers came back."

"What about the burns?" I don't want to know what happens next.

Dandy props his elbows on his knees and stares into the dark at the garden and the woods beyond. "They burned the camp."

"The army?"

"We weren't leaving fast enough. People were trying to pack their things, and they got impatient and lit up a few tents, I think just to show us, but we were crammed so close it started to spread. And they just kept driving us further and further away." His voice breaks. "They had bayonets, Ma."

I scoot over and put my arm around him. His shoulders are shaking, but his eyes are dry. "What then?"

"Dad and I were trying to shove our stuff into sacks before they came for us, but someone—a lady—started screaming. We ran to see what was wrong, and the fire came through. We tried to save our stuff. That's how we got burned. Stupid."

"What about the woman who was screaming?"

"It was Miz Kelly," Dandy said. "We ate with her family most nights. They broke her tent pole and it came down on her baby. We got him out, but I don't know what happened after that. The fire came and we all started running."

He sobs then, once, and I gather him into my arms. "It felt like we were going to run all the way home," he says against my shoulder, "but a bunch of us ended up in some woods outside the city. We were pretty banged up. Dad twisted his knee, so I played up my shoulder and kept us in the woods for an extra day so he could rest.

"The next morning, I guess that was the thirtieth, we started home. It wasn't as easy as the trip down. He had trouble getting on the train, so we waited, and snuck along to the yard where they were stopped and found a place to hide. But it wasn't a direct train, and we weren't in much of a state to mooch food." He grins crookedly. "Would you have fed me?"

"I just did, you fool." I stroke his hair. "And I'll give you more tomorrow, after you've slept." I pause. "How about your dad? You saw him just now, is he willing to talk?"

He laughs. "When is Dad ever willing to talk?"

Daniel's silence is one of the things I love about him, but this is different. I fear it will be like the war all over again, where he had to be drawn out, led back to the man he'd been before the conflict. "I just meant, this seems worse. He was counting on this so much."

"I think he feels...betrayed. He thought they would value what the soldiers did in the war, but Hoover's hiding in the White House with the gates chained shut, and instead of help, he sent tanks." He breaks down again, sobbing like the child he was not so long ago. "Who treats people like that?"

"People with power," I say, fury running through my veins. "They don't like to share it."

It is too simple, perhaps, but it's the best explanation I can give. Rich people, powerful people, they need to keep us down because if we realized we were as good as them, it would be dangerous. *We* would be dangerous.

In the morning, the kids discover their father and bedlam reigns until it is overtaken by hunger. I never went back to bed after talking to Dandy, so I am in the kitchen when they come down, Pearl hanging onto Daniel's hand and the boys flanking their brother, everyone talking at once. I meet Daniel's eyes across the table, understand he is putting on a front for them.

"What happened to your face, Dad?" Toby peers at his black eye. "Did you get in a fight?"

Dandy reaches for toast and elbows his brother. "Who wants to talk about that?" he asks. "What's been happening here?"

Toby objects and Pearl, ever watchful, waves a plate in front of him. "Mama made pancakes."

After the plates are cleared, Dandy asks the boys about fishing, and Daniel's injuries are forgotten.

"Smoke?" I'd put a pack of Luckies aside for such a day. They might be a bit stale, but I don't think Daniel will mind.

"God, yes."

We settle onto the porch, side by side but with distance in between. He takes a cigarette from the red and green pack and lights it, tilting his head back against the chair.

"Dandy told me."

He exhales a plume of smoke. "Good. So you won't ask me."

"Well..." I reach for his free hand. His fingers are tense but slowly relax in mine.

"I don't want to talk about it."

And he doesn't, though that night when he has the worst nightmare he's had in years, it is my arms he seeks until the shaking stops. I hold him and soothe him, remembering his return from the war, hating the things men do to each other.

He improves over the next few days, though he disappears into his thoughts if left on his own for too long. It reminds me of the dark weeks after Teddy's birth, when I couldn't remember how to love my baby, when his every breath caused me to fear it was his last.

I got past it because I had to, and I can see Daniel making the same superhuman effort. He doesn't fool me. He doesn't even fool the children.

34

Claire

Does Irene plan to announce her return, or will she simply appear on the doorstep with her luggage during the first week of September? There will, regretfully, be room for her, but I remain obdurate; I will not give up Esther and Mason Hedges.

No doubt dealing with the same concerns, Harry spends his evenings playing with Thelma and watching Teddy's attempts at walking. Unsuccessful thus far, he is a determined child, and I am certain he will be mobile before his first birthday—which means he will bear more watching than ever.

Finally, on Labor Day, as we stand along Market Street watching the parade with the children, I broach the subject. "Have you heard from her?"

He looks down, his face shaded by his hat. "We spoke last week."

Since when does Harry keep things from me? "And what did she have to say?"

"She called the office, to let me know that Aunt Nora will be shutting the house in a few weeks and she'll be coming back to Philadelphia." He shifts Teddy to his other side after the baby smacks him repeatedly with the small flag he is holding.

"I'll tell Katie to get her rooms ready." A band marches past, all red uniforms and shining brass, drowning any attempt at conversation. Which is good, because what I want to say isn't fit for Harry's ears, much less Teddy's. I have enjoyed the summer and am not looking forward to the return of Irene's silent hostility at dinner. "When does she expect to arrive?"

"She'll be in the city on Friday," he says, "but only temporarily. Aunt Nora sold her house, and she and Mother are going to take an apartment together."

"An apartment." Can I be this fortunate?

"At either the Drake or the Versailles." He shifts, and I can see his lips curl. He isn't sorry to lose his mother's constant presence either.

"Close by," I say, trying not to smile.

"But not too close."

Ava

I follow the unfamiliar sound of whistling and find Daniel on the back step, smoking in the fading light, a mug of tea nearby. He looks more cheerful than he has since before Washington.

Hearing my approach, he pats the place beside him. "Come here."

"What's going on?" I settle myself warily.

"I've found a job."

"That's wonderful!" We had discussed Harry's offer again in bed a few nights ago, but he hadn't been receptive. "Is it Philadelphia?"

He stares at me. "No."

"But you said…"

"I don't want to work in a factory, not for Claire's husband or anyone else," he says. "This is what I am, what I've always been. Why did I think they'd ever give me more?"

Something in his voice scares me. "It's just bad luck," I say. "You and everybody else who went to Washington, you deserve that money."

"But we won't get it." He slams his mug down and a chip splits from the base, skittering across the porch floor. "I didn't get the bonus, and I don't have a job. Only one thing I've ever been good at, and they won't let me do it."

I should say something to cheer him, to jolly him out of the black mood that threatens like a summer storm, but I don't remember how. "What are you going to do?"

His bruises have faded, but his eyes are bloodshot, the creases at their corners no longer only from laughter. "What I'm good at," he says.

"Has the Gracie called you back?" I feel a surge of excitement; maybe things will turn around now.

"Not the Gracie." He stubs the cigarette out carefully. "Another mine."

It means traveling, but having him work away is better than losing him entirely. Some men have hopped trains in the middle of the night, leaving their families to face an unknown future—the Depression divorce Callum once teased me about. It isn't desertion so much as desperation, but there's little difference for those left behind. "How far away is it?"

"Nearby."

He is being cagey. "Daniel, it's not...it's not *that* mine, is it?" Night after night, we hear trucks rumbling away from the mountain where no coal is officially being mined. Dandy went back there when they returned from Washington, but he does not talk about it and I have no idea when my husband's feelings changed. "Daniel?"

"Boy was right," he says. "I told him so."

"But it's illegal. If the company finds out, they'll set the police on you." A finger of cold touches my spine. "That's what you said then."

"It's different now. And the police know. Half their relatives are probably working there."

I put a hand on his arm. "I meant the other kind of police. The CIP."

They are my private nightmare, yet here he is, tempting fate, bringing them—or something like them—back into our lives. "What if there's another brick through the window?"

"If there's coal to be had, and people to buy it, why shouldn't we take it out of the ground and sell it? We need the money."

He's not wrong, and I am not completely against illegality—I can find a way to justify almost anything that will keep my kids fed—but legal, sanctioned mining is dangerous enough, without this added degree of risk. "Is it safe?"

Daniel laughs. "It's a mine. It's never completely safe."

"But the Gracie has precautions." I twist my hands in my apron. "Rules and regulations to keep you safe."

"The same rules and regulations that let our fathers live to a ripe old age?" He cocks his head. "The safest way is men watching out for each other, like it was in the army. The company just wants coal. There are always more men if some get hurt."

"I'd rather you do anything else." I reach around and take a sip of his tea. It's cold; he's been out here thinking for a long time.

"There is nothing else." Daniel puts his arm around me and I lean into his body. Moments of private physical affection are rare, but

I know where the kids are. We are actually alone. "I don't know if you will ever understand, but this is what I'm good at. If you want the truth, I love it. I love the feeling of going down the lift into the tunnels and being enclosed by the earth."

I shudder. It gives me the willies, every time he talks about it, the idea of being so far underground, with no sunlight or fresh air.

"The only feeling like it," he says, his voice low and in my ear, "is being inside my wife."

Claire

Hedges deposits me on the sidewalk just short of the Drake's substantial awning. I should have walked; the fresh air would have done me good, and I would have had more time to prepare. Instead, the building's doorman greets me instantly and opens the front door.

My eyes skim the grand lobby with its deep chairs and light streaming through tall windows. It looks like a nice, comfortable hotel—not the best sort of hotel, the kind Irene would visit, but a very good hotel, the kind where she would choose to live. A pair of elevators with etched doors lay straight ahead. Taking a deep breath, I march toward them, and the left elevator opens at my approach, disbursing several chattering women.

The elevator operator pops his head out. "Ma'am?"

"I'm coming." The outer door slides closed and he shuts the inner gates. "What floor, ma'am?"

"Ten, please." I rub my gloved hands together, more than a bit nervous to see Irene, but there is also a thread of anger beneath my nervousness.

She stopped by a week ago while I was out with the children. When I returned, backing carefully through the door with Teddy's coach, it was to find Katie sobbing in the front hall, being comforted by her mother. Harry's case rested on the bottom step, but he was nowhere in sight.

"I couldn't stop her, ma'am!" Katie wailed through her apron. "She just came in and pointed at things, and Baxter and some other man, they carried it all out."

Teddy began to howl, adding to the general din. His mouth, open wide, displayed four hard-won teeth. I scooped him up and handed him to Thelma. "Can you take your brother up? I'll be there directly."

Mrs. Hedges put an arm around her daughter and led her toward the kitchen. I followed. "What on earth?"

"The other Mrs. Warriner," Mrs. Hedges said. "She let herself in just past noon and directed her two men to take certain items from the house." Her lips were a thin line; this was her first introduction to Irene. "Katie tried to speak to her, but she pushed her. She *pushed* my girl."

Katie dropped into a kitchen chair. "She said she would call the police if we tried to stop her, and that they would never believe colored servants over her." She began to wail again. "I'm so sorry, ma'am, I tried, I really did."

"I know you did. None of this is your fault." I put my hand on her shoulder, meeting Mrs. Hedges' eyes. "I imagine this has disrupted things down here. Why don't you all take the evening off? Mr. Warriner and I will go out with the children, once he's catalogued what's missing."

It was quite a catalog—not only had she cleared out her entire suite upstairs, but she'd taken her favorite pieces from the dining and living rooms, as well, including an entire set of Meissen china. Several hideous knickknacks had disappeared from the front hall, and pale squares on the wallpaper showed where she had removed a few family portraits.

Harry was furious. "It's not that she doesn't have the right to her things, but to have done it without asking—to have upset Katie so badly—it's in poor taste."

I couldn't agree more, but I was so happy to have her gone that it was difficult to share his outrage.

The Drake is perfectly to Irene's taste. The carpets are dark burgundy, with a muted scroll design; the hallways are papered in a discreet gold print, with electric sconces set every ten feet. I follow the marker and turn left. Apartment 1002 is at the end of the hall.

Baxter opens the door, looking abashed to see me. "Good afternoon Mrs. Warriner."

"Good afternoon, Baxter. How lovely to see you again."

He takes my coat and hat, and shows me into a living room that duplicates Irene's private sitting room down to the color of the walls. Did Honora have any say in the decoration of this apartment?

"Darling Claire!" Honora trails layers of mauve chiffon that seem more spring than fall, but her smile is genuine, and her outstretched hands grip mine with a friendly pressure.

"How are you, Aunt Honora?" I sit next to her on the plush sofa. "Are you enjoying life in the city?"

"Do call me Nora," she says. "I was getting lonely rattling around in that big house without Charlie, and Irene seemed to want company."

That was rich since Irene used her sister as an excuse to not return home. "Well, I'm glad you two are enjoying setting up housekeeping. The house isn't the same without Irene, but we're managing."

Honora raises an eyebrow. "I'm sure you are, my dear."

"Claire." Irene is framed in the doorway, waiting for her greeting. I do the expected: a light embrace, kisses on both cheeks, wrinkle my nose to avoid the miasma of her cologne. "Aunt Nora told me you were settling in nicely."

"The French ambassador lives upstairs," Irene says. "He has an entire floor."

"Have you met him yet?"

"Not yet," Honora told me. "Irene is still practicing her French."

"Sister!"

"Well, it's true." Honora rang a bell. "What would you like, Claire—coffee, tea, or is it late enough for a cocktail?"

"Coffee would be lovely," I say. "It's a bit chilly today."

"Did you have other calls," Irene asks, "or is this a special trip?"

"You're my last stop," I say. "I don't know if you remember—it happened around the time you left—but I've been helping Prue Foster organize a Christmas party for the city's orphanages. I met with the events manager at the Bellevue Stratford to discuss which room we can have."

"I haven't heard a peep about this," Honora says. "Tell me more. What can I do?"

An unfamiliar maid enters with a tray, which she puts on the table in front of us. Honora signs for her to leave, and pours the coffee herself.

"Well," I say, "it's a bit of a group effort. Prue Foster, Stella Good, Geneva Rowland, and I, we're organizing it, but things like this tend to draw in a lot of people."

"And I assume you are accepting donations?"

I smile broadly. "Of course, Aunt Nora. You know how this works." I sip my coffee and add a touch more cream. "Every time we hit our fundraising goal, we find something else to add."

"But they deserve it, the poor, tragic little things." Honora gives a decided nod. "Irene, is that Evans in the other room? Tell her to bring my checkbook."

We continue our discussion of the gala until Evans returns, handing a checkbook to each woman. Honora takes hers eagerly, and Irene smiles thinly and places hers on the table.

"All right, then." Honora selects a frosted almond lace cookie and pops it into her mouth. She writes swiftly with her fountain pen, then tears the check free and waves it to dry the ink before handing it to me. "Your turn, sister," she says, and reaches for another cookie.

I avert my eyes as Irene's pen scratches. I hadn't expected a cent from her, but sisterly shaming cannot be ignored. I put both checks into my bag without looking at them.

"How are you and Harry managing?" Irene asks. "And the children, of course."

"We're just fine." I settle my cup back into its saucer. "Thelma's so much better—Max is going to change her braces after the new year. And Teddy's grown so much. You really should visit, Irene, before he forgets you entirely."

"I'd love to meet him," Honora says. "He looks like such a lovely, chubby boy. I adore babies."

Do people wonder about me and Ava the same way I question how Honora and Irene can possibly be related?

"He would love that." I take one of the almond cookies; the flavor is delicate and delicious. "Mrs. Fell still makes these lovely cookies, I see."

"Mrs. Fell is a very deft baker." Irene sits upright in the tufted chair she'd removed from our living room, along with its matching ottoman. "You should remember that."

"Of course," I say. "I'll have to ask her for the recipe. Mrs. Hedges has added variety to our menu, but I don't believe she makes these."

"I'm glad you were able to find a new cook."

"I do hope you haven't been worrying about us." I take my time with the cookie. "Katie was able to find us a new cook and house man almost immediately—I believe you met Mrs. Hedges when you retrieved your things."

"I hadn't intended to keep Mrs. Fell and Baxter permanently." She focuses on her poaching of the servants, rather than my roundabout accusation of theft. "I thought it would be advantageous to have a cook for the summer."

"I had a perfectly good cook," Honora says. "Did you think I intended to let the gulls feed me?"

"Mrs. Fell would have preferred to return to Delancey Place." Irene looks pointedly at me.

"Then she should have stayed." I give her a placid smile. "We assumed you would keep the servants; after a certain age, it's difficult to adjust to change. Harry and I still look at it as an adventure."

Honora snorts and takes a hasty mouthful of coffee. "It's a good thing Mrs. Fell knows how to bake these cookies," she says. "It was our mother's recipe, as I recall, but you never would give it to me, Irene."

The sisters are still squabbling when I take my leave. Before ringing for the elevator, I retrieve the checks from my bag. As expected, Irene's is for twenty dollars. Aunt Nora, on the other hand, has given me five hundred.

Pearl

September 9, 1932

Daddy is working at the bootleg mine, of all places. He needs a job, and they were taking on more men. But he kicked Dandy out because of that mine, and now he's there himself. Sometimes grownups don't make any sense at all.

Ava

Most of the work at the bootleg mine is done at night, so Daniel is back on his old hours. I quickly grow accustomed to having him around during the day, when the children are at school. It is remarkable how working has restored him—at times he is almost playful, waltzing me around the kitchen or coming up behind me when I am standing at the sink.

"What time does Pearl get home?" He shoves the *Times-Tribune* to one side. It no longer holds his interest.

"Not for a half hour, maybe longer." I have a pot on the stove and a sink full of dishes to attend to. "Why?"

"I'd let you take me upstairs," he says, "if I was certain when she was getting home."

Even after six kids, he can make the hair stand up on my arms just by looking at me. "I've got things to do, Daniel."

"There's always the table." His slow smile spreads. "It's a nice old table."

"It's showing its age," I respond, getting into the spirit of his game. "Lots of wear and tear."

He stands, sliding one arm around me to cup my bottom. "I don't know," he says. "I like it. Sturdy. Good legs."

His other hand joins the first, and my pulse beats faster.

"Dance with me?" He backs me up until my thighs meet the table's edge. When he kisses me, I melt and hope Pearl takes her time walking home. Maybe she'll let that nice Jack Polikoff walk with her. She's always a few minutes late when that happens.

"I don't think I know this dance." My face is against his neck.

Laughter rumbles in his chest. "We were born knowing this dance."

"It's good that the men have gotten involved." Daniel draws the covers over us to cut the bedroom's chill. "The boys were just chipping away at it, with no sort of plan."

The boys, as far as I knew, had never needed a plan. It was once men discovered their enterprise that it got ambitious. "What do you mean?"

"We've opened up proper rooms," he says, an excitement in his voice that I haven't heard in months. "It takes time because we can't use explosives."

"Explosives would take all the stealth out of it," I agree, reaching over the side of the bed to retrieve my drawers. "You're being careful?"

"We're being careful." Daniel stretches. His hands, which have so recently explored my body, are nicked and bruised from his labors. "It's difficult to get the supports—unofficially. But Al Denning can still get to the yard where the company stacks the timbers they've removed. We're managing."

I hope it's enough. I had worried about Dandy working the bootleg mine, but boys were never going to get into serious trouble. They didn't have the muscle or the skill to accomplish what their elders have taken on. Which means the risk has increased along with the yield. Even without explosives, how long will it be before someone notices trucks going around the mountain to load the product of a mine that doesn't exist?

"The kids will be home soon." I wriggle into my brassiere, turning to present Daniel with the hooks. "Get dressed."

He pouts and smacks my bottom. "I'd rather stay here."

"Then stay," I say, buttoning my dress. "I'll tell them you're napping. But put some clothes on first."

He sticks a foot out from beneath the quilt. "I've got my socks on, woman, what more do you want?"

Shaking my head, I go back down and reach the bottom of the steps just as Pearl opens the front door.

35

Ava

Something is wrong. The last two weeks, I've been full of energy. This morning, I roll out of bed ahead of Daniel and the others, but it is only habit that gets me to my feet.

Downstairs, I bless Dandy for filling the wood box before bed. I build up the fire and open the kitchen windows. The rain has blown over and the air is fresh and damp-smelling. I wait for the coffee pot and stare out the window, thinking of everything I have to do, wondering where I will find the energy.

Judging the coffee to be warm enough, I pour a cup. The rich, slightly bitter aroma reaches my nose, and my stomach rolls over. For a moment, I see spots. I put the cup down, untasted.

No no no no no no. I can't be.

I fling open the door and stand on the step, my apron pressed to my mouth.

Daniel appears at my shoulder, my abandoned cup in his hand. "What's wrong?"

I swallow hard, find I can speak. "Coffee."

He understands immediately and passes the cup back through the window. "Are you sure?"

I nod, then start to cry. "That's been the tell every time before."

With a few sewing jobs and Daniel working at the other mine, we have just begun to get our heads above water. There are still bills to be paid, but I'd begun to feel a little less frightened of the future. And now—this.

Daniel pulls me back against him. "I'm sorry, Ave," he says. "I didn't mean for it—how are we going to—"

"It's not just you," I say, wiping my eyes. "It was both of us. And we'll find a way. We always do."

"We do." He draws me closer, the hunger that brings us together evident in his kiss. "It just used to be easier."

I kiss him back. What does it hurt now? "We'll figure out something." It is so easy to slip into reassurance mode. We *will* figure out something, but at the moment, I have no idea what. I follow him back into the house, breathing shallowly.

"I'm heading in early." He shrugs into his jacket. "There's an order to fill, and the last thing we need right now is for me to lose this job."

"The kids will be down soon, anyway," I tell him. "I'll pull myself together."

Daniel pours the coffee into his battered thermos, then fills the kettle and puts it back on the hot stove. "Tea's on," he says, kissing me one last time. "I'll see you later."

I go back to the step after he leaves, letting the October breeze cool my flushed face. Another baby. We have been careful, but that works only so well, as we know from experience. How are we going to do this again? I even traded away the baby clothes, certain Teddy was my last.

After what I have done, I don't deserve another child. What kind of mother gives away her baby, even to a needy sister, even for the child's own good? When Claire's letters arrive, filled with news and photographs of Teddy and Thelma, it is easy to think we did the right thing, but at night, or when I am alone—and I am grateful every day that my life gives me so little privacy—regret seeps in. The photographs are just proof of what we've lost.

It's not long before Pearl catches me puking. She understands, my girl, even when I don't want her to. "I thought we were done with babies," she says.

"So did I." I take a deep breath and return to the porch, where we've left our work baskets, to take advantage of the light. "Trust me, so did I."

She sits in the chair next to mine and retrieves the shirt she is mending. "But you're grown-ups. Isn't there any way you can stop it from happening?"

If only our adult powers could control such things. "It's not that easy."

"Well, I don't know that," she says, with a touch of impatience. "Mary Kasky told us what her older sister told her, but it sounded stupid."

Is it that time, already? I look at my daughter and wonder. She hasn't bled yet; at her age, I'd had the curse for a year, and a pretty good idea about the purposes of boys. Pearl keeps close to home, and other than Jack Polikoff, I've never seen her pay attention to boys. "Do you want to know?"

She blinks, then nods her head.

I tell her plainly what I know about the sex act. Awkward as it is, I wish Mama had done the same for me when I was young enough to listen.

"It sounds awful," Pearl says at last. "People like that?"

"It's not awful." I think of Claire and amend. "It can be, if a woman is unwilling or even just not ready. But when it's time and with the right man, it's lovely." I offer a small smile. "You'll have your feelings for each other to make it better, in the beginning, when it's still unfamiliar."

"Hmm." Her mouth twists to one side as she considers my words. "What about babies, though?"

In for a penny. "As Catholics," I tell her, "we're not supposed to prevent babies. Which is another reason to wait for the right man."

Pearl is fixed on the babies. "But it's not impossible to prevent them?"

"Not entirely." I reluctantly explain withdrawal, and about the rubbers we can rarely afford. I do not mention Claire's operation; it is too much information for a girl her age. "The only sure thing is staying away from each other, and that's hard when you're in love."

"So you and Daddy never wanted this many kids?" She stitches quietly, a notch between her brows.

"We wanted kids," I say, hoping she understands. "If I'm honest, I'd have rather had you further apart, but I wouldn't not have had one of you."

"Your life would have been completely different if you didn't have us." Her tone is contemplative.

"My life would have been quiet, and I wouldn't know how to live that way." I pick up a spool and slide green thread across a stub of candle. "It's hard to even think about it, because you're here, and even as babies, you were all such *people*. Of course, our lives would have been easier, but easy isn't the point. This"—I wave my hand at the house, encompassing her scattered siblings in my gesture—"is the point. Family. Being together. It's hard, but I wouldn't change any of it."

It is the truth. In the last year, I've prayed for strength, for money, for my husband and son to find their way home, but I've never prayed for a different life.

"It seems funny," she says, "that all you have to do is marry a man for him to have the right to be inside your body." She raises her eyes. "You might barely know him at that point."

"And that's why I'm telling you this now. Your granny didn't tell me anything until my wedding night, and by then your daddy and I had figured a few things out on our own." I neglect to mention that these discoveries occurred in the woods behind the Gracie, in between his shift and suppertime, and that I emerged from his explorations smeared with coal dust which had to be washed away in ice-cold creek water before Mama saw me and blistered my behind. "It can be a beautiful thing, Pearl, when you're ready."

"How do you know when you are?"

"You'll know," I tell her. "Just don't let anyone rush you."

Pearl

October 13, 1932

Mama's having another baby. She told me that, and a lot more besides. Now I know how babies are made, and more or less what Mr. Nolan was trying to do to me. And maybe what Jacky Polikoff thinks about when he walks me home.

I'll wait. Boys don't look at me like that, but even if they did, I'm not going to do what Mama did. She was only six years older than me when she got married. She and Daddy love each other, but look where it's gotten them.

Ava

Daniel is happy to be underground again, risking himself to bring home a surprising amount of money. The work is good for him, no matter how it makes me feel. He is calm, the jittery energy of misery worn away by physical labor. He and Dandy live together as if nothing had ever happened between them, and they go off to work—to the mine that nearly broke our family apart—singing.

When he's home and awake, he plays with the little boys. They thrive under the extra attention.

I wish Thelma could be here to experience this version of her father. So much of her childhood was spent with Daniel on nights, sleeping through the day, working elsewhere, or bitter and unemployed. This father would dance her around the front room to radio music and call her princess, and our house would be filled with her crystal laughter.

Claire

As the gala grows closer, there are constant claims on my time—calls to donors, whose importance cannot be ignored; visits to the orphanages; meetings with Prue and the other women which often devolve into cocktails and giggling like adolescent girls. I tear myself away to get home to Teddy and Thelma, feeling that I have friends who will not disappear as soon as the gala is over.

When I ready myself for my first solo visit to the Presbyterian Home, Thelma sits on the foot of the bed, swinging her legs.

"Can I come with you, Aunt Claire?"

She's only just gotten in from school; it was a half day and I thought she would want to stay home and play with her brother. "It's not much fun, sweetie," I say. "It's a sad place—just lots of children without parents."

"Like me," she says. "How many?"

"Lots." Does she think of herself as being without parents? "Wouldn't you rather stay with Teddy? Maybe Katie has time to play."

Thelma looks up at me, her eyes wide. "I don't have any friends at school, but maybe one of the orphans wouldn't mind about my legs. Please, aunt."

She is lonely! I am filled with shame—I have been celebrating the friendships I've made, and all the while, Thelma has been missing her brothers and sister. Teddy is her brother, of course, but he is a baby and she is quite mature for her age. She needs friends—even orphan friends, if any can be mustered from those dull-eyed, apathetic children.

"Well, then," I say, feigning enthusiasm, "Hedges will drive us to the orphanage and we'll see if we can find you some friends. I have an idea. Do you know any Christmas carols?"

"Of course."

"That's it, then. We were thinking it would be nice if they sang a few carols at the party, so I'll put you in charge of the program."

Her smile spreads wide and I see the difference between it and her normal, polite expression; the only times I've seen this sunshine smile is when she is with Max.

Once she is bundled into her new blue coat and matching beret, we climb into the Packard. On the front passenger seat is a large basket containing several of Mrs. Hedges' delicious chocolate cakes, to be shared out at the children's evening meal.

When we get there, I say, "I have to talk to Mr. Carson, so I'm going to hand you over to a nice young lady named Miss Abigail. She'll be the one to introduce you to the children, and she can help with the program if you like."

Mr. Carson and Abigail meet us at the door, and Abigail's face lights up at the sight of Thelma. "I was just going to the schoolroom," she says. "Would you like to come with me?"

Thelma takes her hand, and I follow Mr. Carson into his office to drink weak tea and discuss the final plan for the party.

"Isn't it going to be difficult to get people to attend on Christmas Day?" he asks. "I'll be there, certainly, and Miss Abigail and the rest of the ladies who work here, but the other volunteers... Are they willing to be apart from their families on the holiday?"

"Mrs. Foster is hard to resist," I admit. "She leans heavily on the fact that what is a mere inconvenience for them—being separated from their families—is a fact of life for these children." I venture a smile. "It was my idea to charge them a dollar a head for each child they wanted to bring, and five dollars for each adult." It would pay for their food and drink, with a nice packet set aside for a post-holiday treat.

His eyebrows raise. "You're more devious than I gave you credit for, Mrs. Warriner."

"I am large, Mr. Carson," I say, smiling brightly. "I contain multitudes."

Hedges slows the car at the corner so a group of elderly women can cross. Hearing the bells, I look up Twentieth Street and turn to Thelma. "Would you like to stop in at St. Patrick's and light a candle for your granny? It's been almost a year."

She nods, and I lean forward. "You can let us out at the corner here. We'll walk home."

"Yes, ma'am." He pulls to the curb and hops out to open our door.

St. Patrick's is only a half block away, but Thelma drags her feet as we climb the steps and pass between the massive pillars. When I'd gone to fetch her, she'd been leading close to fifty children in a rousing version of *O Come All Ye Faithful*, with two smaller girls clinging to her hands.

I have more or less returned to the church since my niece came to live with me; I promised Ava that Thelma would attend mass regularly, and she is far too young to go alone. Harry doesn't mind going to church without me—and now that Irene is back, they have time for lunch afterward, at her apartment or a restaurant, and I have an excuse not to join them.

The church is echoing and damp, incense lingering in the corners. I put a coin in the box and use the taper to light two small candles in red glass votives so we can each say a prayer for Mama.

Pearl

November 18, 1932

I stopped at the cemetery on my way home from Mrs. Z's and there were flowers on Granny's grave. Today is the first anniversary of her death. I know Mama doesn't visit, so who are they from?

I can't believe it's only been a year. So much has happened that I can barely remember Granny sometimes. Teddy born and gone to aunt's. Thelma getting her legs fixed. Daddy and Dandy, apart and together again. And now another baby.

I hope things are different this time, and Mama doesn't get sad again. I want Thelma to get better, but I also want her to come home. Is it selfish to want life to be easy, for just a little while?

36

Ava

The air is thick with dust. It is difficult to breathe. I can see only a little way by the light of my head lamp, but I can touch the back of the man in front of me, and feel the hand of the man behind me on my own back. The noise is endless.

Down we go, into a dark, echoing chamber where the clang of picks and tools swirls around me, louder still. There is light now, a few lanterns set around. More headlamps.

I move toward the seam, my muscles ready for the work I know best. I swing the pick and—

The shriek of the siren tears me from sleep. For a moment, as I claw my way out of the dream into the similar darkness in the bedroom, I don't know where I am.

It's early, nowhere near dawn yet. The siren wails and a window glows into light across the road. I fumble for my clothes and bang my knee on the bed frame as I shove my feet into shoes.

"Mama, what is it?" Pearl appears in the door, flashlight in her hand.

"I don't know." I take the light. "Nothing, I hope. You stay here with the boys."

"But Mama—"

"No."

As I fly off the porch, I hear a door open and turn to tell Pearl to stay back. Trudy emerges from her house, pulling on her son's heavy coat. She too has a flashlight. "Wait for me."

"Is Hermann there?"

"*Ja*, and Fritz." She takes my hand. "Daniel and your boy?"

I nod, struck by the night sky. It was raining when Daniel left for work, and when I went to bed. Now the sky is black, spangled with stars like sequins on one of Claire's evening dresses. The air is crisp, with almost no wind. It would be beautiful, if not for the siren.

Others joined us as we hurry toward the center of town—mostly women, some with flashlights, others with lanterns. The few men are older, and carry shovels and mining tools. A scattering of boys, too young to work, follow like puppies. We are, for the most part, silent.

A light shows in the guard house at the Gracie, where a window has been smashed to gain access to the siren. A boy emerges at the sight of us, scrubbing his black-smeared face with his sleeve. He is no more than twelve.

"Ceiling fell," he shouts. "Way inside. They're trying to get them out."

His words strike my gut before my brain fully understands. Trudy's arm goes around me as I stagger. She does not let me fall.

We follow the boy around the pile and up a steep path, over the heap of rubble left behind when the Gracie shut down most of its operations. Rocks and debris catch underfoot. I stumble, but keep moving.

Daniel and my son are down there.

I have made this vigil before, twenty years ago, waiting through a day and a night with Mama, Margit, and Claire, for our father and Jake to emerge from the remains of the Gracie no. 1. Jake and a few others made it out, but the rest weren't brought up for days, and when they were, we weren't permitted to see them or prepare their bodies for burial.

I shake myself. *Stop thinking of the past!* This is Daniel, my life. The father of my babies. If I try hard, I can feel him, a pulse deep inside, deeper than the baby.

He is alive. I hold onto that pulse.

"Mother Mary, keep him safe and bring him home." I clamber over the hill, following the sound of voices. "Keep him safe."

A haphazard rescue operation has already begun. A half dozen cars and trucks are idling, their headlights pointed at the mine entrance, which is no more than a reinforced hole in the side of the mountain. Men and boys pass buckets of rubble like a fire brigade, and we quickly join the line. It is eerily quiet but for the rumble of engines and the rhythmic sound of men attacking the wall of earth inside the tunnel.

I reach into my pocket and touch my rosary before taking my place. Once my hands are busy with buckets, I tell the beads in my mind to keep worry at bay.

The crucifix. *Keep them safe.*
One bead. *Bring them home.*
Another. *He's my life.*

Another. *I need him.*

Another. *My babies need him.*

I try to damp down my panic. I don't want to hurt the child. This baby—my miracle baby—is Daniel the price I will pay? Is Dandy?

"No," I whisper. "God, you can keep this baby, just give me my husband and my son."

"Stop that." Trudy takes the bucket as I reach for the next one. "Bargaining with God will not bring them out any sooner."

We huddle near the trucks, taking warmth from the engines, passing the buckets down the line, where a new pile of rubble is rapidly forming. A murmur of prayer rises like mist around us—all the Catholics in the crowd are saying the rosary, and I join them, comforted by the familiar words.

The crowd works steadily, but with little visible progress. The company men arrive and stay well back, arms crossed. They will not help, and they announce through a bullhorn that anyone who assists with the rescue effort will never work at the Gracie again.

"Anyone who would work at the Gracie is already down there," a woman's voice says, and there is a murmur of agreement.

Father Dennis scrambles over the hill, landing, as I had, on his hands and knees. He gets up and skids down the pile to join the men. Father Anton is on his heels.

"Won't you pray with us, Father?" Becky Nordstrom, I think, worrying about her houseful of boys.

He does not even look over his shoulder. "Right now the good Lord wants me to dig."

As the sky lightens, the birds begin to sing. Word has spread, and trucks pull up from nearby towns and point their lights toward the tunnel, spilling more men with tools. They quickly get to work, and a faint sense of hope seeps into me.

Father Dennis makes his way back through the crowd. He is wearing street clothes instead of his black suit, and he is crusted with dirt. He walks among us, touching shoulders, exchanging words. He stops beside Trudy and me. "How are you, ladies?"

"Waiting and praying," I say.

"Keep at it," he tells me. "I'm going to continue digging. My back is as strong as my faith, and God doesn't want me to stand and watch." He looks over at the company men, standing now with the police and the fire brigade, and raises his voice. "Unlike these shameless bastards."

A few of the men duck their heads, and two of the firemen break away and follow the priest.

His words rally the women. Our voices join in prayer again, the sound rising and falling. I feel a hand on my arm and look down to see Pearl with the boys. "I told you to stay home."

"They're ours, too, Mama." Pearl edges in next to me, grunting in surprise at the weight of the bucket.

Toby and George attach themselves to my skirt. "What's happening? Is Daddy out yet? Where's Dandy?"

I step out of line for a moment, squatting down to look into their nearly identical faces. Their eyes are red, but they won't cry in public. "They're not out yet, but don't give up." Squeezing them to me, I say, "Look at all the people who've come to help."

"I brought food," Pearl says over her shoulder. Toby opens the sack and produces a bottle of tea, a loaf of bread, and some cheese. "It's not much, but it's what I could grab before they got too far ahead of me."

"It's perfect." I take a deep swallow of tea. It is light now, and I can see the exhaustion and fear on the faces of the onlookers. Most of us have been down this road before. It never gets any easier, waiting for your loved ones to make it back to the surface.

The ground swells and drops, sickeningly, before the sound of the explosion reaches our ears. Black smoke belches out of the tunnel, spraying the nearest workers with dirt and gravel. Everyone rushes forward, attacking the freshly fallen earth with picks, shovels, even their bare hands.

I keep an arm around the boys and stay close to Pearl. She is a comfort, but she needs my support as much as the young ones. "Any time now," I say, "we'll see them coming out."

There is another rumble under our feet, and my chest absorbs the impact of a second explosion. I look around, wondering why no one is crying out in fear, and realize they haven't felt it. I close my eyes, try to find Daniel.

The pulse is gone.

I take a shaky breath and try harder. Using my free hand, I thumb over my beads, looking for Daniel in the darkness of my mind. All I can feel is a thick, blanketing silence.

Cheering opens my eyes again. A man stumbles out of the tunnel, stands dazed a few feet outside, looking at the crowd. He drops to his knees and two women help him up, weeping loudly.

Other men stagger through the opening. Women and children come forward to claim their own, crying and hugging and crying some more.

One, two, three…then a fourth. A pause. Two more, smaller, holding each other up. One of them is Dandy.

I push to the front, striking a man who tries to hold me back. Dandy falls against me, almost dead weight. The only parts of him not black with dust are the tear-tracks on his cheeks and a large patch of red on the side of his face. I touch him gently and my hand comes away sticky. His hair is clotted with blood.

"How bad are you hurt, baby?" I drop to my knees, stones digging into my flesh, and paw him all over, feeling his joints, his birdlike ribs through the torn shirt. He screams when I touch his left shoulder. "What happened?"

"Mama," he says, tears running down his face, "it's Daddy."

I know what he is trying to tell me, but I continue to examine him, wiping his tears with my fingers. "He'll be out soon. They're working as fast as they can."

"I saw it." Dandy cries harder, burying his face in the shoulder of my coat. "It came down on him and two other men." He sobs until he retches. "When they blew the tunnel, more came down."

He is gone. I knew it when I felt that punch, that second movement of the earth that went unnoticed by the others. That was the second collapse.

Daniel, my darling. My boy. The one I have loved since I was a child, the other part of myself. How am I supposed to go on, half-whole?

I wrap my arms around Dandy then, and gather the rest of the children into my embrace. "Careful of his left side," I say. "I think something's broken." Pain in my knees makes me stand, and I absently pick up one of the rocks. To my left, Trudy is clutching Hetty, both of them watching the tunnel. "Are there others coming out?" Dandy shakes his head. "Mrs. Metzger's brother? Fritz?"

"No." He separates from us and tries to straighten, wincing. "He was on the seam near Daddy. I'm not sure about Fritz." Holding his left arm tight to his body, he takes a deep breath and walks over to the Metzger family, to give them the bad news.

Tears stream down Pearl's face. The boys sob noisily, and the heart comes right out of me. When I chose to marry Daniel, I knew I would repeat at least some of Mama's life. I hadn't planned to repeat every part of it, from the number of children to the vigil at the mine to losing my husband.

"Come on." I take Toby's hand and Pearl takes George's, and we join Dandy. "Dandy, come along." I give Trudy a quick hug. "I'll put tea on, my friend. Come in if you want company."

We walk back to the house, the younger boys snuffling quietly, Pearl and I bracing Dandy on either side. He is stiff in our grasp, whether from pain or grief, I can't be sure. Are they so different? I feel as if I've been struck by the same ton of coal that crushed my husband, so perhaps not.

Once inside, I shoo Pearl and the boys into the kitchen while I help Dandy undress. "Does it hurt anywhere besides your arm?" I ask. "What about your head? There's blood all over your shirt."

"Most of it's not mine." His voice is almost inaudible. "I laid down next to Dad. It's his." He starts to cry again. I wrap a blanket around him, rest my head against his back and let him cry it out.

There is a quiet knock and a neighbor looks in. "The doctor is at the mine now," she says. "The company tried to stop him, but he threatened to quit on them. I told him your boy needed help. He'll be along."

It could be hours before Dr. Kerr reaches us. "Does it hurt bad, Dandy?"

"There's worse hurt than me." He gulps. "I'm okay, Mama."

"Of course you are." I cup his cheek, registering that in his agony, he has gone back to calling me Mama. "I can help with the pain, though." Taking my sewing box from the shelf, I retrieve the brown bottle concealed inside. "Take a good swallow of that."

"It should have been me."

I thought he was asleep, but his voice is alert, if quiet, so as not to wake the kids sleeping in the front room with us. They drank their tea and cried for a while, but exhaustion finally took them. They will wake soon enough, and I will need to think about supper.

"Why would you say that?" I sit on the edge of the bed, smooth back his dark hair, so like his father's. "I don't want to lose you."

"If I could trade places, I would." His voice is stronger now. "It should have been me, not him. He was only there because of me."

I'm not the only one feeling guilty. "Don't you remember how he fought you over that mine? It was his choice to go. It could have just as easily been you, and that would have been no better."

Tears brim. "I should have been able to save him."

"You can't pull a grown man from under a ton of rock. I'm just thankful you got out. You're my baby. I don't know what I would do without you." I meet my boy's eyes and find a man looking back at me. "I'm as much responsible for this as anyone," I tell him. "I should have pushed harder for him to take a job in the city. I thought things would get better."

"It's not your fault, Mama," Dandy says. "How can you even think that?"

"The same way you blame yourself. It doesn't have to make sense." I straighten his covers, the weight of which is kept off his shoulder and arm by a contraption of scrap wood and wire hastily assembled by Toby. "It's going to be a rough road from here on out. We're going to have to hold each other up."

"What comes next?"

"I don't rightly know." I have been thinking over our options while he slept, and as soon as I am able, I need to call my sister. I need to hear her voice. "Maybe we should go to your aunt. I don't know what good it did your granny to stay here after my daddy died, and I don't want your sister to grow up thinking this life is the best she can do, the way I did.

"I loved your father. I loved him more than I have words for, but there are times I think Claire had the right idea, to try and better herself."

"Do you regret it?" Dandy asks. "Daddy, or us?"

I shake my head. "No. I was your dad's wife in my heart since I was Pearl's age, or younger. I just want you all to have more chances than we did." I squeeze his hand a little harder, a warning. "You're never going back underground. I'll break your other arm before I let you even think about it."

"Deal." His mouth quirks. "I never loved it the way he did. I wanted to. I hated it when I started working further underground, and this mine, when the men came and made it bigger, it always...scared me a little."

"Well, that's the end of it, then." I smile at my boy. It will take a while, but he will get past this. "You rest now. I'm going to check on the others, then walk down to the store and call your aunt."

I am a few steps from the bed when he speaks again. "I don't want to be called Dandy anymore. That was my baby name." His voice wobbles. "I'm not a baby."

"No, you're not," I say. "Sleep well, Dan."

"I have to call my sister," I say to the same neighbor who stopped by earlier. "Can you look in on the kids in an hour or so?"

Her knitting needles click quietly, and she nods. "Is Trudy back?"

"I haven't heard anything next door."

"Fritz got out." The needles cease, and she looks up. Her eyes are swollen, though as far as I know, she has not lost anyone. "I don't know how bad he is. He's at the hall with the others."

Then that's where Trudy will be. I'll check on her after I speak to Claire.

Pulling my scarf around my throat, I duck my head and step into the wind. It has been less than twelve hours since I walked this road in the company of my neighbors, yet everything is different. I come within sight of St. Stanislaus and veer off, needing a few moments to get myself together before facing the inevitable crowd at the store.

Dipping my fingers in the font, I make my way, not toward the nave, where a handful of women are clustered in the first pews, but to the shrine to St. Barbara on the left side of the church.

Knees protesting, I kneel in front of the saint and retrieve the rosary from my pocket, but peace is nowhere to be found. I glance up at St. Barbara's beautiful, impassive face. "Patron saint of miners," I mutter. "Fine job you did." If it is blasphemy, I do not care. She is not just the patron saint of miners, but one of the church's Holy Helpers, prayed to by those at risk of sudden or violent death in their labors. I look at the statue again. "I hope to God it was an easy death because he didn't deserve this."

The beads grind between my fingers like bits of gravel. I continue my attempt at prayer, but other thoughts intrude.

This didn't have to happen. If we had gone to Philadelphia, if Daniel had taken the job Harry offered, he would be alive. He knew how I felt about leaving—had he been placating me by insisting he would rather stay? Had all this happened because of my refusal to accept help?

It is my fault. I have brought this on myself and my children out of my own stupid, arrogant pride.

"God forgive me," I say. "Daniel, forgive me."

For the first time since I was torn out of sleep, I allow myself to think about my loss. Some part of me knew, from the moment I heard the siren, that this could be the outcome. As long as I could feel Daniel inside me, glowing like a spark, he was still alive. But with that gone, I am alone. The world without Daniel is a dark and frightening place.

How had Mama done it, with nearly as many children, and even less support? Tears drip off my chin, beading on my wool scarf. I stop fighting and let them flow. I will only have this one opportunity to let it out without witnesses.

Footsteps pause beside me and I look up to Father Anton's narrow face, full of concern. "How are you, Mrs. Kimber?" he asks. "How are the little ones?"

"Hurting," I say honestly. "I'm about to call my sister home, but I need to gather myself before I speak to her."

"Stay as long as you need." His hands, resting lightly on his thighs, are torn and swollen from his efforts at the mine. "The church is here for you."

"Thank you, Father."

"Shall I stop by later and talk to the children?"

"I think they would appreciate that."

I kneel before the shrine, pretending that my tears are from the pain in my knees, until my mind clears. I know what must be done. My pride has no place in this new world.

When I put the rosary back in my pocket, I encounter something else: the stone I'd picked up at the mine when I knew Daniel was gone. I turn it over in my hand. It is not a stone, but a piece of coal. Still just a rock, but with so much potential: heat, money, pain, death. I cross myself, then place the coal carefully at the feet of the saint.

37

Claire

It begins to snow while Thelma is with Max. Looking out the waiting room window at the flakes drifting lazily down, I am glad she agreed to wear a scarf and mittens. It wouldn't do for her to catch cold and miss school, not now that she has finally begun to enjoy it.

I flip through a magazine, ignoring the fashions in its well-thumbed pages. My mind is on the gala, and how to make Christmas happen for several hundred children, not to mention the two living in my house. Thelma has continued to accompany me on my orphanage visits, and the combination of her angelic looks and clumsy metal braces has stirred curiosity in the stone-faced children. They surround her, asking questions and patting her like a doll, and she has in turn persuaded them to participate in the Christmas program.

Her voice is audible through the closed door—not her words, but the lilt, excitement that her braces are being adjusted and she is closer to being freed from her armor, as she has taken to calling it. Listening to her, I smile. I will miss her when she goes home, but I look forward to making a family with just Harry and Teddy.

The door from the hall cracks open and a woman peers in. "Mrs. Warriner?" she asks doubtfully.

"Yes?"

"Your maid telephoned," she says. "She needs you to call home right away."

Katie doesn't even like to answer the phone; I can't imagine her asking the operator to put a call through to the Children's Hospital and leaving such a message. I drop a note on the desk for Max and make my way to the downstairs hall where the public telephones are located.

The phone hasn't finished its first ring when it is snatched up. "Ma'am?"

"Is Teddy all right?"

"Mrs. Kimber called for you," she says thickly. There is a muffled sound that I identify as a sob. "Her husband was killed this morning. She wants you."

I stop myself before I begin to cry. I can't lose control now; this isn't my sorrow, it is Ava's. Good God, it is Thelma's. "I'm going to have to tell Thelma."

"That poor baby girl," Katie says. "I'll have cocoa for you when you get home. It won't fix anything, but it won't make it any worse."

I stay in the protective wooden booth until it begins to feel like a coffin, then I sprint for the elevator. They will be waiting, and I don't want them to come downstairs looking for me. The least I can do is give Thelma the news of her father's death in the privacy of Max's office.

When I burst in, they are sitting on his exam table and he is teaching her a new Christmas carol. I cherish her last moment of innocence before I interrupt. "Thelma, honey, we need to talk before we head home. Max, can I use your office?"

Pearl

November 20, 1932

Daddy is dead.

I keep expecting him to walk in, whistling, and say it was all a mistake, that he hadn't gone to work yesterday, after all. But he won't. He's dead.

Dandy got out, but he's hurt bad and the doctor hasn't come for him yet, if he even will.

Daddy is dead. And I don't know what's going to happen to us.

Ava

Dr. Kerr tended to everyone at the makeshift hospital before setting out on home visits. It was after ten by the time he got to us, but he was able to fix Dandy's dislocated shoulder and gave him an injection to knock him out.

Despite our exhaustion, the rest of us slept very little. When I went to use the outhouse at three, Pearl was dozing on the floor next to Dandy's cot, and Toby was sitting on the back step, smoking. I didn't have the energy to scold him, just sat beside him and bummed the rest of the cigarette for myself.

In the morning, we huddle around the stove in the front room. The boys are worn out but refuse to go back to sleep; Pearl stares at the glow coming through the door of the stove, her eyes shining, but she is done with crying for now. She is too much like me.

It is so quiet that the sound of a motor is audible from far down the road. I put down my mending. "That'll be your aunt." Claire was not home when I called, but Katie assured me she would get word to my sister if she had to take to the streets to find her.

"Will she have Thelma?" Pearl puts her sewing aside; like me, handwork soothes her.

"I hope so."

Pearl opens the door as the Packard stops out front. Claire gets out and quickly opens the rear door. Thelma's movements are halting, but smoother than I expected. She flings herself at me, wailing, and I squat down to hug her. Her braces bang against my sore knees. "Look how much you've grown!" I say, squeezing her tight.

"Where's Daddy?" Thelma's tears are hot on my neck. "I want my daddy."

I smooth her hair, tears perilously close. "I know, sweetheart," I say. "We all do."

"I want him!" Thelma is not to be consoled.

"Your daddy was so proud of you, Thelma, he thought you were such a brave girl."

She squirms free, striking me again with her braces. "I want my daddy. Why isn't he here?"

Pulling her close again, I tell her the truth as I know it, as it was told to me and Claire all those years ago. "The mine took him." There is a deep gasp as she processes this, and she begins to sob again, more quietly. I rub the narrow space between her shoulder blades, waiting for the first wave to pass. I don't know what Claire has told her, beyond the fact of Daniel's death, but it doesn't matter; I have my girl back, and we will mourn together, as a family.

I can't lose her again. Whatever exercises she is doing can be done here, and if she has to have her braces adjusted in the city, I will find the money or beg it from my sister. From now on, we stay together. The process of unraveling started when Dandy left, and it grew worse after Teddy and Thelma went away. Now Daniel is gone for good.

The kids swarm Thelma, hugging her and examining her braces. I heave myself up, dusting off my skirt, and turn to greet Claire and Harry. My sister hugs me close, murmuring words of sympathy and so I am facing the Packard when the door opens on the other side and a familiar figure gets out.

I stiffen. "Why is he here?"

"He thought he might be able to help," she says.

I turn away. "I don't want strangers here."

"We were at his office when Katie called. He was so good with Thelma, I thought it would make the trip easier." Claire glances pointedly at my daughter, almost invisible among her siblings. "She wanted him to come."

"Thelma doesn't need a grown man for a playmate." I hate that I'm taking this out on Claire, but I can't seem to stop myself.

"He was a big help," my sister says, unfazed by my tone. "Traveling with two children isn't easy, but we didn't want to leave Teddy behind—we thought you would want to see him, especially now."

"Teddy?" Max vanishes from my mind. "You brought Teddy?"

Harry comes around the car with my boy. He is dressed in a dark blue sailor suit with white trim, and when he is put down, he toddles unsteadily toward me. I sink down in front of him. "Hello, Teddy."

He looks from me to Claire, and back again. "H'lo." His voice is the same, chirpy and cheerful, but he doesn't recognize me. A hole opens in my chest.

"You're a fine handsome boy," I manage to say, and tousle his hair. "Look at you."

Teddy smiles broadly, knowing full well he is a fine boy, and looks toward Claire. "Ma?"

I kiss him on the forehead, hiding my face in his halo of curls, and tell him the truth as he will learn it. "I'm Thelma's mama."

"How are the children?" Claire looks nearly as wrung out as I feel. One of her first experiences of motherhood should not have been telling a child that her father is dead, but she'd had little choice; it couldn't be left until their arrival.

"About how you'd expect," I say. "Dandy was down there. He got pretty banged up trying to get Daniel out. The rest are just hurting." I take a deep breath. "I don't think we know what's hit us yet." Claire gathers me into her arms again, and this time, I allow myself to cry. It is only for a moment, then I pull myself together and wipe my eyes decisively. "I'm glad you came."

Claire

Watching my sister's face when Teddy calls me Ma reminds me—again, and for the first time—what Ava has done for me. Understanding, Harry rests a hand on my shoulder. "She needs to see him," he says softly. "He's still ours."

"I know."

Walking into the house and seeing Dandy in the cot by the stove, I remember Mama's funeral only a year ago. How much has changed in that time, for me and for Ava. I am a mother; she is a widow. I am gaining confidence daily; she has asked for my help. Some cosmic switch has been flipped, and we have taken each other's places.

I look over my shoulder and see Max hanging back, talking to Harry. For a moment I think about joining their conversation, then I see Dandy, with his father's face, and forget everything else.

Ava

More people pass through the house than attended Mama's vigil. Men, either out of work or keeping well away from the mine, cluster on the front porch, talking and smoking. When I look out the window, I see Harry in their midst. Maybe he has a bottle with him. A year ago it angered me that he'd brought spirits into our home, and now I'm hoping he has. I shake my head.

The kids hold their grief in check while there are people around. Thelma sticks close to Pearl, a handkerchief in her fist, but she has stopped crying. George and Toby are side-by-side as always, still unnaturally subdued. Dandy appears to have aged several years.

He is the man of the house now. For so long, I felt like the only adult, but now it seems my son has grown up to assume the mantle his father couldn't always carry.

I miss Daniel with a fierceness that is almost unbearable, but I have always seen him clearly. He was a man strong in everyday troubles, but he could not face the repeated blows of the Depression and continue to stand. His disappointment at the failure of the Bonus Army, his continued unemployment, the loss of his children, my ability to earn while he could not—the world broke him long before the mine took him.

Tears burn and I retreat to the kitchen before I shame myself in front of my neighbors. Instead of the peace I long for, I find myself face-to-face with Max, coming in the back door.

"I can't believe you came with them." For once Max isn't smiling, but he radiates pleasantness in the face of my hostility. "Thelma needs her family, not a doctor."

His expression doesn't change, but something dims inside him. "I'm sorry," he says formally. "I wanted to offer my condolences and I thought perhaps I could be of some assistance."

"We don't need help," I say. "I'd appreciate it if you would go back out front with Harry. My kids don't need to be confused about you."

He watches as I walk away. Perhaps I've been unkind, but seeing him pop out of Harry's car like a jack-in-the-box, with his ready smile and his easy charm, is too much right now.

"Who were you talking to, Mama?" Pearl has Thelma on her lap, practically inhaling the little girl. It pains me to see how much she missed her sister.

"My Dr. Max," Thelma says, brightening. "He's fixing me."

"There's nothing wrong with you." Dandy sounds so much like Daniel that I flinch.

"Of course, there isn't," I say, "but he's helping her walk better, and we're all very grateful."

"Did he put those ugly things on her legs?"

"They're braces, and they're straightening her legs," I tell him. "See how much better she's doing already?"

His lip comes out, truculent. "I still don't see why he's here."

Neither do I, and it irks me to have to defend Max after I've just finished dressing him down. "He came to pay his respects, and to help Claire with Thelma and Teddy."

"His clothes are funny," Pearl says. "And he needs to comb his hair."

"He does," I agree. "I don't think he stops to look in a mirror that often."

Claire

"What are your plans?" Harry asks Ava in a quiet moment. He looks comfortable here; between Mama's funeral and Ava's visit with us, it's become easier for him. Or maybe I've just stopped being ashamed of my family. "Have you had time to think?"

"I've thought," Ava says, "but that's as far I've gotten. We're hanging onto the house by our fingernails, but Daniel's burial will take everything we have, and quite a lot that we don't."

"We can help—"

"You're not paying for my husband's funeral," she says, not unkindly. "I'm willing to accept help, Harry, but not for this. After that, I'm not so sure."

"You'd be welcome to come to us." Suddenly I want this very much. "We have the room."

Ava laughs. "Can you imagine me arriving with this lot? Where would you put us all?" She lowers her voice. "It's early days, but I'm expecting again."

Another baby! I wonder if this one was planned, and think not. Most prevention isn't effective; that's why there are so many Catholics. "It feels wrong to congratulate you."

"What did Mama say—losses and blessings balance each other out? This baby will have some big shoes to fill." Ava looks gutted, and I wonder how long it's been since she slept. "You'd be giving house room to me and six children, Harry, in addition to your own."

Harry looks gratified that she referred to Teddy as ours. "You could have Mother's suite."

"She'll have a stroke when she finds out."

He blinks. "She might," he agrees. "But it's available."

Ava shakes her head. "I'm not sure what the solution is," she says, "but we can't live with you—not long term, anyway. That's carrying family too far."

Harry takes her hand, something I cannot do without crying. "I understand. And I thank you for calling me family."

"If you weren't family, you wouldn't have Teddy." She looks at the baby, asleep in my arms. "Are you ever going to tell him?"

"When he's older," I say.

Harry polishes his glasses, not looking directly at Ava. "It would help if you were around. He could grow up knowing you and the other children."

"Another reason you'd like us to move."

"I'm selfish." His voice softens. "I want what's best for him, and what's best is to have all his family close by."

38

Ava

I watch from a distance as Max keeps an eye on Thelma, speaks to the little boys, and befriends Dandy to the extent of being allowed to examine his shoulder, but I continue to avoid him. Or he avoids me, I'm not certain which it is. Finally, as I make my way to the kitchen, he catches my arm. "Why are you limping?"

"I scraped my knees." I try to get past him. "It's nothing."

"Let me look." He reaches for his bag.

"I'm fine."

Dandy speaks up. "Let him look, Ma."

Cornered, I sit in the nearest chair. "It's nothing," I say again. "It'll heal on its own."

Max delicately folds my skirt up and makes a tutting sound. "You'll get a nasty infection if these aren't cleaned," he says. "Let me do that much."

"I can do it myself." I sound like a child.

"But you haven't." He retrieves antiseptic and a roll of bandage from his bag. "I can't claim to know you that well, but I think you're more likely to take care of others than yourself. Am I right?"

"The kids need me." I wince at his touch. "What am I supposed to do, put my feet up? In case you haven't noticed, our lives have gone to hell."

"I've noticed." He gently picks grit out of my right knee with a pair of tweezers. "I also know if you end up flat on your back with a raging infection, you'll be no use to anyone."

His logic is as irrefutable as it is annoying. I close my eyes and let him work, tuning out the chatter in the room until I feel the solid weight of a child nestle under my arm. Through the haze of pain, I acknowledge the changes in my girl: she is taller, more solid. "How are you, baby?"

"Sad." She nuzzles against me. "Auntie Claire is nice, but I miss home."

"We've missed you, too," I say, "but I'm glad you're doing so good."

"Miss Thelma is a very brave girl." Max puts the tweezers down and shows us his handkerchief. "That's quite a rock collection."

"Are you done?" I attempt to get up, but he blocks me.

"Not yet." He daubs my knees with antiseptic. It stings, and I wriggle away. "You squirm worse than Thelma. Keep still."

Setting my jaw, I remain motionless, only stirring when he finishes applying light bandages to both knees. "Thank you."

Max's earnest hazel eyes meet mine. "It's the least I can do since I've intruded on your grief." He busies himself with his bag. "Claire wasn't certain if the company would treat your son, that's why I offered to come along. I didn't mean to offend."

Guilt surges through me, but I can't bring myself to apologize. "Thankfully, the doctor didn't listen to the company."

"A dislocated shoulder, he said."

I think of how Dandy screamed when the doctor put his arm back in the socket. It was a sound I did not think could come from a human child, and I never want to hear it again. "He did."

"He's doing well," Max says quietly. "Physically, anyway."

What he does not say comes through loud and clear. "We're all going to take a while to heal."

There is a stir at the door. Mr. Scovill enters, followed closely by his son-in-law, Mr. Butler, and Mr. Henderson, the agent. All three are wearing suits and ties, and remove their hats as they approach.

Mr. Scovill is a tall, portly man with an impressive mustache, while Mr. Butler is short and slight, not only clean-shaven but with very little hair on his head. Mr. Scovill speaks first. "We've come to offer our condolences on the loss of your husband, Mrs. Kimber."

"Thank you." Over the years, I've sewn for both their wives, but I've never spoken with the men other than brief pleasantries at the company picnics.

"We heard your boy was also injured."

I gesture toward Dandy. His arm is in a sling to relieve the strain on his shoulder. "He'll mend, God willing. It could have been worse."

"Indeed," says Mr. Butler.

"As to that," Mr. Scovill says, "I have some unfortunate news." He pauses, and I wonder if it is for effect, or if he truly doesn't know how to tell me. "A crew of our men attempted to reach the chamber where the cave-in occurred." He pauses again, stroking his mustache. "They did not succeed. There was another collapse, and they barely made it out. It appears the entire chamber has come down. That means there is no way for the dead to be …retrieved."

"You won't bring them out?" Even though we weren't permitted to see him, we'd at least been able to bury my father.

Mr. Butler shakes his head. "At this point, we'd have to blast a new passage. There's no saying it would even work, and it's not something we're willing to take on financially, the times being what they are."

And because the company wouldn't go to any trouble for ex-employees who had been driven to theft by those times. "Thank you for telling me."

I watch them leave, avoiding conversation with the other visitors, and realize Mr. Henderson is still here. "Is there something else?"

"I want to offer my personal condolences, Mrs. Kimber, aside from those of the company."

"Thank you." My gaze moves around the room, checking on the kids. "It was kind of you to come."

"There's something else." He turns his hat in his hands. "I find this very difficult, but Mr. Scovill was clear. If Mr. Kimber had died in the company's employ, you would be entitled to compensation, and you would be permitted to stay on, provided you could pay the rent."

"Like we did after my father died," I say. "And the rent is up to date."

"That no longer matters." Mr. Henderson worries at his lip with his rabbity front teeth.

"What do you mean?" I focus on him with difficulty; the room is beginning to spin.

His face is beaded with sweat. "Your family, the other families involved in the…incident, will have a week to vacate your homes."

"And if we don't?"

"The police will put you and your belongings in the street." He tries to take my hand. "Mrs. Kimber, I'm sorry—I know it sounds unfeeling, but—"

"Sounds unfeeling?" I repeat. "I've just lost my husband, and very nearly my son to this damned mine, and now they threaten me with homelessness?" Blood rushes to my head. "I will leave this house when I'm good and ready, and if they attempt to remove me, they will regret it."

Mr. Henderson retreats, blown back by the force of my anger. "Mrs. Kimber, I'm just the messenger."

"Then take a message." I step toward him and he scuttles for the door. "We'll go, but if anyone touches a stick of furniture, or God forbid, one of my children, before that week is up, they won't have to worry about the house because I will burn it to the ground."

Claire

Harry and Max have taken the children to the hotel for a meal. Ava needs to eat, but she won't leave Dandy, and I won't leave her.

"You have to talk to the children, Ava."

"What do you mean?" Her needles click, and it reminds me of my childhood—she and Mama never just *sat*.

"Don't do what she did." I fold my empty hands in my lap. "Talk to them."

She stops knitting. "Sister, what are you on about?"

I have known, ever since Katie told me the news, that this needs to be said, but I haven't been able to find the right words. I chance it and say what comes into my head. "It's not just your loss." I fiddle with the ball of mud-colored wool I wound for her. "It's theirs, too. Mama not talking about what happened was part of why Jake left."

She picks at a dropped stitch and I watch my words sink in.

"It makes it worse, and it took me a long time to forgive her for that."

"I need tea for this conversation." Putting her knitting on the hassock, she hovers a hand over Dandy's forehead before ducking out of the room.

I follow her to the kitchen, where she stands before the stove, hands on hips, having a silent argument with a ton of cast iron. The kettle whistles and she snatches it up before it can wake Dandy, and transfers the water into the old brown teapot.

When we have our tea and our feet are propped up facing the stove, she says, "I wanted to name my firstborn Teddy."

"But you didn't. You waited until she was gone."

"I didn't want to remind her." Ava stares into her mug. "As if she ever forgot. Yesterday was the longest day in the history of the world, and I'm never going to forget a moment of it."

I put my hand over hers. "Tell them that."

"I'll try." She squeezes her eyes shut. "But you know me, full speed ahead."

"Then tell them that—that it's how you cope, but it's okay if their way is different. Let them cry. Let them talk about their father."

Rain pelts the window. I hope Harry gets the children in and out of the car quickly or the house will be full of wet clothing. I close my eyes and listen to the rain; it is a soothing sound, especially this close to the fire.

"Did Jake really leave because of Mama?" Ava sounds uncertain. "How do you know?"

"He told me." I was his pet, the way Teddy was Ava's. We talked about the things I couldn't tell her—my dreams of leaving, his terror of the mine. "After Tata died, he told Mama he didn't want to go back underground. She said that was his life, same as it was Tata's, and he had no choice."

It wasn't a compelling argument for a boy who had just lost his father. Feeling trapped, Jake bolted. I understood, even as I mourned yet another loss that could not be discussed. My eyes are hot with tears. "He told me to get out as soon as I could."

"And you did." My sister's voice cracks.

"Mama pushed me to finish school." I stretch my hands out toward the heat, my bracelets clinking. "I always wondered if she did it because of him."

Ava rests her head on her arms. After a moment she speaks, her voice muffled. "I've spent my life believing I put my family first, and I don't even know our entire story."

Ava

It is almost nine when the Packard draws up in front of the house. Claire leaves with Harry, promising to return in the morning. The kids are red-eyed but calm and, thanks to Harry, well-fed. Dandy is up and moving around, and seems to be in no more pain than I would expect from such an injury.

"Let's stay down here for a little." It's colder than the kitchen, but this won't take long. "There's something we need to talk about."

Pearl flicks on the radio, and dance music fills the room. She snaps it off almost immediately, and I understand—music feels wrong, and she doesn't have the energy to search for something more appropriate.

There is a shelf above the radio. In the center is the portrait of Daniel and me on our wedding day: both of us unimaginably young, his hair slicked back with pomade, mine in a pompadour. To my eyes, we look like children playing dress-up.

"Listen," I say to them, "there are a few things I need to tell you. Some of it you might not understand yet, but it needs to be said."

I take down the photograph of Mama and *her* children, the metal frame cool in my hands. "You've seen this picture all your lives. There were seven of us. By the time Dandy was born, Claire and I were the only ones left here."

"And then Aunt Claire left," Pearl says. "Before Daddy came home, right?"

"Right." I glance at her wedding photo on the shelf beside mine. "It was my mother's life I was living." I see the incomprehension on their faces. "I loved your father, and I don't regret a moment of our life together, but everything could have been very different if we hadn't been so stubborn.

"Your dad was raised the same as I was. The same as you've been. We were scared to try another way. By the time he came back from the war, all we wanted was to be together again. Leaving Scovill Run, getting away from the mines, it never really seemed like something we could do."

The kids are silent. I've never sat them down and talked to them, all together, like this. That is another thing that will have to change.

"We settled," I tell them. "But now we have the chance to try something different." I make eye contact with each of them in turn. "I know it's hard. But your daddy would want us to try. He wouldn't want us to stay here, or for you to be dependent on the company for the only work there is. He would want us to make something of this family, even though he's no longer with us."

"He'll always be with us," Pearl says. "I can feel him right now."

"Me too," says Toby.

Tears bead my eyelashes. Normally I would blink them back, but instead, I let them flow. "That's because he's in every one of you. I can see him." I bite my lip. "Two things you should know about your daddy: he worked hard, and he loved hard. That's the legacy he left you. Not money, not a house. Just that: work hard, love hard."

"Amen," says Dandy.

After that, nothing needs to be said but the obvious. "Let's go to bed."

The bed I shared with Daniel is separated from the other beds by Mama's old quilt, slung over a line.

"Let's push the beds together," Toby suggests.

"Just like when we were little." Pearl throws her weight against it and the bed skids across the floor. The younger boys help, shoving until the two beds meet.

Crawling into the center, I encounter the dent made by Daniel's body. With a deep breath, I settle into it and pat the mattress on either side. Thelma and Pearl climb in on my right, while George, Toby, and Dandy get in on my left.

Once the blankets and quilts are pulled up to our chins, I say, "Try to sleep, okay? The next few days are going to be really hard."

Thelma sniffs loudly and George says, "Hush."

"Let her cry if she wants, George. We've all cried today." Claire's words echo, and I think about what it cost her to speak to me like that. "There's something you need to understand. Everybody grieves in their own way. If you cry, it's okay. If you don't, that's okay too." A tear slips along my nose and I wipe it with the back of my hand. "When my father died, your granny thought it would be better if we didn't see how upset she was."

"Was it?" asks Toby.

"No." I squeeze his hand. "It made it worse."

Rain pounds on the roof. The uneven plink of water into the bucket measures out the seconds until Thelma speaks. "Will we be okay, Mama?"

"Yes, baby. We'll be sad, but we'll be okay." I survey them in the bleak lamplight. "There's one more thing. We're going to have to move."

Pearl slips out of bed to adjust the bucket. "The rent's paid up, isn't it?"

"It doesn't matter." Even saying the words exhausts me.

"Because of what Dad and I were doing?"

"Yes."

"Where will we go?" George squeaks.

"To Philadelphia." I've said it. Now I have to follow through.

Pearl turns toward me. "I thought we didn't take charity."

"We don't," I tell her. "Once we're settled, I'll pay back whatever they've spent helping us."

"What will you do for work?" It is a surprising question from Toby.

"When I was there in the spring, I made your aunt a dress. She says her friends will pay me to sew for them." It won't be enough, not if I sew night and day, not if Pearl sews with me—and I want her in school. But it will be a start.

"There's bound to be something," Dandy says. "Maybe Uncle Harry can give me a job in one of his factories."

"We'll talk about that when the time comes."

"We're building a fort in the woods," George says, out of nowhere. "We can't go until it's finished."

"We have to, stupid!" Toby elbows him. "Didn't you hear Mama?"

"Knock it off, both of you." Dandy's tone is hard. "There's more important things than your fort."

Thelma snuggles against me, warm as a kitten. "I can live at home again." Her voice fades as she drifts off to sleep. On my other side, Toby tries unsuccessfully to stay awake. George's eyes are already closed.

I lower my voice. "Let them sleep. You're both going to be involved in any decisions that have to be made. You're old enough now."

"Why didn't we move before?" Pearl curls around Thelma, stifling a yawn.

"We thought about it." My eyes sting, but if I close them, I won't be able to sleep. "He decided to go into the mine instead."

"It's all he knew," Dandy says. "We talked about it on the way home from Washington."

"Did you?" The house creaks in the wind, and a draft stirs the quilt-curtain.

"After they set the soldiers on us, Dad said he just wanted to come home where he understood how things worked."

Pearl's head droops against the pillow. One down, one to go. Then I can lie awake all night and think about the empty space in my bed, and my life. The full weight of my new reality descends: never again will Daniel wrap himself around me in the night.

"Turn off the lamp."

Dandy complies, and we lay in the dark, listening to the storm until we both fall asleep.

My dreams are filled with darkness and suffocation and I wake repeatedly, gasping for air. When the birds begin their morning song, I clamber out of bed, leaving a tangle of children beneath the covers.

The rain has stopped. Sun streams through the windows and I squint until my eyes adjust to the light. My chest feels hollow, as if my heart has been scooped out. I need to find the strength to continue living.

The kids are waiting for me to make things right, and I will. Somehow. All I feel at the moment is an enormous, exhausting obligation. I want Daniel to walk in and say, "It was all a mistake, I wasn't in the mine."

That isn't going to happen.

This town has taken everything from me: father, mother, brothers, husband. It will not take my kids. Going to Philadelphia— saving our family—is the last thing I can do for the man I have loved since I was a girl.

The thought of moving is terrifying. No work, no place to live, no friends. No one but Claire and Harry, whose charity we will be forced to accept. I have always managed on my own. and if we weren't being evicted, I would find a way to do it again. But the company won't change its mind; the men who committed the crime of trying to feed their families will not be forgiven, even in death. Families have been put out before for less reason and ended up living in the woods. At least that will not happen to us.

Pushing open the back door, I step onto the porch and am struck by the beauty of the day. The rain has taken the dust from the air even as it flattened the last of my garden. The distant rush of the creek reaches me in the stillness. A catbird cries like a colicky baby.

It is a beautiful day, too beautiful for grief, yet grief there is, and will continue to be.

Weeping may endure for a night, but joy comes with the morning.

Mama's voice appears at the most inopportune times, but she always says what I need to hear. Joy will come again. Not this particular morning, but someday. And my job is to settle my family in a place where joy will know how to find us.

Part Three

November 1932 - January 1933

39

Claire

"So we're agreed," Harry says. "They stay with us as long as they need to."

"Of course." I have wanted Ava and her family to come to us since Mama's funeral. I'm only sorry it's taken a tragedy to make it happen. "I'd like to stay and help with the packing, if you don't mind."

"Do you want Teddy with you?"

I do not like him out of my sight—he's with us now at the table in a high chair supplied by the restaurant—but he will only get underfoot and possibly upset Ava and the children. "I suppose he should go back with you."

"I'll keep him occupied while you take Claire out to the house." Max punctures the yolk of his fried egg with a piece of toast.

My husband glances up from his plate. "It will be faster if we leave together."

Something flickers in Max's eyes. "I'm not certain I'd be welcome."

Ava's touchiness had been more than the occasion warranted, though who's to say how I would react in a similar circumstance. "No one needs to know you're there," I say. "I'll just hop out of the car."

He nods and returns to his breakfast. There's something bruised about him today, and I wonder if it's all Ava's doing, or if he's seen in this place the reverse of what he tried to show her at the encampment in Philadelphia.

"You did good yesterday," I tell him. "Maybe not with my sister, but after." He and the young priest had gone to the hall to check on the men there. That is something I will be sure to let Ava know when she is in a better frame of mind; once she moves to Philadelphia, there will be no avoiding Max, and I don't want our relationship spoiled by her rancor.

Pearl

November 23, 1932

I haven't written because it hurts too much to talk about what happened. Worst of all is seeing Mama with the stuffing knocked out of her. I don't know if I ever want to love somebody if losing them does that to you. When Aunt Claire came the morning after, Mama just fell on her. She shook it off quick, but I saw her break and it was scary.

Teddy and Thelma came too, and Thelma's doctor. He seemed nice enough, and Thelma loves him to pieces, but Mama was rotten to him.

The biggest news is that the company won't let us stay on, so we're going to live with Aunt Claire and Uncle Harry. I hope Mama plays nice until we find a place of our own. Thelma says the house is as big as a castle. It better be, to fit all of us.

I don't mind leaving. Wherever we are, we'll be a family, and without Daddy, it may as well be someplace new.

Claire

While Harry supervises the bellboy's loading of the car, I pull Max aside. "When you get back to town, could you drop something off at the house for me?"

"Aside from Teddy, you mean? Of course."

I take several folded sheets from my bag. "Pass these on to Katie. Ava and the children will be staying in Irene's old rooms, but I want them to feel welcome, and that's not likely, not in the state she left them."

He looks over the pages, which represent two hours during which I should have been sleeping, and lets out a low whistle. "No wonder Prue praises you to the skies."

"What do you mean?" His words make no sense to my exhausted brain.

"I mean you've been hiding your light under a bushel all these years, Mrs. Warriner." Smiling makes him look more like the old Max. "Are you leaving anything for Harry to do?"

"Harry will bankroll it," I say with a shrug, knowing my husband will be back in his office at the earliest opportunity. "He doesn't need to worry about beds and children's clothing."

"Understood." Max tucks the list into an inside pocket. "Katie and I will see to everything."

"I don't mean for you to do it!" Katie is perfectly capable, and will likely be offended at any offer of assistance. "You've lost two days at the hospital as it is."

He offers a crooked smile. "I feel like I've overstepped here. Call it my way of making amends."

Pearl

November 24, 1932

It's Thanksgiving today. Aunt Claire made us all come to dinner with her at the Mansion House, and there was so much food! Mama barely ate anything, but the rest of us cleaned up every scrap, and Toby and George fought over who got Mama's plate.

All I could think about was last year at Mrs. Metzger's, where we all told what we were grateful for. Two of the people at that table are dead now, and two more are hurt. I'm not feeling very thankful, but then I look at Dandy and know it could be worse.

November 25, 1932

Granny must have had fun raising Mama and Aunt Claire because they disagree about everything. This time it's about how to pack. Mama wants to take all our stuff and Aunt C says she already has everything we'll ever need. (Thelma told me that Aunt C bought all new bedroom furniture recently and we're probably getting her old stuff, which is still nicer than anything we have).

George is only concerned about the radio, which we wrapped in Granny's quilts and put in a crate, but Mama dug in her heels about the kitchen table, of all things, and said she didn't care if it was mended. She actually got tears in her eyes over a table, and Aunt C backed down when Mama asked if she hadn't lost enough without losing her things, too.

I guess when you're surrounded by nice stuff all the time, maybe you aren't as attached to it. But this is the only place we've ever known, and Mama and Daddy spent their whole marriage here. Aunt C knew when she was beaten, and said to pack whatever she wanted, they would find a place for it.

Ava

Claire has taken over, directing my kids and referring endlessly to a list that she keeps in her pocket. Trudy—who is in the same situation—has become her enthusiastic lieutenant. Who knew my little sister could be so efficient? Once she stops questioning my choices, it is a relief not to think about every aspect of the move; I point to what must be kept and watch it disappear into boxes.

As I am not needed in the house, I decide to visit Father Dennis. Perhaps his Irish common sense will cut through the fog in my head and let me see a way forward. I avert my eyes from St. Barbara's shrine as I pass, not wanting to see if my spiteful lump of coal is still there, and knock on the door to the priests' office.

Father Anton answers, a sympathetic expression slipping over his face at the sight of me. "Mrs. Kimber, you have been in our prayers these last days. Your family is well?"

"We are." I try to look past him. "Is Father Dennis here?"

"Not at the moment. Is there something I can help you with?"

I shake my head. "I need to talk to him."

A bare twitch of his lips. "I am a priest as well as he."

"I know that." I do not have the energy to deal with his wounded feelings. "But he's been a friend of the family since before I was born."

"He is at the rectory," Father Anton says, chastened. "There was a leak in the roof that no one could fix but himself, and then the diocese called from Scranton and would only speak only to him."

Karen Heenan

Clasping his arm, I say, "Be patient. Father Dennis was new here, back when my mother first came. The town didn't accept him right off, but now he's as established as the church itself."

There is a ladder leaning against the back end of the rectory, but Father Dennis is nowhere to be seen. I let myself into the front hall, which smells faintly of damp and strongly of cabbage. "Father? Are you here?"

"In the kitchen." His voice drifts toward me.

The linoleum on the kitchen floor is peeling, as is the paint. There are pots on the floor and Father Dennis is in shirtsleeves and sock feet, staring up at the sagging plaster.

"You should let Father Anton fix it," I suggest meekly.

"That's what he says." He turns toward the stove. "Will you take tea, while I deliberate with the Almighty about the current location of the roofing nails?"

"Let me." I push a chair toward him and swing the kettle off the stove. "Put shoes on while you deliberate, the floor's wet and you're not getting any younger."

"Disrespectful young woman," he mutters, disappearing into the hall and returning with his shoes. "What can I do for you?"

Placing our cups—no better than those in the church office—on the table, I sit beside him. "More of the same, I suppose. Tell me it will be better soon."

He bends to tie his shoes, then curls his hands around the cup. "Hearts don't mend to a schedule, Ava."

I need something more, something to quiet the thoughts that rattle my brain like a child banging on a pot. "I've never been without Daniel, not since we were kids. He's part of who I am."

"And he always will be." Father Dennis spoons sugar into his tea. "Daniel wouldn't want you to buckle, Ava. You're strong, like your mother."

Twenty years ago, my mother buried not only her husband but her youngest son. I choke. "How did she survive losing them both?"

"I don't know," he says. "For the longest time, she wouldn't talk about it. There is tremendous guilt and anger in the loss of a child."

I still have my children. All of them. Losing Daniel is something I will never get over, but the thought that I could have lost Dandy— my baby!—is unfathomable. When I look at him, I see all the phases of his life: tiny, diapered baby; scruffy little boy; gangling ten-year-old, black hair flopping in his eyes.

How had Mama not just given up when Teddy was killed? Suddenly, I think of David, Thelma's twin. Barely there, unknown to the rest of the family, but just as beautiful, just as real, as his sister. In my mind, I have seven children, not six.

I reach for the sugar, unable to think about that. The bowl is crusty, with only a thin dusting of powder at the bottom. I take the barest amount and stir it into my tea. "I worry about how the kids will manage. About how we'll *all* manage."

He turns the chipped cup in his fingers, which are as ragged as the young priest's from digging in the pile. "Sometimes you just have to take a breath, Ava, and put it in God's hands."

His words echo my mother, but I resist them. My whole identity is tied up with being in charge, being the one who knows where to go, how to get there, how to live, how much it will cost, how to keep my people safe. The ground shifts under my feet. I am none of these things, now. Have I ever been, or have I always been a fraud? I want to keep pretending I know what to do, but I also want to continue with the honesty I've shown the kids, sit them down and say, "I don't know what's next."

We fall silent, listening to the uneven drip from the ceiling. The kitchen is warm, and once the roof is mended, it could be a pleasant place. What a shame the two of them are on their own; the house could use a woman's touch, even someone who came in and cleaned regularly. Why had I never seen to it, or asked Pearl? What about Trudy—?

I give up trying to organize the lives of others and concentrate on the mess that is my own life. "This is my home," I say to the priest. "Mama is buried here. Tata and Teddy. Dan is *in* the mountain. How can I leave them?"

"Your home is here," Father Dennis says, placing his hand over his heart. "And Daniel and Lillie will always be with you. Let Claire help, for the sake of the children."

Through the confusion swirling in my head, I feel a small glimmer of something. It isn't hope, not yet, but it *is* gratitude. Gratitude that I had Daniel for as long as I did, that my boy wasn't trapped forever inside that damned mine, that he is *alive* and mostly whole. "I will," I say, closing my eyes in exhaustion. "For their sake."

Claire

The bells began at daybreak. I wake in my bed at the hotel, thinking I have overslept, but they ring the same number over and over: eleven, for the seven men and four boys who perished less than a week ago. Although Father Dennis was unable to convince the company to change their position on bringing out the bodies, he organized a memorial for the day before we are set to leave, so the town can mourn their dead.

We have arranged to meet in the lobby, so we can walk together to the church. The children are scrubbed and quiet, bands of black fabric pinned neatly to their sleeves. Pearl fastens one to my coat.

"I'm not sure I can do this," Ava says, her lips barely moving. "Stop me if I start screaming."

I pull her close in a brief hug. "I'll do my best."

The priest's desire to hold a service is understandable, but most of the bereaved families are readying themselves to move, the same as Ava, with little time to spare for niceties. Some, I think, have already left. But when we walk into the church, it is packed. Whether or not the company has sanctioned this memorial, all those who lost someone in the bootleg mine are present, and miners and their families have come from all over the area to pay their respects.

In the crush of faces, I see Frank, and it surprises me that I can turn calmly toward Thelma, without a flicker of the fear I felt a year ago.

A pew has been saved for us toward the front. People greet Ava quietly, reaching out to take her hand. She speaks to them, never losing her awareness of the children. I am awed by her ability to function in the midst of what must be paralyzing grief.

The young priest, Anton, begins the service. His Slovak accent is strong, and he leads the opening prayer with tears on his cheeks. This is the first disaster he has experienced, according to Ava, but it is unlikely to be his last. When Father Dennis steps forward, he fades gratefully into the shadows.

"We come here today to honor our dead. Those we lost last Sunday, and those who we have lost in the past, and who are still with us every day." His smile is sad. "The mine giveth, and the mine taketh away, and it takes far more than it gives, my friends. Each time, those taken are our men and boys, our fathers and sons, our brothers and cousins and friends."

He rests big hands on either side of the lectern, looking out over the congregation without seeing any of us. "I would like at this time to say the names of those we have lost. As you hear their names, picture them in your mind. Say a prayer for them, and another for those they leave behind."

A murmur runs through the pews. This is not how these services are usually conducted. When Tata died, separate funerals were held as the men were brought out, and the atmosphere had been one of sadness. Here anger simmers under the hastily-assembled black clothing, and most particularly under the black robe of Father Dennis.

"Jakub Andrysiak." The name is unfamiliar, but when I hear *Jakub*, I think of my lost brother, though he detested his Polish name because it tied him to Tata.

"Stanley Becker." One of the town's small German contingent. Most are not Catholic, but there aren't enough of them to merit their own church, and they prefer the Catholics to the Methodists.

"Bogdan Gorecki. Thomas Gorecki." I have a faint memory of Bogdi Gorecki; Thomas must be his son.

"Hermann Jäger." Trudy's brother.

"Daniel Kimber." Beside me, Thelma sobs into her handkerchief. I put my arm around her and Toby snugs in next to her, to be included in my embrace. I do not dare look at Ava.

"Ansel Kraus." Stifled weeping from the cluster of Germans.

"John Polikoff." A gasp from Pearl; one of her classmates?

"Piotr Wiśniewski. Stefan Wiśniewski." I remember them—they were brothers, a few years younger than me. Judging by the weeping coming from the other side of the aisle, both were married, with several children.

"Michael Zabek." A wail like ripping cloth. The source is an elderly woman, white-haired and black-clad. A widow already, and now without a son.

"These are our dead, O Lord. We are confident that death is not the end, nor does it break the bonds forged in life. We pray that you grant mercy upon their souls, for they were taken before their time and their work is yet unfinished. Comfort their families, O Lord, for theirs is the hard task. Their loved ones are with You in Heaven, but here on earth, we mourn their loss."

My cheeks are streaming with tears at the unfairness of it all, these lost souls who wanted nothing more than to feed their families. If Father Dennis asked us to cross the road to the Gracie and lay waste to it, I think we would tear the breaker apart with our bare hands.

40

Pearl

December 1, 1932

I almost don't believe we're here. Up until we drove away, I thought Mama would find a way for us to stay in our house. Except it's not our house, not anymore.

Before we left, she sold our beds to Mrs. Nordstrom, who has new boarders because of the evictions. Mrs. Metzger took my chickens to the rectory. She's going to keep house for the priests. There's no pay, but she can keep Fritz and Hetty with her.

I've only ridden in a car twice before, and it was nothing like Uncle's, which is beautiful inside, with soft gray cushions and tassels like on furniture. There are even little bitty flower vases between the windows, though of course there were no flowers because it's November. The boys rode in the truck with our stuff and Mama fidgeted the whole way because she was afraid they'd freeze to death. (They didn't).

When we had supper that first night, Aunt Claire told us she registered us for the local school, but we wouldn't have to start until the new year, to give us time to get used to things.

I think it's going to take longer than that, but I'm looking forward to school. She even said there's a library within walking distance of the house. A whole library!

Ava

I've never needed an alarm clock in my life. My body knows when to get up and start the day, and now, when I wake in the darkness and have nothing to do, it feels wrong. I've been here before, but as a guest. I don't know how to *live* like this.

The kids have adapted remarkably well. Pearl slumbers peacefully beside me, and across the room, Thelma is face-down on her cot, one arm dangling. In the room beyond ours, the boys sleep soundly. Dandy is unwilling to let his little brothers explore alone, and so the three of them spend their days out of the house, and come home worn out and hungry.

Easing out of bed, I pull on my robe and tuck Thelma's arm under the covers, then trip over Claire's damned dog. It makes an offended noise and jumps onto the bed, nestling into the blanket.

I long for tea, but going downstairs now will throw off the rhythms of this strange household. Two days ago, I flustered poor Mrs. Hedges by appearing in the kitchen at dawn, when she and her husband were having their coffee. I won't make that mistake again.

If someone had told me I would miss life in Scovill Run, I would have laughed. Miss that falling-apart house, the endless work and bone-deep exhaustion at the end of the day? But I miss it all, and the community I have lost besides. I made sure Trudy was well settled, but she is no longer on the other side of the wall. There is no one to talk to here, other than the kids.

For all that Claire insisted she wanted us with her, other than a few days of focused attention which nearly drove me insane, we see her only at meals. She has some society thing, she explains— something to do with orphans and Christmas—but it feels like she's avoiding the problem she invited into her house.

Go ahead, I think. Spend time with your rich friends and leave us to manage.

We *are* managing, each in our own way. I would prefer not to think about Daniel too much—grief renders me skinless, angry in a way I haven't experienced in a lifetime of angers and irritations. It is consuming, and I cannot afford to be consumed.

But the kids need to talk about him, and when they do, I push my feelings down and speak quietly, tell them stories they haven't heard and repeat ones they have. It keeps him alive for them, and for Thelma and the boys, that's especially important. Pearl and Dandy won't forget, but I won't have the young ones grow up not remembering their father.

Later that morning, we are in my room, laughing about a disastrous hunting trip he once took with the boys, when Claire pops her head in. "I'm off," she says breezily. "Can I pick up anything for you while I'm out?"

I follow her into the hall. "You go on," I tell her. "We're fine here."

"I don't know how you do it, Ava. You're so strong." Claire's arms go around me, light as a butterfly, and then her heels clatter down the stairs.

A noise makes me turn. Mrs. Hedges is a few feet away, a duster in her hand. She raises her shoulders a fraction. "Is there a choice?"

That is what irritates me about Claire, her assumption that I possess some great strength to get me through this thing that has torn a hole in the fabric of my world. "If there is," I say, "I'd like to not be the strong one for a while."

She clasps my arm with a thin, brown hand. "I lost my youngest boy two years ago. You stay strong for them, but inside..." Her eyes glisten as her voice trails off.

Inside is a different thing entirely. Sometimes my brain is a dark place, filled with screams like the very pit of hell. Claire wouldn't recognize her strong sister if she could see that.

"I'm very sorry about your son." Her pain is palpable; I am not so locked inside myself that I can't sense it. "Why don't I come down to the kitchen for a cup of tea, and you can tell me about him?"

Claire

Ava seems content to stay in the house, even as the children explore the neighborhood. I feel guilty leaving her alone, but Christmas is three weeks away, and there is still so much to be done.

Katie and her mother transformed Irene's fussy third-floor suite into a welcoming space for my sister's family. The heavy draperies are gone, replaced with net curtains which let in light to show the other changes: an un-fussy walnut bedroom suite, with a small bed alongside for Thelma; a comfortable, overstuffed armchair; a Monet painting of flowers. The second room has twin beds for the boys— the beds Harry and I used to sleep in. If and when they find a place of their own, I will be happy to see those beds leave with them.

In addition to furnishing the rooms, Katie and Max took my list to Gimbels and bought inexpensive clothes for the children. I had to guess at the sizes, and they have an easier return policy than the other stores. I made sure Ava's dress found its way into her closet, where I hope she will eventually acknowledge its presence and wear it.

It occurred to me when we arrived and Katie met us at the door with Teddy that it might be difficult for Ava to share a house with him, and so I have begun to bring him to our meetings. Many of the other volunteers are young mothers, and they are charmed by him. He enjoys riding in the car and thrives on the extra attention.

Prue hasn't given up her campaign for me to learn to drive, and I'm beginning to see her logic. I hate having to call Hedges from whatever he's doing if I need to run across town; it would be so much easier if I could drive myself. Harry said he'll buy me a little roadster like Prue's for my next birthday if I learn to drive.

As I consider this, I marvel at how my life has changed. Last December, I was childless, mostly friendless, and cowed by my mother-in-law. Now I have a son, more acquaintances—if not true friends—than I can shake a stick at, and Irene is close enough to visit, but her space in my house has been filled with people I love.

Ava won't stay forever, I know that. She's too proud, and the children have learned her lessons well. Pearl asked the other day if she could help Katie with the cleaning, to pay her share of the rent. I assured her that we don't want rent, but she gave me her mother's face and I won't be surprised if I come downstairs and find her polishing furniture in the living room or helping Mrs. Hedges with the dishes.

They're good children, all of them. Even the boys, who I can finally tell apart because they keep still long enough at meals for me to notice the minuscule differences between them. George has more freckles; Toby has a cowlick that will not be tamed. They both have wide, gap-toothed smiles and more energy than should be legal in such small bodies. Teddy babbles and grins at them and I am boundlessly grateful that he will grow up knowing his brothers— though hopefully not taking on all their behaviors.

Pearl

December 7, 1932

Thelma was right. Aunt Claire's house is huge! We have two whole rooms and a bathroom to ourselves, and there's always cake in the kitchen if we're hungry. Aunt C doesn't make the cakes. She doesn't cook, either, not ever, and she doesn't clean. There are servants who live in the house who do all that.

Thelma tried to explain them before, but I didn't know she meant real colored people. There's a girl named Katie who I don't think is more than eighteen, and her parents, who are called Hedges and Mrs. Hedges. I wonder if he doesn't get to be a mister because he's a servant or because he's colored? Anyway, I like Katie, she's got the prettiest voice and she loves Thelma and Teddy as much as we do.

Aunt C is helping to organize a big Christmas party, and almost every day she either goes out, like she has a real job, or stays in her sitting room making lists and telephone calls. Katie and I take Thelma to her appointments with Dr. Byrne since Aunt is busy and Mama is staying in, doing what she calls getting used to things.

Ava

I take more comfort from the Hedges family than from my sister: Katie, always cheerful and so good with the kids; Hedges himself, silent but stalwart; and Mrs. Hedges—or Esther, as I learn to call her after our conversation in the kitchen.

Her son, Roy Lee, was fourteen when he was killed. He and some friends had been in the train yards, doing whatever boys do. "Snitching coal, probably," she said, with no emotion in her voice. He was on top of a car when he slipped and fell, breaking his neck. "It was just bad luck. He could just as easily have gotten up."

As Daniel could just as easily have walked out of the mine. "Bad luck," I agree. I stare down at the plain saucer between my hands; the dishes used downstairs are sturdier and more to my liking than the beautiful, breakable stuff Claire prefers.

Esther refills my tea. "Your hands look better. You been using that lotion I put in your bathroom?"

My skin is softer, the knuckles less swollen, after only a few weeks without doing laundry. I flex my hands and take a deep breath, letting it out slowly. "I'm being selfish. Half the families in town lost someone in that mine."

"And they all feel the same. They just aren't as lucky as you."

She is right. However much I hated asking for help, Claire was a godsend. Families in Scovill Run without anyone to take them in would have still been in their houses when Mr. Henderson and his men came, and that does not bear thinking about.

"I worry about the kids. They've lost everything familiar to them, on top of losing their father."

"They haven't lost everything." Esther bends to take a tray of cookies from the oven and the scent of cinnamon fills the air. "You're their home, not some house."

"You make it sound as though my husband had no part in it."

"Of course he did," she says. "But you gave them life. Now you show them how to keep living."

I try. When I flag, Dandy is there to shore me up. It feels wrong to be comforted by one of my kids, but he has an instinct for when I am most fragile. He will smile, or touch my shoulder, and the grief recedes long enough for me to take a breath.

But for all his support, he is still a boy; I can't talk to him about how I feel, and so I creep to the kitchen when everyone has gone out. Esther is uncomfortable with Claire knowing about our friendship, and I understand. Pearl seems to have developed a similar relationship with Katie—they take Thelma to her appointments, something I've encouraged because it gets my daughter's nose out of her books and hopefully stops her from fretting about me.

I have no desire to see Max Byrne. Talking to him has a knife-edge feeling, like I'm on the verge of exposing some protected part of myself. I am grateful for his treatment of Thelma and—in a way which I choose not to examine—for his appearance in Scovill Run. Even though I did not want him there, I learned later from Trudy that he had treated the injured men at the hall, so his efforts weren't wasted on everyone. Just on me.

41

Ava

Any other day at this hour, Esther would be starting her day in the kitchen, but Claire and Harry gave the Hedges family off for Christmas and I volunteered to cook breakfast. Around me, the house is still quiet—no one will be up for at least an hour.

After my first cup of tea, I slip quietly up to the nursery. The door is ajar. I push it wider, so the light falls across the crib. Teddy is on his back, covers thrown completely off, mouth agape in an unchildlike snore. His blond curls are damp, and I have a visceral memory of what a hot baby he was. My hand hovers, wanting to smooth back his hair, afraid of waking him.

"Merry Christmas, darling," I whisper. "Happy birthday."

A year ago, he had been nothing more than a weight in my belly and a nagging backache. A year ago, I had five children, a husband, and a home of my own. I had everything.

I still have five children, but no husband and no home. Something must be done, and soon. Once the holidays are over, I need to find work and a place for us to live. Our rooms here are comfortable, but they are rooms—I won't let the kids take over, and I want my things around me, not stored in a warehouse somewhere.

Teddy sighs and rolls onto his side. I bend closer, letting his scent fill my nostrils. When he opens his eyes, I start back in surprise. He raises chubby hands, asking to be picked up, and I hastily straighten. This day will be hard enough without actually touching him.

When he realizes he isn't going to get his way, he grizzles a bit, then grasps the bars of his crib, slowly getting one leg, then the other, beneath him. He pulls himself upright, watching me with those ridiculous blue eyes.

"Who's my most beautiful boy?" I ask, my eyes stinging.

As always, he responds to the tone of my voice, dropping smartly on his diapered bottom and smiling at me with his four teeth.

I hug myself to hold back the pain. This is my baby, mine and Daniel's. It doesn't matter that I'm carrying another child; Teddy is still *ours*.

Faint voices reach me through the room's other door: Claire and Harry are awake. My sister will be in soon to check on Teddy and bring him down for his bottle. I kiss my fingertips and touch them to his forehead, and steal silently back to the kitchen.

Dandy is there, hunched around a steaming cup of tea, the image of his father. "Where were you?"

"Upstairs," I say vaguely, not wanting him to know I was mooning over the crib. "Hungry?"

His mouth quirks. "Always."

In this place of plenty, it makes no difference if I feed my eldest before the rest of the household is awake. I heat the pan and crack a trio of eggs into hot fat, stepping back to avoid the sizzle. "Is your shoulder bothering you? Is that why you're up?"

Shrugging, he says, "It's Christmas."

"The boys aren't awake yet." I top off his tea and pour myself a cup, add a teaspoon of sugar. "What is it?"

He scrubs his face with his hand. "When Dad and I were in Washington, he told me something."

"Yes?" I slide the eggs onto a plate and push it across the table to him. "What?"

"It was a secret." He digs into the eggs, and I wait while they disappear. "I don't know if I should tell you."

I don't want my boy to betray his father, but I can't believe Daniel kept secrets from me. "You don't have to tell, but if you think I should know, go ahead." I swallow hard. "I'll leave it up to you."

Breakfast will be buffet-style, I decide, not wanting to carry a load of hot plates up to the dining room. Scrambled eggs, sausages, bacon. Stacks of pancakes. The miracle of fresh orange juice.

Dandy is quiet for so long that I have finished my tea and started mixing the pancake batter. "I think you need to know," he says, "even if it makes you mad. He thought you'd hate him, so he never told."

I stop and stare at him. "I couldn't hate your father." Shake him, yes. Shout at him, even. Never hate.

"Teddy was his idea."

"What do you mean?" My voice is loud in the quiet room.

"He wrote to Aunt Claire when you were having...when you were sad. He asked her not to tell you."

And she kept his secret. What had she thought, receiving that letter?

I barely remember how I felt after Teddy was born. I remember crying without knowing why and never having any energy. Days didn't register; weeks were hazy; only a few memories from that time are sharp.

Daniel hadn't been wrong to be scared. If I'd been wholly myself, I would have been frightened, but in the fog of my unhappiness, it didn't seem to matter. The loss of his job, my lack of milk, the fact that the house was always cold. The constant fear of eviction. None of it mattered.

Of course, he had asked Claire. The only surprise was how long she waited to ask me. Then I remembered her letter; she had just lost a baby herself. So she had received his request, asking her to take our child, while she was expecting. I let out a breath, thinking of my sister losing yet another baby, and having that offer in the back of her mind.

For the first time, I truly begin to accept what we have done.

When breakfast is over and gifts have been exchanged, the kids and I go to mass. When we come back, Claire corners me about the party.

"It would mean a lot if you were there," she says. "We've had our Christmas, between last night and this morning, but this is important to me."

I can't look at her right now, not without thinking of Daniel's letter and the secret they had between them. "I think I've had enough Christmas."

There is no such thing as enough Christmas in Claire's books, and she sticks to her guns. "It's going to be wonderful. We've worked on this for months. You should be there."

"Go enjoy your party," I tell her. "I'm not stopping you."

"Don't begrudge, Ava." Claire folds her arms, looking uncannily like Mama. "If someone else is getting something, it doesn't mean you're being deprived. Life isn't pie."

"In my experience," I say, "when someone gets something, it almost always means that my people don't." Claire might have started out poor, but years of Harry's indulgence have taken the edge off her memories. "It just seems silly—all this time and effort for a party."

Claire presses her lips together before responding. "Why do you have to be so *mean* about everything?"

Is that how she sees me? "I can't help it."

"You can help it." I can see she's holding back what she really wants to say. "You just choose not to, the way you choose to be angry all the time."

"We don't need a savior, Claire." Why should I not be angry, when she has my son in a crib off her bedroom, and I am forced to accept her charity? "We need to do this on our own, and I don't think some big party is going to make things better."

She huffs out a breath. "No, *you* need to do it on your own. You're pushing me away as hard as you can."

Somehow I don't think we're still talking about the party. "I'm in your house," I say. "How is that pushing you away?"

"You act like you're here against your will." Her hands go to her hair, but instead of raking her fingers through and spoiling her waves, she drops them to her sides. "I'm doing the best I can."

I sort through the rubble of hats and mittens the kids have left on the hall table. "And you want what? Gratitude?" I let out a breath, calm myself before I say something unforgivable. "I appreciate what you've done. I do. I know it's been a lot of expense and inconvenience for you and Harry. But this isn't how we live. I can't just keep taking things from you."

Her shoulders relax. Whether or not she'd admit it, she needs to hear that I am grateful. "I'm just saying, you don't always have to do it all yourself."

The idea of relying on someone else is so alien that she might as well be speaking Chinese. "I'm managing just fine," I say crisply. "Stop undermining me by giving the kids things they shouldn't get used to having."

"We're leaving at noon," is all she says. "Stay home if you must, but don't spoil the children's fun."

"I'm not likely to spoil anything for your orphans."

"Not those children. Yours. They deserve this treat just as much." Claire looks directly at me, and there is a steely determination in her gaze. "Thelma has been involved with this almost from the beginning. She's been to the orphanages. She knows the children. The boys will enjoy it—they're still young enough, and God knows Dandy and Pearl deserve a break from acting like adults." She checks to make sure none of them are in earshot. "They're carrying the weight of the world on their shoulders, Ava. Let them have this."

I spread my hands. "I didn't say they couldn't go."

"You know they won't go without you." Claire bites her lip. "You can handle the punch," she says. "You can stay in a corner and pour drinks, that way you don't have to be in the middle of everything."

I don't want to serve drinks to a bunch of rich people. I want to stay home alone and take a bath. I want to retreat into the hot water and think of Daniel, think of my birthday baby who is no longer mine. "Fine," I say when it appears she will otherwise stand there all day. "If it will make you leave me alone."

Claire

Harry drops me at the stone portico on Broad Street. "Are you sure you don't want me to come in with you?"

The hotel's many windows glow with warmth. I look north to the clock tower atop City Hall—it's just after four. "I'm fine," I say. "I just want to look things over. Come back with them in an hour or so. Don't let Ava change her mind."

I wave him off, happy to be on my own. The chaos of opening presents and then having words with my sister has taken some of the luster from the day and I need to calm down. I intend to enjoy myself.

"Merry Christmas, madam." The uniformed doorman's genial smile belies the fact that he is working on Christmas. "Are you here for the big party upstairs?"

"Merry Christmas," I return. "I am. Is anyone here yet?"

He nods. "Mrs. Foster and a few of her ladies are just ahead of you. They've gone up to the Cameo room."

Originally we were given the Clover room, but the Hangley-Martenson engagement imploded while I was in Scovill Run and when the larger space became available, Prue jumped at the chance. The room is frequently used for society functions and I know it well, but I still visited to make notes of additional decorations that would be required and how to rearrange the seating. Stella and Marie handled most of it, knowing I needed to spend time with my family, but I hadn't been able to keep away entirely.

My heels click on the mosaic floor, echoing in the nearly-empty lobby. Glass arches lead to darkened spaces which, on any other day, would be a bustling dining room, a cafe, and the sweet Viennese tea room. Several clerks are huddled behind the marble reception desk, but when they see I know where I'm going, they return to their tasks.

A sign has been posted by the elevator bank: "Orphans' Society Christmas Party: 19th Floor." I pass a gloved finger over a smudge on the brass frame and step into the nearest open car.

A twelve-foot blue spruce, covered in silver tinsel and shining ornaments, dominates the room. The glittering star at its pinnacle nearly disappears into the domed ceiling. It is a fairyland, and for a moment, I am a child, walking in and seeing the tree and Santa's throne alongside.

"It's perfect." Prue appears from nowhere and captures my arm. "When I came up with this hare-brained scheme, I had no idea what you were capable of."

"It's hardly all me." Wrapped gifts are piled around the bottom of the tree, one for each child on my list of attendees, and another twenty put aside for unexpected additions. "It's been a group effort."

"Whatever." Her lipstick is as red as Santa's suit, her enormous smile slightly alarming to the uninitiated. "I'm going to have a party for all the volunteers after the holidays are over, to say thank you."

The idea of a party at the Foster house no longer terrifies me. "I shall look forward to it."

Before the others arrive, I check on the arrangement of tables and chairs—there needs to be seating for hundreds of children, even though they will be on stage in shifts, singing carols—and making sure the drinks tables and buffet are properly spaced for crowd control.

While the party is intended for the children, there will be a fair number of adults in attendance—all our volunteers are bringing their families, and some of our biggest donors, including Aunt Nora, have paid to attend.

A wave of sound rolls over me, and I turn toward the elevators, where Mr. Carson and Abigail are shepherding the first group of children into the room.

Ava

The slightly uneven strains of "Away in a Manger" drift over the room. The drinks table is deserted, all eyes on the singing children. I lean my elbows on the table, taking the weight off my feet. I have given in and worn the green print dress and shoes from my spring visit, but the dress is tight and my pleasure in it is gone.

It was a good idea to come. Thelma knows half the orphans in attendance, and George and Toby appear to be forming a gang with the orphan boys. Pearl and Dandy stand side-by-side, listening to the carols and keeping an eye on the young ones.

"Claire should be proud," Max Byrne says at my elbow. For some reason, he is wearing a green tunic with striped leggings and shoes with curling toes.

"What are you supposed to be?" I busy myself rearranging punch cups for my invisible customers, trying not to gawk.

"Isn't it obvious?" He touches a finger to his cap. "May I have a drink, or are you here to guard it from marauding elves?"

"Punch or eggnog?"

"Eggnog."

I ladle the creamy liquid into a cup and hand it to him. Our fingers brush and I take another step back. "Don't you feel ridiculous?"

"Why should I?" His curly hair works rather well with the cap, I have to admit. "It's not about how I feel, anyway."

I shake my head slowly. "Did you just happen to have this hanging in your closet?"

"I borrowed it from a friend who works at the Forrest Theatre." He grins, looking no older than Toby. "Should I keep it?"

Why doesn't he take his eggnog and leave? "You'd probably wear it."

"I probably would." He leans against the table, watching the performance. "They've worked so hard for this to come off."

"Claire's done nothing but talk about it since we got here." Her single-mindedness surprised me; I'd never thought of her as able to focus on anything.

"I'm sure," Max said. "This is almost all her doing."

"She introduced me to some red-haired woman, said she was the organizer."

"Prue Foster had the idea, but Claire executed it." He holds out his cup for a refill. When I angle myself so he is out of my line of sight, he comes around the table. "Thelma's thrilled to have her family here."

My eyes close. "What's left of her family."

"I'm sorry." He sounds contrite. "I put my foot in it all the time with you."

When the carol is over, Thelma makes her way through the crowd. "Did you see my friends, Mama?" she crows. "Weren't they good, Dr. Max?"

I am stunned when she jumps into his arms and allows him to swing her around. "They were very good."

"Can they come visit when we find a house, Mama?" she asks over his shoulder. Her cheeks are rosy and she looks healthier than she has in years.

"We'll see."

Max deposits her gently on the carpet and points toward the tree. "There's one last performance," he says, "and then you and your brothers and sisters should head back here and keep your mama company."

Thelma streaks off clumsily toward the stage, her oversized bow bobbing through the crowd.

"She does like you." I try not to think about what it felt like to see my daughter in Max's arms.

"I love her like she's my own." His eyes are alight. "Can't help it."

There is a moment where it is still possible to hold my tongue, to stop myself from lancing the boil of my misery and showering him with its poison. "But she's not yours," I say, crossing my arms over my chest. "She's not yours, and she's not Claire's. She's mine. *My* child. Just because I let one go doesn't mean I'm handing them out to everyone who asks."

"I never meant that," Max says, stricken. "But it's hard not to get attached, she's a sweet girl."

"While the two of you have been playing pretend with my daughter, I've been worrying about her, worrying about the others, worrying about Daniel." I stop for breath. "I don't have to worry about him anymore, but I'm twice as worried about the kids."

"I'm sure they'll be fine, once they've had time to adjust." He tidies the cups into rows, avoiding my gaze. "They're good, smart children, a credit to their parents."

"And here I've been waiting all this time for someone to tell me that." I move the cups back where they were. "I didn't know they were good, smart children until you told me."

"What's wrong?" he asks. "I know you've been through a lot, but you don't need to take it out on me. I just want to help—I want to be your friend."

Max is like a less-endearing version of Claire's dog, begging for my attention, all of which must be given to my kids. There is nothing left over for a grown man who can't manage his own affairs. "I don't have time for friends," I tell him. "I don't know where you got the notion that I would want them."

"From you," he says. "I thought we *were* friends."

I purse my lips, feel the unaccustomed stickiness of lipstick. "You're my daughter's doctor. I've been polite."

"And now you've stopped."

"Stopped?"

"Being polite." Max is angry. "Between your husband and your home, you've had an enormous loss, but you've landed on your feet, as best you can. You'll build a new life, with new friends."

"All I need are my kids." I back away again. "Why won't you understand that?"

He takes a step toward me. "Maybe because I don't believe it."

"What should I say to convince you?" I take a deep breath. "That I send Thelma with Pearl so I don't have to talk to you? Is that enough?"

For a second, he looks like a disappointed boy, but he rallies quickly. "That would indeed be enough, Mrs. Kimber. I'll continue to treat Thelma, of course, but I'll make myself scarce in the future."

There is a quivering in my midsection: the baby has chosen this moment to announce himself. Why do they always pick up on my internal state and become acrobats?

358

"I'll leave you be." He touches his cap and turns away, but not before I see the pain in his eyes. "Merry Christmas."

The kids surge around me when the performance ends. Thelma leans heavily against my hip, unwilling to admit she is tired; Toby and George remain alert, despite their yawns. Pearl moves behind me and briefly rubs my shoulders. I roll my head from side to side, loosening the tension in my neck.

I've had enough—of Christmas, of people, of wearing an expression that has nothing at all to do with how I feel. What are we waiting for now?

The room is plunged into darkness, and hundreds of children squeal. For a few long moments, nothing happens, and then, very faintly, we hear bells. The sound seems to come from the roof garden. A gust of wind blows through the room, and there are more squeals and a stir of movement.

A point of light in the darkness. The star at the top of the tree glows gold, then the rest of the tree ripples into brightness, all the way to the bottom. The electric lights glint off the tinsel and glass ornaments, and the whole tree shimmers like a mirage.

Everyone catches their breath, and tears burn at the corners of my eyes. It is lovely, and the children—all of them—deserve this. I put my arm around Thelma and the others crowd around me.

George looks up. "Is Santa here?"

"There's no Santa, dummy!" Toby says.

Madness fills the room as the children stream toward the tree, shouting and pushing. The golden throne at its base is occupied now by a portly man in a red suit. I know, from all those conversations I tried to ignore, that it is Prue Foster's husband, but he looks like Santa from an old Christmas card with a long, fur-trimmed coat, straggling white beard, and high black boots.

"Shows what you know!" George and Toby begin to scuffle, until Dandy swats them.

Max Byrne darts forward with a microphone. "There's only one Santa, and there are an awful lot of you. Let's not run him down, okay?" He points to the floor in front of the tree. "Two lines, boys and girls, and be ready to tell Santa your name and what you want for Christmas."

Though my kids have already had their gifts, they still join the throng around the stage to watch the goings-on. Pearl maneuvers to the front and speaks to Max, who drops his cap on her head. She tips her head back and laughs, then calls to Dandy, and they join Max to hand out presents.

Safe in my corner, I slip off my shoes and watch as the orphans sit on Santa's lap, one after another, and whisper in his ear. He hugs each one, then passes them on to Max, who directs the handing out of gifts by Pearl, Dandy, and several other older children.

This is not what I expected. There is something almost magical at work here. I could watch these happy children all night. Knowing they are going back to homes with no parents, possibly no siblings, makes their joy even more touching.

And it makes my meanness even more shameful.

Her holiday over, Katie claims Teddy for the nursery as soon as we walk in. Pearl and Dandy push the little ones toward their beds while Harry, Claire, and I remain in the hall, shedding coats and hats and trying not to yawn as openly as the kids.

"I'm proud of you, my girl." Harry hugs my sister to him. "Who needs a drink?"

Claire colors prettily. "I would hurt someone for a martini, but first I need to get these shoes off." We mount the stairs together, leaning on the rail for support.

"I'm off to bed," I say at the landing.

"After this, I think we're all worn out." She slips off her shoes, curling her toes in the hall runner. "It went rather well, didn't it?"

"It did." I put a hand on her arm. "I want to apologize."

"For what?" She looks tired but happy, a solid-through happiness I haven't seen in her since we were young.

"I thought your party was silly," I tell her. "It wasn't. It was magic, what you did tonight."

She flushes again. "It's no more than they deserve."

"Well, I didn't take it seriously." My grip tightens, then I step away. "You gave those kids—and mine—something they'll never forget."

42

Claire

"Where did you get to during the party?" I ask Harry over breakfast. There was a significant span of time when he and several other husbands disappeared. I have my suspicions but bide my time before asking for confirmation.

"A few of the fellows went downstairs to find a little quiet." He looks abashed. "I didn't think we'd be missed."

That means someone had let them into the Clover Club and they'd settled in to have drinks poured by an amenable waiter. "You could have at least—"

"I have to make a call later today," Harry interrupts smoothly, "but I think I may have found a house for you, Ava."

The fragile china cup pauses halfway to my sister's lips. "You have?"

"I was talking to George Howe while you were upstairs making merry. He owns some houses not too far from here, and he's looking for tenants."

"If it's near here, we can't afford it." Ava carefully places the cup back into its saucer. "Even if you help at first, which I grant you'll have to do until I find work. You can't be paying our rent forever."

"You might be able to afford this sooner than you think." Harry polishes his glasses and sets them back on his nose, smiling delightedly. "From what George told me, he bought the entire row a year or so ago. Some of the houses were in pretty rough shape. He's had his workmen making them over one at a time between other jobs, but the work is still ongoing. Most people wouldn't be willing to live near a construction site."

Unsaid is the fact that George Howe is a friend and would be willing to give Ava a break on the rent if they are good tenants. I squeeze Harry's hand under the table, his disappearance forgiven. "That sounds lovely!" I say. "I do so want you within walking distance."

Some people might not be willing to live on such a block, but Ava is ready to go anywhere, short of a coal mine, that will give her privacy and independence again. She glances at the children. They are silent, watching her.

"I'd be willing to look at it."

Ava

Before Harry can talk to Mr. Howe, I receive a telephone call of my own. When Katie comes for me, I can't imagine who would call, but I immediately recognize the voice, full of confidence and money. "Hello, Mrs. Foster. I hope you enjoyed the rest of your holiday?"

"It was lovely, Mrs. Kimber, thank you so much." There is a delicate pause. "I know you're just settling in, and I can't imagine you would say yes, but it never hurts to ask."

"Ask what, exactly?" If it involves one of her charitable endeavors, she'll be hearing a swift no; charity, for the foreseeable future, begins at home.

Prue laughs. "I suppose it would help to know that! My husband and I are giving a party on New Year's Eve, and while I do have something to wear, I was wondering if you could find the time to put together a little number like that blue one you made for Claire? She stopped traffic in that dress."

I'd asked my sister how the dress had gone over and her response was noncommittal; I give more weight to Prue Foster's opinion.

"I could," I say, "but this is the last stretch of time I have to spend with my kids before they start school."

"So it will cost me," she says good-naturedly. "Understood. Do I buy the cloth, or do you?"

"You can buy it if you get exactly what I tell you and bring it here this afternoon." I am taken aback by her swift agreement. "I'll need to get your measurements and then you can come back tomorrow late afternoon for a fitting."

"Done," she says gleefully. "Tell me how many yards, and where you got Claire's fabric. I'll be at the house by one o'clock."

I duck out of the alcove and nearly collide with Pearl, wandering down the hall with her nose in a book. "What is it, Mama?"

"I may need your help this afternoon," I say, bemused. "I just got an order from my first dressmaking client."

She drops her book and whoops, and we do a little dance together in the hallway.

Mrs. Prudence Foster will have a new dress for her party, and I will have earned my first money in this strange new world.

Pearl

December 27, 1932

My notebook ran out before Christmas, so I haven't written. Aunt Claire gave me a diary for Christmas, with a proper lock and key, and I was going to save it for 1933, but I need to write down what's happened so far.

Uncle Harry thinks he's found us a place to live, and Mama just got asked to make a gown for one of Aunt C's lady friends. It needs to be done by New Year's Eve, so she's going to use aunt's sewing machine and she promised to let me try it. Or at least help with the hand sewing.

It was so sad to wake up on Christmas without Daddy, but aunt and uncle tried their best to make up for it. There were presents, even better ones than last year, and then we went to mass. Uncle's mother came for lunch. She came to the party later, too, not that she spoke to any of us. She did try to speak to Aunt C, but I don't think it went well. Aunt said something sharp and turned away, and Mrs. Warriner just stood there with her teeth in her mouth.

Christmas was hard for Mama, because it's not just Christmas for her, it's Teddy's birthday. She was tight around the mouth all day, and it surprised me to pieces when she decided to come to the orphan party.

If I write about that, I'll use up half this diary. I put its key on the chain with the gold cross which was Aunt C's other present. I hope it's not disrespectful, but there's no other place to keep it. It won't be long before Toby is old enough to pry, and even though I don't have any secrets, I like having someplace for my private thoughts. And now I can even manage more than a few lines a day because if I run out of pages, Aunt C will buy me another one.

Ava

Prue Foster is a whirlwind, arriving promptly with a large wrapped parcel and a suitcase of charm. "I don't suppose I could have the *exact* dress you made for Claire?"

"Do you want my sister to throw me out?" I shake my head. "You'll have something that suits you better. Your shoulders are lovely—I'll make sure to show them off." I walk around her, looking at the statuesque figure and making changes in my head to the basic pattern I used for Claire's dress. "Is there anything you'd like to hide?"

She laughs, clapping both hands on her bottom. "It's not likely, what with styles the way they are, but do your best."

Lips pressed tight, I circle her again. "Maybe not *hide*, but it can be de-emphasized."

I open the parcel to find yards of deep purple satin, even better quality than I had chosen for Claire. There is also a smaller cut of the same fabric, but in scarlet. I shake it out and it spreads across the table like blood.

"I couldn't resist," she says. "It's too divine. Could you line the back drape in this, so there's just a hint of red when I move?"

"I'm not certain how that will look." Other than absolutely awful. Very few people can successfully wear that shade, and Mrs. Foster isn't one of them. I don't even know yet if she has the skin for a backless dress.

"I know," Mrs. Foster says. "It's ghastly, but I adore it. No one will tar you with the brush of my bad taste. I'll make sure I tell them how good you are, and how reasonable for a rush job." She grins conspiratorially. "You may think you're overcharging me, but you haven't met my friends."

Stroking the satin, I say, "I'm very much looking forward to making their acquaintance."

Claire

Following the sound of voices to the dining room, I find Ava deep in conversation with Prue Foster over a large puddle of aubergine satin. My sister has a tape measure slung around her neck and a determined look on her face.

I lean into the room. "I can't believe you're out and about already. I'm still recovering."

"Priorities, darling," Prue says, not looking up. "I'm taking advantage of your sister and getting a gown made for New Year's Eve."

"In five days?"

"It's not impossible," Ava says crisply. "So long as I can use your machine, Claire."

"Of course you can."

She smiles. "Now, Mrs. Foster, let's go upstairs so I can measure you. After that, Claire will give you tea for your trouble and I don't want to see you again until tomorrow afternoon."

"It's no trouble at all." Prue's mouth curls up at the corners. "Didn't I tell you, Claire, that I wanted a dress like yours?"

Prue is getting what she wants, but I am willing to bet my sister is also getting something from the deal.

Ava

Measurements completed, I hand Mrs. Foster off to Claire and commandeer the dining room again. Most of my supplies are packed away, but the shop thoughtfully included two spools of purple thread in the package, and Claire has plenty of pins in the sewing box she never opens. I had left the gown pattern here, knowing there was no use for it in Scovill Run, and I pin the pieces to sheets of newspaper. Mrs. Foster isn't as slender as my sister, but it isn't difficult to draft the pattern up to her size.

Clearing my mind to focus on the task, I make short work of the basic bodice. It occurs to me how to draw attention away from Mrs. Foster's abundant backside and I unfurl the red satin again to see how much there is. Nearly two yards—she has no idea how to calculate yardage. I spread the purple satin across the table, blessing people who have parties large enough to require tables of this size.

Without weights, the satin is slippery. I look around. The silver salt and pepper shakers will do for a start, and the smaller candlesticks. Once the fabric is held in place, I lay out the new pattern pieces, humming contentedly. Satin is a notoriously unflattering fabric on a less-than-perfect figure, but bias cut is forgiving and I hope for the best. I am looking forward to using that wondrous electric machine again.

If I get everything cut out, Pearl can help with the basting, and later with the finish work. She has a lovely touch with a rolled hem, but this gown is going to have to hang for a day or two for the bias to stretch before it can be hemmed.

Conversation rises in the hall, and then the door closes. A few minutes later, my sister pops her head in. "Katie has set up the machine. It's ready whenever you are."

"Thank you." The pinned pieces of the dress, including the scarlet drape, are folded on the sideboard, and the table is covered with diamond-shaped pieces of fabric in both colors.

"What's all that?"

"The not-yet-patented Ava Kimber bottom distracter." I show Claire a rough sketch of a long, harlequin-pieced scarf that will start at the front neckline, drape over Mrs. Foster's very nice shoulders, and flutter distractingly down her back.

"It's gorgeous," Claire says. "In a slightly alarming way."

"That's exactly what I'm going for. It suits her—she's a bit alarming."

"I wouldn't know where to start." She watches, fascinated, as I pin the pieces together. Mama taught us both, but Claire's skills never progressed beyond basic mending.

"Sometimes I make it up as I go along," I say, around a mouthful of pins. "It usually works. This one had better."

"I almost forgot—I came in to tell you, Harry talked to George Howe. He has a house, and it will be available after the first of the year."

43

Ava

Naturally, all the kids want to see the house, but Dandy and I go alone. I need to make a decision, and the fewer voices clamoring for my attention during that process, the better. Dandy reminds me more and more of his father; he will keep quiet, answer my questions honestly, and support whatever I decide.

We turn off Delancey Place onto Nineteenth Street and walk a few short blocks before turning onto Ringgold. It is a narrow block with tall brick houses that seem to lean toward each other across the street, like trees.

"Harry says these houses were built during the Civil War for mill workers." I pull the slip of paper from my pocket; it is damp and creased from my nervous handling. "We're looking for number twenty-two."

"Who lives here now?"

"I don't know." There is a sign on the first house denoting "Howe & Lescaze," and I gesture toward it. "Our landlord, apparently."

"He's a builder?"

"An architect." The red brick houses have white steps that run sideways up to the front door. There is another entrance beneath the stairs, leading to a lower level. Some houses have shutters; others do not. A few show signs of being actively worked on. "He built that big office building on Market Street, the Savings Fund Building, I think it's called."

"The Philadelphia Savings Fund Society," Dandy says. "It's almost all glass. I saw an ad for it in the paper, it said the offices were designed to be lit by the sun."

I stop in front of the next-to-last house and look up. "Well, that's not what this was designed for." Two narrow windows on each floor, bracketed by black-painted shutters, and one on the ground level by the steps.

Despite its unassuming front and being connected to its neighbors on both sides, it seems enormous compared to the house where I have spent my life. Four floors of space—what would we even do with it all? "It's too much," I say, shaking my head. "We need something smaller."

"Uncle Harry says we can afford it." Dandy is twitching with excitement. "Why do we need a small house?"

"Because we're small people." I shove the paper back into my pocket and turn, wishing desperately for Daniel. "I don't know how to live in a place like this."

My son's arm around my shoulders surprises me. "We're *not* small people," he says. "We've just had small lives. And maybe that can change." He lopes toward the steps, towing me behind him. "Let's at least look in the windows."

I nod, unable to speak. He sounds so much like his father. We stoop to peer in the ground floor window, which opens onto an empty space, with a kitchen beyond.

"We could put a wall up there, divide it so you could use that empty part for your dressmaking. Your customers could come right in this lower door here." He runs his hand over the brick. "I could make a sign, *A. Kimber, Dressmaker*, to put by the door."

"Dreamer!" My heart beats faster at the thought. Climbing the steps, which need a good scrubbing, I stand on tiptoe to look in the first-floor window. It is a bright room with a fireplace on one wall and two large back windows. There is a curved staircase, with light filtering down from above.

It is a warm, welcoming house. If I can quell the panicky belief that we don't deserve all this, it could be a good home. A floor for Dan and the boys, a floor for myself and the girls—and the baby, when he comes. A room for us to be together. A kitchen, with room for the table Daniel repaired. Space for my sewing machine. For my business.

"It's perfect." I look up at Dandy. "Let's go tell the others before I come to my senses." Dandy picks me up and swings me around, whooping like a boy. "Put me down, you lunatic child!"

"Not until you promise you won't change your mind." He swings me once more and then sets me gently on my feet. "Let's go home, Ma."

"No," I say. "*This* is home, or it will be, soon enough. Let's go back to your aunt's."

Claire

Everything happens so quickly that I can barely reconcile myself to it. When Ava came back and told Harry she liked the house, he was on the phone with George Howe before she finished speaking. Within two days, she signed a lease for a suspiciously low rent and Harry organized a truck to bring their things from storage in the days after the new year.

"I think they're rushing into this." I am snuggled against him under the blue satin quilt. The novelty of sharing a bed hasn't worn off. Why had I accepted Irene's furniture placement all those years? Why had he? "Do you think she's ready?"

"You can't keep them here forever," he says softly. "Is it your sister who's not ready, Claire, or you?" He strokes my hair. "Ava needs her independence."

"She's been independent since she was born." I sigh, knowing he's right. "I just like having them here."

A year ago, I couldn't have imagined living with my sister and her family, as I couldn't have imagined the house without Irene's dour presence. But now, hearing the children's voices makes me happy, and I like keeping an eye on Ava, making sure she isn't concealing too much grief behind her smooth façade.

"Look at it from her angle," he says. "She'd probably just begun to feel better about Teddy, and now she has to see him every day, with you as his mother."

That is enough to put my selfish thoughts aside. I can't add to Ava's burdens, not when she has another baby on the way. I don't know whether to feel happy or sad about that and decide, as Mama would have said, to offer it up to God and make the best of whatever comes. Ava must wonder at my sudden about-face, but she doesn't question it, and even accepts the secondhand furniture I press on her with something resembling grace.

In the days before the move, we clean the house on Ringgold Place from top to bottom. Between the lot of us, it doesn't take more than two days—it wasn't dirty as much as neglected. Mr. Howe, the landlord, sent two men to paint the walls. Katie and Pearl do the heavy cleaning, while Dandy and Hedges carry things up and down the narrow, twisting staircase. Even Toby and George, excited to have a home of their own again, manage to haul buckets of water without spilling and wipe the insides of the windows with vinegar.

Dandy and Ava put their heads together about the empty space on the ground floor, which my nephew is certain he can turn into a work area for Ava's dressmaking business. He tells Harry about his plans, and Harry sends over a long table from one of his factories.

Standing in the small space, with Ava's treadle machine under the high window and the cutting table off to one side, I can almost believe it is happening. My sister will have a home, and if I have any say in the matter, she will have a business, as well.

Ava

Harry and Claire ask me to accompany them to the Fosters' New Year's Eve party. The fact that I have nothing to wear to such a gathering never occurred to them. I am content to stay with the kids—between completing Mrs. Foster's dress and preparations for the move, I am worn out. Toby pleads to stay up until midnight, but I have every intention of being asleep long before then.

"I'll let you know how Prue's dress goes over," Claire promises, before vanishing in a cloud of French perfume.

After a quiet supper in the kitchen, Hedges builds up the fire in the living room and I sit on the davenport between Thelma and Dandy. The little boys toast themselves on the rug, and Pearl has Teddy on her lap and a book on the arm of her chair. She is almost done reading *Alice in Wonderland*. When the boys beg again to stay up until midnight, she tells them they can, unless she finishes the book first.

"You said Alice was a silly girl's book," she reminds them, pinching the scant number of pages and winking at me. "Tweedle-Dum and Tweedle-Dee, that's who you two are."

"I like the cat," George says. "He's like Toby."

Toby grins. "I wish I could disappear and leave my smile in the air. It would scare people spitless."

Pearl is done before ten, and Thelma and George are asleep. Toby is paging through the book, looking at the illustrations, yawning hugely.

"Can we move tomorrow, Mama?" Pearl asks. "I like it here, but I want to go home."

"We can't go home," Toby says faintly. His head has fallen forward onto the book.

"It will be," Dandy says before I can. "You'll start school soon, and make new friends."

"You should go back to school, Dan. You're not too old."

"Sorry, Ma." He rubs his fingers through his hair. "Going to school would feel like I was pretending to be a kid. I want to pay my way."

"You do already." I pat his arm and smile at Pearl. "Both of you. I'm lucky to have you."

My daughter wipes away a tear. "I miss Daddy."

"I do, too," I tell her. "Every day. But he wouldn't want us to be sad. We can't help missing him, and we shouldn't try. What we can do is make him proud of who we become next." My low back twinges and I force myself up from the cushions. "Let's get them into bed."

Reaching our room, I remove Thelma's braces and help my near-sleepwalking girl into her nightgown. She sits on the bed and falls back, instantly asleep. "Would you put Teddy down?" I ask Pearl. "I'd love a bath before I turn in."

She hoists him higher and kisses his cheek. "Is it hard, Mama?" she asks "Being with him, knowing he's not yours anymore?"

"I carried him for nine months." I take my robe off its hook and turn off the bedroom lamp. "Part of him will always be mine. But he'll have a good life here, and Harry and Claire have promised to tell him the truth when he's old enough to understand."

"At least we can see him," Pearl says. "I missed him almost as much as Thelma when you went away."

"I know you did. I feel bad I didn't take it serious, how upset you were." Pearl leans against me and I squeeze her shoulder. "I was so upset myself, I forgot how it felt to be you."

"What do you mean?"

"I took care of Claire and my brother Teddy when I was your age. If Granny had come home without them one day, I wouldn't have known what to do." I hope someday Pearl finds a man who recognizes her strength and lets her use it.

After she leaves, I sit on the edge of the tub and wait for it to fill. It is shameful, but my favorite part of the house on Ringgold Place—besides its very existence—is the bathtub. A tub of my own: a place to hide away when the world gets too noisy.

It's been little more than a month, but already I can no longer remember my husband's smile or the sound of his voice, his scent, or how it felt to be in his arms. It's too soon—have I been so willfully busy that I've forced him from my memory?

I slip into the scented water and close my eyes, trying to summon him. I think back to our one-night honeymoon, the first real bathtub I'd ever seen, and the first time we saw each other naked. I was in the tub, luxuriating in the hot water—no bath salts or bubbles there—and he came in, wearing just his one-piece underwear. I noted it needed mending and vowed I would take better care of him, now that he was mine.

"How's the water?" He sat on the edge of the high iron tub and put his cold hand on my wet shoulder. I shivered, not completely from the cold.

"Hot." I brought my knees up to my chest. I had thought many times about Daniel seeing me without clothes, and now that he had, I was shy and uncertain of myself.

"You look like a mermaid." He stroked my shoulder again. "Beautiful."

I giggled in spite of my nerves. "And you look like a coal miner." I inspected the grime under his nails and embedded in his knuckles. "Does this ever wash out?"

"Let me in and we'll find out." He shucked his underwear and climbed in behind me.

I had a quick impression of a lean, rangy body, pale as my own, with dark hair in places I was afraid to look at. When his arms came around me, I relaxed against him with a sigh. It would be all right. We would figure it out together.

Water laps at the edge of the tub. I snap out of my memories and sit up, the image of Daniel clear in my mind. The feel of his arms around me in the hotel tub, what had happened after.

I know how to find him now. It just takes hot water, and time.

Claire

The hotel band is taking a last break before midnight. Someone has put a record on the phonograph, but most people stop to catch their breath and drink champagne. I step back from Harry, letting my fingers trail down his arm until they tangle with his. "Can we sit?"

"Of course," He leads me back to our table. "I'm proud of you, you know."

"What?"

"I'm proud of you," he repeats, sliding a drink toward me. "You've accomplished so much in the last year. You've changed."

I start to object, then stop. I *have* accomplished things. I *have* changed. The old Claire would have demurred, but I feel the need to take credit for what I have done. "I think some of it came from losing Mama," I say slowly. "I was an adult before that, but losing her made me grow up. And of course, there's Teddy." I don't mention what came before Teddy; Harry knows what those repeated losses took from me, and even motherhood—at last—does not entirely change that.

"There's Ava, too." He lights a cigarette and watches the remaining dancers, giving me time to gather my words.

"I always thought of her as my second mother. It wasn't fair to her." Ava, in this past year, has proved herself to be a woman like me, sometimes right, sometimes wrong. Also still growing up, and learning at long last that she doesn't have to do everything on her own. "She's had a hard time."

"But she's coming through it." He stubs out his cigarette in a small glass ashtray with the Warwick Hotel logo. "I've always been a bit frightened of your sister."

"Join the club." I still have trouble accepting the swift unraveling of Ava's world. "It's been painful, seeing her so lost."

Prue spins by in her husband's arms, the harlequin-patterned scarf fluttering behind her. It should have been ridiculous, but because of Ava's skill and Prue's conviction, it is not; she has been garnering admiring glances all night. I smile in satisfaction and suspect my sister will soon be very busy in her new workroom. Sliding my bangles up and down my arm, I continue, "She accepted the life we were born into. She wanted it—or at least she wanted enough of it that she was willing to risk the rest. I never was."

Harry's hand covers mine, warm and reassuring, "I'm glad," he says. "You've brought more to my life than I could have ever imagined."

"You thought I was a little blonde ornament when we met."

"And you were," he agrees, squeezing my fingers so I know it is in fun. "But you were so much more. You were the reason I left politics, did you know that?"

"What? No, why?" During our very first walk by the river, he'd mentioned his desire to run for office, and it confused me when he stepped down after one term. How had it been my fault?

"If I'd been single, or if I'd married someone else, it might never have occurred to me to be unhappy with what we were doing, but you made me see things differently. I wanted to help people, and that seemed to be the last item on their agenda." Harry rubs a finger over his mustache, thinking. "Watching you organize this whole Christmas gala—"

"It was just a party. It wasn't a big deal."

"It was a huge deal, for the children and you. You wouldn't have taken that on last year. If Prue Foster had managed to persuade you to help, you would have found a quiet corner to hide in, or invitations to write, or you would have asked me to send a check and gone out and bought a new dress to wear to the party. But instead, you gave two hundred children the best Christmas they've had in years. *You* did that."

I sniff back tears, touched by his unexpected praise. "Even though I drove your mother out of the house?"

"The change has been good for her." He smiles with no evidence of resentment. "She and Aunt Nora have been genteelly fighting since they were born. They may as well end as they began. The house doesn't need two mistresses, and I only need one wife."

Ava

It is nearly eleven when I emerge from the bathroom. Pearl is snug in bed with another book. *The Good Earth*, this time. Claire lent it to me, but I haven't found time to read it yet. Thelma sleeps soundly in the glow from the silk-shaded lamp.

"Is it good?"

"So good, Mama." She closes the book. "You have to read it."

"Maybe once we've moved, and things calm down." I pull my nightgown over my head, shed my robe, and work my arms into the sleeves. Mama's lessons die hard. "I'm glad you like to read."

Pearl leans over and turns off the bedside lamp. "I like to see other places," she says, "even if it's just in books."

I pull the covers up under my chin. The faint light from outside shows the outlines of the furniture, but little else. It isn't as dark as Scovill Run, but it's better than the front-facing rooms, which feel too exposed. As we settle in, I ask, "Do you want to continue to take Thelma to her doctor's appointments after we move? We can change them so they're after school."

"Yes, please." Pearl rolls onto her side. "I like Dr. Max."

Good. I'm hoping for a few dress orders after this party, and if I don't have to stop sewing for Thelma's appointments, I will have more time to visit with the customers. Pearl can be trusted to relay accurate messages. It will also limit my contact with Max's abrasive charm—though the last time I saw him, he had been far from charming. Then again, I had been far from kind.

He's stayed away since Christmas, which means I've never had the chance to apologize. I *should* apologize, but it is easier not to. I have enough on my plate without having to deal with Max Byrne.

44

Ava

Everything is packed—nothing left in the closet this time—and the kids are finishing breakfast. I come upstairs to use the bathroom, then sit on the bed, looking around the rooms that have cradled and protected us during this most fragile time. It is not just the rooms that have cradled us, but Claire. She came when I needed her most, and found a way forward when all I could see was darkness. Even more surprising, her mad scheme of promoting me to her friends as a dressmaker seems to have worked. I cannot see far ahead, not yet, but there is enough light now to at least see possibilities.

I look forward to the light, much in the way I look forward to the arrival of my last child. Babies have a way of keeping you from too much reflection. I will have no choice then but to look to the future.

There is one thing I must do before leaving, but I haven't been able to find a way to broach the subject. It seems easiest to absent myself from the family group and wait for Claire to find me. One of the kids will offer, but she will come herself, feeling my need, as I would feel hers.

Less than five minutes pass before she appears in the doorway. "The natives are getting restless downstairs. Are you ready?"

"Almost." I pat the bed beside me. "I need to ask you something." I look at the painting on the wall, something vivid and smeary, which my sister has assured me is very good, and which I take to mean is very expensive. The rug is also colorful, and likely valuable. I look at anything but Claire. "Did Daniel ever write to you?"

She blinks. "Not that I recall."

"Try a little harder," I say, recognizing the blink for what it is. "Dandy told me Teddy was Daniel's idea. He has no reason to lie."

"Wait here." Claire bounds up and leaves the room. I stay put, suddenly exhausted by keeping up the appearance of being in control.

A few minutes later, she returns with a quilted satin box. The box is filled with letters. She riffles through them, slides one out, and hands it to me.

I take it, not sure if I want to read what Daniel wrote. Through the paper, I can see his familiar scrawl, and when I unfold it, all I can I see are his fingerprints. "Oh, God." I clap my hands over my face and bend double. "What has happened to my life?"

She puts a tentative hand on my shoulder. "It's like Mama always said. Sometimes you just have to trust that the Lord knows what he's doing."

The last thing I want right now is to have Claire quoting Mama at me—even if she's right. What I want is for my sister to disappear, so I can hold the letter to my face and see, foolishly, if I can smell Daniel on the paper. I want to touch his fingerprints and try to understand what made him ask Claire for help, when I could not.

There's no point in tearing myself apart, wondering why. I'll never know, not really, and I might not even if Daniel had lived. No matter how well a couple knows each other, there are always mysteries.

I bring my hands down with a sigh. "God doesn't give you more than you can handle," I quote in return, "unless He wants to know what you're made of."

We stare at each other for a long moment before dissolving into helpless, exhausted laughter, and the subject of Teddy is closed forever.

Pearl

January 12, 1933

I feel guilty about how much I love it here. Should I be this happy without Daddy? Mama says however we feel is right, and that everyone grieves differently, but I hate that he's missing all this. I think he would have liked it here. And he could have gotten a job with our landlord, like Dandy has, working on the houses on our street or elsewhere in the city. He didn't have to stay underground, risking his life for the company. They never cared about him.

School here is different than Scovill Run. I don't feel like I'm just killing time until I have to go to work. The teachers actually encourage us. When Miss Rodney asked my favorite subject, I told her how much I like to read, and she wrote down a few books for me. I'm going to get them from the library next time I go with Thelma. One of them is called *The Secret Garden*, and Miss Rodney says if I like that one, there are other books by the same writer. And she's a lady! It's not just Miss Alcott and her *Little Women*, or Miss Buck. There are a lot of lady writers in the world.

I would like to be one of them, but first I need to read a whole lot more and figure out how it's done.

Ava

Between our old furniture and the pieces Claire insisted on giving us, the house comes together quickly. I am unsettled at how *nice* it all is, and how unworthy I feel of having a home like this. I remind myself this is what I wanted—a house with curtains at the windows, where coal dust doesn't seep through every crack, and where we aren't all crammed together like sardines.

We spend our evenings in the sitting room. Our old davenport and chairs are arranged to face the fire, and although the window seat has no cushions, Pearl sits there regardless, lost in her stories. The radio plays softly on a table between the front windows and Dandy has hung a shelf over it, so Mama and Daniel's photos watch over us.

The upstairs is still incomplete, but we have sufficient beds and a chest of drawers on each floor. There is even a rug in the room I share with the girls, found forgotten in Claire's attic. It is a luxury to not put my bare feet on the cold floor when I get up in the morning.

I value early mornings as I always have, sitting alone at the table with that first cup of tea, an old plaid shirt of Daniel's thrown over my shoulders to keep off the chill until the stove heats the room. Most of the time I am too tired or busy to brood, but in the mornings, until I hear the kids' footsteps on the stairs, I close my eyes and pretend my life is whole again.

With my sewing machine and Harry's table, I can get to work almost immediately, but I want my workroom to be a space where customers will feel comfortable, and that will take time. Until then, I will meet with them at Claire's house.

Dandy finished the wall between the workroom and the kitchen and hung a door pulled from a pile of trash outside one of the other houses. It looked leprous and peeling when he dragged it through to the back yard, but once he sanded off the old finish and painted it white, it was quite presentable. He stayed up late covering the walls with soft lilac-gray paint procured from who-knows-where and produced from a similar source three cheap picture frames to display photos of women in glamorous gowns Pearl tore from the magazines in Max Byrne's office.

My sister is possibly more excited about my business than I am. One afternoon I take delivery of a proper dress form, something I've always wanted, and she has already insisted on loaning me her electric sewing machine. When I object, she says, "You've already used it more than I ever have."

The house's noises still catch me unawares. A creak on the stairs—is it the house breathing, a kid trying to be stealthy, or a ghost from the strange history of the houses on this street? Pearl told me all about the Underground Railroad, and it makes me proud to know that escaped slaves may have passed through our home on their way to freedom.

Where are the kids, anyway? School lets out at three, but they don't usually drift home until suppertime. Depending on the day, Pearl has either gone with Thelma to her therapy appointment or dropped her at Claire's while she goes to the library. Toby and George have taken to the city in the way they once took to the woods. Day by day, their territory widens, and I realized that my kids—all of them—know Philadelphia far better than I do.

Toby, still fascinated with cars, has become Mason Hedges' protégé, following him to the garage and going with him whenever there is a reason to take the Packard out. George, without a singular fascination of his own, follows along. Often they come home with grease on their hands and faces, ecstatic to have been permitted to look under the hood or pass tools to Hedges as he works on the car.

At least they will have a skill. I would rather have my sons be car mechanics than miners.

My eldest son will be neither miner nor mechanic. Dandy encountered our landlord while scavenging lumber from the building site's trash pile, and Mr. Howe inquired as to his intentions. When he told me, I worried that Mr. Howe would object to the renovations, or to my running a business out of the house, but Dandy said he was more interested that he knew how to frame a wall and hang a door.

"He offered me a job, Ma."

I haven't seen my son this worked up in a long time, and I pour only a bit of cold water on his excitement. "I was still hoping you'd go back to school."

"I'm not a schoolboy," he says with a shake of his head. "And I'm not going to be Dad, either."

"I know you're not. You'll have chances he never did."

"Including this one." He gives me his father's smile, the smile that convinces me that up is down. "This is a good opportunity. I'll be starting with the crew working on this block, but I'd like to work on one of his skyscraper buildings. Wouldn't that be something?"

He's always been good with his hands, and building is a solid, practical job. There will always be a need for men to build things.

"You have my blessing." I kiss his forehead. "You don't need it, since you're a man grown, but you have it anyway."

Claire

It is tempting, whenever I notice a need in the Kimber household, to simply fill it, as I would in my own home. But even though Ava has softened more than I thought possible, I know better than to push. The dress form could be justified for her business, but carpets in the bedrooms could not—at least not until I found that lovely second-hand rug and had Hedges conceal it in the attic for us to discover.

I drop in frequently before the children get home to drink tea and watch Ava sew. My sister's mastery of fabric still confounds me; she is better by far than even our mother, and when asked, cannot explain her knowledge. "It just makes sense," she says with a shrug, tearing a width of fabric with a sound that sets my teeth on edge.

One thing is still missing from the house, and I decide to remedy it whether or not she approves. I arrive just as the Wanamaker delivery truck turns out of the narrow street. Ava stands coatless on the top step, her arms crossed. On seeing me, her face assumes its familiar glare.

"Claire, you have to stop all this." She gestures at the crate sitting just inside the door. "I'm making money now. It may not be much, but we're managing."

I run lightly up the steps and pull her inside, closing the door against the cold. "It's not an extravagance," I tell her. "The baby will be here before you know it, and you don't have a high chair."

The chair I purchased is plainer than the cherrywood colonial in which Teddy sits each evening, but Ava will be less likely to object, as fancy equates to expensive in her mind. She does not need to know that it cost just as much.

She raises a shoulder. "Someone always just holds the babies."

"Wouldn't it be nice if everyone could eat, without a baby on their lap?" I shake my head. "Teddy loves his high chair, and if you're going to be hard-headed about it being a gift, consider that I would appreciate a place to put him if you ever invite me to dinner. Not that you have."

Ava shoves the crate aside for Dandy to open and leads me downstairs. "It's a wonderful house," she says, "but the kitchen isn't exactly built for dinner parties."

I take two mugs from their hooks and fill them. "We did grow up together, remember? Bumping elbows with my nieces and nephews isn't going to kill me."

"Esther—Mrs. Hedges—is a far better cook than I am." She reaches for her mug and sits under the back window.

I wonder at her use of my cook's first name but can only hold so many thoughts at once. "Mrs. Hedges is no better a cook than you are, she simply has a better budget, and fewer claims on her time." I smile triumphantly. "Harry has a dinner at the Union League on Thursday, no wives allowed, so Teddy and I will be at loose ends. He would very much enjoy sitting in your new chair."

Ava

I send Pearl to the butcher for a chicken. There is more meat in our diet now; though it costs more to eat this way, I saw how rapidly the kids filled out in the short month at Claire's house, and I will not deprive them if there is a way around it. I would rather they be cold than hungry.

While I prepare the bird, Pearl chops vegetables. "I think it's nice that we can have Aunt Claire for dinner," she says. "She's done so much for us."

"She has." I rub butter onto the chicken skin a little too enthusiastically. "I wish I could accept it a little better."

Pearl puts down the knife and turns to me. "She knows that," she says. "She knows you."

"She does." And so does my daughter.

Scraping the vegetables into the pot, Pearl reaches for the bread I baked this morning while I was altering a dress for Lavinia Thorndyke. "Can I ask a question, Mama?"

"Of course." I close the oven door and lean against the table, one hand going to my low back.

"Would you—" She ducks her head, her hair swinging forward. It has gotten longer, and it suits her. "Would you ever get married again?"

I sit back, trying to decide how to honestly answer her unexpected question. She deserves more than a reminder of how recently her father died, although that is my first instinct. I am getting better at holding my tongue.

"I can't imagine that I would," I say slowly. "Why? Are you thinking about getting married?"

"I don't know if I ever want to," Pearl says, dropping into a chair. "I love babies, but I don't know if I want my own." She looks up at me, tears beading her lashes. "I don't want you to think I'm ungrateful—"

"I wouldn't change a thing about my life," I tell her. "That doesn't mean you should do what I did. I loved your father, but if I hadn't known him, maybe I would have been brave like Claire and found another path."

It strikes me as I say it, the truth of those words. It took courage for my sister to stand up to her family and tell us she wanted to leave Scovill Run. It took courage to choose marriage to someone so different from herself, and find a way to make it work.

I had always believed Claire took the easy way out, but now her bravery makes me feel small.

Supper is a raucous affair, the boys alternately showing off for their aunt and shoving food in their mouths like they haven't been fed in days. "Slow down," I scold, when they reach for seconds. "The rest of us haven't finished yet."

Toby's lip comes out. "Grownups eat too slow."

"Save room," Claire advises. "I brought dessert."

Earlier I had asked Pearl to make cookies, and she shook her head. "Aunt will bring something," she said. "I stopped in after school and saw a bakery box."

Once the chocolate cake has been reduced to crumbs, I send the kids upstairs to do their homework and listen to the radio while Claire and I remain at the table. I ignore the dishes in the sink and the unfinished dress on my sewing table and decide to enjoy this time with my sister without doing anything else. Stillness is as strange as being alone, but I'm getting used to it.

"He likes the chair." I nod at Teddy, whose head has fallen forward. A thread of drool connects his lower lip to his bib.

Claire smiles. "He likes being in the center of everything."

Teddy is the center of her life, and we have done this for her. I will never know exactly what drove Daniel to write that letter, but in the end, it was for the best. Certainly, it has been for Claire—she has blossomed in the last year, and part of it has been from finally achieving her dream of motherhood.

"Your workroom is coming along." She pushes back her chair and wanders through the open door. "You don't mind if I poke around?"

"Go ahead." I follow her. "Thank you again for lending me your machine."

"It's not a loan." She pulls the chain and light floods over the two machines, side by side. "I told you. This way there's a machine for both you and Pearl, if it gets busy."

"I don't want her to spend her life hunched over a machine," I say. "It's not her dream."

Claire's plucked eyebrows lift. "Is it yours? It's a skill that allows you to feed your family, but is it your dream to spend your days sewing and making nice to women like Prue and Lavinia Thorndyke?"

It may not have been my dream, but it is, I realize, a gift—and a gift that has always been mine. As the space has come together and the ladies—even Lavinia Thorndyke—come calling with their requests and their scented envelopes of neatly folded cash, dressmaking has become something more than extra income. It is a way to support my family, on my own and on my terms. That is as close to a dream as I have ever allowed myself to have.

When Hedges knocks on the front door at eight, Dandy scoops Teddy up and carries him out to the car. Claire and I follow more slowly, still talking. All the words we held back for a dozen years have returned to us.

Mama always said family stays together. I was never sure if she meant it as a blessing or a curse, but we'll find out. It is a strange place I find myself in, needing Claire more than she needs me. She already knows how to mother; we were taught by the best. What we are learning now is how to be sisters again. We have found our way back to each other, and that's as good a place to start as any.

She says goodnight to the kids, then hugs me. "Come over tomorrow, if you have time. I'll be in all day."

"I'll try." I remain on the top step until Claire turns to wave, as I know she will, and then I shut the door.

Author's Note and Acknowledgments

I've always been interested in the Great Depression. Listening to stories from my great-grandmother, aunts, and my dad growing up, I can't help but feel that as an era, it's underrepresented in fiction and film, bracketed as it is by the more colorful and dramatic Roaring Twenties and WWII.

Much of what we see about the Depression is male-centered unless it's that Dorothea Lange photo of the Migrant Madonna, or the Dust Bowl and subsequent trek to California and (hopefully) prosperity. I wanted to write about the people who tried to stay put, who were so dirt poor already that the Depression shouldn't have made much of a difference. I also wanted to write about women, because much of the strain of keeping families fed, housed, and together fell on them. It was a lot to carry, and they did the best they could. They were often more employable—albeit at lower wages—than their husbands, and I wondered what that might have done to their marriages.

As an only child, not married until my mid-forties, and with no children, I was confounded when this story presented itself. Researching history is one thing—one of my favorite things—but researching the emotional trauma of a woman who has had multiple miscarriages, and on the flip side, a woman with multiple children, left me questioning where to start.

This makes it sound like I had a difficult time writing this book, or perhaps that I didn't enjoy it. Nothing could be further from the truth. The first germ of the idea appeared one night as I was falling asleep when I heard the words, "dear sister" and a somewhat different form of Claire's letter to Ava unspooled in my mind. I had no idea what it meant, but I was smart enough to get out of bed and write it down.

I worked on it for a bit, getting to know the characters, but *A Wider World* needed to be written next, not only because it was the sequel to *Songbird*, but because Robin Lewis, the main character, was even louder than Ava and Claire, and he was followed by *Lady, in Waiting*.

There may be more Tudor Court books in my future, but the sisters had waited long enough. When I came back to the story, the problems that had hung me up earlier—whether to write in first or third person, whether to tell the story solely from Ava's point of view or through both sisters—had disappeared. I knew how the story was supposed to sound; I just needed help getting inside the sisters.

When I first came up with the idea of Claire asking for Teddy, I wondered if readers would believe it. But desperation will make people do things that would be considered terrible in more "normal" situations. Unsure if their little ones would be able to survive, parents left children at orphanages; some children were abandoned; others were sold outright. Requesting to adopt a sister's child seemed mild in comparison, while still exploring the heartbreak of such a decision.

Back to Philadelphia. It was an absolute joy, when I started writing Claire's sections of the book, to wander *my* city with new eyes, seeing what places I could use, what places had changed, and what had disappeared entirely.

Apparently, I'm older than I realize because I knew Wanamaker's *as* Wanamaker's (it's now Macy's). I remember the toy department and the Christmas display. I remember the elevators, although by the time I shopped there, they were self-service. I had lunch once in the Crystal Tea room and I was made to feel poor and not quite welcome at Bonwit Teller.

I have, at various times, lived around the corner from both St. Patrick's and St. Mark's churches. Claire lives in my favorite house on Delancey Place. And Ava and her family moved into the very house I once rented on Ringgold Place, now called Waverly Street.

A city is like a stage set, with layers of curtains with scenes painted on, shifting in the breeze so you can see the places underneath. I'm grateful for this book—it allowed me to revisit my city with a new appreciation.

In some instances, social media can be a curse, but in others, it's a research tool. Public thanks to Christy Vasquez and Christa Short for talking to me about childbirth and mothering large families, respectively. Thanks to Karla Kizer for answering questions about

OB/GYN matters. Thanks to Deepika Prakash for founding Patternreview.com, an online sewing community where I met and became friends with many of the women who helped me, and which has also enriched my knowledge of vintage fashion. Thanks are also due to several friends, not named for reasons of privacy, for sharing their journeys toward childbirth, adoption, and the pain of their miscarriages so openly. I hope I have done justice to their feelings and experiences.

This book should have been dedicated to Dianne Dichter, my friend and first reader, who I had in mind while writing it. Thank you for the angry text messages, and for letting me know I made you cry. That is every author's dream.

And of course, all the love and thanks I can muster to Mario Giorno: husband, friend, reader, and bottomless well of patience. Are you happy I've finally stopped talking about the Tudors—for now?

About the Author

As an only child, Karen Heenan learned young that boredom was the ultimate enemy. Shortly after, she discovered perpetual motion and since then, she has rarely been seen holding still.

Since discovering books, she has rarely been without one in her hand and several more in her head. Her first series, *The Tudor Court*, stemmed from a lifelong interest in British history, but she's now turned her focus closer to home and is writing stories set in her native Philadelphia.

She lives in Lansdowne, PA, just outside Philadelphia, where she grows much of her own food, makes her own clothes, and generally confuses the neighbors. She is accompanied on her quest for self-sufficiency by a very patient husband and an ever-changing number of cats.

One constant: she is always writing her next book.

Follow her online at karenheenan.com and sign up for her newsletter to receive a free novella and updates on what's next.

Made in the USA
Monee, IL
19 July 2024

62163449R10236